# *Down River*

## John Hart

St. Martin's Paperbacks

This is a work of fiction. All of the characters, organizations, and events portrayed in this novel are either products of the author's imagination or are used fictitiously.

DOWN RIVER

Copyright © 2007 by John Hart.
Excerpt from *The Last Child* copyright © 2008 by John Hart.

Cover design by Honi Werner

For information address St. Martin's Press, 175 Fifth Avenue, New York, NY 10010.

Library of Congress Catalog Card Number: 2007021540

ISBN: 0-312-94566-3
EAN: 978-0-312-94566-4

Printed in the United States of America

St. Martin's Press hardcover edition / October 2007
St. Martin's Paperbacks edition / October 2008

St. Martin's Paperbacks are published by St. Martin's Press, 175 Fifth Avenue, New York, NY 10010.

10 9 8 7 6 5 4 3

More praise for John Hart's
## *Down River*

"Hart takes his time, snaring the reader with evocative storytelling and lush prose along with the usual quota of conflict and murder."
—*Boston Globe*

"Sometimes, early success can be a curse for a writer.... That's definitely not the case with John Hart...With *Down River,* he's only gotten better."
—*Winston-Salem Journal*

"Hard-boiled and rich...[an] intricate, haunting story... simply superb." —*Library Journal* (starred review)

"Engrossing...expertly evokes John Grisham and John Berendt." —*Mystery Scene*

"With its keen appraisals of human foibles and its emphasis on North Carolina history and flavor, *Down River* falls squarely in the league of the best of Southern novels."
—*South Florida Sun-Sentinel*

...and Hart's *New York Times* bestseller
## *The King of Lies*

"A seething, roiling, boiling North Carolina murder story... crossbreeds enough Grisham-style intrigue and Turow-style brooding to make for a sulfurous mix."
—Janet Maslin, *The New York Times*

"*The King of Lies* moves and reads like a book on fire."
—Pat Conroy

MORE...

St. Martin's Paperbacks Titles by
# John Hart

*The King of Lies*

*Down River*

*The Last Child*
**Available from St. Martin's Griffin**

*For Katie, as always*

# *Acknowledgments*

I would describe my books as thrillers or mysteries, but they revolve, also, around family. This is not by accident. We all have families. Good ones, bad ones, absent ones, indifferent ones. For my purposes, it almost doesn't matter. The leap is easy to make, and readers can relate, regardless. I have often said that family dysfunction makes for rich literary soil, and it truly does. It is fertile ground, the perfect place to cultivate secrets and misdeeds, grow them into explosive stories. Betrayals cut more deeply, pain lingers longer, and memory becomes a timeless thing. For a writer, this is a gift.

So first and foremost, I'd like to thank my own family for putting up with it. My parents are not evil people—they are wonderful. So are my in-laws, my siblings, my wife, and my children. They have been incredibly supportive throughout this process, and I could not have done it without them. This is especially true of Katie, my wife, to whom this book is dedicated. I love you, baby. Thanks for always being there.

The good people at Thomas Dunne Books/St. Martin's Press have also come to feel a bit like family. Special thanks to my editor, Pete Wolverton, a tireless advocate and collaborator. Katie Gilligan, another keen-eyed editor, also has my sincere gratitude. You two make a great team. There are others whom I have come to know, and whose support has been invaluable: Sally Richardson, Matthew Shear, Thomas Dunne, Andy Martin, Jennifer Enderlin, John Murphy, Lauren Manzella, Christina Harcar, Kerry Nordling, Matt Baldacci, Anne Marie Tallberg, and Ed Gabrielli. Thank you all. Thanks also to Sabrina Soares Roberts, who copyedited the manuscript, and to the people who worked so hard in producing the book: Amelie Littell, Cathy Turiano, Frances Sayers, and Kathie Parise. It takes a lot of people to bring a book to publication, and I know that I have not mentioned everyone. Nevertheless, you have all been fabulous.

I would also like to give a shout-out to the VHPS sales force, hard-working, dedicated professionals who do more to ensure a book's success than most readers will ever know. Thanks for your energy and support.

My agent, Mickey Choate, deserves a special place on this page. Thanks, Mickey. You've been a good friend and adviser. Thanks, as well, to Jeff Sanford, my film agent, who is knowledgeable and sure and not scared to tell a good story.

The town of Salisbury also merits a special mention. Like my family, Salisbury does not deserve the darkness I have inflicted upon it. It's a great town, and I am proud to have been raised there. I do encourage all readers to remember that while the town is real, the people I create are not: not the judges or police officers, not the sheriff or his deputies. I did, however, borrow three names from real people: Gray Wilson, my brother-in-law, Ken Miller, with whom I once worked, and Dolf Shepherd, whom I knew as a boy. Thanks to Gray and Ken, for lending their names, and to Dolf's family, who gave me permission to use his.

Thanks to the following people, who tried to make magic happen: Brett and Angela Zion, Neal and Tessa Sansovich, Alex Patterson, and Barbara Sieg. You went beyond the call, all of you, and I won't forget you.

Writing a book requires a lot of time in isolation. Thanks

to the following friends, who have gone out of their way to keep me sane: Skipper Hunt, John Yoakum, Mark Witte, Jay Kirkpatrick, Sanders Cockman, Robert Ketner, Erick Ellsweig, James Dewey, Andy Ambro, Clint Robins, and James Randolph, who also checked my law.

I would also like to thank Peter Hairston and the late Judge Hairston for allowing me the opportunity to spend some time with them at Cooleemee Plantation, a truly remarkable place.

Finally, a special thanks to Saylor and Sophie, my girls.

# *One*

The river is my earliest memory. The front porch of my father's house looks down on it from a low knoll, and I have pictures, faded yellow, of my first days on that porch. I slept in my mother's arms as she rocked there, played in the dust while my father fished, and I know the feel of that river even now: the slow churn of red clay, the back eddies under cut banks, the secrets it whispered to the hard, pink granite of Rowan County. Everything that shaped me happened near that river. I lost my mother in sight of it, fell in love on its banks. I could smell it on the day my father drove me out. It was part of my soul, and I thought I'd lost it forever.

But things can change, that's what I told myself. Mistakes can be undone, wrongs righted. That's what brought me home.

Hope.

And anger.

I'd been awake for thirty-six hours and driving for ten. Restless weeks, sleepless nights, and the decision stole into me like a thief. I never planned to go back to North Carolina—I'd buried it—but I blinked and found my hands on the wheel, Manhattan a sinking island to the north. I wore a week-old beard and three-day denim, felt stretched by an edginess that bordered on pain, but no one here would fail to recognize me. That's what home was all about, for good or bad.

My foot came off the gas as I hit the river. The sun still hung below the trees, but I felt the rise of it, the hard, hot push of it. I stopped the car on the far side of the bridge, stepped out onto crushed gravel, and looked down at the Yadkin River. It started in the mountains and stretched through both Carolinas. Eight miles from where I stood, it touched the northern edge of Red Water Farm, land that had been in my family since 1789. Another mile and it slid past my father's house.

We'd not spoken in five years, my father and me.

But that was not my fault.

I carried a beer down the bank and stood at the verge of the river. Trash and flat dirt stretched away beneath the crumbling bridge. Willows leaned out and I saw milk jugs tied to low limbs and floating on the current. They'd have hooks near the mud, and one of them rode low in the water. I watched it for motion and cracked the beer. The jug sank lower and turned against the current. It moved upstream and put a V in the water behind it. The limb twitched and the jug stopped, white plastic stained red by the river.

I closed my eyes and thought of the people I'd been forced to leave. After so many years, I'd expect their faces to pale, their voices to thin out, but that's not how it was. Memory rose up, stark and fresh, and I could not deny it.

Not anymore.

When I climbed up from beneath the bridge, I found a young boy on a dusty bike. He had one foot on the ground and a halting smile. He was maybe ten, in blown-out jeans and old canvas high-tops. A bucket hung from his shoulder by a knotted rope. Next to him, my big German car looked like a spaceship from another world.

"Morning," I said.

"Yes, sir." He nodded, but did not get off of the bike.

"Jug fishing?" I asked him, gesturing down the to the willows.

"Got two yesterday," he said.

"Three jugs down there."

He shook his head. "One of them is my daddy's. It wouldn't count."

"There's something pretty heavy on the middle one." His face lit up, and I knew that it was his jug, not his old man's. "Need any help?" I asked.

"No, sir."

I'd pulled some catfish out of the river when I was a boy, and based on the unmoving pull on that middle jug, I thought he might have a monster on his hands, a black-skinned, bottom-sucking beast that could easily go twenty pounds.

"That bucket won't be big enough," I told him.

"I'll clean him here." His fingers moved with pride to a thin knife on his belt. It had a stained wooden handle with pale, brushed-metal rivets. The scabbard was black leather that showed white cracks where he'd failed to oil it properly. He touched the hilt once and I sensed his eagerness.

"All right, then. Good luck."

I took a wide path around him, and he stayed on his bike until I unlocked my car and climbed in. He looked from me to the river and the grin spread as he shrugged off the bucket and swung one narrow leg over the back of the bike. As I pulled onto the road I looked for him in the mirror: a dusty boy in a soft yellow world.

I could almost remember how that felt.

I covered a mile before the sun made its full assault. It was too much for my scorched eyes and I pulled on dark glasses. New York had taught me about hard stone, narrowness, and gray shadow. This was so open. So lush. A word fingered the back of my mind.

*Verdant.*

So damn verdant.

Somehow, I'd forgotten, and that was wrong in more ways than I could count.

I made successive turns, and the roads narrowed. My foot pressed down and I hit the northern edge of my father's farm doing seventy; I couldn't help it. The land was scarred with emotion. Love and loss and a quiet, corrosive anguish. The entrance rushed past, an open gate and a long drive through rolling green. The needle touched eighty, and everything bad crashed down so that I could barely see the rest of it. The good stuff. The years before it all fell apart.

The Salisbury city limit came up fifteen minutes later and I slowed to a crawl as I pulled on a baseball cap to help hide my face. My fascination with this place was morbid, I knew, but it had been my home and I'd loved it, so I drove through town to check it out. It was still historic and rich, still small and Southern, and I wondered if it had the taste of me even now, so many years after it had spit me out.

I drove past the renovated train station and the old mansions stuffed with money, turned my face away from men on familiar benches and women in bright clothes. I stopped at a light, watched lawyers carry large cases up broad stairs, then turned left and lingered in front of the courthouse. I could recall the eyes of every person on the jury, feel the grain of wood at the table where I'd sat for three long weeks. If I closed my eyes now, I could feel the crush of bodies on the courthouse steps, the near physical slap of fierce words and bright, flashing teeth.

*Not guilty.*

The words had unleashed a fury.

I took a last look. It was all there, and wrong, and I could not deny the resentment that burned in me. My fingers dug at the wheel, the day tilted, and the anger expanded in my chest until I thought I might choke on it.

I rolled south on Main Street, then west. Five miles out I found the Faithful Motel. In my absence, and unsurprisingly, it had continued its roadside spiral into utter decay. Twenty years ago it did a booming business, but traffic trailed off when the church moms and preachers drove a stake through the triple-X drive-in across the street. Now it was a dump, a long strip of weathered doors with hourly rates, weekly tenants, and migrant workers shoved in four to a room.

I knew the guy whose father ran it: Danny Faith, who had been my friend. We'd grown up together, had some laughs. He was a brawler and a drinker, a part-time pair of hands on the farm when things got busy. Three weeks ago he'd called me, the first person to track me down after I'd been hounded out of town. I had no idea how he'd found me, but it couldn't have been that hard. Danny was a stand-up guy, good in a tight corner, but he was no deep thinker. He'd called me for help, and asked me to come home. I'd told him no. Home was lost to me. All of it. Lost.

But the phone call was just the beginning. He could not have known what it would do to me.

The parking lot was pure dirt, the building long and low. I killed the engine and entered through a filthy glass door. My hands found the counter and I studied the only wall ornament, a ten-penny nail with a dozen yellowed-out air fresheners in the shape of a pine tree. I took a breath, smelled nothing like pine, and watched an old Hispanic guy come out of a back room. He had finely groomed hair, a Mr. Rogers sweater, and a large chunk of turquoise on a leather thong around his neck. His eyes slid over me with practiced ease, and I knew what he saw. Late twenties, tall and fit. Unshaven, but with a good haircut and an expensive watch. No wedding ring. Scarred knuckles.

His eyes flicked past me, took in the car. I watched him do the math.

"Yes, sir?" he said, in a respectful tone that was rare in this place. He turned his eyes down, but I saw how straight he kept his back, the stillness in his small, leathery hands.

"I'm looking for Danny Faith. Tell him it's Adam Chase."

"Danny's gone," the old man replied.

"When will he be back?" I hid my disappointment.

"No, sir. He's gone three weeks now. Don't think he's coming back. His father still runs this place, though. I could get him if you want."

I tried to process this. Rowan County made two kinds of people: those who were born to stay and those who absolutely had to leave. Danny was the former.

"Gone where?" I asked.

The man shrugged, a weary, lips-down gesture, palms turned up. "He hit his girlfriend. She fell through that window." We both looked at the glass behind me, and he gave another near Gallic shrug. "It cut her face. She swore out a warrant and he left. No one has seen him around since. You want I should get Mr. Faith?"

"No." I was too tired to drive anymore, and not ready to deal with my father. "Do you have a room?"

"*Sí.*"

"Just a room, then."

He looked me over again. "You are sure? You want a room here?" He showed me his palms a second time.

I pulled out my wallet, put a hundred-dollar bill on the counter.

"*Sí,*" I told him. "A room here."

"For how long?"

His eyes were not on me or on the hundred, but on my wallet, where a thick stack of large bills was about to split the seams. I folded it closed and put it back in my pocket.

"I'll be out by tonight."

He took the hundred, gave me seventy-seven dollars in change, and told me room thirteen was open if I didn't mind the number. I told him that the number was no problem. He handed me the key and I left. He watched me move the car down the row to the end.

I went inside, slipped the chain.

The room smelled of mildew and the last guy's shower, but it was dark and still, and after days without sleep, it felt about right. I pulled back the bedcover, kicked off my shoes, and dropped onto the limp sheets. I thought briefly of hope and anger and wondered which one was strongest in me. Nothing felt certain, so I made a choice. Hope, I decided. I would wake to a sense of hope.

I closed my eyes and the room tilted. I seemed to rise up, float, then everything fell away and I was out, like I was never coming back.

I woke with a strangled noise in my throat and the image of blood on a wall, a dark crescent that stretched for the floor. I heard pounding, didn't know where I was, and stared wide-eyed around the dim room. Thin carpet rippled near the legs of a battered chair. Weak light made short forays under the curtain's edge. The pounding ceased.

Someone was at the door.

"Who is it?" My throat felt raw.

"Zebulon Faith."

It was Danny's father, a quick-tempered man who knew more than most about a lot of things: the inside of the county jail, narrowmindedness, the best way to beat his half-grown son.

"Just a second," I called out.

"I wanted to talk to you."

"Hang on."

I went to the sink and threw some water on my face, pushed the nightmare down. In the mirror, I looked drawn-out, older than my twenty-eight years. I toweled off as I moved to the door, felt the blood flow in me, and pulled it open. The sun hung low. Late afternoon. The old man's face looked hot and brittle.

"Hello, Mr. Faith. It's been a long time."

He was basically unchanged: a little more whittled down, but just as unpleasant. Wasted eyes moved over my face, and his lips twisted under dull whiskers. The smile made my skin crawl.

"You look the same," he said. "I figured time would have taken some of the pretty-boy off your face."

I swallowed my distaste. "I was looking for Danny."

His next words came slowly, in a hard drawl. "When Manny said it was Adam Chase, I didn't believe him. I said no way would Adam Chase be staying here. Not with that big old mansion full of family just sitting out there at the river. Not with all that Chase money. But things change, I reckon, and here you are." He lowered his chin and foul breath puffed out. "I didn't think you had the nerve to come back."

I kept my sudden anger in check. "About Danny," I said.

He waved the comment away as if it annoyed him. "He's sitting on a beach in Florida somewhere. The little shit. Danny's fine." He stopped speaking, closing down the subject of his son with an offhand finality. For a long moment he just stared at me. "Jesus Christ." He shook his head. "Adam Chase. In my place."

I rolled my shoulders. "One place is as good as another."

The old man laughed cruelly. "This motel is a rattrap. It's sucking the life out of me."

"If you say so."

"Are you here to talk to your father?" he asked, a sudden glint in his eyes.

"I plan to see him."

"That's not what I meant. Are you here to *talk* to him? I mean to say, five years ago you were the crown prince of Rowan County." A despicable grin. "Then you had your little trouble and you're just up and gone. Near as I can tell, you've never been back. There's got to be a reason after all this time, and talking sense into that prideful, stubborn son of a bitch is the best one I can think of."

"If you have something to say, Mr. Faith, why don't you just say it?"

He stepped closer, brought the smell of old sweat with him. His eyes were hard gray over a drinker's nose, and his

voice thinned. "Don't be a smart-ass with me, Adam. I remember back when you was just as much a shit-brain kid as
my boy, Danny, and the two of you together didn't have the
sense to dig a hole in the dirt with a shovel. I've seen you
drunk and I've seen you bleeding on a barroom floor." He
looked from my feet to my face. "You've got a fancy car and
a big-city smell on you, but you don't look no better than
anyone else. Not to me. And you can tell your old man I said
that, too. Tell him that he's running out of friends."

"I don't think I like your tone."

"I tried to be polite, but you'll never change, you Chases.
Think you're so much better than everyone else around here,
just because you have all that land and because you've been
in this county since creation. None of it means you're better
than me. Or better than my boy."

"I never said I was."

The old man nodded, and his voice quivered with frustration and anger. "You tell your daddy that he needs to stop being so goddamn selfish and think about the rest of the people
in this county. I'm not the only one that says so. A lot of people around here are fed up. You tell him that from me."

"That's enough," I said, stepping closer.

He didn't like it, and his hands seized up. "Don't you talk
down to me, boy."

Something hot flared in his eyes, and I felt a deep anger
stir as memories surged back. I relived the old man's petti-
ness and disregard, his quick and ready hands when his
son made some innocent mistake. "I'll tell you what," I
said. "Why don't you go fuck yourself?" I stepped even
closer, and as tall as the old man was, I still rose above
him. His eyes darted left and right when he saw the anger
in me. His son and I had cut a wide swath through this
county, and in spite of what he'd said, it had rarely been
me bleeding on some barroom floor. "My father's business
is no business of yours. It never has been and it never will

be. If you have something to say, I suggest that you say it to him."

He backed away, and I followed him out into the molten air. He kept his hands up, eyes on me, and his voice was sharp and harsh. "Things change, boy. They grow small and they die. Even in Rowan County. Even for the goddamn Chases!"

And then he was gone, walking fast past the flaking doors of his roadside empire. He looked back twice, and in his hatchet face I saw the cunning and the fear. He gave me the finger, and I asked myself, not for the first time, if coming home had been a mistake.

I watched him disappear into his office, then went inside to wash off the stink.

It took ten minutes to shower, shave, and put on clean clothes. Hot air molded itself around me as I stepped outside. The sun pressed down on the trees across the road, soft and low as it flattened itself against the world. A mist of pollen hung in the yellow light and cicadas called from the roadside. I pulled the door shut behind me, and when I turned I noticed two things almost at once. Zebulon Faith leaned, cross-armed, against the office wall. He had two guys with him, big old boys with heavy shoulders and thick smiles. That was the first thing I saw. The second was my car. Big letters, gouged into the dusty hood.

*Killer.*

Two feet long if it was an inch.

So much for hope.

The old man's face split and he pushed words through the smile. "Couple of punk kids," he said. "They took off that way." He pointed across the empty street, to the old drive-in parking lot that was now a sea of weed-choked Tarmac. "Damned unfortunate," he finished.

One of the guys elbowed the other. I knew what they saw: a rich man's car with New York plates, a city boy in shined shoes.

They had no idea.

I moved to the trunk, put my bag inside, pulled out the tire iron. It was two feet of solid metal with a lug wrench on one end. I started across the parking lot, the heavy rod low against my leg.

"You shouldn't have done it," I said.

"Fuck yourself, Chase."

They came off the porch, moving heavily, Zeb Faith in the middle. They fanned out, and their feet rasped on hard-baked earth. The man on Faith's right was the taller of the two, and looked scared, so I focused on the man to the left, a mistake. The blow came from the right, and the guy was fast. It was like getting hit with a bat. The other followed almost as quickly. He saw me droop and stepped in with an upper-cut that would have broken my jaw. But I swung the iron. It came up fast and hard, caught the man's arm in midswing and broke it as cleanly as anything I'd ever seen. I heard bones go. He went down, screaming.

The other man hit me again, caught me on the side of the head, and I swung at him, too. Metal connected on the meaty part of his shoulder. Zebulon Faith stepped in for a shot, but I beat him to it, delivered a short punch to the point of his chin and he dropped. Then the lights went out. I found my-self on my knees, vision clouded, getting the shit kicked out of me.

Faith was down. So was the man with the broken arm. But the other guy was having a time. I saw the boot arcing in again and I swung with all I had. The tire iron connected with his shin and he flopped onto the dirt. I didn't know if it was broken, didn't really care. He was out of it.

I tried to stand up, but my legs were loose and weak. I put my hands on the ground, and felt Zebulon Faith standing over me. Breath sawed in his throat, but his voice was strong enough. "Fucking Chases," he said, and went to work with his feet. They swung in, swung out. Swung in again, and came back bloody. I was down for real, couldn't find the tire iron, and the old man was grunting like he was at the end of an all-night screw. I curled up, tucked my face down, and sucked in a lungful of road grit.

That's when I heard the sirens.

# *Two*

The ambulance ride was a blur, twenty minutes of white gloves, painful swabs, and a fat paramedic with sweat hanging from his nose. Light flashed red and they lifted me out. The hospital solidified around me: sounds I knew and odors I'd smelled one time too many. The same ceiling they'd had for the past twenty years. A baby-faced resident grunted over old scars as he patched me up. "Not your first fight, is it?"

He didn't really want an answer, so I kept my mouth shut. The fighting started somewhere around age ten. My mother's suicide had a lot to do with that. So did Danny Faith. But it had been a while since my last one. For five years I'd moved through my days without a single confrontation. No arguments. No hard words. Five years of numbness, now this: three-on-one my first day back. I should have gotten in the car and left, but the thought never occurred to me.

Not once.

When I walked out, three hours later, I had taped ribs, loose teeth, and eighteen stitches in my head. I hurt like nobody's business. I was pissed.

The doors slipped shut behind me, and I stood, bent to the left, favoring the ribs on that side. Light spilled out across my feet, and a few cars passed on the street. I watched them for a couple of seconds, then turned back to the lot.

A car door opened thirty feet away, and a woman climbed out. She took three steps and stopped at the hood of the car. I recognized every part of her, even at that distance. She was five eight, graceful, with auburn hair and a smile that could light a dark room. A new pain welled up inside me, deeper, more textured. I thought I'd have time to find the right approach, the right words. But I was empty. I took a step and tried to hide the limp. She met me halfway, and her face was all hollow places and doubt. She studied me from top to bottom, and her frown left little question of what she saw.

"Officer Alexander," I said, forcing a smile that felt like a lie.

Her eyes moved over my injuries. "Detective," she corrected me. "Bumped up two years ago."

"Congratulations," I said.

She paused, looked for something in my face. She lingered on the stitches in my hairline, and for an instant, her face softened. "This is not how I thought we would meet again," she said, eyes back on mine.

"How then?"

"At first, I saw a long run and a hard embrace. Kisses and apologies." She shrugged. "After a few years with no word, I imagined something more confrontational. Screaming. Some swift kicks, maybe. Not seeing you like this. Not the two of us alone in the dark." She gestured at my face. "I can't even slap you."

Her smile failed, too. Neither of us could have seen it happening like this.

"Why didn't you come inside?"

Her hands settled on her hips. "I didn't know what to say. I thought the words would come to me."

"And?"

"Nothing came."

I couldn't respond at first. Love dies hard, if at all, and there was nothing to say that had not been said many times in the far past of that other life. When I did speak, the words came with difficulty. "I had to forget this place, Robin. I had to push it down."

"Don't," she said, and I recognized the anger. I'd lived with my own for long enough.

"So what now?" I asked.

"Now, I take you home."

"Not to my father's house."

She leaned closer and a glimmer of the old warmth appeared in her eyes. A smile flirted on the lines of her mouth. "I wouldn't do that to you," she said.

We moved around her car, and I spoke over the roof. "I'm not here to stay."

"No," she said heavily. "Of course not."

"Robin . . ."

"Get in the car, Adam."

I opened the door and sank into the car. It was a big sedan, a cop car. I looked at the radios and the laptop, the shotgun locked to the dash. I was wiped. Painkillers. Exhaustion. The seat seemed to swallow me up, and I watched the dark streets as Robin drove.

"Not much of a homecoming," she said.

"Could have been worse."

She nodded, and I felt her eyes on me, brief glances when the road straightened out. "It's good to see you, Adam. It's hard but good." She nodded again, as if still trying to convince herself. "I wasn't sure that it would ever happen again."

"Me either."

"That leaves the big question."

"Which is?" I knew the question, I just didn't like it.

"Why, Adam? The question is why. It's been five years. Nobody's heard a word from you."

"Do I need a reason for coming home?"

"Nothing happens in a vacuum. You should know that better than most."

"That's just cop talk. Sometimes there is no reason."

"I don't believe that." Resentment hung on her features.

She waited, but I did not know what to say. "You don't have to tell me," she said.

A silence fell between us as wind bent around the car. The tires hammered against a sudden spot of rough pavement.

"Were you planning to call me?" she asked.

"Robin—"

"Never mind. Forget it."

More wordless time, an awkwardness that daunted both of us.

"Why were you at that motel?"

I thought about how much to tell her, and decided that I had to square things with my father first. If I couldn't make it right with him, I couldn't make it right with her. "Do you have any idea where Danny Faith might be?" I asked.

I was changing the subject and she knew it. She let it go. "You know about his girlfriend?" she asked. I nodded and she shrugged. "He wouldn't be the first bottom-of-the-heap reprobate to hide from an arrest warrant. He'll turn up. People like him usually do."

I looked at her face, the hard lines. "You never liked Danny." It was an accusation.

"He's a loser," she said. "A gambler and a hard drinker with a violent streak a mile wide. How could I like him? He dragged you down, fed your dark side. Bar fights. Brawls. He made you forget the good things you had." She shook her head. "I thought you'd outgrow Danny. You were always too good for him."

"He's had my back since the fourth grade, Robin. You don't walk away from friends like that."

"Yet you did." She left the rest unsaid, but I felt it.

*Just like you walked away from me.*

I looked out the window. There was nothing I could say that would take away the hurt. She knew I'd had no choice.

"What the hell have you been doing, Adam? Five years. A lifetime. People said you were in New York, but other than that, nobody knows anything. Seriously, what the hell have you been doing?"

"Does it matter?" I asked, because to me it did not.

"Of course it matters."

She could never understand, and I didn't want her pity. I kept the loneliness bottled up, kept the story simple. "I tended bar for a while, worked in some gyms, worked for the parks. Just odd jobs. Nothing lasted more than a month or two."

I saw her disbelief, heard the disappointment in her voice. "Why would you waste your time working jobs like that? You're smart. You have money. You could have gone to school, become anything."

"It was never about money or getting ahead. I didn't care about that."

"What, then?"

I couldn't look at her. The things I'd lost could never be replaced. I shouldn't have to spell that out. Not to her. "Temporary jobs take no thought," I said, and paused. "Do that kind of stuff long enough, and even the years can blur."

"Jesus, Adam."

"You don't have the right to judge me, Robin. We both made choices. I had to live with yours. It's not fair to condemn me for mine."

"You're right. I'm sorry."

We rode in silence. "What about Zebulon Faith?" I finally asked.

"It's a county matter."

"Yet, here you are. A city detective."

"The sheriff's office took the call. But I have friends there. They called me when your name came up."

"They remember me that well?"

"Nobody's forgotten, Adam. Law enforcement least of all."

I bit down on angry words. It's the way people were: quick to judge and long to remember.

"Did they find Faith?" I asked.

"He ran before the deputies arrived, but they found the other two. I'm surprised you didn't see them at the hospital."

"Are they under arrest?"

Robin looked sideways at me. "All the deputies found were three men lying in the parking lot. You'll have to swear out a warrant if you want somebody arrested."

"Great. That's great. And the damage done to my car?"

"Same thing."

"Perfect."

I watched Robin as she drove. She'd aged, but still looked good. There was no ring on her finger, which saddened me. If she was alone in this world, part of it was my fault. "What the hell was that all about anyway? I knew I'd have a target on my back, but I didn't expect to get jumped the first day back in town."

"You're kidding, right?"

"No. That old bastard has always been mean-spirited, but it's like he was looking for an excuse."

"He probably was."

"I haven't seen him in years. His son and I are friends."

She laughed bitterly, and shook her head. "I tend to forget that there's a world outside of Rowan County. No reason for you to know, I guess. But it's been the deal around here for months. The power company. Your father. It's torn the town in two."

"I don't understand."

"The state is growing. The power company plans to build a new nuclear facility to compensate. They're looking at numerous sites, but Rowan County is the first choice. They need the water, so it has to be on the river. It would take a thousand acres, and everybody else has agreed to sell. But they need a big chunk of Red Water Farm to make it work. Four or five hundred acres, I think. They've offered five times what it's worth, but he won't sell. Half the town loves him. Half the town hates him. If he holds out, the power company will pull the plug and move on to some other place."

She shrugged. "People are getting laid off. Plants are closing. It's a billion-dollar facility. Your father is standing in the way."

"You sound like you want the plant to come."

"I work for the city. It's hard to ignore the possible benefits."

"And Zebulon Faith?"

"He owns thirty acres on the river. That's seven figures if the deal goes through. He's been vocal. Things have gotten ugly. People are angry, and it's not just the jobs or the tax base. It's big business. Concrete companies. Grading contractors. Builders. There's a lot of money to be made and people are getting desperate. Your father is a rich man. Most people think he's being selfish."

I pictured my father. "He won't sell."

"The money will get bigger. The pressure, too. A lot of folks are leaning on him."

"You said that it's gotten ugly. How ugly?"

"Most of it is harmless. Editorials in the paper. Harsh words. But there have been some threats, some vandalism. Somebody shot up some cattle one night. Outbuildings were burned. You're the first one to get hurt."

"Other than the cows."

"It's just background noise, Adam. It'll work out soon, one way or another."

"What kind of threats?" I asked.

"Late-night phone calls. Some letters."

"You've seen them?"

She nodded. "They're pretty graphic."

"Could Zebulon Faith be behind any of it?"

"He leveraged himself to buy additional acreage. I'm thinking that he needs that money pretty badly." She cut her eyes my way. "I've often wondered if Danny might not be involved. The windfall would be enormous and he doesn't exactly have a clean record."

"No way," I said.

"Seven figures. That's a lot of money, even for people that have money." I looked out the window. "Danny Faith," she said, "does not have money."

"You're wrong," I said.

She had to be.

"You walked out on *him*, too, Adam. Five years. No word. Loyalty only goes so far when that kind of money is on the table." She hesitated. "People change. As bad as Danny was for you, you were good for him. I don't think he's done that well since you left. It's just him and his old man, and we both know how that is."

"Anything specific?" I didn't want to believe her.

"He hit his girlfriend, knocked her through a plate glass window. Is that how you remember him?"

We were silent for a while. I tried to drown out the clamor she'd unleashed in my mind. Her talk of Danny upset me. The thought of my father receiving threats upset me even more. I should have been here. "If the town is torn in two, then who is on my father's side?"

"Environmentalists, mostly, and people who don't want things to change. A lot of the old money in town. Farmers without land in contention. Preservationists."

I rubbed my hands over my face and blew out a long breath.

"Don't worry about it," Robin said. "Life gets messy. It's not your problem."

She was wrong about that.

It was.

R obin Alexander still lived in the same condo, second floor in a turn-of-the-century building, one block off the square in downtown Salisbury. The front window faced a law office. The back window looked across a narrow alley to the barred windows of the local gun shop.

She had to help me out of the car.

Inside, she turned off the alarm, clicked on some lights,

and led me to her bedroom. It was immaculate. Same bed. The clock on the table read ten after nine.

"The place looks bigger," I said.

She stopped, a new angle in her shoulders. "It got that way when I threw out your stuff."

"You could have come with me, Robin. It's not like I didn't ask you."

"Let's not start this again," she said.

I sat on the bed and pulled off my shoes. Bending hurt, but she didn't help me. I looked at the photographs in her room, saw one of me on the bedside table. It filled a small silver frame; and in it, I was smiling. I reached for it, and Robin crossed the room in two strides. She picked it up without a word, turned it over, and placed it in a dresser drawer. When she turned, I thought she would leave, but she stopped in the door.

"Go to bed," she said, and something wavered in her voice. I looked at the keys she still held.

"Are you going out?"

"I'll take care of your car. It shouldn't spend the night out there."

"You worried about Faith?"

She shrugged. "Anything's possible. Go to bed."

There was more to say, but we didn't know how to say it. So I stripped out of my clothes and crawled between her sheets; I thought of the life we'd had and of its ending. She could have come with me. I told myself that. I repeated it, until sleep finally took me.

I went deep, yet at some point I woke. Robin stood above me. Her hair was loose, eyes bright, and she held herself as if she might fly apart at any second. "You're dreaming," she whispered, and I thought that maybe I was. I let the dark pull me under, where Robin called my name, and I chased eyes as bright and wet as dimes on a creek bed.

I woke alone in cold and gray, put my feet on the floor. There was blood on my shirt so I left it; but the pants were okay. I found Robin at the kitchen table, staring down at the rusted bars on the gun shop windows. The shower smell still clung to her; she wore jeans and a pale blue shirt with turned cuffs. Coffee steamed in front of her.

"Good morning," I said, seeking her eyes, remembering the dream.

She studied my face, the battered torso. "There's Percocet, if you need it. Coffee. Bagels, if you like."

The voice was closed to me. Like the eyes.

I sat across from her, and the light was hard on her face. She was still shy of twenty-nine, but looked older. The laugh lines had gone, and her face had thinned, compressing once-full lips into something pale. How much of that change came from five more years of cop? How much from me?

"Sleep okay?" she asked.

I shrugged. "Strange dreams."

She looked away, and I knew that seeing her had been no dream. She'd been watching me sleep and crying to herself.

"I stretched out on the sofa," she said. "I've been up for a few hours. Not used to having people over."

"Glad to hear it."

"Are you?" The mist seemed to blow off of her eyes.

"Yes."

She studied me over the rim of her mug, her face full of doubt. "Your car's outside," she finally said. "Keys on the counter. You're welcome to stay here as long as you'd like. Get some sleep. There's cable, some decent books."

"You're leaving?" I asked.

"No rest for the wicked," she said, but did not get up.

I rose to pour a cup of coffee.

"I saw your father last night." Her words pounded into my back. I said nothing, couldn't let her see my face, didn't want her to know what her words were doing to me. "After I got your car. I drove out to the farm, spoke to him on the porch."

"Is that right?" I tried to keep the sudden dismay from my

voice. She should not have done that. But I could see them there, on the porch—the distant curl of dark water and the post my father liked to lean against when he stared across it.

Robin sensed my displeasure. "He would have heard, Adam. Better he learn from me that you're back, not from some idiot at the lunch counter. Not from the sheriff. He should know that you've been hurt, so that he wouldn't wonder if you didn't show up today. I bought you some time to heal up, get yourself together. I thought you'd appreciate it."

"And my stepmother?"

"She stayed in the house. She didn't want anything to do with me." She stopped.

"Or with me."

"She testified against you, Adam. Let it go."

I still didn't turn around. Nothing was happening as I'd hoped. My hands settled on the counter's edge and squeezed. I thought of my father, and of the rift between us.

"How is he?" I asked.

A moment's silence, then, "He's aged."

"Is he okay?"

"I don't know."

There was something in her voice that made me turn around. "What?" I asked, and she raised her eyes to mine.

"It was a quiet thing, you understand, very dignified. But when I told him that you'd come home, your father wept."

I tried to hide my dismay. "He was upset?" I asked.

"That's not what I meant."

I waited.

"I think he wept for joy."

Robin waited for me to say something, but I couldn't answer. I looked out the window before she could see that tears were rising in my eyes, too.

Robin left a few minutes later to catch the seven o'clock briefing at the police station. I took some Percocet and pulled her sheets around me. Pain tunneled through my head; hammer blows at the temples, a cold nail at the hairline. In all of my life, I'd seen two things make my father cry. When my mother died, he'd wept for days; slow, constant tears, as if they welled from the seams of his face. Then tears of joy, once.

My father had saved a life.

The girl's name was Grace Shepherd. Her grandfather was Dolf Shepherd, the farm's foreman and my father's oldest friend. Dolf and Grace lived in a small cottage on the southern edge of the property. I never knew what had happened to the child's parents, only that they were gone. Whatever the reason, Dolf stepped up to raise the girl by himself. It was a trial for him—everybody knew it—but he'd been doing well.

Until the day she'd wandered off.

It was a cool day, early fall. Dry leaves clattered and scraped under a dull, heavy sky. She was barely two, and let herself out the back door while Dolf thought she was upstairs, sleeping. It was my father who found her. He was high in one of the pastures when he saw her on the dock below the house, watching leaves spin on the surging current. I'd never seen my father move so fast.

She went in without a splash. She leaned too far and the water just swallowed her up. My father hit the river in a loose dive, and came up alone. I made it to the dock as he went back down.

I found him a quarter mile downstream, cross-legged in the dirt, Grace Shepherd on his lap. Her skin shone as pale as something already dead, but she was round-eyed and wailing, her open mouth the only slash of color on that bleak riverbank. He clutched the child as if nothing else mattered; and he was weeping.

I watched for a long second, sensing, even then, that the moment was a sacred thing. When he saw me, though, he smiled. "Damn, son," he'd said. "That was a close one."

And then he'd kissed her head.

We wrapped Grace in my jacket as Dolf arrived at a run. Sweat poured down his face and he stopped, uncertain. My father handed the child to me, took two quick steps, and dropped the girl's grandfather with a single blow. The nose was shattered, no question, and Dolf bled there on the river-bank as his oldest friend trudged, wet and weary, to the house up on its hill.

That was my father.

The iron man.

# *Three*

I slept some of the pain away, and woke to a thunderstorm that rattled the old windows and put jigsaw shadows on the wall every time the lightning flashed. It swept through town, dropped sheets of water, then boiled south toward Charlotte. The pavement still steamed when I went outside to get my bag from the car.

I laid my fingers on gouged paint and traced the word.

*Killer.*

Back inside, I stalked the small rooms. Restless energy burned through me, but I felt at odds with myself. I wanted to see home, but knew how the seeing would hurt. I wanted to speak to my father, but feared the words that would come. His words. Mine. Words you can't take back or forget; the kind that scar deep and heal thin.

Five years.

Five damn years.

I opened a closet door, closed it without seeing what was inside. I drank water that tasted of metal, stared at books, and my eyes passed over it without seeing it; but it must have registered on me. It must have had some impact. Because as I paced, I thought of my trial: the hate that burst against me each day; the arguments built to hang me; the confusion among those who knew me best, and how it was compounded when my stepmother took the stand, swore her oath, and tried with her words to bury me.

Most of the trial was a blur: accusations, denials, expert testimony on blunt force trauma and blood spatter. What I remembered were the faces in the courtroom, the ready passions of people who once professed to know me.

The nightmare of every innocent man wrongly accused.

Five years ago, Gray Wilson was nineteen years old, right out of high school. He was strong and young and handsome. A football hero. One of Salisbury's favored sons. Then someone bashed a hole in his skull with a rock. He died on Red Water Farm and my own stepmother said I did it.

I circled the room, heard those words again—*not guilty*— and felt the violent thrust of emotion they put into me: the vindication and relief, the simple conviction that things could go back to the way they'd been. I should have known that I was wrong, should have felt it in the dank air of the slam-packed courtroom.

There was no going back.

The verdict that should have been an ending, was not. There was also the final confrontation with my father and the short, bitter goodbye to the only place I'd ever called home. A forced parting. The town didn't want me. Fine. Just dandy. As much as it hurt, I could live with that. But my father made a choice, too. I told him that I didn't do it. His new wife told him that I had. He chose to believe her.

Not me.

Her.

And he told me to leave.

My family had been on Red Water Farm for more than two hundred years, and I'd been groomed since childhood to take over its management. My father was easing back; Dolf, too. It was a multimillion-dollar operation and I was all but running it when the sheriff came to lock me away. The place was more than a part of me. It was who I was, what I loved, and what I was born to do. I couldn't stay in Rowan County if the farm and my family were not a part of my life. I couldn't be Adam Chase, the banker, or Adam Chase, the pharmacist. Not in this place. Not ever.

So I left the only people I'd ever loved, the only place I'd called home. I sought to lose myself in a city that was tall and gray and ceaseless. I planted myself there, and breathed in the noise and the flow and the pale white fuzz of endless, empty days. For five years, I succeeded. For five years I pounded down the memories and the loss.

Then Danny called, and blew everything apart.

It was on the fourth shelf, thick and spine-out. Pale. White. I pulled it from the shelf, a heavy sheaf, bound in plastic.

*State v. Adam Chase.*

Trial transcript. Every word said. Recorded. Forever.

It was heavily used, smudged, and folded at the corners. How many times had Robin read it? She'd stood by me during the trial, sworn that she believed me. And her faith had almost cost her the only job she'd ever cared about. Every cop in the county thought I'd done it. Every cop but her. She'd been un-flinching, and in the end, I'd left her.

*She could have come with me.*

That was truth, but what did it matter? Her world. My world. It could not have worked. And here we were, all but strangers.

I let the transcript fall open in my hands; it did so easily, spread itself to the testimony that almost damned me.

*WITNESS: A witness called by The State, having been first duly sworn to tell the truth, was examined and testified as follows:*

DIRECT EXAMINATION OF JANICE CHASE BY THE
DISTRICT ATTORNEY FOR THE COUNTY OF ROWAN

*Q: Will you please state your name for the Court?*

*A: Janice Chase.*

*Q: How are you related to the defendant, Mrs. Chase?*

*A: He is my stepson. His father is my husband. Jacob Chase.*

*Q: You have other children with Mr. Chase?*

*A: Twins. Miriam and James. We call him Jamie. They're eighteen.*

*Q: They are the defendant's half siblings?*

*A: Adopted siblings. Jacob is not the natural father. He adopted them shortly after we were married.*

*Q: And where is their natural father?*

*A: Is that important?*

*Q: Just trying to establish the nature of these relationships, Mrs. Chase. So the jury will understand who everybody is.*

*A: He's gone.*

*Q: Gone where?*

*A: Just gone.*

*Q: Very well. How long have you been married to Mr. Chase?*

*A: Thirteen years.*

*Q: So, you've known the defendant for a long time.*

*A: Thirteen years.*

*Q: How old was the defendant when you and his father were married?*

*A: He was ten.*

*Q: And your other children?*

*A: They were five.*

*Q: Both of them?*

*A: They are twins.*

*Q: Oh. Right. Now, I know this must be difficult for you, testifying against your own stepson . . .*

*A: It's the hardest thing I've ever done.*

*Q: You were close?*

*A: No. We've never been close.*

*Q: Um. . . . Is that because he resented you? Because you'd taken his mother's place?*

*Defense Counsel: Objection. Calls for speculation.*

*Q: Withdrawn.*

*A: She killed herself.*

*Q: I beg your pardon.*

*A: His mother killed herself.*

*Q: Um . . .*

*A: I'm no homewrecker.*

*Q: Okay . . .*

*A: I just want to be clear on that up front, before his lawyer tries to make this out like something it's not. We were never close, that's true, but we're still family. I'm not making this up and I'm not out to get Adam. I have no agenda. I love his father more than anything. And I've tried with Adam. We just never got close. It's that simple.*

*Q: Thank you, Mrs. Chase. I know that this is difficult for you. Tell us about the night that Gray Wilson was killed.*

*A: I saw what I saw.*

*Q: We'll get to that. Tell us about the party.*

I closed the transcript and replaced it on the shelf. I knew the words. The party had been at midsummer: my stepmother's idea. A birthday party for the twins, their eighteenth. She'd hung lights in the trees, engaged the finest caterer, and brought a swing band up from Charleston. It started at four in the afternoon, ended at midnight; yet a few souls lingered. At two A.M., or so she swore, Gray Wilson walked down to the river. At roughly three, when all had left, I came up the hill, covered in the boy's blood.

He was killed by a sharp-edged rock the size of a large man's fist. They found it on the bank, next to a red-black stain in the dirt. They knew it was the murder weapon because it had the boy's blood all over it and because it was a perfect match, in size and shape, for the hole in his skull. Somebody bashed in the back of his head, hit hard enough to drive bone shards deep into his brain. My stepmother claimed that it was me. She described it on the stand. The man she'd seen at three o'clock in the morning had on a red shirt and a black cap.

Same as me.

He walked like me. He looked like me.

She didn't call the cops, she claimed, because she did not realize that the dark liquid on my hands and shirt was blood. She had no idea that a crime had been committed until the next morning when my father found the body halfway in the river. The way she told it, it wasn't until later that she put it all together.

The jury debated for four days, then the gavel came down and I walked out. No motive. That's what swung the vote. The prosecution put on a great show, but the case was built entirely on my stepmother's testimony. It was a dark night. Whoever she saw, she saw from a distance. And I had no reason in the world to want Gray Wilson dead.

We barely knew each other.

I cleaned the kitchen, took a shower, and left a note for Robin on the kitchen table. I gave her my cell number and asked her to call when she finished her shift.

It was just after two when I finally turned onto the gravel drive of my father's farm. I knew every inch of it, yet felt like an intruder, like the land itself knew that I'd surrendered my claim upon it. The fields still glistened from the rain, and mud filled the ditches that ran beside the drive. I steered past pastures full of cattle, through a neck of old forest, and then out into the soy fields. The road followed a fence line to the top of a rise, and as I crested the ridge I could see three hundred acres of soy spread out below me. Migrants were at work in the field, baking in the hot sun. I saw no supervisor, no farm truck; and that meant no water for the workers.

My father owned just north of fourteen hundred acres, one

of the largest working farms left in central North Carolina. Its borders had not changed since the original purchase in 1789. I drove through soy fields and rolling pasture, crossed over swollen creeks, and passed the stables before I topped the last hill and saw the house. At one point it had been surprisingly small, a weathered old homestead; but the house I remembered from childhood was long gone. When my father remarried, his new wife brought different ideas with her, and the home now sprawled across the landscape. The front porch, however, was untouched, as I knew it would be. Two centuries of Chases had stood on that porch to watch the river, and I knew that my father would never allow it to be torn down or replaced. "Everybody has a line," he'd said to me once, "and that porch is mine."

There was a farm truck in the driveway. I parked next to it, saw the water-coolers in the back, their sides wet with condensation. I switched off the ignition, climbed out, and a million pieces of my old life coalesced around me. A slow, warm childhood and my mother's bright smile. The things my father liked to teach me. The calluses that grew on my hands. Long days in the sun. Then the way things changed, my mother's suicide, and the black months fading to gray as I fought through its aftershock. My father's remarriage, new siblings, new challenges. Then Grace in the river. Adulthood and Robin. The plans we made all blown to bits.

I stepped onto the porch, stared over the river, and thought of my father. I wondered what was left of us, then went in search of him. His study stood empty and unchanged: pine floors, overflowing desk, tall bookshelves and piles of books on the floor next to them, muddy boots by the back door, pictures of hunting dogs long dead, shotguns next to the stone fireplace, jackets on hooks, hats; and a photograph of the two of us, taken nineteen years earlier, half a year after my mother died.

I'd lost twenty pounds in the months since we'd buried her. I'd barely spoken, barely slept, and he decided enough was enough and it was time to move on. Just like that. *Let's do something,* he'd said. *Let's get out of the house.* I did not even look up. *For God's sake, Adam. . . .*

He took me hunting on a bright, fall day. High, blue sky, leaves not yet turned. The deer came in the first hour, and it was unlike any deer I'd ever seen. Its coat shone pale white under antlers wide enough to carry a grown man. He was massive, and presented himself, head up, fifty yards out. He stared in our direction, then pawed the ground, as if impatient.

He was perfect.

But my father refused the shot. He lowered his rifle and I saw that tears brimmed in his eyes. He whispered to me that something had changed. He couldn't do it. *A white deer is a sign,* he said, and I knew that he was talking about my mother. Yet, the animal hung in my sights, too. I bit down hard, let out half a breath, and I felt my father's eyes. He shook his head once, mouthed the word, *No.*

I took the shot.

And missed.

My father lifted the rifle from my hands and put an arm over my shoulder. He squeezed hard and we sat like that for a long time. He thought that I'd chosen to miss, that in the last second I, too, had come to believe that life was more precious somehow, that my mother's death had had this effect on both of us.

But that wasn't it. Not even close.

I wanted to hurt that deer. I wanted it so badly my hands shook.

That's what ruined the shot.

I looked again at the photograph. On the day it was taken, I was nine years old, my mother fresh in the ground. The old man thought we'd rounded the corner, that that day in the woods had been our first step, a sign of healing. But I knew nothing of signs or forgiveness. I barely knew who I was.

I put the photo back on the shelf, squared it just so. He

thought that day was our new beginning, and kept the photo all these years, never guessing that it was a great, giant lie.

I'd thought that I was ready to come home, but now I was no longer sure. My father was not here. There was nothing for me here. Yet, as I turned, I saw the page on his desk, fine stationery next to an expensive burgundy pen my mother had once given him. "Dear Adam," it read. Then nothing else. Emptiness. How long had he stared at that blank paper, I wondered, and what would he have said, had the words actually come?

I left the room as I'd found it, wandered back into the main part of the house. New art adorned the walls, including a portrait of my adopted sister. She was eighteen the last time I'd seen her, a fragile young woman who'd sat every day in the courtroom, yet had been unable to meet my eyes. She was my sister, and we'd not spoken since the day I left, but I didn't hold that against her. It was as much my fault as hers. More, really.

She'd be twenty-three now, a mature woman, and I looked again at her portrait: the easy smile, the confidence. It could happen, I thought. Maybe.

The picture of Miriam turned me to thoughts of Jamie, her twin brother. In my absence, responsibility for the crews would have fallen to him. I went to the big staircase and yelled his name. I heard footsteps and a muffled voice. Then, stocking feet at the top of the stairs, followed by jeans grimed at the cuff, and an impossibly muscular torso beneath pale, thin hair spiked with some kind of gel. Jamie's face had filled out, lost the angles of youth, but the eyes had not changed, and they crinkled at the corners when they settled on me.

"I do not freakin' believe it," he said. His voice was as big as the rest of him. "Jesus, Adam, when did you get here?" He came down the stairs, stopped and looked at me. He stood six four, and had me by forty pounds, all of it muscle. The last time I'd seen him he'd been my size.

"Damn, Jamie. When did you get huge?"

He curled his arms and studied the muscles with obvious pride. "Gotta have the guns, baby. You know how it is. But look at you. You haven't changed at all." He gestured at my face. "Somebody kicked your ass, I see, but other than that you could have walked out of here yesterday."

I fingered the stitches.

"Is that local?" he asked.

"Zebulon Faith."

"That old bastard?"

"And two of his boys."

He nodded, eyelids drooping. "Wish I'd been there."

"Next time," I said.

"Hey, does Dad know you're back?"

"He's heard. We haven't spoken yet."

"Unreal."

I held out my hand. "Good to see you, Jamie."

His hand swallowed mine. "Fuck that," he said, and pulled me into a bear hug that was ninety percent painful backslapping.

"Hey, you want a beer?" He gestured toward the kitchen.

"You have the time?"

"What's the point of being the boss if you can't sit in the shade and drink a beer with your brother? Am I right?"

I thought about keeping my mouth shut, but I could still see the migrants, sweating in the sun-scorched fields. "Someone should be with the crews."

"I've only been gone an hour. The crews are fine."

"They're your responsibility—"

Jamie dropped a hand on my shoulder. "Adam, you know that I'm happy to see you, right? But I've been out from under your shadow for a long time. You did a good job when you were here. No one would deny that. But I manage the daily operations now. You would be wrong to show up all of a sudden and expect everybody to bow down to you. This is my deal. Don't tell me how to run it." He squeezed my shoulder with steel fingers. They found the bruises and burrowed in. "That would be a problem for us, Adam. I don't want there to be a problem for us."

"Okay, Jamie. I get your point."

"Good," he said. "That's just fine." He turned for the kitchen and I followed him. "What kind of beer do you like? I've got all different kinds."

"Whatever," I said. "You pick." He opened the refrigerator. "Where is everybody?" I asked.

"Dad's in Winston for something. Mom and Miriam have been in Colorado. I think that they were supposed to fly in yesterday and spend the night in Charlotte." He smiled and nudged me. "A couple of squaws off shopping. They'll probably be home late."

"Colorado?"

"Yeah, for a couple of weeks. Mom took Miriam to some fat farm out there. Costs a fortune, but hey, not my call, you know." He turned with two beers in his hands.

"Miriam has never been overweight," I said.

Jamie shrugged. "A health spa, then. Mud baths and eel grass. I don't know. This is a Belgian one, some kind of lager, I think. And this is an English stout. Which one?"

"The lager."

He opened it and handed it to me. Took a pull on his own. "The porch?" he asked.

"Yeah. The porch."

He went through the door first, and when I emerged into the heat behind him, I found him leaning against our father's post with a proprietary air. A knowing glint appeared in his eyes, and his smile thinned into a statement.

"Cheers," he said.

"Sure, Jamie. Cheers."

The bottles clinked, and we drank our beer in the still and heavy air. "Cops know you're back?" Jamie asked.

"They know."

"Jesus."

"Screw 'em," I said.

At one point, Jamie raised his arm, made a muscle and pointed at his bicep.

"Twenty-three inches," he said.

"Nice," I told him.

"Guns, baby."

Rivers find the low ground—it is what they are made to do—and looking over the one that defined our border I thought that maybe the talent had rubbed off on my brother. He talked about money he'd spent and about the girls he'd laid. He counted them up for me, a slew of them. Our conversation did not venture beyond that until he asked about the reason for my return. The question came at the end of his second beer, and he slipped it in like it meant nothing. But his eyes couldn't lie. It was all he cared about.

*Was I back for good?*

I told him the truth as I knew it: doubtful.

To his credit, he covered his relief well. "Are you sticking around for dinner?" he asked, draining the beer.

"Do you think that I should?"

He scratched at his thinning hair. "It might be easier with just Dad here. I think he'll forgive you for what happened, but Mom won't be happy. There's no lie in that."

"I'm not here to ask for forgiveness."

"Damn, Adam, let's not start this up again. Dad had to choose a side. He could believe you or he could believe Mom, but he couldn't believe both of you."

"This is still my family, Jamie, even after all that's happened. She can't very well tell me to stay away."

Jamie's eyes grew suddenly sympathetic. "She's scared of you, Adam."

"This is my home." The words sounded hollow. "I was acquitted."

Jamie rolled massive shoulders. "Your call, bro. It'll be interesting either way. I'm just glad to have a front-row seat."

His smile was patently false; but he was trying. "You're such an ass, Jamie."

"Don't hate me 'cause I'm beautiful."

"Tomorrow night, then. May as well do it all at once." But that was only part of it. I was feeling the pain, a profound ache that still had room to grow. I thought of Robin's dark bedroom, and then of my father and the note he had been unable to complete. The time would be good for everyone.

"So, how's Dad?" I asked.

"Ah, he's bulletproof. You know how he is."

"Not anymore," I said, but Jamie ignored me. "I'm going to walk down to the river, then I'll be out of here. Tell Dad that I'm sorry I missed him."

"Say hello to Grace," he said.

"She's down there?"

"Every day. Same time."

I'd thought a lot about Grace, but was less sure of how to approach her than anyone else. She was two years old when she came to live with Dolf, still a child when I'd left, too young for any kind of explanation. For thirteen years I'd been a large part of her world, and leaving her alone is what felt most like a betrayal. All of my letters had come back unopened. Eventually, I'd stopped sending them.

"How is she?" I asked, trying not to show how much the answer mattered.

Jamie shook his head. "She's a wild Indian, no mistake, but she always has been. She's not going to college, looks like. She's working odd jobs, hanging around the farm, living off the fat of the land."

"Is she happy?"

"She should be. She's the hottest thing in three counties."

"Is that right?" I asked.

"Hell, I'd fuck her." He winked at me, not seeing how close he was to a beating. I told myself that he meant nothing by it. He was just being a smart-ass. He'd forgotten how much I loved Grace. How protective of her I'd always been.

He wasn't trying to start something.

"Good to see you, Jamie." I dropped a hand on the hard lump of his shoulder. "I've missed you."

He folded his massive frame into the pickup truck. "Tomorrow night," he said, and jolted off toward the fields. From the porch I saw his arm appear as he draped it through the window. Then he tossed a wave, and I knew that he was watching me in the rearview mirror. I stepped onto the lawn and watched until he was gone. Then I turned down the hill.

Grace and I had been close. Maybe it was that day on the riverbank, when I'd held her, wailing, as my father hammered Dolf into the dirt for letting her wander off. Or the long walk back to the house, as my words finally calmed her. Maybe it was the smile she'd given me, or the desperate grip around my neck when I'd tried to put her down. Whatever the case, we'd bonded; and I'd watched with pride as she took the farm by storm. It was as if that plunge in the river had marked her, for she was fearless. She could swim the river by age five, ride bareback by seven. At ten, she could handle my father's horse, a big, nasty brute that scared everyone but the old man. I taught her how to shoot and how to fish. She'd ride the tractor with me, beg to drive one of the farm trucks, then squeal with laughter when I let her. She was wild by nature, and often returned from school with blood on her cheek and tales of some boy who'd made her angry.

In many ways, I'd missed her the most.

I followed the narrow trail to the river and heard the music long before I got there. She was listening to Elvis Costello.

The dock was thirty feet long, a finger bone stroking the river in the middle of its slow bend to the south. She was at the end of it, a lean brown figure in the smallest white bikini I'd ever seen. She sat on the side of the dock, holding, with her foot, the edge of a dark blue canoe and speaking to the woman who sat in it. I stopped under a tree, hesitant about intruding.

The woman had white hair, a heart-shaped face, and lean arms. She looked very tan in a shirt the color of daffodils. I watched as she patted Grace's hand and said something I could not hear. Then she gave a small wave and Grace pushed with her foot, skimming the canoe out into the river. The woman dipped a paddle and held the bow upstream. She said last words to the younger woman, then looked up and saw me. She stopped paddling and the current bore her down. She stared hard, then nodded once, and it was like I'd seen a ghost.

She drove the canoe upstream, and Grace lay down on the hard, white wood. The moment held such brightness, and I watched the woman until the curve in the river stole her away. Then I walked onto the dock, my feet loud on the wood. She did not move when she spoke.

"Go away, Jamie. I will not swim with you. I will not date you. I will not sleep with you under any circumstances. If you want to stare at me, go back to your telescope on the third floor."

"It's not Jamie," I said.

She rolled onto her side, slid tinted glasses down her nose, and showed me her eyes. They were blue and sharp.

"Hello, Grace."

She declined to smile, and lifted the glasses to hide her eyes. She rolled onto her stomach, reached for the radio, and turned it down. Her chin settled on the back of her folded hands, and she looked out over the water.

"Am I supposed to jump up and throw my arms around you?" she asked.

"No one else has."

"I won't feel sorry for you."

"You never answered my letters."

"To hell with your letters, Adam. You were all I had and you left. That's where the story ends."

"I'm sorry, Grace. If it means anything, leaving you alone broke my heart."

"Go away, Adam."

"I'm here now."

Her voice spiked. "Who else cared about me? Not your stepmother. Not Miriam and not Jamie. Not until I had tits. Just a couple of busy old men that knew nothing about raising young girls. The whole world was messed up after you left, and you left me alone to deal with it. All of it. A world of shit. Keep your letters."

Her words were killing me. "I was tried for murder. My own father kicked me out. I couldn't stay here."

"Whatever."

"Grace—"

"Put some lotion on my back, Adam."

"I don't—"

"Just do it."

I knelt on the wood beside her. The lotion was hot out of the bottle, cooked in the sun and smelling of bananas. Grace was beneath me, a stretch of hard, brown body that I could not relate to. I hesitated, and she reached behind herself and untied the top of her bikini. The straps fell away and for an instant, before she lay back down, one of her breasts hung in my vision. Then she was flat on the wood, and I knelt unmoving, completely undone. It was her manner, the sudden woman of her, and the certain knowledge that the Grace I'd known was lost forever.

"Don't take all day," she said.

I put the lotion on her back but did a bad job of it. I couldn't look at the soft curves of her, the long legs slightly parted. So I looked over the river as well, and if we saw the same thing, we could not have known. There were no words for that moment.

I'd barely finished when she said, "I'm going for a swim." She retied her top and stood, the smooth plane of her stomach inches from my face. "Don't go away," she said, then turned and split the water in one fluid motion. I stood and watched the sun flash off of her arms as she stroked hard against the current. She went out fifty feet, then turned, and swam back. She cut through the river like she belonged in it, and I thought of the day she'd first went in, how the water had opened up and taken her down.

The river ran off of her as she climbed up the ladder. The weight of water pulled her hair back, and for a moment I saw something fierce in her naked features. But then the glasses went back on, and I stood mutely as she lay back down and let the sun begin to bake her dry.

"Should I even ask how long you plan to stay?" she said.

I sat next to her. "As long as it takes. A couple of days."

"Do you have any plans?"

"One or two things," I said. "Seeing friends. Seeing family."

She laughed an unforgiving laugh. "Don't count on a whole lot of this. I have a life, you know. Things I won't drop just because you decide to show up unannounced." Then, without skipping a beat, she asked me, "Do you smoke?" She reached into the pile of clothes next to her—cutoffs, red T-shirt, flip-flops—and came out with a small plastic bag. She pulled out a joint and a lighter.

"Not since college," I said.

She lit the joint, sucked in a lungful. "Well, I smoke," she said tightly. She extended the joint toward me, but I shook my head. She took another drag, and the smoke moved out over the water.

"Do you have a wife?" she asked.

"No."

"A girlfriend?"

"No."

"What about Robin Alexander?"

"Not for a long time."

She took one more drag, stubbed the joint out, and dropped the charred end back into the plastic bag. Her words were soft around the edges.

"I've got boyfriends," she said.

"That's good."

"Lots of boyfriends. I date one and then I date another." I didn't know what to say. She sat up, facing me. "Don't you care?" she asked.

"Of course I care, but it's none of my business."

Then she was on her feet.

"It *is* your business," she said. "If not yours, then whose?" She stepped closer, stopped an inch away. Powerful emotions emanated from her, but they were complex. I didn't know what to say, so I said the only thing that I could.

"I'm sorry, Grace."

Then she was against me, still wet from the river. Her arms circled my neck. She clutched me with sudden intensity. Her hands found my face, squeezed it, and then her lips pushed against mine. She kissed me, and she meant it. And when her mouth settled against my ear, she squeezed me even tighter, so that I could not have stepped away without forcing her. Her words were barely there, and still they crushed me.

"I hate you, Adam. I hate you like I could kill you."

Then she turned and ran, down the riverbank, through the trees, her white suit flashing like the tail of a startled deer.

# *Four*

Some time later, I closed the door of my car as if I could shut off the world. It was hot inside, and blood pounded where the stitches held my skin together. For five years I'd lived in a vacuum, trying to forget the life I'd lost, but even in the world's greatest city the brightest days had run shallow.

But not here.

I started the car.

Everything here was so goddamned real.

Back at Robin's, I cut the tape from my ribs and stood under pounding water for as long as I could. I found the Percocet and took two, thought about it, and then swallowed another. Then, with all of the lights off, I climbed into bed.

When I woke it was dark outside, but a light shone from the hallway. The drugs still had a grip on me, and deep as I'd been, the dream still found me: a dark curve of red spatter, and an old brush too big for small hands.

Robin stood next to the bed, dark against the light. She was very still. I couldn't see her face. "This doesn't mean anything," she told me.

"What doesn't?"

She unbuttoned her shirt, then slipped it off. She wore nothing else. Light spilled through the gaps between her fingers, the space between her legs. She was a silhouette, a paper doll. I thought of the years we'd shared, of how close we'd come to forever. I wished that I could see her face.

When I lifted the blanket, she slipped in, on her side, and put a leg over me. "Are you sure?" I asked.

"Don't talk."

She kissed the side of my neck, rose to kiss my face, and then covered my mouth. She tasted as I remembered, felt the same: hard and hot and eager. She rolled on top of me, and I winced as her weight came onto my ribs. "Sorry," she whispered, and shifted all of her weight onto my hips. A shudder moved through her. She rose above me and I saw the side of her face in the hall's light, the dark pit of one eye and the dark hair that gleamed where the light touched it. She took my hands and placed them on her breasts.

"This doesn't mean anything," she repeated; but she was lying, and we both knew it. The communion was immediate and total.

Like stepping off a cliff.

Like falling.

When next I woke, she was getting dressed.

"Hey," I said.

"Hey yourself."

"Want to talk?" I asked.

She whipped on her shirt, started on the buttons. She could not bring herself to look at me. "Not about this."

"Why not?"

"I needed to figure something out."

"Do you mean us?"

She shook her head. "I can't talk to you like this."

"Like what?"

"Naked, tangled in my sheets. Put on some pants, come into the living room."

I pulled on pants and a T-shirt, found her sitting in a

leather club chair with her legs drawn up beneath her. "What time is it?" I asked.

"Late," she said.

A single lamp burned, leaving most of the room in shadow. Her face was pale and uncertain, eyes filled up with hard gray shadow. Her fingers twisted together. I looked around the room as silence stretched between us. "So, how've you been?" I finally asked.

Robin came to her feet. "I can't do this. I can't make small talk like we saw each other last week. It's been five years, Adam. You didn't call or write. I didn't know if you were alive, dead, married, still single. Nothing." She ran her fingers through her hair. "And even with all of that, I still haven't moved on. Yet here I am sleeping with you, and you want to know why? Because I know that you're going to leave; and I had to find out if it was still there between us. Because if it was gone, then I'd be okay. Only if it was gone."

She stopped talking, turned her face away, and I understood. She'd let her guard down and now she hurt. I stood up. I wanted to stop what was coming, but she spoke over me.

"Don't say anything, Adam. And don't ask me if it's gone, because I'm about to tell you." She turned to face me, and lied for the second time. "It's gone."

"Robin . . ."

She shoved her feet into untied running shoes, picked up her keys. "I'm going for a walk. Get your stuff together. When I get back we'll see about finding you a hotel room."

She slammed the door behind her, and I sat down, awed again by the force of the passions that had grown in the wake of my flight northward.

When she returned, twenty minutes later, I had showered and shaved; everything I owned was either on my back or in the car. I met her in the foyer, by the door. Her face was flushed. "I found a room at the Holiday Inn," I told her. "I didn't want to leave without saying goodbye."

She closed the door and leaned against it. "Hang on a second," she said. "I owe you an apology." A pause. "Look, Adam. I'm a cop, and that's all about keeping control. You understand? It's about logic, and I've trained myself that way since you left. It's all I had left." She blew out a hard breath. "What I said back there, that was five years' worth of control slipping away in under a minute. You didn't deserve it. You don't deserve to be tossed out in the middle of the night either. Tomorrow's soon enough."

There was no irony in her.

"Okay, Robin. We'll talk. Just let me get my bag. Do you have any wine?"

"Some."

"Wine could be nice," I said, then went outside to collect my things. I stood in the parking lot. The sky spread out, a low blackness propped up by small-town light. I tried to figure out how I felt about Robin and the things she'd said. Everything was happening so fast, and I was no closer to doing what I'd come here to do.

I dropped my duffel in the foyer and walked toward the living room. I heard Robin's voice, saw that she was on her cell. She held up a hand, and I stopped, realizing that something was wrong. It was all over her.

"Okay," she said. "I'll be there in fifteen minutes."

She snapped the phone closed, reached for the gun in its shoulder holster, shrugged it on.

"What is it?" I asked.

Her features closed down as she spoke. "I have to go out," she said.

"Something serious?"

She stepped closer. I felt the change in her, the sudden rise of an unyielding intellect. "I can't talk about it, Adam, but I think that it is." I started to speak, but she cut me off. "I want you to stay here. Stay by the phone."

"Is there a problem?" I was suddenly wary; there was something in her eyes.

"I want to know where to find you," she said. "That's all."

I tried to hold her gaze, but she glanced away. I didn't know what was going on, but I did know this: that was her third lie tonight. I didn't know what it was about, but it could not be good. "I'll be here," I said.

Then she left.

No kiss. No goodbye.

All business.

# *Five*

I stretched out on the sofa, but sleep was an impossible dream. I sat up when Robin opened the door. Strain showed on her face. Fatigue and what looked like anger.

"What time is it?" I asked.

"After midnight."

I noticed all of the things that were not right: red mud on her shoes, a leaf tangled in her hair. Her face was flushed, with spots of brighter color in the hollow places. The kitchen lamp put pinpricks in her eyes.

Something was very wrong.

"I have to ask you a question," she said.

I leaned forward. "Ask," I said.

She perched on the edge of the coffee table. Our knees were close, but we did not touch. "Did you see Grace today?"

"Did something happen to her?" Adrenaline jolted through me.

"Just answer me, Adam."

My voice was too loud. "Did something happen to her?" We stared at each other. She didn't blink.

"Yes," I finally said. "I saw her at the farm. At the river."

"What time?"

"Four. Four thirty, maybe. What's going on, Robin?"

She blew out a breath. "Thanks for not lying to me."

"Why would I lie to you? Just tell me what the hell is going on. Did something happen to Grace?"

"She's been attacked."

"What do you mean?"

"Somebody assaulted her, maybe raped her. It happened this afternoon. Early evening, perhaps. Down by the river. It looks like someone dragged her off the trail. They'd just found her when I got the call."

I surged to my feet. "And you didn't tell me?"

Robin rose more slowly. Resignation moved in her voice. "I'm a cop first, Adam. I couldn't tell you."

I looked around, grabbed my shoes, started pulling them on. "Where's Grace now?"

"She's at the hospital. Your father is with her. So are Dolf and Jamie. There's nothing you can do."

"Screw that."

"She's sedated, Adam. It won't make a difference if you're there or not. But you saw her this afternoon, right before it happened. You may have seen something, heard something. You need to come with me."

"Grace comes first."

I turned for the door. She put her hand on my arm, pulled me to a stop. "There are questions that need to be answered."

I pulled my arm away, ignored her sudden anger, and felt my own emotion rise. "When you got the call, you knew it was Grace? Didn't you?"

She did not have to answer. It was obvious.

"You knew what that would mean to me and you lied about it. Worse, you tested me. You knew that I'd seen Grace and you tested me. What? Did Jamie tell you that I was there? That I saw her at the river?"

"I won't apologize. You were the last to see her. I had to know if you'd tell me that."

"Five years ago," I spat out. "Did you believe me then?"

Her eyes drifted left. "I would not be with you if I thought you'd killed that boy."

"So, where's the trust now? Where's the goddamn faith?"

She saw the rage in me, but didn't flinch. "It's what I do, Adam. It's who I am."

"Screw that, Robin."

"Adam—"

"How could you even think it?"

I turned violently away; she raised a hand to stop me, but could not. I tore open the door and was through, into the thick night that held such perfect ruin.

# *Six*

It was a short drive. I passed the Episcopal church and the old English cemetery. I took a left at the water tower, ignored the once grand homes that had decayed and been cut up into low-rent apartments; then I was into the medical district, among the doctors' offices, pharmacies, and glass-front stores selling orthopedic shoes and walkers. I parked in the emergency room lot, and headed for the double doors. The entrance was lit, everything else dark. I saw a figure leaning against the wall, the glow of a cigarette. I looked once and glanced away. Jamie's voice surprised me.

"Hey, bro."

He took a last drag and flicked the butt into the parking lot. I met him near the door, under one of the many lights.

"Hey, Jamie. How is she?"

He shoved his hands into the pockets of his jeans and shrugged. "Who knows? They won't let us see her yet. I think that she's conscious and all, but she's like, catatonic."

"Is Dad here?"

"Yeah. And Dolf."

"What about Miriam and your mom?"

"They've been in Charlotte. Flew in from Colorado last night and stayed to shop. They should be here before long. George went in to pick them up."

"George?" I asked.

"George Tallman."

"I don't understand."

Jamie waved a hand. "It's a long story. Trust me."

I nodded. "I'm going in. I need to talk to Dad. How's Dolf holding up?"

"Everybody's a mess."

"You coming?"

His head moved. "I can't handle it in there."

"See you in a bit, then." I turned for the door, and felt his hand on my shoulder.

"Adam, wait." I turned back, and he looked miserable. "I'm not just out here to have a smoke."

"I don't understand."

He looked up and then to the side, at everything but my face. "It's not going to be pretty in there."

"What do you mean?"

"Dolf found her, okay? She didn't come home and he went looking for her. He found her where she'd been dragged off the trail. She was bloody, barely conscious. He carried her home, put her in the car, and drove her here." He hesitated.

"And?"

"And she talked. She hasn't said a word since she's been here—at least not to us—but she talked to Dolf. He told the cops what she said."

"Which was what?"

"She's out of it, confused maybe, and she doesn't remember much, but she told Dolf the last thing she does remember is that you kissed her, then she told you that she hates you, and then she ran away from you."

His words crashed down on me.

"The cops say that she was attacked maybe a half mile from the dock." I saw it all on his face. Half a mile. An easy run.

It was happening again.

"They think that I had something to do with it?"

Jamie looked like he'd rather be anywhere but here. He

seemed to twist inside his own body. "It's pretty bad, isn't it, bro? Nobody has forgotten why you left."

"I would never hurt Grace."

"I'm just saying—"

"I know what you're saying, damn it. What's Dad saying?"

"Not a word, man. He's gone into some kind of weird shutdown. I've never seen anything like it. And Dolf—Jesus—he looks like somebody hit him with a brick. I don't know. It's ugly." He paused. We both knew where this would go. "I've been out here for an hour. I just thought you should know . . . before you walk in there."

"Thanks, Jamie. I mean it. You didn't have to."

"We're brothers, man."

"Are the police still here?"

He shook his head. "They hung out for a long time, but it's like I said, Grace isn't really talking. I think they're out at the farm, Robin and some guy named Grantham. He works for the sheriff. He's the one asking all the questions."

"The sheriff," I said, feeling the emotion move into my face: the dislike, the memories. It was the Rowan County sheriff who'd filed the murder charge against me.

Jamie nodded. "Same one."

"Wait a minute. Why is Robin involved in this? She works for the city."

"I think she does all the sex cases. Some kind of partnership with the sheriff's office when it's out of her normal jurisdiction. She's always in the paper. That Grantham, though, don't let him fool you. He's only been around for a few years, but he's sharp."

"Robin questioned me." I still could not believe it.

"She had to, man. You know what it took for her to stand by you when everyone and his brother wanted you strung up? She almost got fired for it." Jamie shoved his hands deeper into his pockets. "You need me to go in with you?"

"You offering?"

He didn't answer, just looked embarrassed. "No problem," I said, and turned away.

"Hey," Jamie said. I stopped. "What I said before, about being glad to have a front-row seat . . . I didn't mean it. Not like this."

"It's cool, Jamie. No sweat."

I went in through the double doors. Lights hummed. People looked up and then ignored me. I rounded a corner and saw my father first. He sat like a broken man. His head hung loosely and his arms wrapped around his shoulders as if they had too many joints. Dolf sat beside him, very erect, and stared at the wall in utter stillness. The skin beneath his eyes had pulled away in pale, pink crescents, and he, too, looked reduced. He saw me first, and twitched as if caught doing something he should not.

I stepped farther into the waiting area they occupied. "Dolf." I paused. "Dad."

Dolf pushed himself to his feet and rubbed his hands on his thighs. My father looked up, and I saw that his face looked shattered, too. He held my eyes and straightened his back as if will alone could reconstitute a broken frame. I thought of what Robin had said, that my father wept when he heard that I'd come back. I saw nothing like that now. His fists were white and hard. Cords stretched the skin of his neck.

"What do you know about this, Adam?"

I'd hoped that this would not happen, that Jamie had been wrong. "What do you mean?"

"Don't be smart with me, son. What do you know about this?" He raised his voice. "About Grace, goddamn it."

For an instant I froze, but then I felt the palsy in my hands, the disbelief that made my skin burn. Dolf looked traumatized. My father stepped closer. He was taller than I, still wide through the shoulders. I searched his face for reason to hope and found nothing. So be it.

"I'm not going to have this discussion," I said.

"Oh, yes, you damn well are. You're going to talk to us, and you're going to tell us what happened."

"I have nothing to say to you about this."

"You were with her. You kissed her. She ran from you. Don't deny it. They found her clothes still on the dock." He'd made up his mind. The calm was a veneer. It wouldn't last. "The truth, Adam. For once. The truth."

But I could tell him nothing; so I said the only thing that still mattered to me. Knowing my father and what would come, I said it.

"I want to see her."

He lunged for me. He caught me by the shirt and slammed me against the hard hospital wall. Every detail of his face was plain, but mostly I saw the stranger in him, the pure and crushing hatred as the last of his faith in me fell away. "If you did this," he said, "I will fucking kill you."

I didn't fight back. I let him hold me against the wall until the hatred shrank into something less total. Like pain and loss. Like something in him just died.

"You should not have to ask me," I said, removing his hands from my shirt. "And I should not have to answer."

He turned away. "You are not my son," he said.

He showed me his back, and Dolf could not meet my eyes; but I refused to be made small. Not now. Not again. So I fought the overwhelming urge to explain. I stood my ground and, when my father turned, I held his eyes until he looked away. I sat on one side of the waiting area and my father sat on the other. At one point, Dolf made as if to cross the room to speak with me.

"Sit down, Dolf," my father said.

Dolf sat.

Eventually, my father climbed to his feet. "I'm going for a walk," he said. "I need some unspoiled air." When the sound of his feet faded away, Dolf came to sit beside me. He was just over sixty, a hardworking man with massive hands and iron hair. Dolf had been around for as long as I could remember.

My entire life. He'd started on the farm as a young man, and when my father inherited the place, he'd kept Dolf on as the number two man. They were like brothers, inseparable. It had always been my belief, in fact, that without Dolf, neither my father nor I would have survived my mother's suicide. He'd held us together, and I could still remember the weight of his hand on my narrow shoulder in the hard days after the world vanished in a flash of smoke and thunder.

I studied his uneven face, the small blue eyes and the eyebrows dusted with white. He patted my knee and leaned his head against the wall. In profile, he looked like he'd been carved from a hunk of dried beef.

"Your father is a passionate man, Adam. He acts in the moment, but usually calms down and sees things differently. Gray Wilson was murdered and Janice saw what she saw. Now you're back and someone's done this to Grace. He's worked up. He'll get over it."

"Do you really think words can make this right?"

"I don't think you did anything wrong, Adam. And if your father was thinking straight, he'd see it that way, too. You need to understand that when Grace came to me, I had no idea what to do. My wife left when my own daughter was young. I knew nothing about nothing. Your father helped me. He feels responsible." He spread his palms. "He's a proud man, and prideful men don't show their hurt. They lash out. They do things they eventually regret."

"That changes nothing."

Dolf shook his head again. "We all have regrets. You do. I do. But the older we get, the more there are to carry around. That much weight can break a man. That's all I'm saying. Give your old man a chance. He never believed you killed that boy, but he couldn't just ignore the things his own wife said."

"He threw me out."

"And he's wanted to make it right. I can't count the times he wanted to call you, or write you. He even asked me once if I'd drive to New York with him. He said there were things to say, and not all things should be trusted to paper."

"Wanting is not the same as doing."

"That's true."

I thought of the blank page I'd found on my father's desk. "What stopped him?"

"Pride. And your stepmother."

"Janice." The name came with difficulty.

"She's a decent woman, Adam. A loving mother. Good for your father. In spite of everything, I still believe that, just as she believes what she saw that night. I can promise that these five years have not been easy on her, either. It's not like she had a choice. We all act on what we believe."

"You want me to forgive him?" I asked.

"I want you to give him a chance."

"His loyalty should be to me."

Dolf sighed. "You're not his only family, Adam."

"I was his first."

"It doesn't work that way. Your mother was beautiful and he adored her. But things changed when she died. You changed most of all."

"I had my reasons."

A sudden brightness moved into Dolf's eyes. The manner of her death hit us all hard. "He loved your mother, Adam. Marrying again was not something he did lightly. Gray Wilson's death put him in a difficult place. He had to choose between believing you and believing his wife. Do you think that could be easy or anything but dangerous? Try to see it like that."

"There's no conflict today. What about now?"

"Now is . . . complicated. There's the timing. The things Grace said."

"What about you, then? Is today complicated for you?"

Dolf turned in his seat. He faced me with blunt features and a level gaze. "I believe what Grace told me, but I know you, too. So, while I don't know what, exactly, to believe, I do think that this will all be sorted out in time." He looked away. "Sinners usually pay for their sins."

I studied his raw face, the chapped lips and the drooping eyes that ill-concealed the grief. "You honestly believe that?" I asked.

He looked up at the humming lights, so that a bright, gray sheen seemed to cover his eyes. His voice drifted, and was pale as smoke.

"I do," he said. "I absolutely do."

# *Seven*

Ten minutes later, the cops materialized in the door. Robin appeared subdued, while the other cop made small, eager movements. Tall and round-shouldered, he was somewhere north of fifty, in faded jeans and a red jacket. Brown hair spread thinly over a narrow forehead and sharp nose. A badge hung on his belt and small, round glasses flashed over washed-out eyes.

"Can we talk outside?" Robin asked.

Dolf sat up straighter, but said nothing. I got up and followed them out. Jamie was nowhere to be seen. The other cop held out a hand. "I'm Detective Grantham," he said. We shook hands. "I work for the sheriff, so don't let the clothes fool you."

His smile broadened, but I knew better than to trust it. No smile could be real tonight. "Adam Chase," I said.

His face went flat. "I know who you are, Mr. Chase—I've read the file—and I will make every effort to keep that knowledge from coloring my objectivity."

I kept my calm, but it took some effort. No one knew a thing about me in New York. I'd grown used to it. "Are you capable of that?" I asked.

"I never knew the boy that was killed. I know he was liked, that he was a football hero and all that; that he had a lot of family around here. I know that they made a lot of noise about rich men's justice. But that was all before my time. You're just like anybody else to me, Mr. Chase. No preconceptions."

He gestured at Robin. "Now, Detective Alexander has told me about your relationship to the victim. None of us likes to see cases like this, but it's important to move as quickly as possible when something like this does occur. I know that it's late and that you're probably upset, but I'm hoping that you can help me out."

"I'll do what I can."

"That's good. That's just fine. Now, I understand that you saw the victim today?"

"Her name is Grace."

He smiled again, and this one had an edge on it. "Of course," he said. "What did you and Grace talk about? How was her state of mind?"

"I don't know how to answer that," I said. "I don't know her anymore. It's been a long time. She never responded to my letters."

Robin spoke. "You wrote to her?"

I could feel the sudden hurt in her voice.

*You wrote to her, but not to me.*

I turned to Robin. "I wrote to her because she was too young to understand my reasons for leaving. I needed her to understand why I was no longer there for her."

"Just tell me about today," Grantham said. "Tell me the rest of it."

I pictured Grace: the heat of her skin beneath my palm, the fierce resentment, the undertones of something more. I knew what this cop was looking for. He had his story from Grace and wanted corroboration; to hell with objectivity. Part of me wanted to give it to him. Why? Because screw it.

"I rubbed lotion on her back. She kissed me. She said that she hates me." I looked Grantham in the eye. "She ran away."

"Did you chase her?" Grantham asked.

"It wasn't that kind of running away."

"It doesn't sound like the kind of reunion most would expect, either."

My voice came low and hard. "Thinking that I raped Grace Shepherd is like saying I raped my own daughter."

Grantham did not blink. "Yet, daughters are raped with great consistency by their fathers, Mr. Chase."

I knew that he was right. "It's not like it sounds," I said. "She was angry at me."

"Why?" Grantham asked.

"Because I left her. She was making a point."

"What else?"

"She said that she had lots of boyfriends. She wanted me to know that. She wanted me to hurt, too, I think."

"Are you saying that she's promiscuous?" Grantham asked.

"I'm not saying anything like that. How would I know something like that?"

"She told you."

"She also kissed me. She was hurt. She was lashing out. I was her family and I left her when she was fifteen years old."

"She's not your daughter, Mr. Chase."

"That's irrelevant."

Grantham looked at Robin, then back at me. He clasped his hands in front of his waist. "Very well. Go on."

"She was wearing a white bikini and sunglasses. Nothing else. She was wet, just out of the river. When she ran away, she ran south along the bank. There's a trail that's been there forever. It leads to Dolf's house, about a mile down."

"Did you assault Ms. Shepherd?"

"I did not."

Grantham pursed his lips. "Okay, Mr. Chase. That'll do for now. We'll speak again later."

"Am I a suspect?" I asked.

"I rarely speculate on such things this early in an investigation. However, Detective Alexander has stated, quite emphatically, that she does not believe you capable." He paused, looked at Alexander, and I saw flakes of dried skin on his glasses. "Of course, I have to consider the fact that you and Detective Alexander apparently have some kind of relationship. That complicates matters. We'll have a better idea about all of this once we can speak to the victim"—he caught himself—"to Grace."

"When will that be?" I asked.

"Just waiting for the doctor to clear it." Grantham's cell phone chirped and he looked at the caller ID. "I need to get this." He answered the phone and walked away. Robin moved next to me, yet I found it hard to look at her. It was like she had two faces: the one I saw above me in the half-light of her bedroom and the one I'd seen most recently, the cop.

"I shouldn't have tested you," she said.

"No."

"I apologize."

She stood in front of me, and her face was the softest I'd seen since my return. "It's complicated, Adam. For five years, all I've had is the job. I take it seriously. I'm good at it but it's not all good. Not all the time."

"What do you mean?"

"You get isolated. You see shadows." She shrugged, dug deeper for the explanation. "Even the good guys will lie to a cop. Eventually, you get used to it. Then you start to expect it." She was struggling. "I know it's not right. I don't like it either, but it's who I am. It's what I became when you left."

"You never doubted me, Robin, not even during the worst of it."

She reached for my hand. I let her take it.

"She was so innocent," I said. I spoke of Grace.

"She'll get over this, Adam. People get over worse."

But I was already shaking my head. "I'm not talking about what happened today. I'm talking about when I left. When she was a child. It was like a light came off of her. That's what Dolf used to say."

"How so?"

"He said that most people walk in light and dark. That's the way the world usually works. But some people carry the light with them. Grace was like that."

"She's not the child you remember, Adam. She hasn't been for a long time."

There was something in Robin's voice. "What do you mean?" I asked.

"About six months ago, a state trooper caught her doing one-twenty down the interstate at two in the morning on a stolen motorcycle. She wasn't even wearing a helmet."

"Was she drunk?" I asked.

"No."

"Was she prosecuted?"

"Not for stealing the bike."

"Why not?"

"It was Danny Faith's bike. I guess he didn't know that she's the one who took it. He reported it stolen but wouldn't press charges. They locked her up, but the D.A. dropped the case. Dolf hired a lawyer to handle the speeding charge. She lost her license."

I could picture the bike, a big Kawasaki that Danny had had forever. Grace would be very small on it, but I could see her, too: the speed, the torrent of noise, and her hair straight out behind her. Like she'd looked the first time she'd ridden my father's horse.

Fearless.

"You don't know her," I said.

"A hundred and twenty miles an hour, Adam. Two in the morning. No helmet. It took the patrolman five miles to catch up with her."

I thought of Grace now, damaged in one of those antiseptic rooms behind me. I rubbed at my eyes. "What am I supposed to feel, Robin? You've seen this before."

"Anger. Emptiness. I don't know."

"How can you not know?"

She shrugged. "It's never been someone I love."

"And Grace?"

Her eyes were impregnable. "I've not known Grace for some time, Adam."

I was silent, thinking of Grace's words on the dock.

*Who else cared about me?*

"Are you okay?" Robin asked.

I was not, not even close. "If I could find the guy that did this, I'd kill him." I showed her my eyes. "I would kill that motherfucker dead."

Robin looked around; no one was close. "Don't say that, Adam. Not here. Not ever."

Grantham finished his phone call and met us at the hospital door. We walked in together. Dolf and my father were speaking to the attending physician. Grantham interrupted them.

"Can we see her yet?"

The doctor was a young, earnest-looking man with black-framed glasses and a thin nose. He seemed small and prematurely bent; he held a clipboard against his chest as if it could armor him from the injuries that surrounded him. His voice was surprisingly firm.

"Physically, she's sound enough. But I don't know that she'll be responsive. She has not really said anything since she came in, except for once in the first hour. She asked for somebody named Adam."

People turned as one: my father, Dolf, Robin, and Detective Grantham. Eventually, the doctor looked at me as well. "Are you Adam?" he asked. I nodded, and my father's mouth opened in the silence. The doctor looked uncertain. "Maybe if you spoke to her. . . ."

"We need to speak to her first," Grantham said.

"Very well," the doctor said. "I will need to be in the room as well."

"No problem."

The doctor led us down a narrow hall with empty gurneys

along the wall. We rounded a corner and he stopped next to a pale wooden door with a small window in it. I caught a glimpse of Grace under a thin blanket.

"The rest of you wait out here," he said, then held the door for the detectives.

Cool air moved against my face and then they were inside. Dolf and my father watched through the window while I paced small circles and thought of the last thing Grace had said to me. Five minutes later the door opened. The doctor looked at me.

"She's asking for you," he said.

I started for the door, but Grantham stopped me with a hand against my chest. "She wouldn't speak to us. We've agreed to let you in because the doc here thinks it will help her snap out of it." I met his gaze and held it. "Don't do anything to make me regret this."

I leaned against his hand until he was forced to move it. I stepped past him, into the room, still feeling his fingers there, and how he'd pushed hard at the last second. The door swung on silent hinges; the two old men crowded against the glass. Then she was before me, and I felt my resentment wither and die. None of that mattered.

Hospital light sucked the color out of her. Her chest rose and fell, with long pauses where I felt that none should be. Strands of blond hung across her cheek, and there was dried blood in the shell of her ear. I looked at Robin, whose face was closed.

I walked around the bed. Stitches pierced her lips. She had massive bruising, her eyes so swollen that they were barely open, just a glimmer of blue that looked too pale. Tape secured a tube to the back of her hand, which felt brittle when I took it. I tried to find some hint of her in those eyes, and when I said her name, the slice of blue expanded minutely, and I knew that she was there. She stared at me for a long time.

"Adam?" she asked, and I heard all of the things I knew she felt, the subtle nuance of pain and loss.

"I'm here."

She rolled her head away, not wanting me to see the tears that slipped, thick and silent, down her face. I straightened so that she could see me when she opened her eyes. It took her a while. Grantham shifted his feet. No one else moved.

She did not look at me again until the tears had ceased, but when our eyes met, I knew they would come again. The battle was there, in her face, and I watched helplessly as she lost it. She held up her arms and I leaned into them as the dam burst again; and she grasped me as she began to sob. Her body was hot and shaking; I put my arms around her as best as I could. I told her not to worry. I told her that everything would be okay. Then she leaned her mouth against my ear one more time and whispered something so quietly I could barely hear her.

"I'm sorry," she said.

I pulled away so she could see my face. I nodded because I had no words; then she pulled me back down and held me as the tremors racked her.

I looked up, and found my father's face in the window. He rubbed a hand across his eyes and turned away, but not before I saw the palsy in his fingers. Dolf watched him go, and then shook his head, as if in great sadness.

I returned my attention to Grace, and tried with my arms to swallow her up. Eventually, she drifted back to whatever shelter her mind had made for itself. She never said another word, just rolled onto her side, and closed her eyes.

The cops got nothing.

Back in the hall, Grantham crowded me again. "I think that we need to step outside," he said.

"Why?"

"You know why." His hand settled around my arm. I jerked it away and he grabbed for it again.

"Just a minute now," Dolf said.

Grantham got control of himself. "I told you not to piss me off," he said.

"Come on, Adam," Robin said. "Let's go outside."

"No." It was all settling upon me: Grace's lost innocence, the suspicions that dogged me, and the darkness that hung above my return to this place. "I'm not going anywhere."

"I want to know what she said." Grantham stopped short of actually touching me. "She said something to you. I want it."

"Is that true?" Robin asked. "Did she speak to you?"

"Don't ask me, Robin. It's not important."

"If she said anything, we need to know what it is."

I took in the faces around me. What Grace had said was for me, and I felt no need to share it. But Robin put her hand on my arm. "I have vouched for you, Adam. Do you understand what that means?"

I pushed lightly past her and looked in on Grace. She had curled into a ball, her back to the world outside. I still felt the hot slide of her tears as she'd pressed against me. I spoke to Grantham, but put my eyes on my father. I told them exactly what she said.

"She said that she was sorry."

My father slumped.

"Sorry for what?" Grantham asked.

I'd told them the truth, exactly what she'd said; but interpreting that apology was not my problem. So, I offered an explanation that I knew he would accept, even though it was a lie.

"When we were at the river, she said that she hated me. I imagine that she was apologizing for that."

He looked thoughtful. "That's it?" he asked. "That's all she said?"

"That's it."

Robin and Grantham looked at each other and there was a moment of unspoken communication between them. Then Robin spoke. "There are a few other things we'd like to discuss with you. Outside, if you don't mind."

"Sure," I said, and turned for the exit. I took only two steps before I heard my father say my name. His hands were palms up, his face drawn down by the realization that Grace would be unlikely to embrace the man who'd so abused her. There was no forgiveness in my face as I met his eyes. He took half a step and said my name again, a question, a plea, and for a moment I thought about it; he was in pain, full of sudden regret and of the years that had marched so implacably between us.

"I don't think so," I said, and walked out.

# *Eight*

Ilooked for Jamie as we hit the night air, and I saw him at the edge of the lot. He sat behind the wheel of a darkened truck. He took a swallow from a bottle and did not get out. An ambulance pulled in, lights off.

"I need a cigarette," Grantham said, and walked off to find one.

We watched his back, and stood in the kind of awkward silence that troubled people know so well. I heard a horn, a light burst from Jamie's truck. He pointed to his right, at the entrance to the emergency lot. I turned to see a long, black car slide through the narrow, concrete barrier and pull to a stop. The engine died. Two doors opened and they stepped out: Miriam, my sister, and a thickset man in black boots and a police uniform. They both saw me at the same time and stopped. Miriam looked startled and stayed by the car. The man with her grinned and came over.

"Adam," he said, and took me by the hand, pumping it fiercely.

"George."

George Tallman had been a hanger-on for as long as I could remember. He was a few years my junior, and had been much better friends with Danny than with me. I retrieved my hand and studied him. He was six feet two, maybe two ten, with thick, sandy hair and round, brown eyes. He was solid, not fat, and had a handshake he was proud of.

"The last time I saw you with a gun, George, you were drunk and trying to shoot beer cans off a stump with an air rifle."

He glanced at Robin and his eyes narrowed. The smile fell off. "That was a long time ago, Adam."

"He's not really a cop," Robin said.

For an instant George looked angry, but it passed. "I do school outreach," he said. "Give presentations to the kids, talk about drugs." He looked at Robin. "And I am a cop." His voice remained even. "Bullets and everything."

I heard tentative footsteps and turned to see Miriam. She looked pale in loose slacks and a long-sleeved shirt. She gave me a nervous smile, but her eyes were not without hope. She had matured, but did not look like her portrait. "Hello, Miriam," I said.

"Hi, Adam."

I gave her a hug, felt the bones of her. She squeezed back, but I could tell that doubt still troubled her. She and Gray Wilson had been good friends. My trial for his murder had cut her deeply. I gave her an extra squeeze, then let her go. The moment I stepped away, George filled the void. His arm settled across her shoulders and he pulled her against his side. This surprised me. He used to follow Miriam around like a barely tolerated puppy.

"We're engaged," he said.

I looked down, saw the ring on her hand: a small diamond in yellow gold. Five years, I reminded myself. Things change. "Congratulations," I said.

Miriam looked uncomfortable. "This is not really the time and place to talk about that," she said.

He squeezed her tighter, blew out through his nose, and looked up from the ground. "You're right," he said.

I glanced back to the car, a shining, black Lincoln. "Where's Janice?" I asked.

Miriam began. "She wanted to come—"

"We took her home," George interrupted.

"Why?" I asked, knowing the answer.

George hesitated. "The hour," he said. "The circumstances."

"Meaning me?" I said.

Miriam shrank under the words, as George finished the
thought. "She says this damns you like the trial failed to do."

Miriam spoke. "I told her that was unfair."

I let it go. I let it all go. I studied my sister: the bent neck,
the thin shoulders. She risked a glance, then dropped her
eyes again. "I told her, Adam. She just wouldn't listen."

"Don't worry about it," I said. "How about you? Are you
okay?"

Hair moved on her head as she nodded. "Bad memories,"
she said, and I understood. My unexpected return was baring
old wounds.

"I'll get over it," she said, then turned to her fiancé. "I
need to speak to my father. I'm glad to see you, Adam."

They left, and I watched them. At the door, Miriam
looked back at me; her chin settled on her shoulder and her
eyes were large and black and troubled.

I looked at Robin. "You don't care for George, I take it."

"Lack of commitment," she said. "Come on. We still have
things to discuss."

I followed her to Grantham's car, which was parked on
the side street. The cigarette was half-smoked and stained
his face orange each time he took a drag. He dropped the
butt in the gutter and his face fell into shadow.

"Tell me about the trail by the river," he said.

"It goes south, along the river, to Grace's house."

"And beyond that?"

"It's old, a Sapona Indian trail, and it goes for miles. It runs
beyond Grace's house to the edge of the farm, then through a
neighboring farm and several small properties with fishing
cabins on them. After that, I don't know."

"How about to the north?"

"It's about the same."

"Do people come through there? Hikers? Fishermen?"

"Occasionally."

He nodded. "Grace was attacked about a half mile from the dock, where the trail bends hard to the north. What can you tell me about that area?"

"The trees are thick there, but not deep. It's really just a band of forest along the river. Above the trees, it's pasture."

"So, whoever did this most likely came along the trail."

"Or off the river," I said.

"But you'd have seen that."

I was already shaking my head. "I was only on the dock for a few minutes. But there was a woman."

"What woman?"

I described what I'd seen: the white hair, the canoe. "But she went upstream, not down."

"Do you know her?"

I pictured the face, a middle-aged woman that looked young. Something familiar. "No," I said.

Grantham made a note. "We'll check on it. She may have seen something. Someone in another boat, a man. He could have seen Grace, and put a boat ashore downriver. She's beautiful, half-dressed on a lonely stretch of river . . ."

I pictured her swollen face, the tattered lips held together by knotted, black thread. No one who saw her in that hospital room could know how beautiful she truly was. Suspicion flared in me. "Do you know her?" I asked.

Grantham studied me with the stillest eyes I'd ever seen. "It's a small county, Mr. Chase."

"May I ask how you know her?"

"That's hardly relevant."

"Nevertheless . . ."

"My son is about her age. Does that satisfy you?" I said nothing, and he continued evenly. "We were talking about a boat. Someone that may have seen her from the river and laid in wait."

"He'd have to know that she'd walk home that way," I said.

"Or he could have been coming to her, then met her on the trail. He could have seen you two on the dock and waited. Is that possible?"

"It's possible," I said.

"Does D.B. seventy-two mean anything to you?" He slipped the question in, and for a long moment I could not speak.

"Adam?" Robin said.

I stared as something loud and tribal began to thunder in my head. The world turned upside down.

"Adam?"

"You found a ring." I could barely drive out the words. The effect on Grantham was immediate. He rocked onto the balls of his feet.

"Why would you say that?" he asked.

"A gold ring with a garnet stone."

"How do you know that?"

My words came in some other man's voice. "Because D.B. seventy-two is engraved on the back of it."

Grantham shoved his hand into a coat pocket, and when it reappeared it held a rolled-up plastic bag. He allowed it to unfurl from his fingers. It glistened in the hard light, and streaked mud shone on its sides. The ring was there: heavy gold, a garnet stone. "I'd very much like to know what it means," Grantham said.

"I need a minute."

"Whatever it is, Mr. Chase, I suggest you tell me."

"Adam?" Robin sounded hurt, but I couldn't worry about that. I thought of Grace, and of the man who was supposed to be my friend.

"This can't be right." I ran the film in my head, the way it could have been. I knew his face, the shape of him, the sound of him. So I could fill in the blanks, and it was like watching a movie, a horror show, as my oldest friend raped a woman I'd known from the age of two.

I pointed at the ring in the plastic bag.

"You found that where it happened?" I asked.

"It was at the scene, where Dolf found her."

I walked away, came back. It could not be true.

But it was.

Five years. Things change.

And there was nothing good left in my voice. "Seventy-two was the number of his football jersey. The ring was a gift from his grandmother."

"Go on."

"D.B. stands for his nickname. Danny Boy. Number seventy-two." Grantham nodded as I finished. "D.B. seventy-two. Danny Faith."

Robin stood silent; she knew what this was doing to me.

"Are you certain?" Grantham asked.

"Do you remember those fishing cabins I told you about? The ones downriver from Dolf's house?"

"Yes."

"The second one down is owned by Zebulon Faith." They both looked at me. "Danny's father," I said.

"How far down from where she was attacked?" Grantham asked.

"Less than two miles."

"Well, all right."

"I want to be there when you talk to him," I said.

"Out of the question."

"I did not have to tell you. I could have had the conversation myself."

"This is a police matter. Stay out of it."

"It's not your family."

"It's not yours either, Mr. Chase." He stepped closer, and

although his voice was measured, the anger spilled over the lines. "When I want something else from you, I'll tell you about it."

"You wouldn't have him without me," I said.

"Stay out of it, Mr. Chase."


I left the hospital as a low moon pushed silver through the trees. I drove fast, my head full of blood and grim rage. Danny Faith. Robin was right. He'd changed, crossed the line, and there was no going back. What I'd said to Robin was true.

I could kill him.

When I got to the farm, it felt off: the road too narrow, turns in the wrong places. Fence posts rose up from colorless grass, barbed wire dark and tight between them. I passed the turn for Dolf's house before I knew it was there. I backed up, hung right onto a long stretch where I'd once taught Grace to drive. She'd been eight years old, and could barely see over the wheel. I could still hear the way she laughed, feel the disappointment when I told her she was going too fast.

Now she was in the hospital, fetal and broken. I saw the stitches in her lips, the thin slivers of blue when she tried to open her eyes.

I slammed my open palm against the wheel, then gripped it with both hands and tried to bend it in half. I pushed hard on the gas, heard the slam and bang of rocks on the undercarriage. One more turn, then over a cattle guard that made the tires thump. I slid to a stop in front of a small, two-story house with white clapboards and a tin roof. My father owned it, but Dolf had lived here for decades. An oak tree spread over the yard, and I saw an old car on blocks in the open barn, its engine in parts on a picnic table under the tree.

I jerked the key out of the ignition, slammed the door, and heard the high whine of mosquitoes, the slap and stutter of bats diving low.

I locked my hands into knots as I crossed the yard. A single light hung above the porch. The knob rattled and the door swung away from me. I turned on lights, went in, and stood in Grace's room, absorbing the things she loved: posters of fast cars, riding trophies, a picture taken on a beach. There was no clutter. The bed. The desk. A row of utilitarian footwear, like snake boots and hip-waders. There were more pictures on the mirror above the dresser: two of different horses and one of the car I'd seen in the garage—her and Dolf smiling, the car on a flatbed.

The car was for her.

I turned away and pulled the door shut. I brought in my bag and tossed it on the guest-room bed. I stared at a blank spot on the wall and thought for what felt like a very long time. I waited for some kind of calm, but it never came. I asked myself what mattered, and the answer was Grace. So I searched Dolf's kitchen for a flashlight. I pulled a shotgun from the gun cabinet, cracked it, loaded it, then saw the handgun. It was an ugly, snub-nosed thing that looked about right. I put the long gun back, lifted out a box of .38 caliber shells and extracted six of them. They were fat, heavy, and slipped into the machined holes as if they'd been greased.

I paused at the door, knowing that once I stepped outside, there'd be no stopping. The gun was warming in my hand, heavy. Danny's betrayal shot dark holes through me, dredged up the kind of rage I'd not felt in years. Was I planning to kill him? Maybe. I really didn't know. But I'd find him. I'd ask some hard damn questions. And by God, he would answer them.

I went down the hill, across the pasture, and didn't need the light until I hit the trees. I turned it on and followed the narrow footpath until it intersected the main trail. I put the light on it. Except for the roots that rose above it, it was beaten smooth.

I went to the hard turn in the trail that Grantham had mentioned, saw the broken branches and bruised vegetation. I followed the ground as it sloped to a shallow depression filled with churned leaves and grasping red earth, a snow angel in the mud.

I was close to the spot where my father had pulled Grace from the river all those years ago, and as I stared at the signs of her resistance my finger found its way into the trigger guard.

I passed the boundary of my father's farm, the river on my left; then the neighboring farm, the first cabin, empty and dark. I kept an eye on it. Nothing. Then I was back in the woods, and the Faith cabin was ahead. A half mile. Fifty yards. And moonlight pushed deeper into the trees.

Thirty yards out I left the trail. The light was too much, the trees thinning. I found the darkness of the deeper forest, and angled away from the river so that I would cut the clearing above the cabin. I stopped at the edge of the trees, settled into the low growth. I could see everything: the gravel drive, the dark cabin, the car parked at the door, the shed next to the woods.

The cops.

They'd left their cars on the drive above me, and were on foot, almost to the cabin. They moved like I thought cops would move, bent at the waist, weapons low. Five of them. Their shapes blurred into one another, separated. They accelerated across the last gap, reached the car, divided. Two moved for the door. Three split for the back. Close. Damn they were close. Black on black. Part of the cabin.

I waited for the sound of splintered wood, forced myself to breathe, and saw something wrong: a pale face, motion. It was by the shed at the edge of the woods, someone peering around the corner, then pulling back. Adrenaline slammed through me. The cops were pressed against the sides of the door and one of them, Grantham maybe, had his pistol in a two-handed grip, barrel at the sky. And it looked like he was nodding. Like he was counting.

I looked back at the shed. It was a man in dark pants. I couldn't make out his face, but it was him. Had to be.

Danny Faith.

My friend.

He ducked low and turned in a dead sprint for the trees, for the trail that would lead him away. I didn't think. I ran, down the edge of the clearing, toward the shed, the gun in my hand.

I heard cop sounds at the cabin, voices, crashing wood. Someone yelled "Clear!" and it was echoed.

We were alone, the two of us, and I could hear him thrashing through brush, limbs snapping into place behind him. I made for the tree line, the shed coming up; then I was there, and I saw the glow of fire shining through the cracks of the door and through the dirt-smeared windows. The shed was on fire. Raging on fire. I was next to it when the windows blew out.

The concussion threw me into the dirt. I rolled onto my back as flames poured skyward and turned night to day. I could see everything to the edge of the woods. The trees still guarded their blackness. But he was out there, and I went after him.

I was at the edge of the trees when I heard Grantham shout my name. I saw him at the cabin door, then plunged into the trees, half-blind. But I'd grown up in woods like this, knew them, so that even when I fell I popped up like I was on a spring. But then I went down hard and the gun spun out of my hand. I couldn't find it, couldn't waste the time, so I left it.

I saw him on the trail, the flicker of his shirt as he rounded a bend. I was up to him within seconds. He heard me, turned, and I hit him in the chest at a dead run. I landed on top of him, and saw how wrong I'd been. I felt it as my hands went around his neck. He was too thin, too brittle to be Danny Faith; but I knew him, and my fingers ground deeper into the withered neck.

His face showed his own bitter hatred as he struggled beneath me. He twisted to bite me, couldn't reach, and I felt his fingers on my wrists as he tried to force my hands away. His knees rose up; his heels drummed the hard-packed clay. Part of me knew that I was wrong. The rest of me didn't care. Maybe it had been Danny. Maybe he was at the cabin, arrested and in cuffs. But maybe we'd all been wrong, and it was not Danny Faith that had raped my Grace. Not Danny, but this miserable old fuck. This sorry, worthless, undeserving motherfucker kicking in the dirt as I crushed the life out of him.

I squeezed harder.

His hands left my wrists and I felt them fumbling at his waist. When I felt something hard between us I realized the mistake I'd made. I rolled off of him as the gun hammered away, two enormous concussions that split the dark and blinded me. I kept rolling, off the trail and into the dampness under the trees. I found a wide trunk and put my back to it. I waited for the old man to come and finish the job. But the shot never came. There were voices and lights, badges glinting, and shotgun barrels as smooth as glass. Grantham was standing over me, his light in my face. I tried to stand, then something crashed into my head and I was on my back.

"Put this cocksucker in handcuffs," Grantham said to one of the deputies.

The deputy grabbed me, flipped me onto my stomach, and slammed his knee into the center of my back.

"Where's the gun?" Grantham demanded.

"It was Zebulon Faith," I said. "His gun."

Grantham looked around, shone his light down the trail. "All I see out here is you," he said.

I was shaking my head. "He set the fire and ran. He shot at me when I tried to stop him."

Grantham glanced at the river, at the slow roll of water that looked like sucking black tar, then upslope, to the oily glow of the burning shed. He shook his head and spat in the dirt.

"What a mess," he said, then walked away.

# *Nine*

They stuffed me in the back of a cop car, then watched the shed burn to the ground. Eventually, firemen put water on the smoking debris, but not before my arms went numb. I thought about what I'd almost done. Zebulon Faith. Not Danny. Feet drumming clay and the fierce satisfaction I'd felt as the life began to fade out of him. I could have killed him.

I felt like that should trouble me.

The air in the car grew close, and I watched the sun rise. Grantham poked through the soaking ash with a white-haired fireman. They picked up objects and then let them fall. Robin's car rolled out of the trees an hour after dawn. She passed me on the cratered road, and lifted a hand from the wheel. She spoke for a long time with Detective Grantham, who pointed at things amid the ruin, then at the fire marshal, who came over and spoke some more. Several times they looked at me, and Grantham refused to hide his displeasure. After about ten minutes, Robin got into her car and Grantham walked uphill to where I sat in his. He opened my door.

"Out," he said.

I slipped across the seat and put my feet on the damp grass.

"Turn around." He made a motion with his finger. I turned and he removed the handcuffs. "A question, Mr. Chase. Do you have any ownership interest in your family's farm?"

I rubbed my wrists. "The farm is held as a family partnership. I had a ten percent interest."

"Had?"

"My father bought me out."

Grantham nodded. "When you left?"

"When he kicked me out."

"So, you have nothing to gain if he sells."

"That's right."

"Who else has an interest?"

"He gave Jamie and Miriam ten percent each when he adopted them."

"What's a ten percent stake worth?"

"A lot."

"How much is a lot?"

"More than a little," I said, and he let it go.

"And your stepmother? Does she have ownership?"

"No. She has no interest."

"Okay," Grantham said.

I studied the man. His face was unreadable, his shoes black and destroyed. "That's it?" I asked.

He pointed at Robin's car. "If you have questions, Mr. Chase, you can talk to her."

"What about Danny Faith?" I asked. "What about his father?"

"Talk to Alexander," he said.

He shut my door and walked to the driver's side; turned the car around and drove back into the trees. I heard the car bottom out in a rut, then I walked down to speak with Robin. She did not get out, so I slid in next to her, my knee touching the shotgun locked to the dash. She was tired, still in last night's clothes. Her voice was drawn.

"I've been at the hospital," she said.

"How's Grace?"

"Talking a bit."

I nodded.

"She says it wasn't you."

"Are you surprised?"

"No, but she didn't see a face. Inconclusive, according to Detective Grantham."

I looked at the cabin. "Did they find Danny?" I asked.

"No sign." She stared at me. When I turned back, I knew what she was going to say before the words left her mouth. "You should not have been here, Adam."

I shrugged.

"You're lucky nobody got killed." She peered through the glass, clearly frustrated. "Jesus, Adam. You don't think right when you get like this."

"I didn't ask for this to happen but it did. I'm not going to sit on my hands and do nothing. This happened to Grace! Not some stranger."

"Did you come here to do harm?" she asked.

I thought of Dolf Shepherd's pistol lying out there in the leaves. "Would you believe me if I said no?"

"Probably not."

"Then why bother to ask? It's done."

We were both stripped-down, nerves exposed. Robin had her cop face on. I was getting to recognize it pretty well. "Why did Grantham let me go?" I asked. "He could have made my life hell."

She thought about it, then pointed at the pile of black ash. "Zebulon Faith was running a methamphetamine lab in the shed. He was probably using the money to cover the debt on the property he's bought. He had it rigged to burn. He must have known that the police were coming in. We'll find something to that effect. A motion sensor up the road. A phone call from one of the trailers you pass on the way in. Something that told him to get out. There's not much left."

"Enough?" I asked.

"For a prosecution? Maybe. Juries are fickle."

"And Faith?"

"He'd have disappeared completely, with nothing but circumstantial evidence linking him to the lab." She faced me, pivoting in her seat. "If it goes to trial, Grantham will need you to put Zebulon Faith at the scene. He weighed that into his decision to cut you loose."

"I'm still surprised he did it."

"Crystal meth is a big problem. A conviction will play well. The sheriff is a politician."

"And if Grantham thinks I had something to do with Grace's rape? Would he sell her out, too?"

Robin hesitated. "Grantham has reason to doubt that you were involved with the assault on Grace."

There was a new tension in her face. I knew her too well. "Something's changed," I said.

She thought about it, and I waited her out. Finally, she relented.

"Whoever attacked Grace left a scrap of paper at the scene. A message."

Cold filled me up. "And you've known this all along?"

"Yes." Unrepentant.

"What did it say?"

" 'Tell the old man to sell.' "

I stared at her in disbelief.

"That's what it said."

My mind went red, and I got out of the car, started walking.

I should have killed him.

"Adam." I felt her hands on my shoulders. "We don't know that it was Zebulon Faith. Or Danny, for that matter. A lot of people want your father to sell. More than one person has made threats. The ring could be a coincidence."

"I somehow doubt that."

"Look at me," she said. I turned. She stood on a depression in the earth, a low place, and her head barely reached my chest. "You got lucky today. You understand? Somebody could have been killed. You. Faith. It should have ended worse than it did. We will handle this."

"I don't owe you any promises, Robin."

Sudden bitterness twisted her mouth. "It wouldn't matter if you did. I know what your promises are worth."

Then she turned, and as she left the darkness beneath the trees, the day fell upon her shoulders like a weight. She disappeared into her car and threw dirt from her rear tires as she slewed the car around. I stepped onto the road behind her, watched her taillights flare as she slammed her way out.

It took half an hour to find Dolf's gun, but eventually I saw it, one black patch among the millions. I found the path next, and followed the river, my feet soundless on the soft earth. The river moved, as always, but its voice was hushed, and after a time I ceased to hear it. I put the violence behind me, sought some kind of peace, a stillness that went beyond mere numbness. Being in the woods helped. Like memories of Robin in the early days, my father before the trial, my mother before the light winked out of her. I walked slowly and felt rough bark under my fingers. I rounded a bend in the trail and stopped.

Fifteen feet away, its head lowered to drink, was a white deer. Its coat shone, still damp from the night air, and I saw a quiver in its shoulder, where it took the weight of its thick neck, and of the antlers that spanned five feet from tip to tip. I held my breath. Then its head came up, turned my way, and I saw those great, black eyes.

Nothing moved.

Moisture condensed around its nostrils.

It snorted, and some strange emotion stirred in my chest: comfort shot through with pain. I did not know what it meant, but I felt it, like it could tear me open. Seconds rolled over us and I thought back to the other white deer and how I'd learned, at age nine, that anger could take away pain. I reached out a hand, knowing that I was too far away to touch it, that too many years had passed to take that day back. I stepped closer, and the animal tilted its head, scraped an

antler against one of the trees. Otherwise, it stood perfectly
still and continued to regard me.

Then the sound of a shot crashed through the forest. It
came from far away, two miles, maybe. It had nothing to do
with the deer; but still, the animal rose. It leapt out and arced
above the river, the weight of its antlers pulling it down by
the head; and then it hit, surging across the current, lunging
as it drew near the opposite bank. It powered up the slick
clay, and at the top, it stopped and turned. For a moment, it
showed one wild, black eye, then it tossed its head once and
slipped into the gloom; a pale flicker, a slash of white that, in
places, looked gray. For no reason that I could explain, I
found it suddenly hard to breathe. I sat down on the cold,
damp ground, and the past filled me up.

I saw the day my mother died.

*I didn't want to kill anything. I never had. That was my
mother in me, or so the old man would say if he knew.
But death and blood was part of what it took to go
from boy to man, no matter what my mother had to say
about it. I'd heard the argument more than once: quiet
voices late at night, my parents arguing over what was
right and wrong in the raising of their boy. I was eight,
and could drill a bottle cap from sixty yards out; but
practice was just practice. We all knew what was out
there.*

*The old man killed his first deer when he was eight,
and his eyes still went glassy when he talked about it,
about how his own father had dragged hot blood across
his forehead that day. It was a baptismal, he'd say, a thing
that stretched through time, and I woke on the designated
morning with a stomach full of cold and dread and
nausea. But I geared up, and met Dolf and my father
outside in the dark air. They asked if I was ready. I said
that I was, and they flanked me as we climbed the fence
and set out for the deep and secret woods.*

*Four hours later we were back at the house. My rifle smelled of burned powder, but there was no blood on my forehead. Nothing to be ashamed of, they said, but I doubted their sincerity.*

*I sat on the tailgate of my father's truck as he walked inside to check on my mother. He came down with a heavy step.*

*"How is she?" I asked, knowing what his answer would be.*

*"Same." His voice was gruff, but could not hide the sadness.*

*"Did you tell her?" I asked, and wondered if my failure might bring her some rare joy.*

*He ignored me, began to strip down his rifle. "She asked me for a cup of coffee. Take her one, would you?"*

*I didn't know what was wrong with my mother, only that the light had died out of her. She'd always been warm and fun, a friend on the long days that my father worked the land. We played games, told stories. Laughed all the time. Then something changed. She went dark. I'd lost count of the times I'd heard her crying, and was scared by the many times that my words to her had fallen into a blank-eyed silence. She'd wasted down to nothing, her skin stretched tight, and I feared that one day I might see her bones if she passed before an undraped window.*

*It was scary stuff, and I knew what none of it meant.*

*I entered the quiet house, smelled the coffee my mother liked. I poured a cup, and was careful on the stairs. I spilled none of it.*

*Until I opened her door.*

*The gun was already against her temple, her face hopeless and white above the pale pink robe she wore.*

*She pulled the trigger as the door swung wide.*

*My father and I never talked about it. We buried the woman we loved, and it was like I'd always known: death and blood was part of what it took to go from boy to man.*

*I killed a lot of deer after that.*

# *Ten*

I found Dolf on the porch, rolling a cigarette. "Morning," I said, and stood against the rail, watching his deft and busy fingers. He studied me as he licked the paper and ran the cigarette between his fingers one last time. He took a match from his shirt pocket, struck it with a thumbnail. His eyes settled on the pistol still tucked under my belt. He blew out the match.

"That mine?" he asked.

I pulled out the pistol and set it on the table. The sweet tobacco smell surrounded me as I bent, and his face looked etched in the sharp light. "Sorry," I said.

He picked up the gun and sniffed the barrel; then he laid it back down. "No harm done." He leaned back in the chair and it creaked beneath him. "Five years is a long time," he said casually.

"Yep."

"Guess you came home for a reason. Want to tell me about it?"

"No."

"Maybe I can help you."

It was a good offer. He meant it. "Not this time, Dolf."

He gestured downriver. "I smelled the fire. Thought maybe I could see the glow, too."

He wanted to talk about it, wanted to know, and I didn't blame him.

"Sound travels down the river." He took a drag. "I can smell the smoke on you."

I sat in the rocker next to his and put my feet up on the rail. I looked once again at the gun and then at Dolf's coffee cup. I thought of my mother and of the white deer.

"Somebody's hunting the property," I said.

He rocked slowly. "It's your father."

"He's hunting again? I thought that he'd sworn it off."

"Sort of."

"What does that mean?"

"There's a pack of wild dogs hanging around. They showed up after the first of the cattle was shot. They smell blood from miles off. Find the carcasses at night. They've got a taste for it now. We can't seem to drive them off. Your father is determined to kill every last one of them. It's his new religion."

"I thought that cattle had been shot at only once."

"That's all we reported to the sheriff. It's more like seven or eight times now."

"What kind of dogs?" I asked.

"Hell, I don't know. Big ones. Little ones. Dirty, skulking bastards. They're all mean as hell. But the leader—damn—now he's something else. Looks like a cross between a German shepherd and a Doberman. Hundred pounds, maybe. Black. Fast. Smart as hell. Doesn't matter where your father comes from, how quiet he is, that black one always sees him first. Fades away. Your old man can't get a shot. Says that dog's the devil himself."

"How many in the pack?"

"Maybe a dozen at first. Your old man killed two or three. It's down to five or six now."

"Who killed the others?"

"That black one, I think. We found 'em with their throats torn out. All males. Rivals, I guess."

"Jesus."

"Yep."

"Why aren't you reporting the shootings?"

"Because the sheriff is useless. He was useless five years ago and he's found no reason to change, far as I can tell. First time we called him, he walked once around the carcass, then suggested that it might be best for all concerned if your father just sold. That about settled it for your dad and me."

"Is anybody still at the hospital?"

"They won't let us see her, so no point hanging around. We came home a few hours ago."

I stood up, walked to the corner of the porch. The sun was rising above the treetops. I debated how much to tell Dolf, decided he ought to know everything. "It was Zebulon Faith," I said. "Him or Danny. They're the ones that did it."

Dolf was silent for a long moment. I heard his chair creak again and felt his footsteps on the old floor. He stood next to me and put his hands on the rail, looked out to where a low mist was rising from the river.

"Wasn't Zebulon Faith," he said.

I turned, not sure what to think; he picked a piece of tobacco off of his tongue as I waited for him to explain. He took his time about it.

"He's mean enough to do it, I reckon, but he went in for prostate cancer three years ago." He looked at me. "The old boy can't get it up anymore. He's impotent. No lead left in the pencil."

"How can you know that?" I asked.

Dolf sighed, kept his eyes on the river. "We had the same doctor, got diagnosed about the same time; we went through it together. Not like we were friends or anything, but we talked once or twice." He shrugged. "Just one of those things."

"Are you sure?"

"Pretty much."

I thought about Dolf fighting off a cancer while I struggled for meaning in some faraway city I had no business being in. "I'm sorry, Dolf."

He spit out another piece of tobacco, shrugged off my sympathy. "What makes you think it was one of them?" he asked.

I told him everything I knew: Danny's ring, the fire, my fight with Zebulon Faith.

"Maybe a good thing you didn't kill him," Dolf said.

"I wanted to."

"Don't blame you."

"Could have been Danny that did it."

Dolf thought about it, spoke with reluctance. "Most people have a dark streak in them somewhere. Danny is a good enough kid in a lot of ways, but his streak is closer to the surface than most."

"What do you mean?"

He studied me. "I spent a lot of years watching you swing at shadows, Adam. Lashing out. Untouchable in a lot of ways. It killed me to see you like that, but I could understand it. You saw things no boy should see." He paused and I looked away. "When you'd come home bloodied up, or when your dad and I bailed you out, there was always a sadness in you, a quietness. Damn, son, you'd look all but lost. That's a hard thing for me to say to you, but there it is. Now Danny, he was different. He'd have this look of barely restrained glee. That boy, he got in fights because he enjoyed it. Big damn difference."

I didn't argue. In a lot of ways, Danny's dark streak formed the bedrock of our friendship. I'd met him six months after my mother killed herself. I was already fighting, cutting school. Most of my friends had pulled away from me. They didn't know how to handle me, had no idea what to say to a boy whose mother blew her own head off. That hurt, too, but I didn't whine about it. I pulled deeper into myself, gave up on everybody. Danny came into my life like a brother. He had no money, bad grades, and an abusive father. He hadn't seen his mother or a square meal in two years.

Consequence meant nothing to Danny. He flat-out did not give a shit.

I wanted to feel like he did.

We hit it off. If I got into a fight, he backed me up. I did the same. Older kids. Kids our age. It didn't matter. Once, in the eighth grade, we stole the principal's car and parked it in plain view at the massage parlor by the interstate. Danny went down for that: expelled for two weeks, juvenile record. He never mentioned my name.

But he was a grown man now, and his father stood to make a pile of money. I had to wonder how deep that dark streak ran.

Seven figures, Robin had said.

Deep enough, I guessed.

"You think he could have done it?" I asked. "Attacked Grace?"

Dolf thought about the question. "Maybe, but I doubt it. He's made some mistakes, but I still say he's a good enough kid. Are the police looking for him?"

"Yes."

He nodded. "Guess we'll see then."

"There was a woman with Grace before she was attacked."

"What woman?" Dolf asked.

"In a blue canoe, one of the old wooden ones like you never see anymore. She had white hair, but looked too young for that, somehow. They were talking."

"Were they?" His eyebrows came together.

"Do you know her?"

"I do."

"Who is she?"

"Did you tell the police about her?"

"I did."

He spit over the rail. "Sarah Yates. But you didn't hear that from me."

"Who is she?"

"I haven't spoken to Sarah in a long time. She lives across the river."

"You can do better than that," I said.

"That's really all that I can tell you, Adam. Now come here. I'll show you something."

I let it go, followed him off of the porch and into the yard. He led me to the barn and put a hand on the old MG that sat on blocks in the center of it. "You know, until this car, Grace has never asked me for a single thing. She'd wear the seat out of her pants before she complained of a draft." He rubbed his hand on the car's fender. "This is the cheapest convertible she could find. It's temperamental and undependable, but she wouldn't trade it for the world." He studied me again. "Do those words describe anything else in this barn? Temperamental. Undependable."

I knew what he meant.

"She loves you, Adam; even though you left, and even though the leaving damn near killed her. She wouldn't trade you for anything else."

"Why are you telling me this?"

"Because she's going to need you now more than ever." He put his hand on my shoulder and squeezed. "Don't leave again. That's what I'm telling you."

I stepped back, so that his hand fell away; and for a moment there was a twitch in his gnarled fingers. "That's never been up to me, Dolf."

"Your dad's a good man who's made mistakes. That's all he is. Just like you. Just like me."

"And last night?" I asked. "When he threatened to kill me?"

"It's like I said. Violent and more than a little blind. The two of you. Just the same."

"It's not the same," I said.

Dolf straightened and turned up his lips in the most forced smile I'd ever seen. "Ah, forget it. You know your own mind well enough. Let's go eat some breakfast." He turned and walked away.

"That's the second time you've lectured me about my father in the past twelve hours. He doesn't need you fighting his battles."

"It's not supposed to be a battle," he said, and kept walking.

I looked at the sky, then at the barn, but in the end I had nowhere else to go. We returned to the house, and I sat at his kitchen table and watched as he poured two coffees and took bacon and eggs out of the refrigerator. He cracked six eggs into a bowl, added some milk, and whipped it all with a fork. He put the bowl aside and opened the bacon.

It took a few minutes for us both to calm down.

"Dolf," I finally said. "Can I ask you a question?"

"Shoot." His voice was as calm as could be.

"What's the longest you've ever heard of a deer living?"

"A whitetail?"

"Yes."

Dolf dropped half the side of bacon into the pan. "Ten years in the wild, longer in captivity."

"You ever heard of one living twenty years?"

Dolf put the pan on the stove, and the bacon began to snap and sizzle. "Not a normal one."

Light fingered through the window to place a pale square on the near black wood. When I looked up, he was studying me with open curiosity. "Do you remember the last time my father took me hunting?" I asked. "That white buck I shot at and missed?"

"It's one of your old man's favorite stories. He says that the two of you reached an understanding out there in the woods. A thing unspoken, he'd call it. A commitment to life in the shadow of death, or something like that. Damn poetic, I always thought."

I thought of the photograph my father kept in his study,

the one taken on the day we saw the white deer. It was taken in the driveway after a long, silent walk back from the deep woods. My father thought it was a new beginning. I was just trying not to cry.

"He was wrong, you know. There was no commitment."

"What do you mean?" Dolf asked.

"I wanted to kill that deer."

"I don't understand."

I looked up at Dolf and felt the same overwhelming emotions I'd felt in the woods. Comfort. Pain. "My father said that deer was a sign. He meant that it was a sign from her."

"Adam—"

"That's why I wanted to hurt it." I squeezed my hands, feeling pain as the bones ground together. "That's why I wanted to kill it. I was angry. I was furious."

"But why?"

"Because I knew it was over."

"What was?"

I couldn't meet his eyes. "Everything good."

Dolf did not speak, but I understood. What could he possibly say? She'd left me, and I did not even know why.

"I saw a deer this morning," I said. "A white one."

Dolf sat down on the other side of the table. "And you think that maybe it's the same?"

I shrugged. "I don't know, maybe. I used to dream about the first one."

"Do you want it to be the same?"

I did not answer him directly. "I read up on white deer a few years back, the mythology of white deer. There's quite a bit of it, going back a thousand years. They're very rare."

"What kind of mythology?"

"Christians talk of a white stag that carried a vision of Christ between his antlers. They believe it's a sign of impending salvation."

"That sounds nice."

"There are legends that go back much further. The ancient Celts believed something entirely different. Their legends speak of white deer leading travelers deep into the secret parts of the forest. They say a white deer can lead a man to new understanding."

"That's not too bad, either."

I looked up. "They say it's a messenger from the dead."

# *Eleven*

We ate in silence. Dolf left and I got myself cleaned up. In the mirror, I looked haggard, my eyes somehow older than the rest of me. I pulled on jeans and a linen shirt, then I walked back outside, where I found Robin sitting on the picnic table holding part of a carburetor. She stood when she saw me. I stopped on the porch.

"Nobody answered when I knocked," she said. "I heard the water running and decided to wait."

"What are you doing here?" I asked.

"I came to apologize."

"If it's about earlier—"

"It's not," she said.

"What, then?"

A shadow crossed her face. "It was Grantham's call." She looked down and her shoulders drew in. "But that's no excuse. I should not have let it go this far."

"What are you talking about?"

"If this had been in the city, or in some crowded place, he probably would not have felt the need—"

"Robin."

She straightened, as if to receive punishment. "She wasn't raped."

I was speechless.

"She was attacked, but not raped. Grantham wanted that kept quiet until he saw how you all reacted."

*Not raped.*

My voice grated. "How who reacted?"

"You. Jamie. Your father. Any of the men who could have done it. He was watching you."

"Why?"

"Because sexual assault doesn't always end in rape, because it is not always as random as people might think, and because of where it happened. The odds of a chance encounter way out here are slim."

"And because he thinks I'm capable."

"Most people are bad liars. If you knew that there had been no rape, it might have shown. Grantham wanted a look."

"And you went along with it."

She looked miserable. "It's not an uncommon tactic, withholding information. I had no choice."

"Bullshit."

"That's your emotion talking."

"Why did you decide to tell me?"

She looked around as if for some kind of help. Her palms turned to catch light from the low-hanging sun. "Because things look different in the light of day. Because I made a mistake."

"Zebulon Faith is impotent," I said. "Maybe that's why she wasn't actually raped."

"I don't want to talk about the case," she said. "I want to talk about us. You need to understand why I did what I did."

"I understand perfectly."

"I don't think that you do."

I stepped away from her and my hand found the edge of the open door. She knew that I was going to close it between us. Maybe that's why she said what she did. "There's something that you should probably hear," she said.

"What?"

Robin looked up. "Grace has never been sexually active."

"But she told me—"

"The doctor confirmed it, Adam. In spite of what she said to you, it's pretty clear that she has not had a lot of boyfriends."

"Why would she tell me that?"

"I think it's like you said, Adam."

"What?"

"I think she wanted to hurt you."

The road to my father's house was baked hard, and red dust settled on my shoes as I walked it. The road bent to the north and then rounded east before cresting the small rise that eventually sloped to the river. I looked down on the house and on the cars parked before it. There were a few of them, and one I recognized. Not the car itself, but the license plate, J-19C, a J tag, the kind issued to sitting judges.

I walked down, stood next to the car. There was a Twinkie wrapper on the seat.

I knew the bastard.

Gilbert T. Rathburn.

Judge G.

Gilley Rat.

I stepped away from the car as the front door to the house swung open. The judge backed through it like a dog was after him. One hand clutched a sheaf of papers, the other, his belt. He was a tall man and fat, with a fine, woven hairpiece and glasses that flashed small and gold on his red, round face. His suit was expensive enough to camouflage much of his size, but his tie still looked narrow. My father followed him outside.

"I think you should reconsider, Jacob," the judge said. "It makes all of the sense in the world. If you would just let me explain further—"

"Is there some problem with my diction?" The judge deflated slightly and my father, sensing this, took his eyes off of him and saw me standing in the drive. Surprise flashed across his face, and his voice dropped as he pointed a finger at me. "I'd like to see you in my study," he said, then turned back to the judge. "And don't you go talking to Dolf about this, either. What I say goes for him, too." Without waiting for a reply he turned back into the house.

The screen door slammed shut behind him, and the judge shook his head before turning to face me as I stood in the shade of a pecan tree. He looked me up and down, studied me over the top of his glasses, as his neck swelled out and over his collar. We'd known each other for years. I'd appeared in his courtroom once or twice back when I was young and he still sat on the bench of the lower court. The charges had never been very serious, mostly drinking and brawling. We'd never had a real problem, until five years ago, when he signed off on the felony arrest warrant for Gray Wilson's murder. He could not hide the contempt in his eyes. "This is an unfortunate decision," he said. "You showing your face in Rowan County again."

"Whatever happened to 'innocent until proven guilty,' you fat bastard?"

He stepped closer, topping my height by a good four inches. Moisture beaded on his face and in the hair along the side of his head. "The boy was killed on this farm, and your own mother identified you leaving the scene."

"Stepmother," I said, and matched the man's hard stare.

"You were seen covered in his blood."

"Seen by one person," I said.

"A reliable witness."

"Jesus," I said in disgust.

He smiled.

"What are you doing here, Rathburn?"

"No one's forgotten, you know. Even without a conviction, people remember."

I tried to ignore him.

"We take care of our own," he said as I opened the screen door and looked back. His finger pointed at me, and his watch gleamed on his doughlike wrist. "That's what life in this county is all about."

"You mean that you take care of your own campaign contributors. Isn't that right?"

A deep flush crept up the fat man's neck. Rathburn was an elitist bigot. If you were rich and white, he was usually the judge you'd want. He'd often come to my father for campaign money, and had always left empty-handed. I had no doubt that his presence here had something to do with the money at stake on the river. He'd have his finger in the pie somewhere.

I watched him search for words, then squeeze into his car when nothing came to him. He turned in the grass of my father's lawn, then blew dust up the hill. I waited until he was gone from sight, then closed the door and went inside.

I stopped in the living room and heard a floorboard squeak upstairs. Janice, I thought, then walked to my father's book-lined study. The door stood open, and I knocked on the frame out of long habit. I stepped inside. He stood at the desk, back to me, and his weight was on his hands. He'd lowered his head to his chest, and I saw the length of his neck, the sunburned creases there.

The sight churned up memories of how I'd played under the desk as a child, memories of laughter and love, as if the house had been steeped in it.

I felt my mother's hand, as if she was still alive.

I cleared my throat, saw how his fingers squeezed white against the dark wood. When he turned, I was struck by the redness of his eyes, the pallor of his face. For a long moment we stood like that, and it seemed like a thing unknown to us, a nakedness.

For that instant his features were fluid, but then they firmed, as if he'd come to some decision. He pushed himself off of the desk and crossed the worn rug. He put his hands on my shoulders and pulled me into a fierce embrace. He was wiry and strong, smelled of the farm and of so many memories. My head spun and I fought to hold the anger that sustained me. I did not return the embrace, and he stepped back, hands still on my shoulders. In his eyes I saw the same raw loss. He let go when we heard a rustle at the door and a startled voice.

"Oh. I'm sorry."

Miriam stood in the doorway. She could look neither of us in the eyes, and I knew that she was embarrassed.

"What is it, Miriam?"

"I didn't know that Adam was here," she said.

"Can it wait?" my father asked.

"Mom wants you," she said.

My father blew out a breath of obvious frustration. "Where is she?"

"In the bedroom."

He looked at me. "Don't go away," he said.

After he left, Miriam lingered in the doorway. She'd come to the trial, sat quietly on the front row every day, but I'd seen her only once afterward, the briefest goodbye as I'd thrown what I could into the trunk of my car. I recalled her last words. *Where will you go?* she'd asked. And I'd said the only thing I could. *I honestly don't know.*

"Hello, Miriam."

She raised a hand. "I'm not sure what to say to you."

"Don't say anything, then."

She showed me the top of her head. "It's been hard," she said.

"It's okay."

"Is it?"

Something unknowable moved through her. She'd been unable to look at me during the trial, and had fled the courtroom when the prosecutor mounted the enlarged autopsy photos on an easel for the jury to see. The wound was vividly displayed, the shots taken under bright lights with a high-resolution camera. Three feet tall, the first photo showed hair spiked with blood and dirt, shards of bone and brain matter gone to wax. He'd positioned it for the jury to see, but Miriam sat in the front row, just a few feet away. She'd covered her mouth and run down the center aisle. I always imagined her in the grass beyond the sidewalk, heaving out her insides. It's where I'd wanted to be. Even my father had been forced to look away. For her, though, it must have been unbearable. They'd known each other for years.

"It's okay," I repeated.

She nodded, but looked like she might cry. "How long are you here for?"

"I don't know."

She slipped further into her loose clothing and leaned against the door frame. She still had not met my eyes. "This is weird," she said.

"It doesn't have to be."

She was already shaking her head. "It just is."

"Miriam—"

"I gotta go." And then she was gone, her footsteps a whisper on the bare wood floors of the long hallway. In the silence I heard voices from above, an argument, and my stepmother's escalating voice. When my father returned I saw that his face had hardened. "What did Janice want?" I asked, knowing the answer already.

"She wanted to know if you'd be joining us for dinner tonight."

"Don't lie to me."

He looked up. "You heard?"

"She wants me out of the house."

"This has been difficult for your stepmother."

I fought to remain civil. "I would not want to inconvenience her."

"This is bullshit," he said. "Let's get out of here."

He turned for the back of his study and the door leading outside. His hand settled on one of the rifles propped in the corner and the morning sun flooded the room as the door opened under his hand. I followed him out. His truck was parked twenty feet away. He put the rifle on the gun rack. "For those damn dogs," he said. "Get in."

The truck was old, and smelled of dust and straw. He drove slowly, and pointed the truck upriver. We crossed through cornfields and soy, a new planting of loblolly pines, and into the forest proper before he spoke again. "Did you get a chance to speak to Miriam?"

"She didn't really want to talk."

My father waved a hand, and I saw a quick twist of displeasure on his face. "She's twitchy."

"It was more than that," I said, and could feel his eyes on me as I stared straight ahead. He turned my way, and when he spoke, it was of the dead boy.

"He was her friend, Adam."

I lost my temper. I couldn't help it. "You don't think I know that! You don't think I remember that!"

"It'll work out," he said weakly.

"What about you?" I asked. "A pat on the back doesn't make it all right."

He opened his mouth again and then shut it. The truck crested a hill with a view of the house. He pulled to a stop and switched off the ignition. It was quiet.

"I did what I felt I had to do, son. No one could move forward with you still in the house. Janice was distraught. Jamie and Miriam were affected. I was, too. There were just too many questions."

"I can't give you answers I don't have. Somebody killed him. I told you that it wasn't me. That should have been enough."

"It wasn't. Your acquittal didn't erase what Janice saw."

I turned in my seat and studied the man. "Are we going to start this again?"

"No, son. We're not." I looked at the floor, at the straw and the mud and the tattered, dead leaves. "I miss your mother," he finally said.

"Me, too."

We sat through a long silence as the sun streamed in. "I understand, you know."

"What?"

He paused. "How much you lost when she died."

"Don't," I said.

More wordless time, most of it thick with memories of her and of how good we three had been.

"There must have been some part of you that thought I was capable of murder," I said.

He scrubbed both hands over his face, ground at his eyes with the callused palms. There was dirt under his fingernails, and truth all over him when he spoke. "You were never the same after she died. Before that, you were such a sweet boy. God, you were perfect, a pure joy. After she died, though, you changed, grew dark and distrusting. Resentful. Distant. I thought you'd come out of it with time. But you started fighting in school. Arguing with teachers. You were angry all the time. It was like a goddamn cancer. Like it just ate all that sweetness away."

He palmed his face again; hard skin rasped over the creases. "I thought you'd work it out. I guess there was always the chance you'd pop. I just didn't think it would happen like that. You'd put a car into a tree, get seriously hurt in a fight maybe. When that boy was killed, it never occurred to me that you might be responsible. But Janice swore that she saw you." He sighed. "I thought that maybe you'd finally come undone."

"Because of my mother?" I asked, and he did not see the ice in me. He nodded, and something violent thumped in my chest. I'd been falsely accused, tried for murder, and driven out. He was blaming this on my mother's death. "If I was so messed up, why didn't you get me some help?"

"You mean like a shrink?"

"Yeah. Anything."

"All a man needs are his feet on the ground. We thought we could get you there. Dolf and me."

"And that's worked out for you, has it?"

"Don't you judge me, boy."

"Like it worked for Mom?"

His jaw muscles bulged before he spoke. "Now you need to shut your damn mouth. You're talking about something way over your head."

"Fuck this," I said, and opened the door to the truck. I walked down the road and heard his door slam behind me.

"Don't walk away from me," he said.

I felt his hand on my shoulder, and without conscious thought I turned and punched him in the face. He went down in the dirt, and I stood over him. I saw a flash of color, my mother's last second on this earth, and spoke the thought that had tormented me for the past few years.

"It was supposed to be you," I said.

Blood spread from his nose, down the right side of his mouth. He looked small in the dirt, and I saw the day she did it: the way the gun leapt out of her lifeless hand, how the coffee scalded my fingers when I dropped the cup. But there had been an instant, a flash on her face as the door swung wide. Surprise, I thought. Regret. I used to think it was imagination on my part.

But not now.

"We came back to the house," I said. "We came back from the woods and you went to check on her. She asked *you* to bring her coffee."

"What are you talking about?" He smeared the blood on his face, but made no effort to rise. He didn't want to hear it, but he knew.

"The gun was against her head when I opened the door. She wanted *you* to see her die."

My father's face went white.

"Not me," I said.

I turned to walk away.

And I knew that he would let me go.

# *Twelve*

I left the road and went back to Dolf's house by the trails and footpaths I still remembered. The place was empty, so no one saw how I slumped in the corner, how I almost broke. No one saw how I fought to pull myself together and no one saw me throw my stuff in the car; but Dolf pulled up as I was leaving, and I stopped out of respect for his raised hand and because of the blunt dismay in his face as he read my intentions through our open windows.

He climbed out of the truck and put his hands on the roof of my car. He leaned in close and I saw him take in the bag on the backseat. His eyes lingered on my face before he spoke.

"This is not the way, Adam. Whatever he said to you, running now is not the answer."

But he was wrong; nothing had changed. Distrust was everywhere and my choices still came down to grief or anger. Next to that, the numbness sounded pretty good.

"It's been great to see you, Dolf. But it's not going to work. Tell Grace that I love her." I pulled away and saw him standing in the drive, watching me go. He raised a hand and said something but I missed it. It didn't matter. Robin had turned on me. My father was lost.

It was done.

Over.

I followed the narrow roads back to the river, to the bridge that spanned the border of Rowan County. I parked where I had parked before and I walked to the water's edge. The jugs were still there, and I thought of the lost boy my father pined for, of a time when nothing was more complicated than keeping a scabbard oiled or taking a catfish off the line. I wondered if there was any of that boy left in me, or had the cancer, indeed, eaten him all away? I could remember how it felt. One day in particular. I was seven, and it would be more than a year before a strange, dark winter bled the heat out of my mother.

We were at the river.

We were swimming.

*Do you trust me?* she asked.

*Yes.*

*Come on,* she said.

We were holding on to the edge of the dock. The sun was high, her smile full of mischief. She had blue eyes with yellow spots that made them look like something on fire. *Here we go,* she said, then slipped beneath the water. I watched her legs scissor twice, then she was gone beneath the dock.

I was confused, but then her hand appeared. Squeezing it, I held my breath and let her draw me under the dock. The world went dark, then I rose beside her into the hollow place beneath the boards. It was quiet, green in the way that the forest could be. Light slanted between boards. Her eyes danced, and when light touched them, they flamed. The space was hidden and hushed. I'd been on the dock a hundred times but I'd never been under it. It was like a secret. It was like . . .

Her eyes crinkled and she put a hand on my face.

*There is such magic in the world,* she said.

And that was it.

It was like magic.

I was still pondering this when Dolf's truck coasted to a stop on the road above me. He moved down the bank like an old man.

"How'd you know I'd be here?" I asked.

"I took a chance." He picked up a handful of stones and started skimming them across the water.

"If I cross that bridge now, there's no coming back."

"Yep."

"That's why I stopped."

He threw another rock. It sank on the second skip.

"You're not very good at that," I said.

"Arthritis. It's a bitch." He threw another one; it sank immediately. "Want to tell me the real reason that you're here?" he asked, and put another rip in the water. "I'll do anything I can for you, Adam. Anything I can to help."

I picked up four stones. The first one skipped six times. "You have enough on your plate, Dolf."

"Maybe I do and maybe I don't. Doesn't really matter. The offer stands."

I studied the asymmetry of his face. "Danny called me," I said. "Three weeks ago."

"That right?"

"He said that he needed my help with something. He asked me to come home."

Dolf bent for more rocks. "What did you tell him?"

"I asked him what he wanted, but he wouldn't get specific. He said that he'd figured out how to fix his life, but needed my help to do it. He wanted me to come home, to talk about it face-to-face." Dolf waited for me to finish. "I told him I couldn't do it."

"What'd he say?"

"He got insistent and he got pissed. He said he needed me and that he'd do it for me if the situations were reversed."

"But he wouldn't say what he wanted?"

"Nope."

"You think he wanted you to talk to your father about selling? Try to talk him into it?"

"Money can fix a lot of problems."

Dolf weighed what I'd said. "So, why did you come home?"

"There were times that Danny could have walked away from me when I was in trouble, but he never did. Not once. When I thought of Danny and me, it was a lot like you and Dad. Tight, you know. Dependable. I felt bad, like I let him down."

"Friendships can be difficult."

"And they can die." I shook my head. "I don't know how I could have been so wrong about him. I keep coming back to the money." I threw another stone, thought about Grace. "It's messed up."

We fell silent, watched the river.

"That's not the only reason I came home."

Dolf caught the change in my tone, perked up. "What's the other reason?"

I looked down on him. "Can't you guess?"

I saw it register. "To make peace with your father."

"I'd buried this place, you know. Just moved on as best I could. I had jobs, a few friends. Most days I never thought about this place. I'd trained myself against it. Talking to Danny, though, it got me thinking. Wheels started turning. Memories came back. Dreams. It took a while to get my head straight, but I figured it was probably time."

He hitched at his belt and could not look me in the face. "Yet, here you are, throwing stones in the river and debating which way to go. That way." He pointed north. "Or back home."

I shrugged. "What do you think?"

"I think that you've been gone for too long." I said nothing. "Your dad feels the same, whether he told you so or not."

I threw another stone, but did so poorly.

"What about Grace?" Dolf asked.

"I can't leave her now."

"I guess it's really that simple then."

"I guess it is."

I put the fourth stone in my pocket and left the bridge behind me.

I followed Dolf back to the farm, then climbed into his truck when he said that he had other things to show me. We drove past the stable, and I saw Robin there along with Grantham. They were in clean clothes, but still looked tired, and I was amazed by their tenacity. They were talking to some of the workers and making notes on spiral binders.

"That's not what I want to show you," Dolf said.

I watched Robin as we passed. She looked up and saw me. "How long have they been there?"

"An hour, maybe. They want to speak with everybody."

We rolled out of sight. "There's no interpreter," I said.

"Robin speaks Spanish."

"That's new," I said, and Dolf grunted.

We crossed the main part of the farm and turned onto one of the gravel roads that ran to the far northeast corner of the property. We crested a hill and Dolf stopped the truck.

"Jesus." I was looking at a vineyard, countless rows of lush green vines that filled the hollow beneath us. "How many acres?"

"Four hundred under vine," Dolf said. "And it has been one hell of a job." He nodded, gesturing through the windshield. "That's just over a hundred acres there."

"What the hell?"

Dolf chuckled. "It's the new cash crop, the future of North Carolina agriculture, or so they say. But it ain't cheap. That vineyard went in three years ago and we won't see any profit for at least two more, maybe even four. Even then, there's no guarantees. But the soy market has stalled, beef is depressed, and loblolly doesn't grow any faster just because you want it to. We're rotating in corn and we've leased land for a cell tower, which pays well, but your father worries about the future." He pointed at the vines. "There it is. We hope."

"Was this your idea?"

"Jamie's," Dolf said. "It took him two years to convince your father, and there's a whole lot riding on it."

"Should I even ask?"

"It took a fortune to get the vines in, and we sacrificed producing crop. The farm's lost a lot of cash flow." Dolf shrugged. "We'll see."

"Is the farm at risk?"

Dolf eyed me. "How much did your old man pay for your ten percent?"

"Three million," I said.

"That's about what I figured. He says we're okay, but he's tight-lipped about his money. It has to be hurting, though."

"And this is all riding on Jamie?"

"That's right."

"Damn," I said. The risks were enormous.

"It's make-or-break, I guess."

I studied the older man. The farm was his life. "You okay with that?"

"I turn sixty-three next month." He looked at me sideways and nodded. "But your dad's never let me down before, and I don't think he's planning to now."

"And Jamie?" I asked. "Has he ever let you down?"

"It is what it is, Adam. Guess we'll see."

We were silent for a moment.

"Is my father going to sell to the power company, Dolf?"

There was a hard edge in his voice when he answered. "You worried about missing out on the windfall?"

"That's not fair."

"You're right, Adam. It's not. But I've seen what this money has done to folks around here." He stared through the glass, his eyes distant. "Temptation," he said. "It's making people crazy."

"So, do you think he'll do it?"

Something shifted behind the old man's gaze, and he looked away from me, down to the long rows of promising vine. "Did your father ever explain to you why this place is called Red Water Farm?"

"I always assumed it was because of the clay in the river."

"Thought not." Dolf started the truck and turned around.

"Where are we going?"

"The knob."

"Why?"

"You'll see."

The knob was the highest point on the farm, a massive upheaval of granite that could pass for a small mountain. Most of it was wooded slope, but the peak was barren, the soil too thin for much to grow. It commanded a view of the river's northern approach, and was the most inaccessible part of the property.

Dolf started speaking when we reached the bottom of the knob, and his voice rose as the truck slammed its way up the weathered track that led to the top. "Some time ago this was all Sapona Indian country. There was a village nearby, probably on the farm, although its exact location has never been determined. Like most Indians, the Sapona didn't want to give up their land." He gestured up the track ahead of us. "Their final fight happened right up there."

We came out of the woods and onto the plateau. It was covered with thin grass. At the northern edge, the granite rose out of the earth to form a jagged wall thirty feet high and a quarter mile long. The outcropping was riddled with cracks and deep fissures. Dolf parked at the base of it and got out. I followed him.

"By the best count, there were maybe three hundred people living in that village, and they all fled here at the end. Women and children. Everybody." Dolf plucked a long blade of grass from the stony soil and shredded it between his fingers as he waited for his words to settle into me. Then he started walking along the stony face. "This was the high ground," he said, and gestured at the rock face with a grass-stained finger. "The last good place to fight. You can see everything for miles around from up there."

He stopped and pointed to a narrow fissure in the stone, at the very base of the wall. I knew the spot, for my father had often warned me to avoid it. It was deep.

"When it was over," he continued, "they threw the bodies in there. The men had been shot, of course, but most of the women and children were still alive. They threw them in first and piled the dead on top. Legend says that so much blood soaked into the water table that the springs ran red for days after. That's where the name comes from."

I felt the warmth fade out of me. "How do you know that?"

"Some archaeologists from Washington excavated the pit in the late sixties. I was here when they did it. So was your daddy."

"How have I not heard about it?"

Dolf shrugged. "It was a different time. Nobody cared so much. It wasn't news. Plus, your grandfather only agreed to the excavation if they kept it quiet. He didn't want a bunch of drunk idiots up here getting themselves killed looking for arrowheads. There are some dusty papers on it, I'm sure. Maybe at the university in Chapel Hill or somewhere in Washington. But it was never news. Not like it would be today."

"Why did my father never tell me?"

"When you were young, he didn't want to scare you. Didn't want you worrying about ghosts and such, or the nature of mankind, for that matter. Then when you were older, Jamie and Miriam were too young. By the time you were all grown, I guess he just failed to get around to it. It's no mystery, really."

I edged closer to the pit, and my feet scraped on the raw granite. I leaned forward, but was not close enough to see down into the crack. I looked back at Dolf.

"What does this have to do with my father selling?"

"Your old man is like those Sapona. As far as he's concerned, some things are just worth killing for." I looked hard at the man. "Or dying," he said.

"That right?" I asked.

"He'll never sell."

"Even if the farm goes bankrupt over Jamie's vines?"

Dolf looked uncomfortable. "It won't come to that."

"You willing to bet on it?"

He declined to answer. I moved closer and leaned out over the cruel mouth, looked down the shaft. It was deep, lined with sharp protrusions of hard stone; but the sun angled in. I thought that I saw something down there.

"What did those archaeologists do with the remains?" I asked.

"Tagged 'em. Hauled 'em off. Sitting in boxes somewhere, I'd imagine."

"You sure?"

"Yes. Why?"

I leaned farther and squinted into the gloom. I got down on the warm stone and hung my head over the edge. I saw a pale, smooth curve, and below that a hollow place, and a row of small white objects, like pearls on a string; and a large dark hump of what appeared to be stained, rotting cloth.

"What does that look like to you?" I asked.

Dolf got down next to me. He stared for a good minute, wrinkled his nose, and I could tell that he smelled it, too, the faintest lick of something foul. "Jesus Christ," he said.

"Do you have any rope in the truck?"

He rolled onto his side and the metal rivets of his jeans rasped on the stone. "Are you serious?"

"Unless you have a better idea."

"Jesus Christ," Dolf repeated, then got up and went to the truck.

I tied the rope off with a clove hitch and dropped the loose coil over the edge. It flicked against the stone as it went down.

"Any chance you have a flashlight?"

He pulled one out of the truck, handed it to me. "You don't have to do this," Dolf said.

"I'm not sure what I see down there. Are you?"

"Pretty sure."

"Positive?"

He did not answer, so I turned my back to the hole and grasped the rope. His hand gripped my shoulder. "Don't do this, Adam. There's no need."

I smiled. "Just don't leave me."

Dolf muttered something that sounded like "dumb ass kid."

I got down on my belly and slid my legs over the edge. I planted my feet, let them take what weight they could, put the rest on the rope. I caught Dolf's eye once, and then I was in, the lip of the crevasse seeming to fold over me.

Cold crept up and the air thickened. I descended past layers of rock, and the descent tore the warm, bright world away. The sun abandoned me, and I felt them, three hundred of them, some still alive when they went in. For an instant, my mind got away from me. It was real, as if I could hear the crack of shot on rock, the high screams of women tossed in alive to spare the cost of a bullet. But that was centuries ago, a faint vibration in the ancient stone.

I slipped once, heard the rope sigh as my weight came onto it. I swung away from the wall, and the void tried to suck me down, but I didn't stop. Ten feet more and the smell overwhelmed me. I forced a breath, but the stench was thick. I put a light on the body, saw twisted sticks of legs, and moved the light up. It struck the exposed curve of forehead bone, what had looked, from above, like an upturned bowl. I saw the hollow sockets, the tattered flesh, and teeth.

And there was something else.

I looked closer, saw denim turned to black, and a once white shirt now eggplant with seepage and decay. I almost threw up, and it wasn't because of the colors or the smells.

I saw insects, thousands of them. They moved beneath the cloth.

And they made the scarecrow dance.

* * *

Four hours later, under a vault of clear, sweet air, they hauled Danny Faith out of the ground. There was no pretty way to do it. They went down with a body bag, and used the winch on one of the sheriff's trucks. Even over the whine of it, I heard the scrape of the vinyl bag, the apologetic knock of bone on rock.

Three people followed the body out: Grantham, Robin, and the medical examiner. They wore respirators, but still looked as fragile and gray as charred paper. Robin refused to meet my eyes.

No one but me was saying for sure that it was Danny, but it was. The size was right, and the hair was hard to mistake. It was red and curly, not something you saw that often in Rowan County.

The sheriff made an appearance while the body was still in the hole. He spent ten minutes talking to his people, then to Dolf and to my father. I could see the animosity between them, the distrust and dislike. He spoke to me only once, and the hatred was there, too: "I can't stop you from coming back," he said. "But you shouldn't have gone down there, you dumb shit." He left right after that, like he'd done the only important job and still had better things to do.

I caught myself rubbing my hands on my thighs, like I could abrade away the smell or the memory of the damp rock. My father watched me, and I shoved my hands into my pockets. He seemed as stunned as I, and moved close every time Grantham approached with yet another question. By the time Danny left the knob for the last time, my father and I stood less than five feet apart, and our own troubles seemed reduced next to the awkward sack that refused to lie flat in the back of the sheriff's truck.

But the body wasn't there forever. The trucks dropped away and quiet descended again. We stood in a rough line by the broken stone, the three of us, and Dolf's hat was in his hand.

Danny Faith was no more than three weeks dead; but for

me, in some strange way, he'd been resurrected. Grace had been hurt, yes, but Danny had nothing to do with it. I felt the hatred slip away. In its place rose bittersweet relief, quiet regret, and no small amount of shame.

"Can I give you a ride back?" my father asked.

The wind moved his hair as I stared at him. I loved the man, but could not see a way past our problems. Worse, I did not know if I still had the energy to search one out. Our words came with cost. His nose was swollen where I'd punched him. "Why, Dad? What else is there to say?"

"I don't want you to leave."

I looked at Dolf. "You told him?"

"I'm tired of waiting for you two to grow up," Dolf said. "He needs to know how close he is to losing you for good. Life is too damn short."

I spoke to my father. "I'm staying for Grace's sake. Not for you or anything else. For Grace."

"Let's just agree to be civil, okay? Let's agree to that and see what the future brings."

I thought about it. Danny was gone, and I guessed that there were still things to say. Dolf understood, and turned without speaking. "Meet us at the house," my father called after him. "I think we can all use a drink." Dolf's truck coughed once before the engine caught.

"Civil," I said. "Nothing has been resolved."

"Okay," my father said, then, "You really think it's Danny?"

"Pretty sure," I said.

We stared for a long time at the black, black hole. It wasn't the fact of Danny's death or the questions that his death raised. The rift between us was as raw as ever, more so, and we were both reluctant to face it. It was easier to contemplate the dark slash in the earth, the sudden wind that pressed the thin grass flat. When my father finally chose to speak, it was of my mother's suicide, and of the things I'd said.

"She didn't know what she was doing, Adam. It didn't matter if it was you or me. She'd chosen her moment for reasons we can never understand. She wasn't trying to punish anyone. I have to believe that."

I felt the blood leave my face. "This does not seem like the time to talk about it," I said.

"Adam—"

"Why did she do it?" The question tore itself free.

"Depression does strange things to the mind." I felt him looking at me. "She was lost."

"You should have gotten her some help."

"I did," he said, and that stopped me. "She'd been seeing a therapist for most of that year, for all of the good that it did. He told me that she was improving. That's what he said, and a week later she pulled the trigger."

"I had no idea."

"You weren't supposed to. No kid should know that about his mother. Know that dredging up a smile took everything she had." He waved a hand in disgust. "That's why I never sent you to see a shrink." He sighed. "You were tough. I thought you'd be okay."

"Okay? Are you serious? She did it in front of me. You left me there, in the house."

"Somebody had to go with the body."

"I scrubbed her brains off the wall."

He looked appalled. "That was you?"

"I was eight years old."

He seemed to fall away from me. "It was a hard time," he said.

"Why was she depressed? She'd been happy all of my life. I remember. She was full of joy and then she died inside. I'd like to know why."

My father looked at the hole, and I knew that I had never seen such distress in his features. "Forget it, son. No good can come of it now."

"Dad—"

"Just let her lie, Adam. What matters now is you and me."

I closed my eyes and when I opened them I found my

father standing before me. He put his hands on my shoulders again, as he had in his study.

"I named you Adam because I didn't think that I could love anything more, because I was as proud on the day you were born as the good Lord must have been when he looked down on Adam himself. You are all that I have left of your mother, and you are my son. You will always be my son."

I looked the old man in the eyes, found a hard place in my heart that all but destroyed me.

"God cast Adam out," I said. "He never came back to the garden."

Then I turned and let myself into my father's truck. I looked at him through the open window. "How about that drink?" I asked.

# Thirteen

We drank bourbon in the study. Dolf and my father took it with water and sugar. I drank it neat. In spite of all that had happened, no one knew what to say. There was too much. Grace, Danny, the turbulence of my return. Harm seemed to lurk around every corner, and we spoke little, as if we all knew that it could still get worse. It was like a taint in the air, and even Jamie, who joined us ten minutes after the bourbon was poured, sniffed as if he could smell it.

After careful consideration, I told them what Robin had said about Grace. I had to repeat myself. "She was not raped," I said again, and explained the nature of Grantham's deception. My words dropped into the room with enough weight to take the floor from beneath us. My father's glass exploded in the fireplace. Dolf covered his face. Jamie went rigid.

Then I told them about the note. "Tell the old man to sell."

That sucked the air out of the room.

"This is intolerable," my father said. "All of it. Every damn piece of it. What in God's name is happening here?"

There were no answers, not yet, and in the painful silence I carried my glass to the sideboard for another drink. I tipped two fingers' worth into my glass and patted Jamie on the shoulder. "How you doin', Jamie?"

"Pour me another," he said. I filled his glass, and was almost back to my seat when Miriam appeared in the door.

"Robin Alexander is here," she said. "She wants to talk to Adam."

My father spoke. "By God, I'd like to talk to her as well." There was no mistaking the metal of his anger.

"She wants to talk to him outside. She says it's a police matter."

We found Robin in the yard. She looked unhappy to see all of us there. Once upon a time she had been a part of this family in every way that mattered.

"Robin." I stopped on the edge of the porch.

"May I speak with you in private?" she asked.

My father answered before I could. "Anything you want to say to Adam, you can say to all of us. And I'd appreciate the truth this time."

Robin knew that I'd told, that was clear in the way that she looked at the group of us, as if she was assessing a possible threat. "This would be easier if it was just the two of us."

"Where's Grantham?" I asked.

She gestured at her car, and I could see the silhouette of a man. "I thought that this might go better if it was just me," she said.

My father stepped past me, down onto the grass, and he towered over Robin. "Anything that you have to say regarding Grace Shepherd or events that happened on my property you will, by God, say in my presence. I've known you a long time, and I am not scared to say how disappointed I am in you. Your parents would be ashamed."

She eyed him calmly, and did not flinch. "My parents have been dead for some time, Mr. Chase."

"May as well say it here," I said.

No one moved or spoke. I was pretty sure what she wanted to talk about.

Then a car door slammed, and Grantham appeared around

Robin's shoulder. "Enough is enough," he said. "We'll do this at the station."

"Am I under arrest?" I asked.

"I am prepared to take that step," Grantham said.

"On what grounds?" Dolf demanded, and my father raised a hand, silencing him.

"Just what the hell is going on?" my father asked.

"Your son lied to me, Mr. Chase. I don't take well to lies or to liars. I'm going to talk to him about that."

"Come on, Adam," Robin said. "Let's go to the station. Just a few questions. A few discrepancies. It won't take long."

I ignored everyone else. Grantham disappeared, as did my father. The communication between Robin and me was complete; she understood that, too. "This is the line," I said. "Right here."

Her determination wavered, then firmed. "Would you step to the car, please?"

And that was that.

My heart broke, the last of my hope for us died, and I got into the car.

I watched my family as Grantham turned the car around. I saw shock and confusion. Then I saw Janice, my stepmother. She stepped onto the porch as the dust rose behind us.

She looked old, like she'd aged twenty years in the past five. She raised a hand to shield her eyes from the sun, and even at a distance, I saw how it shook.

# *Fourteen*

They took me into town, past the local college and the shops that surrounded it; then down the main drag with the lawyers' offices, the courthouse, and the coffee shops. I watched Robin's condo slide past. People were out beneath a pink sky, shadows stretching out. Nothing had changed. Not in five years; not in a hundred. There were storefronts that dated back to the past century, businesses in the fifth generation of the same family. And here was one other thing that had not changed: Adam Chase, under suspicion.

"Want to tell me what this is all about?" I asked.

"I think you know," Grantham replied.

Robin said nothing. "Detective Alexander?" I asked. Her jaw tightened.

We moved onto a side street that led to the tracks. The Salisbury Police Department was on the second block, a new, two-story brick building with cop cars in the lot and flags on a pole. Grantham parked the car and they led me in through the front. It was all very cordial. No cuffs. No cell. Grantham held the door.

"I thought that this was a county case," I said. "Why aren't we at the sheriff's office?" The sheriff's office was four blocks away, in the basement under the jail.

Grantham answered. "We thought you might prefer to

avoid those particular interrogation rooms . . . given your previous experience there."

He was talking about the murder case. They'd picked me up four hours after my father found Gray Wilson's body, feet in the water, shoes thumping against a slick, black root. I never learned if he was with Janice when she went to the cops. I never had the chance to ask and liked to think he'd been as surprised as I was when the cuffs came out. They transported me in one of the sheriff's marked cars. Rips in the seat. Face prints and dried spit on the glass divider. They took me to a room under the jail and hammered me for three days, hours at a stretch. I denied it, but they didn't listen, so I shut up. I never said another word, not once, but I remembered the feel of it, the weight of all those floors above you, all that concrete and steel. A thousand tons, maybe. Enough to squeeze moisture out of the concrete.

"Considerate of you," I said, and wondered if I was being sarcastic.

"It was my idea." Robin had still not looked at me.

They took me to a small room with a metal table and a two-way mirror. It may have been in a different building, but it felt the same: small, square, and shrinking by the second. I took a breath. Same air. Warm and moist. I sat where Grantham told me to sit. I disliked the look on his face, and guessed it was habitual when seated on the cop side of bolted-down furniture on the blind side of two-way glass. Robin sat beside him, hands folded tightly on the gray steel.

"First things first, Mr. Chase. You are not under arrest, not in custody. This is a preliminary interview."

"I can call an attorney?" I asked.

"If you think you need an attorney, I will certainly allow you to call one." He waited, perfectly still. "Would you like to call an attorney?" he asked.

I looked at Robin, at Detective Alexander. The bright lights put a shine on her hair and hard lines on her face. "Let's just get this farce over with," I said.

"Very well." Grantham turned on a tape recorder and stated the date, time, and names of everyone present. Then he leaned back and said nothing. The silence stretched out. I waited. Eventually, he leaned into me. "We first spoke at the hospital on the night that Grace Shepherd was attacked. Is that right?"

"Yes."

"You had seen Ms. Shepherd earlier that day?"

"Yes."

"On the dock?"

"That's right."

"You kissed her?"

"She kissed me."

"And then she went south along the trail?"

I knew what he was doing, establishing a pattern of coop-eration. Getting me used to it. The repetition. The pacing. The acquiescence on established issues. Harmless issues. Just a couple of guys chewing the fat.

"Can we cut to the chase?" I asked.

His lips compressed when I broke his rhythm; then he shrugged. "Very well. When you told me that Ms. Shepherd ran away from you, I asked you if you chased her and you told me that you did not."

"Is that a question?"

"Did you pursue Ms. Shepherd after she ran from you?"

I looked at Robin. She looked small in the hard chair. "I did not attack Grace Shepherd."

"We've spoken with every worker on your father's farm. One of them is prepared to swear that you did, in fact, chase Ms. Shepherd after she ran from the dock. He is quite cer-tain. She ran, you followed. I want to know why you lied to us about that."

The question was no surprise. I'd always known that some-one might have seen. "I didn't lie. You asked me if I chased her and I said that it wasn't that kind of running away. You filled in the blanks yourself."

"I have no patience for word games."

I shrugged. "I was unhappy with how our conversation ended. She was distraught. I wanted to speak further. I caught up with her a hundred feet into the trees."

"Why didn't you tell us that?" Robin asked. It was her first question.

I met her eyes. "Because you would ask about the conversation." I thought of the last words that Grace had given to me, the way she shook under the shade of the low branches. "And that's nobody's business," I said.

"I'm asking," Grantham said.

"It's personal."

"You lied to me." Angry now. "I want to know what you said."

I spoke slowly, so that he would not miss a single word. "No fucking way."

Grantham rose from his seat. "Ms. Shepherd was assaulted a half mile from that spot, and you misinformed us about your actions at the time. Since you've been back, you've also put two men in the hospital and been implicated, at least peripherally, in arson, a methamphetamine lab, and the discharge of a firearm. We just retrieved a corpse from your father's farm, a body that you, coincidentally, discovered. Things like this happen infrequently in Rowan County. To say that I am intrigued by you would be a massive understatement, Mr. Chase. A massive understatement."

"You said that I'm not in custody. Is that right?"

"That is correct."

"Then here is my answer." I held up one hand, middle finger extended.

Grantham sat back down. "What do you do in New York, Mr. Chase?"

"That is none of your business," I said.

"If I contact the authorities in New York, what will they tell me about you?"

I looked away.

"What brings you back to Rowan County?"

"None of your business," I said. "The answer to every question you ask, except 'May we call you a cab?' is 'None of your business.'"

"You're not helping yourself, Mr. Chase."

"You should be investigating the people that want my father to sell, the ones making threats. That's what Grace's assault is really about. Why, in the name of God, are you wasting your time with me?"

Grantham flicked a glance at Robin. His lips drew down. "I was not aware that you knew about that," he said.

Robin spoke quickly. "It was my call," she said. "They had a right to know."

Grantham pinned Robin with those washed-out eyes, and his anger was unmistakable. She'd stepped over a line, but refused to waver. Her head was up, eyes unblinking. He returned his attention to me, but I knew that the matter was not closed. "Can I assume that everyone has this information now?" he asked.

"You can assume whatever you want," I said.

We stared at each other until Robin broke the silence. She spoke softly. "If there is anything else that you want to tell us, Adam, this is the time."

I thought of my reasons for returning and of the things that Grace had said to me. Then I thought of Robin, and of the passion we'd known such a short time ago; her face above me in the half-light, the lie in her voice when she told me that it meant nothing; and I saw her at the farm, when she'd asked me to please step to the car, the way that she'd pushed our past down deep and draped herself in cop.

"My father was right," I said. "You should be ashamed of yourself."

I stood up.

"Adam . . ." she said.

But I walked out, walked to the hospital. I slipped past the nurses' station and found Grace's room. I was not supposed to be there, but sometimes you just know what's right. So I passed through the dark crack of her door and pulled a chair close to her bed. She opened her eyes when I took her hand, and she returned the pressure that I gave her. I kissed her forehead, told her that I would stay the night; and when sleep reclaimed her, it left a trace of comfort on her face.

# *Fifteen*

I woke at five and saw light glinting in her eyes. When she smiled, I could tell that it hurt. "Don't," I said, and leaned closer. A tear welled out of one eye. "Don't be sad."

She shook her head, the smallest movement. Her voice broke. "I'm not sad. I thought I was alone."

"No."

"I was crying because I was scared." She went rigid under the sheets. "I've never been scared to be alone."

"Grace . . ."

"I'm scared, Adam."

I stood and put my arms around her. She smelled of antiseptic, hospital detergent, and fear. Muscles clenched in her back, long hard straps; and her arms had strength that surprised me. She was so small under the sheet.

"I'm okay," she finally said.

"Sure?"

"Yes."

I sat back down. "Can I get you anything?"

"Just talk to me."

"Do you remember what happened?"

She moved her head on the pillow. "Just the sense of somebody stepping out from behind a tree; and something swinging at my face—a board, a club, something wooden. I remember falling through some bushes, then being on the ground. A shape standing over me. Some kind of mask. The wood coming down again." She lifted her arms as if protecting her face, and I saw matching contusions on her forearms. Defensive wounds.

"Do you remember anything else?"

"A little bit of being carried home, of Dolf's face in the porch light, his voice. Being cold. A few minutes at the hospital. Seeing you there."

Her voice trailed away, and I knew where her mind had gone. "Tell me something good, Adam."

"It's over," I said, and she shook her head.

"That's just the absence of bad."

What could I tell her? What good had I seen since my return?

"I'm here for you. Whatever you need."

"Tell me something else. Anything."

I hesitated. "I saw a deer yesterday morning."

"Is that a good thing?"

The deer had been in my head all day. White ones were rare, exceptionally so. What were the odds of seeing two? Or of seeing the same one twice?

"I don't know," I said.

"I used to see a huge one," Grace said. "It was after the trial. I'd see him at night, on the lawn outside of my window."

"Was it white?" I asked.

"White?"

"Never mind." I was suddenly at a loss, back in time. "Thanks for coming to the trial," I said. She'd been there every day, a sunburned child in faded clothes. At first, my father had refused her the right to be there. Not proper, he'd said. And so she'd walked. Thirteen miles. After that, he'd surrendered.

"How could I not be there?" More tears. "Tell me something else good," she said.

I searched for something to give her. "You're all grown up," I finally said. "You're beautiful."

"Not that it matters," she said blackly, and I knew that she was thinking of what had happened between us at the river, after she'd run from the dock. I could still hear her words: *I'm not as young as you think I am.*

"You took me by surprise," I said. "That's all."

"Boys are so stupid," she said.

"I'm a grown man, Grace."

"And I'm not a child." Her voice was sharp, as if she'd cut me with it if she could.

"I just didn't know."

She rolled onto her side, showed me her back. And I saw it again, saw how badly I'd handled it.

*She was barely into the trees before I knew that I had to go after her. She owned a corner of my soul that I'd learned to shy from; a locked place. Why? Because I'd left her. Knowing how it would hurt, I'd gone to a distant place and sent letters.*

*Empty words.*

*But I was here now. She was hurting now.*

*So I ran after her. For a few hard seconds she continued to fly, and the soles of her feet winked brown and pink, then dark red as the trail dipped and she hit damp clay. When she stopped, it was sudden. The bank dropped away beside her, and for an instant it looked like she might take to the river, like she might step left and drop away. But she did not, and the hunted-animal look faded from her eyes in seconds.*

*"What do you want?" she asked.*

*"For you to not hate me."*

*"Fine. I don't hate you."*

*"I want you to mean it."*

*She laughed and it cut, so that when she turned to leave, my hand settled on her shoulder. It was hard and*

*hot, and she stopped when I touched her. She froze,
then spun back to me, pressed into me like she could
own me. Her hands found the back of my head and she
kissed me hard, rocked her body against mine. Her
bathing suit was still wet, and the water trapped in it
had warmed; I felt it soaking into me.*

*I took her shoulders, pushed her back. Her face was
full of defiance and of something else.*

*"I'm not as young as you think I am," she said.*

*I was undone yet again. "It's not age," I told her.*

*"I knew that you'd come back. If I loved you
enough, you'd come back."*

*"You don't love me, Grace. Not like that."*

*"I've loved you my whole life. All I needed was the
courage to tell you. Well, I'm not scared anymore. I'm
not scared of anything."*

*"Grace—"*

*Her hands settled on my belt.*

*"I can show you, Adam."*

*I grabbed her hands, grabbed hard and pulled them
away. It was all wrong. The words she'd said, the look
growing on her face as my rejection sank into her. She
tried one more time and I stopped her. She stumbled
back. I watched her features collapse. She flung up a
hand, then turned and ran, her feet flashing red, as if
she was running over broken glass.*

Her voice was small. It barely made it over her shoulder.
"Did you tell anybody?" she asked.

"Of course not."

"You think I'm a silly girl."

"Grace, I love you more than anyone else in the world.
What does it matter what shape the love is?"

"I think I'm ready to be alone now," she said.

"Don't make it like this, Grace."

"I'm tired. Come see me later."

I stood, and thought of embracing her again; but she was locked up. So I patted her on the arm, on a place unmarred by contusions, bandages, or needles placed under her skin.

"Get some rest," I told her, and she closed her eyes. But when I looked back in from the hallway, I saw that she was staring at the ceiling, and that her hands were clenched on the washed-out sheets.

I walked into the diffuse light of another dawn. I had no car, but there was a breakfast joint not too far away. It opened at six, and a couple of cars pulled around back after I'd been waiting a few minutes for the place to open. A metal door slammed against the cinderblock wall, someone kicked a bottle that clattered over concrete. Lights came on and sausage fingers flipped the sign from CLOSED to OPEN.

I took a booth by the window and waited for the smell of coffee. The waitress came over after a minute, and the ready smile slid off of her face.

She remembered me.

She took my order, and I kept my eyes on the plaid sleeve of her polyester shirt. It was easier for both of us that way. The old man with the fat fingers recognized me, too. They spoke in whispers by the cash register, and it was clear to me that accused was the same as convicted, even after five years.

The place filled up as I ate: blue-collar, white-collar, a little bit of everything. Most of them knew who I was. None of them spoke to me, and I wondered how much of that came from mixed feelings over my father's stubbornness and how much came from the belief that I was some kind of monster. I turned on my cell phone, and saw that I had missed three calls from Robin.

The waitress shuffled over and stopped as far away as she could without being obvious. "Anything else?" she asked. I told her no. "Your check," she said, and put it on the table's edge. She used her middle finger to push it toward me.

"Thanks," I said, pretending that I'd not just been flipped off.

"Anytime."

I sat longer, sipping the last of the coffee, and watched a police cruiser pull up to the curb. George Tallman climbed out of it. He dropped some change into a newspaper machine, then looked up and saw me through the glass. I gave him a wave. He nodded back, then made a call from his cell phone. When he came into the restaurant, he slipped into my booth and put his paper on the table. He held out his hand and I shook it.

"Who'd you call?" I asked.

"Your dad. He asked me to keep an eye out." He raised an arm to get the waitress's attention. He ordered a massive breakfast and gestured at my empty coffee cup. "More?" he asked.

"Sure."

"And more coffee," he told the waitress, who rolled her eyes.

I studied him there in his uniform, a navy jumpsuit with lots of gold trim and jangling metal; then I looked out the window, saw the big dog sitting upright in the backseat of his car.

"Are you on the canine unit, too?" I asked.

He grinned. "The kids love the dog. Sometimes I take him with me."

The breakfast came.

"So, you and my dad get along pretty well?" I asked.

George cut his pancakes into neat squares, and laid his knife and fork carefully on the dry edge of the plate. "You know my story, Adam. I come from nothing. Deadbeat dad. On-and-off mom. I'll never have money or position, but Mr. Chase has never looked down on me or acted like I wasn't good enough for his daughter. I'd do anything for your father. Guess you should know that up front."

"And Miriam?" I asked.

"People think I'm into Miriam for the money."

"There's always the money," I said.

"We can't pick who we love."

"So, you do love her then?"

"I've loved her since high school, maybe longer. I would do anything for Miriam." His eyes filled with sudden conviction. "And she needs me. Nobody has ever needed me before."

"I'm glad that it's all good."

"It's not all good, don't misunderstand me. Miriam is . . . well, she's a fragile woman, but like good china, you know. Fragile, beautiful." He lifted his heavy hands from the table, held his fingers as if he was holding teacups by tiny handles. "I have to be gentle." He lowered the pretend cups to the table and lifted his hands, fingers spread. He smiled. "But I enjoy that."

"I'm happy for you."

"Your stepmother was slow to approve." His voice dropped, so that I almost missed his next words. "She thinks I'm a worker bee."

"What?"

"She told Miriam that you *date* the worker bees, you don't marry them." I sipped my coffee and George picked up his fork. He looked as if he was waiting for something. "So do I have your approval?" he asked.

I put down the coffee. "Are you serious?" He nodded and I felt sorry for him. "I'm not entitled to an opinion, George. I've been gone a long time. I left under suspicion. You're a cop, for God's sake."

"Miriam is glad to have you back."

I was already shaking my head. "You have no idea how Miriam feels about me."

"Then let's just say that she's conflicted."

"It's not the same thing," I said, and George looked uncomfortable.

"I've always looked up to you, Adam. Your approval would mean a lot to me."

"Then God bless you both."

He held out his hand again and I shook it; his face was beaming. "Thank you, Adam." He went back to his breakfast, and I watched the food disappear.

"Any word on Zebulon Faith?" I asked.

"He's gone to ground, looks like. But he'll turn up. People are looking for him."

"And what about Danny?" I asked. "What do you think about that?"

"A hell of a place to end up, but I'm not surprised."

"Why not?"

George wiped syrup off his chin and leaned back. "You and Danny were tight, okay, so don't get pissed or anything."

"You were friends, too."

He shook his head. "Early on, maybe. But Danny got cocky after you left. Suddenly, all the women wanted him. Nobody was as cool as he was. He was easy to dislike. Things changed even more when I became a cop." He looked out the window, pursed his lips. "Danny said I was a joke. He told Miriam that she shouldn't date a joke."

"Guess he remembered a different George Tallman."

"Fuck him, then. That's what I say."

"He's dead, George. Why don't you tell me why that fact doesn't surprise you?"

"Danny liked the ladies. The ladies liked him. Single ones and married ones. Probably some pissed-off husbands that would like to take a chunk out of Danny. And Danny was a gambler. Not Wednesday night poker, either. I mean the real deal. Bookies. Borrowed money. He's run the gamut. But you should probably talk to your brother about that."

"Jamie?"

George's mouth tightened in distaste. "Yeah. Jamie."

"Why? Jamie is over his gambling problem. He licked it years ago."

George hesitated. "Maybe you'd better ask him."

"You won't tell me?"

"Look, I don't know what happened with Jamie before you left. I had nothing to do with that. All I know is what I see now. Jamie wants to be the same kind of player Danny was. Problem is, he's half as charming and twice as bad at cards. So, yeah, he gambles. Heavily, from what I've heard. But I don't need to add to our problems. Talk to him about it if you want, but don't mention my name."

A rusted-out pickup pulled into the lot and disgorged three men in dirt-rimed boots and greasy farm caps. They sat at the counter and fingered dog-eared menus. One of them stared at me and made a face like he was about to spit on the floor.

"I take it that you and Robin don't exactly get along," I said.

George shook his head and blinked. "I know you guys have a history, but I don't like mincing words, so I'm just going to say it. She's way too intense. Supercop, you know."

"And she doesn't like you?"

"I'm easy, Adam. I like the uniform. I like working with kids and riding around with the dog. I'm a happy guy. Alexander is all about the bust."

I pretended that I wasn't bothered. "She's changed," I said.

"No shit."

Everyone at the counter was staring at me now, the whole group of them, like they wanted to kick my ass. I understood; the boy had been well liked. I gestured and George followed the motion. "You seeing this?" I asked.

He studied the group, and I was impressed by the force of his personality, the cop in him. He stared them down until they looked away. His face softened when he looked back. "People are idiots," he said.

I heard a horn outside, and saw one of the farm trucks pull to a stop in the lot. It was Jamie. He honked again.

"Your ride," George said.

"Guess he's not coming in." I stood and dropped some bills on the table. "Good seeing you, George."

George gestured at Jamie. "Remember what I said. I don't need any more problems with your brother. We're going to be family soon."

"No worries."

"Thanks."

I started to turn, stopped. "One question, George."

"Yeah?"

"These bookies you're talking about. They heavy hitters? I mean, heavy enough to kill somebody over an unpaid debt?"

He wiped his mouth. "I imagine that would depend on the size of the debt."

I left, and didn't look back. Outside, the day had spread into another towering sky, a vault of blue so vast and still that it seemed unreal. In the truck, Jamie looked pale and swollen, with circles that spread beneath his eyes. A beer bottle was wedged between his massive legs. He saw me looking.

"I'm not drinking early, if you're wondering. I'm still up from last night."

"Want me to drive?"

"Sure. What the hell."

We switched places. I moved the seat up an inch and another empty bottle rolled under my feet. I tossed it into the back. Jamie rubbed a hand over his face and looked at himself in the visor mirror. "Jesus. I look like crap."

"You okay?"

He eyed George through the window. "Let's get out of here," he said. I put the truck in drive and pulled into thin traffic. I felt him looking at me.

"Go ahead," I said.

"What?"

"You can ask me."

His voice rose. "What the hell, Adam? What did the cops want with you?"

"I guess that's been the topic of conversation around the house."

"No shit, bro. It's not like anybody's forgotten the last time the cops took you away. Dad's been telling everyone to calm down, but it hasn't been easy. I'll tell you that for nothing. Everybody's unsettled."

I'd known it was coming, so I explained without losing my temper. Jamie looked doubtful.

"What did you and Grace talk about that was so damned secret?"

"That's none of your business, either," I said. I glanced sideways. He was cross-armed and angry. "Is this why you've been up all night drinking?" I asked. "You wondering about your brother again? Having doubts?"

"No."

"Then what?"

"Danny, mostly," Jamie said. "He was good people, you know. I thought he was still down in Florida, beaching it for a while. And all the time he was in that hole." He drained the beer.

"Don't lie to me, Jamie."

"I'm not lying," he said, but that was false, too. I let it go.

"Danny got into a fight with his girlfriend and hit her," I said. "That's why he was in Florida. Do you know anything about that? Who the girl was?"

"No idea. He had a bunch of them."

"What about his gambling?" I asked, studying him now. "Do you think that could have had something to do with it? Maybe he owed the wrong people."

Jamie looked uncomfortable. "You know about that, huh?"

"How bad was it?"

"Pretty bad at times, but not always. You know how it can be. Up one day, down the next." He laughed, but it sounded nervous. "Things turn fast. But he could handle it. Tried not to spread himself too thin."

"Any idea who took his bets?"

"Why would I know anything about that?" Defensive.

I wanted to push, but eased off. We drove in silence. I

turned out of town, crossed over a creek, and opened up on the empty roads. The truck shook beneath us, and I could tell that my questions had upset him. He sank lower, his jaw twisted, and when he spoke, he did not look at me.

"I didn't mean it, you know."

"Mean what?"

"When I said I'd fuck her. I didn't mean it."

He was talking about Grace.

"What about your telescope on the third floor?" I asked.

He shook his head. "She said that? Damn! Miriam caught me once looking at Grace with binoculars. Just once, okay? And shit. That's not a crime. She's hot. I was just looking." He twitched, like something just occurred to him. "Do the cops know about that?"

"I don't know, but I'm sure they'll talk to Grace. As far as I can tell, she has no reason to do you any favors."

"Fuck."

"Yeah. You've said that once or twice."

"Pull the truck over," Jamie said.

"What?"

"Pull the fucking truck over."

I slowed down, pulled onto the dirt shoulder, put the truck in park. I killed the engine.

Jamie rose in his seat, turned to face me. "Do we need to go?" he asked.

"What?"

"Do we need to step out of this car and go a few rounds? Because I'm thinking that maybe we do."

I leveled a gaze at him. "You're drunk," I said.

"I've had your back for five years. People bad-mouth you, say you're a goddamn killer, and I tell them to shut the hell up. I've been on your side. That's a brother thing. Now, I don't need this calm thing you're doing. I don't buy it. You've been dancing around me since you got in this truck. Just say it. Whatever it is. You think I had something to do with Grace?

Huh? Or with Danny? You want to come back here like nothing ever happened, like nothing's changed? You want to run the farm again? Is that it? Just say it."

He was defensive, and I knew why. The gambling was nothing new—it had happened before—and my questions about Danny had upset him. Sometimes I hated being right.

"How much did you lose?" It was a guess, but a good one. He froze, and I knew. "Dad had to cover you again, didn't he? How much this time?"

He slumped again, suddenly frightened and young. He'd gotten into a hole once his last year of high school. He'd hooked up with a bookmaker in Charlotte and gone heavy on a round of NFL playoff games. The engine ticked as it cooled. "A little over thirty thousand," he said.

"A little over?"

"Okay. Fifty thousand."

"Jesus, Jamie."

He sunk lower, all animosity gone.

"Football again?"

"I thought the Panthers were going to break out. I kept doubling down. It wasn't supposed to happen like that."

"And Dad covered it."

"It was three years ago, Adam." He held up a hand. "I haven't gambled since."

"But Danny has?"

Jamie nodded.

"You still want to go a few rounds?" I asked.

"No."

"Then don't fuck with me, Jamie. You're not the only one that had a bad night."

I started the truck, pulled back onto the road. "I want the name of his bookie," I said.

Jamie's voice was small. "There's more than one."

"I want them all."

"I'll find them. They're written down somewhere."

We drove in silence for a mile, until a convenience store appeared ahead of us. "Can you pull in here?" Jamie asked. I stopped at the store. "Give me a minute."

Jamie went inside. He came back out with a six-pack.

# *Sixteen*

I drove to the farm, took the turn for Dolf's house. There were cars there; Janice was on Dolf's porch. I stopped in the drive. "What's going on?" I asked. Jamie just shrugged. "You getting out?"

"I'm not that drunk," Jamie said.

I climbed out and Jamie slid across the seat. I put my hands on the window frame. "I misjudged Danny. Now he's dead. The cops should look into these bookies. Maybe there's something there."

"The cops?"

"I want those names."

"I'll find them," he replied, then waved once to his mother and turned the truck around.

I took the long walk.

My stepmother watched me approach. Young when she'd married my father, she was still shy of her fifties. She sat alone on the porch, and looked haggard. She'd lost weight. Once lustrous hair had faded to brittle yellow; her cheekbones looked hawkish and sharp. She rose from the rocking chair as my feet landed hard on the lowest step. I stopped halfway up, but she stood between the door and me, so I went to her.

"Adam." She found the courage to step in my direction. There had been a time when she would have swept forward and laid her light, dry lips on my cheek, but not now. Now she was as distant and cold as a foreign shore. "You're home," she said.

"Janice." I'd imagined this moment a thousand times. The two of us, speaking for the first time since my acquittal. Sometimes, when I saw it, she apologized. Other times, she struck me or cried out in fright. Reality was different. It was uncomfortable and nerve-racking. She held herself under tight control and looked as if she might simply turn and walk away. I could not think of a single thing to say. "Where's Dad?"

"He told me to wait out here. He thought that it might help us get reacquainted."

"I didn't think you'd want much to do with me."

"I love your father," she said woodenly.

"But not me?" For better or worse, we'd been family for almost twenty years. I could not hide the hurt, and for an instant her face reflected some unknown pain of her own. It did not last.

"You were acquitted," she said, "which must make me a liar." She sniffed and sat down. "Your father has made it plain that there is to be no more talk of misdeeds by members of this family. I choose to honor his wishes."

"Why don't I think you mean that?"

Some of the old steel flashed in her eyes. "It means that I will breathe the same air as you, and keep my tongue still. It means that I will tolerate the presence, in my home, of a liar and a killer. Don't mistake it for anything other than that. Don't you ever." She held my eyes for a long moment, then fished a cigarette from a pack on the table beside her. She lit it with trembling hands, twisted her lips to blow the smoke sideways. "Tell your daddy I was civil."

I gave her one last look and went inside. Dolf met me and I hooked a thumb toward the closed door. "Janice," I said.

He nodded. "I don't think she's slept since you came back into town."

"She looks bad."

An eyebrow shot up. "She accused her husband's son of murder. You cannot imagine the hell those two have endured."

His words stopped me. In all this time, I'd not once considered what the trial had done to them as a couple. In my mind, I'd always seen them as unchanged.

"But your father put her on notice. He told her that their marriage would be in the most severe danger she could imagine if she did anything but make you feel welcome."

"I guess she tried," I said. "What's going on in there?"

"Come on." I followed Dolf through the kitchen and into the living room. My father was there, along with a man I'd never seen. He was in his sixties, with white hair above an expensive suit. Both men rose as we entered. My father held out his hand. I hesitated, then shook it. He was trying. I had to acknowledge that.

"Adam," he said. "Glad to have you back. Everything okay? We went to the sheriff's department but couldn't find you."

"Everything's fine. I stayed with Grace last night."

"But they told us . . . Never mind. I'm glad she had you there. This is Parks Templeton, my attorney."

We shook hands and he nodded as if something important had been decided. "Good to meet you, Adam. I'm sorry that I didn't make it to the police station in time last night. Your father called as soon as you left with Detective Grantham, but it's an hour up here from Charlotte; and then I went to the sheriff's office. I expected to find you there."

"They took me to Salisbury P.D. as a courtesy. Because of what happened five years ago."

"I suspect that was not entirely true."

"I don't understand."

"If I could not find you, that gave them extra time alone with you. I'm not surprised." I thought back to my time in the interview room, the first thing that Robin had said to me.

*It was my idea.*

"They knew you'd come?" I asked.

"Me or someone like me. Your father had me on the phone before you were off the property."

"I don't need a lawyer," I said.

"Don't be ridiculous," my father said. "Of course you do. Besides, he's here for the family as well."

Parks spoke. "A body was found on the property, Adam, discovered in an out-of-the-way place that few people know about. They'll be looking at everyone, and they'll be looking hard. Some people may try to take advantage of the situation to pressure your father."

"You really believe that?" I asked.

"It's a six-tower nuclear facility and it's an election year. The forces at work are beyond anything you can imagine—"

My father interrupted. "You're overstating things, Parks."

"Am I?" the lawyer asked. "The threats have been graphic, but up until yesterday they were just threats. Grace Shepherd was attacked. A young man is dead, and none of us know the reason why. Putting your head in the sand now won't make it go away."

"I refuse to accept that corruption spreads as thickly in this county as you'd have us believe."

"It's not just the county, Jacob. It's Charlotte. Raleigh. Washington. Nothing remotely like this has happened in decades."

My father waved the comment away, and Dolf spoke up. "That's why you called Parks, isn't it? Let him do the doubting for you."

"There will be an investigation," Parks said. "This is the match dropping, right here. It's going to get hot. Reporters will be all over this place."

"Reporters?" I asked.

"Two came to the main house," my father said. "That's why we're here."

"You should put a man on the gate," I said.

"Yes," Parks said. "A white man, not a migrant. Someone

that cleans up well and knows how to be respectful but firm. If this is going to be on the news, I want the face of Middle America staring out."

"Jesus." Dolf sat down in disgust.

"If the police or anyone else wants to talk about anything, you direct them to me. That's what I'm here for. That's what you're paying me for."

My father looked at Dolf. "Do it," he said.

Parks pulled a chair from the card table by the window and dragged it across the rug. He sat in front of me. "Now, tell me about last night. I want to know what they asked you and I want to know what you said."

I told him, and the other men listened. He asked about the river, about Grace. He wanted to know what was said between us. I repeated what I said to the cops. "It's not relevant," I told him.

"That's for me to judge," he said, and waited for my answer.

It was a small thing, I knew, but not to Grace; so I looked out the window.

"This is not helpful," the attorney said.

I shrugged.

I drove into town to buy something nice for Grace, but changed my mind by the time I hit the city limit. Danny did not attack Grace; that had finally sunk in. That meant that whoever did was still out there. Maybe it was Zebulon Faith. Maybe not. But shopping would get me no closer to an answer.

I thought of the woman I'd seen in the blue canoe. She'd been with Grace moments before the attack. She'd been on the river. Maybe she'd seen something. Anything.

What was her name again?

*Sarah Yates.*

I stopped at the first pay phone I saw. Someone had ripped the cover off of the phone book, and many of the pages were torn, but I found the listings for Yates. There was less than a page of them. I scanned for a Sarah Yates but there was no such listing. I ran down the names more slowly. Margaret Sarah Yates was on the second column. I had no plan to call.

I drove to the historic district and parked in the shade of hundred-year-old trees. The house was all about tall columns, black shutters, and wisteria vines as thick as my wrist. The door was armored by two hundred years of lead paint and had a brass knocker shaped like a swan's head. When the door opened, it was as if the wall had shifted. The crack that appeared and then widened was at least twelve feet tall; the woman standing in it looked more like five. A smell of dried orange peels rolled over me.

"May I help you?" Age had bent the woman's back, but her features were sharp. Dark eyes appraised me from beneath light makeup and white, lacquered hair. Seventy-five, I guessed, trim in a tailored suit. Diamonds flashed at ears and throat, while behind her, an antique silk runner stretched off into a world of serious money.

"Good morning, ma'am. My name is Adam Chase."

"I know who you are, Mr. Chase. I admire what your father is doing to protect this town from the greed and short-sightedness of others. We need more men like him."

I was momentarily undone by her frankness. Not many women would stand and chat with a stranger once tried for murder. "I'm sorry to bother you, but I'm trying to contact a woman named Sarah Yates. I thought that she might live here."

The warmth dropped off of her face. The dark eyes hardened and the teeth disappeared. Her hand moved up on the door. "There is no one here by that name."

"But your name—"

"My name is Margaret Yates." She paused, and her eyelids flickered. "Sarah is my daughter."

"Do you know—"

"I have not spoken to Sarah in more than twenty years."

She put some of her weight on the door. "Ma'am, please. Do you know where I can find Sarah? It's important."

The door stopped moving. She pursed dry lips. "Why do you want her?"

"Someone I care about was attacked. It's possible that Sarah saw something that could help me find who did it."

Mrs. Yates considered, then waved a hand vaguely. "She's in Davidson County, last I heard. Over across the river."

I could shoot an arrow from Red Water Farm and hit Davidson County on the other side of the river. But it was a big county. "Any idea where?" I asked. "It really is important to me."

"If this porch were the bright center of the world, Mr. Chase, then Sarah would have found the place farthest from it." I opened my mouth, but she cut me off. "The darkest, farthest place." She took one step back.

"Any message?" I asked. "Assuming that I find her."

The small body sagged, and the emotion that touched her face was as soft and quick as a moth's wing beating once. Then the spine locked and the eyes snapped up, brittle and tight. Blue veins swelled beneath the paper skin, and her words popped like dry grass burning. "It's never too late to repent. You tell her that."

She crowded me and I stepped back; she followed me out, finger up and eyes gone crazy-bright.

"You tell her to beg our Lord Jesus Christ for forgiveness."

I found the stairs.

"You tell her," she said, "that hellfire is eternal."

Her face overflowed with some unknowable emotion, and she pointed at my right eye as the fire in her voice snapped once more, then died. "You tell her."

Then she turned for the great mouth of a door, and by the time it inhaled her, she was a much older woman.

I drove down shaded lanes and left the armored walls behind me. Thick lawns dwindled to weed and earth as I hit the poor side of town. Houses grew short and narrow and flaked, then I was through and onto long roads that ran wild into the country. I crossed into Davidson County, the bridge humming beneath me. I saw the long, slow brown, and a fat man with no shirt drinking beer on the shore. Two kids with stained lips picked blackberries from a thicket on the road-side.

I stopped at a bait shop, found an S. Yates in the phone book and tracked down the address. The drive pierced a dense tree line eight miles from the nearest traffic light. I made the turn, and the drive straightened into a long descent toward the river. I came out of the trees and saw the bus, which sat on blocks under a gnarled oak. It was pale purple with faded flowers painted on the sides. In front of it, fifteen acres had been cleared and cultivated.

I got out of the car.

The bus shifted as someone moved inside. A man stepped down onto the bare dirt. He was in his sixties, wearing cutoff jeans, untied boots, and no shirt. He was sunburned and lean, with gray hair on his chest, small, callused hands, and dirty nails. Long, gray hair, either damp or unwashed, framed a lined, brown face. He moved sideways, one arm bent, and his smile stretched wide.

"Hey, man. What's happening?" He walked to me. The smell of burned marijuana hung on him.

"Adam Chase," I said, holding out my hand.

"Ken Miller."

We shook hands. Up close, the smell was stronger: earth, sweat, and pot. His eyes were red, his teeth large and yellow and perfectly straight. He looked from me to the car and I saw him take in the word gouged into the hood. He pointed. "Bummer, man."

"I'm looking for Sarah Yates." I gestured at the bus. "She at home?"

He laughed. "Oh, hey man." The laughter grew in him. One hand rose, palm out, the other cupped his stomach. He bent at the waist, trying to speak through the laughter. "No, man. You got it all wrong. Sarah lives through there, in the big house." He got control of himself and pointed toward the next tree line. "She just lets me crash here, you know. I take care of the garden. Help her out when she needs it. She pays me a little, lets me crash."

I looked at the field of green. "That's a lot of work to sleep in a bus."

"No, this is cool. No phone, no hassles. Easy living. But I'm really here for the education."

I looked a question at him.

"Sarah's an herbalist," he stated.

"A what?"

"A healer." He waved an arm at the long rows of plants in the field. "Dandelion weed, chamomile, thyme, sage, catnip."

"Uh-huh."

"Holistics, man."

I pointed to the other side of the clearing, where a gap broke the trees. "Through there?"

"The big house. Straight up."

The big house was about fifteen hundred square feet, a log home with a green tin roof streaked orange at the edges. The logs had weathered gray; the chinking looked like river bottom. I parked behind a van with a bumper sticker on the back that said, GODDESS BLESS.

Shadows filled the porch and my skin chilled as I crossed to the door. I knocked, doubting that she was home. The cabin had that empty feel, and there was no canoe at the dock. I looked over the river, trying to guess exactly where we were. I put the location somewhere north of the farm; couple miles maybe. I walked down to the dock.

There was a wheelchair there, and I stared for a long second. It looked very out of place. I sat down on the dock to wait. It took about twenty minutes. She rounded the northern bend in an easy slide, the bow sweeping in, the current taking the stern out until she caught it with a firm stroke.

I stood, and the sense of knowing her welled up. She was an attractive woman, with ageless skin and a direct gaze. She locked it upon me when she was ten feet out, and did not look away, even as the canoe sidled up against the side of the dock.

I took the rope from her hand and tied it off on a cleat. She lay the paddle down and studied me. "Hello, Adam," she said.

"Do I know you?"

She flashed small teeth. "No, you don't." She waved a hand. "Now step back." She put her hands on the side of the dock and heaved herself up, turning so that she sat on the edge. Her legs twisted away beneath her, thin, lifeless sticks in loose jeans worn, in places, to the color of sand. I saw wasted skin at the ankles.

"Can I help you?" I asked.

"Of course not." Anger snapped in her voice, so that she sounded very much like her mother. She pushed herself back and her legs slid lifelessly behind her. She grabbed the arms of the wheelchair and pulled herself into the seat. She reached down for one of her legs, then fastened those lamplight eyes on me. "No need to stare, young man."

"I'm sorry," I said, and looked for something of interest on the other side of the river. I could sense her behind me, working to position her feet and legs.

"No harm in it, I guess. I don't see people that often. Sometimes, I forget there's something to stare at."

"You handle a canoe better than most."

"It's my only real exercise. Now, that's better." I turned around. She was situated in her chair. "Let's go up to the house." Her hands gripped the wheel rims and she turned without waiting for an answer. She propelled the chair uphill with strong, abrupt strokes. At the cabin, she turned for the rear. "Ramp's in the back," she said. Inside, she maneuvered to the refrigerator and pulled out a pitcher. "Tea?"

"Sure."

I watched as she handled the job with economical precision. Glasses in low cupboards. Ice from a separate freezer. I looked around the cabin. It had a large central room dominated by a fieldstone fireplace; the stones were brown and irregular, probably cleared from the soil beyond the trees. The space was spartan and clean. She handed me a glass. "I can't abide sugar," she said.

"That's okay."

She rolled for the front door, spoke over her shoulder. "Did you meet Ken on the way in?" she asked.

We went outside. I took a chair and sipped tea that was raw and bitter. "Interesting man."

"Once upon a time, he made more money than you'd believe. Seven figures in a year, sometimes. Then something changed. He gave it all to his kids and asked me if he could live out here for a while. That was six years ago. The canoe was his idea."

"Unusual place to live."

"It was there when I bought the place. I lived in it myself until I got the cabin built." She reached up and pulled a joint from her shirt pocket. She lit it with a cheap lighter, sucked in a deep breath, and let the smoke run out over her pale pink lips. She offered it to me and I declined. "Suit yourself," she said, and I watched her take another toke, how she sucked in multiple, small breaths, tightened her jaw before exhaling.

She settled lower in the wheelchair, studied the bright world with a contented air. "So, you know Grace?" I asked.

"Fine girl. We talk from time to time."

"Do you sell her pot?"

"Goodness, no. I'd never sell pot to that girl. Not in a million years." She took another drag, and when she spoke, her words were compressed. "I give it to her." There was laughter in her face. "Oh, don't look so serious. She's old enough to know her own mind."

"She was attacked the other day, you know. Right after the last time you saw her."

"Attacked?"

"Beaten badly. It happened a half mile south of the dock. I was hoping that you might have seen something. A man in a boat or on the trail. Anything like that."

The laughter vanished, and bleakness settled in the place it had been. "Is she okay?"

"She will be. She's in the hospital."

"I went north," she said. "I saw nothing unusual."

"Does Ken Miller know who she is?"

"Yes."

"Do you know him well?"

She waved a hand. "He's harmless."

She pulled one more time on the joint, and when the smoke left her lungs it carried much of her vitality with it. "Nice car," she said, but the words had no meaning. The car just happened to be in her field of vision.

"How do you know me?" I asked. Her eyes cut my way, but she didn't answer.

"Tell me how you found me," she said instead.

"Your mother thought you were over this way."

"Ah," she said, and there was dark history in that single sound.

I turned my seat to face her. "How do you know me, Sarah?"

But she was stoned, her eyes burnished bright and empty. She was seeing something that I could not, and her words drifted. "There are things in this world of which I do not speak," she said. "Promises, promises."

"I don't understand."

She crushed the joint out and dropped it on the unswept boards. Her eyelids drooped, but life moved behind the pale green irises, something knowing and wild enough to make me wonder what she saw. She gestured with a bent finger and I leaned closer. She took my face in her hands and kissed me on the mouth. Her lips were soft, slightly parted, and tasted of the joint she'd smoked. It was not a chaste kiss, nor was it overly sexual. Her fingers fell away and she smiled with such mournfulness that I felt an overwhelming sense of loss. "You were such a lovely boy," she said.

# *Seventeen*

She left me without another word, rolled the chair inside, and closed the door. I got in the car, passed through the trees and thought of Sarah's mother, whose message I had failed to deliver. They were family gone to ash, the bond between them as bloodless as time can make a thing. Maybe that's why I felt a kinship, why I thought of once precious bonds charred to light gray nothing.

I slowed as Ken Miller stepped out of the shade and waved me down. He leaned into the window. "Everything okay?" he asked. "She need anything?"

His face was open, but I knew how meaningless that could be. People show you what you want to see. "Do you know Grace Shepherd?" I asked.

"I know who she is." He nodded through the trees. "Sarah talks about her."

I watched him closely. "She was assaulted, almost killed. You know anything about that?"

His reaction was unscripted. "I'm truly sorry to hear that," he said. "She sounds like a fine girl." He seemed innocent and concerned.

"The police may want to talk to Sarah." A quick jolt of worry flashed across his face. I watched his eyes roll left, to the long purple bus. That's where his stash would be. "I thought you might like to know."

"Thanks."

I turned on my cell phone as I drove back into Salisbury. It rang almost immediately. It was Robin. "I'm not sure that I'm speaking to you right now," I said.

"Don't be stupid, Adam. You lied to us. The questions had to be asked. It's better that I was there than not."

"You said that going to Salisbury P.D. instead of the sheriff's office was for my sake. Did you mean that?"

"Of course. Why else would I do it?" I recognized the truth in her voice and some small part of me loosened. "I'm walking a thin line, Adam. I recognize that. I'm trying to do what's right."

"What do you want?" I asked.

"Where are you?"

"In the car."

"I need to see you. It'll only take a minute." I hesitated. "Please," she said.

We met in the parking lot of a Baptist church. The steeple rose against the blue sky, a needle of white that dwarfed us. She got right to the point. "I understand that you're angry. The interview could have gone better."

"A lot better."

Conviction crystallized her voice. "You chose to mislead us, Adam, so let's not pretend that you're on some moral high ground here. I'm still a cop. I still have responsibilities."

"You should have never been a part of that."

"Let me explain something to you. You left me. Get it? You . . . left . . . me. All I had left was the job. For five years, that's all I've had. And I've worked my ass off. Do you know how many female officers have made detective in the past ten years? Three. Just three, and I'm the youngest in the history of the entire department. You've been back for a couple of days. You understand? I'm who I am because you left. It's my life. I can't turn it off and you should not expect me to. Not when you made me like this."

She was angry and defensive. I thought about what she'd said. "You're right," I said, and meant it. "This is just bad all around."

"It may get a little easier."

"How so?"

"Grantham wants me off the case," she said. "He's angry."

A large crow settled atop the steeple. It spread its wings once, then dropped into black-eyed stillness. "Because you told me the truth about Grace?"

"He says I'm biased toward you and your family."

"Life gets complicated."

"Well, I'm about to make it more so. I asked around. Grace had a boyfriend."

"Who?"

"Unknown. The girl I talked to knew almost nothing. He was a secret for some reason; but there were issues there. Something that made Grace unhappy."

"Who told you this?"

"Charlotte Preston. She was in Grace's class. She works at the drugstore now."

"Did you ask Grace about it?"

"She denies it."

"What about Danny's ring? Or the note? Those don't add up to a frustrated boyfriend."

"I'm sure that Grantham is working on that."

"Why are you telling me this?" I asked.

"Because I'm angry, too. Because it's you and because I'm confused."

"Is there anything else you want to tell me?"

"The body is Danny Faith. Dental records confirm it."

"I knew it."

"Did you know that he called your house?" She put a keen edge on her words, and her attention was complete. "It's on his cell phone records. We just pulled them. Did you talk to him?"

She wanted me to say no. It was too damning, and there could be no easy explanation from where she stood. The timing was pretty bad. I hesitated, and Robin drilled in on it. I saw cop rise in her like a tide. "I spoke with him three weeks ago," I said.

"Forensics thinks he died three weeks ago."

"Yeah. Strange, I know."

"What did you talk about, Adam? What the hell is going on?"

"He wanted a favor."

"What favor?"

"He wanted me to come home. He wanted to talk about it in person. I told him I wouldn't come. He got pissed."

"Why did you come, then?"

"That's personal," I said, and meant it. I wanted my life back, and that included Robin. But she was not making it easy. She was a cop first, and while I understood that, it still cut.

"You need to talk to me, Adam."

"Robin, I appreciate what you've said, but I'm not sure where we stand. Until I know for certain, I'll proceed as I see fit."

"Adam—"

"Grace was assaulted, Danny killed, and every cop in the county is looking at me and my family. How much of that comes from what happened five years ago, I don't know; but I do know this. I'll do whatever I have to do to protect the people I love. I still know this town, still know these people. If the cops aren't going to look deeper than Red Water Farm, then I'll have to do it myself."

"That would be a mistake."

"I've been railroaded once. I'm not going to let it happen again. Not to me or anyone else in my family."

My cell phone rang, so I held up a finger. It was Jamie, and he was stressed-out.

"It's the cops," he said.

"What about them?"

"They're searching Dolf's house!" I looked at Robin as Jamie yelled in my ear. "It's a freakin' raid, man!"

I closed the phone slowly, watching Robin's face. "Grantham is searching Dolf's house." Distaste filled my voice. I could see five steps down the road. "Did you know about that?"

"I knew," she said calmly.

"Is that the reason that you called me? So that Grantham could do this without me around?"

"I thought it would be best if you were not there when he conducted the search. So, yes."

"Why?"

"Nothing could be gained if you and Grantham have another difficult encounter."

"So you lied to me to protect me from myself? Not to help Grantham?"

She shrugged, unapologetic. "Sometimes you can kill two birds with one stone."

I stepped closer, so that she seemed very small. "Sometimes, maybe. But you can't have it both ways forever. One of these days, you are going to need to make a choice about what's more important to you. Me or the job."

"You may be right, Adam, but it's like I said. You left me. This has been my life for five long years. I know it. I trust it. A choice may be out there somewhere, but I'm not ready to make that choice today."

Her face refused to soften. I blew out a breath. "Damn it, Robin." I took a step and turned. I wanted to punch something. "What are they looking for?"

"Danny was killed with a .38. The only pistol registered to anyone at Red Water Farm is owned by Dolf Shepherd, a .38. Grantham is looking for that."

"Then I have a problem."

"What's that?"

I hesitated. "My fingerprints are all over that pistol."

Robin studied me for a long time. To her credit, she did

not ask me why. "Your fingerprints are on record. It won't take very long."

I opened the door to my car.

"Where are you going?"

"Dolf's."

Robin moved for her car. "I'll follow you."

"What about Grantham?"

"I don't work for Grantham," she said.

Four police cars blocked the driveway, so I pulled off into a field and walked. Robin fell in behind me and as we crossed over the steel bars of the cattle guard, dry mud crunched beneath my shoes. I did not see Grantham, and guessed that he was in the house. A uniformed deputy guarded the porch and another slouched by the cars. The front door stood open, wedged with a rocking chair turned flat against the house. Dolf, Jamie, and my father stood together next to Dolf's truck. The old men looked furious; Jamie chewed on a fingernail and nodded at me. I looked for Parks Templeton and found him in his long, expensive car. He had a cell phone to his ear, one leg hanging out of the open car door. He did a double take when he saw us, and hung up the phone. We reached my father at the same time.

Parks aimed a finger at Robin. "Tell me that you have not been speaking to her."

"I know what I'm doing."

"No, you do not."

"Let's talk in a minute," I said to Robin. She turned away and mounted the steps to the porch. I turned back to Parks. "Can you do anything about this?" I gestured at the house.

"We've been through that," my father said. "The warrant is legal."

"How long have they been here?"

"Twenty minutes."

I spoke to Parks. "Tell me about the warrant."

"There's no need—"

"Tell him," my father said.

Parks drew himself up. "It's limited in scope. That's good. It gives the police the authority to seize any handguns and handgun ammunition on the premises."

"That's it?" I asked.

"Yes."

"That should have taken two minutes. They're looking for a .38. It's right there in the gun cabinet."

The lawyer put a finger across his lips, tapped once. "How do you know they're looking for a .38?"

"Because that's what killed Danny. I learned that from her." I gestured at the house, held the lawyer's eyes until he was forced to nod. It was good information. "They should have had it by now," I said. "They should be gone."

For a moment no one spoke. I wish that it had stayed like that.

"I hid it," Dolf finally said.

"What?" Jamie slipped off the hood of the truck. Sudden anger boiled off him. "You hid it? No reason to hide a gun unless you've got something to hide."

The disquiet slid off Dolf's face, replaced by a look of weary resignation. Jamie stepped closer. "I'm always answering to you," Jamie said. "Got you looking over my shoulder. Now, why don't you answer to me? Only one reason to hide a gun, Dolf. That's plain enough. Why don't you just tell us?"

"What are you saying?" my father asked.

Dolf peered out at Jamie from beneath heavy lids, and there was such regret in his eyes. "Danny was decent enough, and I know you loved him, boy—"

"No, you don't," Jamie said. "Don't you 'boy' me. Just explain it. Only one reason to hide a gun, and that's because you knew they'd come looking for it."

"You're drunk," Dolf said. "And that's ignorant talk."

Parks interrupted, and his voice was strong enough to give Jamie pause. "Illuminate us," he said to Dolf.

Dolf looked to my father. He nodded, and Dolf spit on the ground, hitched his thumbs into his belt. He stared at Parks, then at Jamie. "That's not the only reason to hide a gun, Jamie, you big, dumb lummox. A man might hide a gun to keep somebody else from using it. To keep a smart man from doing a stupid thing."

Dolf's eyes cut to me, and I knew that he was thinking about how I took the gun from his cabinet and how I almost killed Zebulon Faith. He'd hidden it for my sake.

"He's right," I said, relieved. "That's a good reason."

"How about you explain that?" Parks said to me.

My father spoke before I could. "He doesn't have to explain anything. We did that five years ago. He won't have to do it again. Not here. Not ever."

I felt my father's eyes on me, the force of what he said. What it meant. It was the first time he'd stood up for me since Janice said that she saw me dripping with blood. Parks went rigid as the color rose in his face. "You are limiting my value to you, Jacob."

"At three hundred dollars an hour, I make the rules. Adam will tell you what he thinks you need to know. I will not have him questioned again."

Parks tried to return my father's stare, but lost his nerve after a few seconds. He threw up a hand and stalked off. "Fine," he said. I watched him all the way back to his car. Suddenly my father was embarrassed, as if by the act of protecting me. He patted Dolf on the shoulder, fastened an eye on Jamie.

"You drunk?" he asked.

Jamie was still mad; you could see it. "No," he said. "I'm hungover."

"Well, keep it together, boy."

Jamie climbed into his truck, slumped in the seat, and lit a cigarette. That left the older men and me. My father led us a few steps away. He looked apologetic. "He's not usually like this," he said, then looked at Dolf. "You okay?"

"It'll take more than that boy's got to ruin my day," Dolf said.

"Where'd you hide the gun?" I asked.

"In a coffee can in the kitchen."

"They'll find it," I said.

"Yep."

I studied Dolf's face. "Is there any chance that it can be linked to Danny's death?"

"I can't imagine how."

"Do you have any handguns?" I asked my father.

He shook his head and his gaze went to some distant place. My mother had killed herself with one of his handguns. It was a stupid question, insensitive, but when he spoke, his face was a rock. "What a mess," he said.

He was right, and I wondered how it all fit. Danny's death, now clearly considered a homicide; the attack on Grace; Zebulon Faith; the power plant; the rest of it. I looked at Dolf's house, full of strangers. Change was coming, and no way would it be the good kind.

"I have to go," I said.

My father looked old.

I nodded at the house. "Parks is right about one thing. They're looking to pin Danny's death on somebody, and for whatever reason, Grantham seems to be looking at us. That means that he'll be looking at me in particular." No one contradicted me. "I need to talk to somebody."

"Talk to who?"

"Something just occurred to me. It may be nothing, but I need to check it out."

"Can you tell us what it is?" Dolf asked.

I thought about it. Until Danny's body was found in that hole, everybody thought he was in Florida. His father. Jamie. There had to be a reason for that, and I thought I might find it at the Faithful Motel. It was a place to start, at any rate. "Later," I said. "If it pans out." I took two steps and stopped, turned back to my father. His face was heavy and filled with sadness. I spoke from the heart. "I appreciate what you said to Parks."

He nodded. "You are my son."

I looked at Dolf. "Tell him why you hid the gun, would you? There's no reason for that to be a secret between us."

"All right."


I got in the car, wondering how my father would feel when Dolf told him just how close I'd come to killing Zebulon Faith. Given the way that we all felt about Grace, I thought he'd probably understand. It was the least of our problems.

I turned off the farm and onto smooth, black pavement. The road was cooked; it shimmered under the sun. I went back to the Faithful Motel and found Manny behind the counter. "It's Manny, right?"

"Emmanuel."

"Is your boss here?" I asked.

"No."

I nodded. "When I was here before, you told me about Danny. You said that he'd gotten into a fight with his girlfriend and then gone to Florida when she took out a warrant."

"*Sí.*"

"Can you tell me the girl's name?"

"No. But she has a cut here now." He drew a finger across his right cheek.

"What does she look like?"

"White. Kind of fat. Trashy." He shrugged. "Danny would sleep with anybody."

"What were they fighting about?"

"He was breaking up with her."

I had a sudden flash of intuition. "It was you that called the police," I said. "That first day I came."

A smile cracked the seamed, brown face. "*Sí.*"

"You may have saved my life."

He shrugged. "I need the job. I hate the boss. This is life."

"Did the police search this place?" I was thinking of drugs.

"They search. They find nothing. They look for Mr. Faith. They find nothing."

I waited for more, but he was finished. "You told me that Danny is in Florida. How do you know that?"

"He sent a postcard." No hesitation, no sign of dishonesty.

"Do you still have it?"

"I think so." He turned for the back room, came back, and handed me a postcard. I took it by the edges; it was a picture of blue water and white sand. It had the name of a resort in the upper-right corner, and a slogan in pink letters across the bottom: SOMETIMES IT'S JUST RIGHT. "It was on the bulletin board," Emmanuel told me.

I looked at the back. In printed letters it read, "Having a blast. Danny."

"When did you get this?" I asked.

Emmanuel scratched at his cheek. "He had the fight with the girl and then he left. Maybe four days after that. Two weeks ago. Two and a half weeks. Something like that."

"Did he pack anything?"

"I did not see him after he hit the girl."

I asked a few more questions, but they led nowhere. I debated whether or not to tell him that Danny Faith was dead, but decided against it. It would hit the papers soon enough.

"Listen, Emmanuel. If the police find Mr. Faith, he may be going away for a while." I paused, to make sure he was following me. "You might want to start looking for another job."

"But Danny—"

"Danny won't be running the motel. It will probably close."

He looked very troubled. "This is true, what you say?"

"Yes."

He nodded, stared at the counter for so long I wasn't sure that he was planning to look up. "The police search everywhere," he finally said. "But there is a storage unit. It's by the interstate, the one with the blue doors. There was a maid, Maria. She's gone now. He made her sign the papers. It is in her name. Number thirty-six."

I digested this. "Do you know what's in that storage unit?" I asked.

The old man looked ashamed. "Drugs."

"How much drugs?"

"Much, I think."

"Were you and Maria together?"

"*Sí.* Sometimes."

"Why did she leave?" I asked.

Emmanuel's face twisted in disgust. "Mr. Faith. Once she signed the documents for him, he threatened her."

"Threatened to call INS?"

"If she told anybody about the storage unit, he would make a call. She was illegal. She got scared. She's in Georgia now."

I held up the postcard.

"I'd like to keep this."

Emmanuel shrugged.

I called Robin from the parking lot. I still had doubts about her loyalties, but she had information that I wanted, and I thought I might have something to trade. "Are you still at Dolf's house?"

"Grantham drove me out of there pretty damn quick. He was pissed."

"Do you know the self-storage facility by the interstate? It's on the feeder road south of exit seventy-six."

"I know it."

"Meet me there."

"Thirty minutes."

I drove back into town and stopped at the copy shop two blocks off the square. I copied the postcard, front and back, then asked the clerk for a bag. She brought me a paper one,

and I asked if she had anything plastic. She found a Ziploc in
a desk drawer. I folded the copy into my back pocket and put
the card in the bag, zipped it up. The bright sand looked very
white through the plastic and the logo caught my eye.

SOMETIMES IT'S JUST RIGHT.

I drove to the storage facility and parked on the dirt verge
of the feeder road. I got out and sat on the hood. Cars flew
by on the interstate above me; the big trucks rumbled and
screamed. I looked over the storage facility, long rows of
squat buildings that flashed in the sun. They nestled in a depression beside the interstate. Metal doors painted blue broke
the long facades. Grass grew tall along chain-link fencing.
Barbed wire leaned out from the top.

I waited for Robin and watched the day make its long slide
into late afternoon. It took her an hour. When she climbed
out of the car, the wind took her hair, wrapped it across her
face so that she had to flick it away with a finger. The gesture
struck me hard and with unexpected force. It reminded me
of a windy day we'd spent on the riverbank seven years ago.
She was kneeling on a blanket, we'd just made love, and a
sudden wind had licked up off the water to bend her hair
across her eyes. I'd pushed the hair back, and pulled her
down. Her mouth was soft, the smile easy.

But that was a lifetime ago.

"Sorry," she said. "Cop stuff."

"Like what?" I slipped off the hood.

"Salisbury P.D. and the sheriff's office use the same forensics lab. They've worked up the bullet that killed Danny Faith.
Chest wound, by the way. They're just waiting for a compari-
son sample." Her eyes were steady. "It won't be long," she
said.

"Meaning?"

"They found Dolf Shepherd's .38."

Although I knew they'd find it, a pit opened up in my
stomach. I waited for her to say more. A yellow moth moved
above tall grass.

"Will your friend at ballistics help you out?" I finally asked.

"He owes me."

"Will you let me know what he says?"

"That depends on what he tells me."

"I can give Zebulon Faith to you," I said, and that stopped her. "I can give him to you on a plate."

"If I share my information?"

"I want to know what Grantham knows."

"I can't make blind promises, Adam."

"I need to know. I don't think I have much time. My prints are on the gun."

"A gun that may or may not be the murder weapon."

"Grantham knows I spoke to Danny right before he died. It's enough for an arrest warrant. He'll bring me in and hammer me. Just like the last time."

"You were in New York when Danny was killed. You'll have alibis, witnesses that can put you there at the time of death."

I shook my head.

"What the hell does that mean?"

"No alibi," I said. "No witness."

"How is that possible?"

"It had been five years, Robin. That's what you have to understand first. I'd buried this place so deep I couldn't see it anymore. It's how I got through the days. I forgot. I made an art of forgetting. That changed after Danny called. It was like he'd put a demon in my head. It wouldn't shut up. It wanted me to go home. It told me that it was time. If I tried to think, I heard the voice. When I closed my eyes, I saw this place. It made me insane, Robin. Day after day. I thought of you, of my father. I thought of Grace and of the trial. That dead kid and the way that this town just chewed me up and spit me out.

"Suddenly, I couldn't stand my life. It was so empty, such a goddamn sham, and Danny's voice tore down everything I'd built. I didn't go to work. I stopped seeing friends. I locked myself away. It just ate at me until I found myself on the road."

I lifted my hands, let them drop. "No one saw me, Robin."

"Demons in the head and no alibi is not something you should ever say again. Grantham has already put in a request with N.Y.P.D. They'll check up on you. They'll be thorough. They'll find where you worked. They'll find out that you quit and when you quit. You need to think hard about that alibi. Grantham's going to wonder if you didn't drive down here and kill Danny. He'll hold your feet to the fire. He'll roast you if he can."

I held her gaze. "I didn't kill anybody."

"Why are you home, Adam?"

I heard the answer in my head. *Because everything that I love is here. Because you refused to come with me.*

I didn't say it, though. I pointed at the bright, aluminum buildings and told her what Emmanuel had said about Zebulon Faith and the drugs. "Number thirty-six. He'll give you all the probable cause you need."

Her voice was empty. "Good information."

"He may have cleaned it out. He's had time."

"Maybe." She looked away, and the wind stirred dust on the road. When she looked back, she'd gone soft around the edges. "There's something else I need to tell you, Adam. It's important."

"Okay."

"The phone call looks bad. The timing makes it worse. Prints on the gun. All the violence and coincidence. No alibi . . ." She trailed off, looked suddenly fragile. "You may be right about the warrant . . ."

"Go on."

"You said I had to make a choice. You or the job." Wind licked at her hair again. She looked uncertain and her voice fell. "I took myself off the case," she said. "I've never dropped a case before. Not ever."

"You did that because Grantham's coming after me?"

"Because you were right when you said I had to make a choice." For an instant, she looked proud, then her features collapsed. I knew that something was happening, but I was slow and confused. Her shoulders rolled inward and something wet moved on her face. When she looked up, her eyes were silver bright, and I saw that she was crying. Her voice broke into a sob. "I've really missed you, Adam."

She stood on the roadside, breaking, and I finally understood the depths of her conflict. Two things mattered to her: the person she'd become and the thing she'd thought was lost. Being a cop. And us. She'd tried to keep them both, tried to walk the line, but the truth had finally caught up with her: there comes a time to choose.

So she did.

And she chose me.

She was naked in the cold and I knew that she would not say another word without some sign from me. I didn't have to think about it, not even for a second. I opened my arms, and she slipped into that space as if she'd never left it.

I drove us to her place, and this time it was different, like the apartment was too small to hold us. We were in one room, then another, clothes on the floor behind us as we slammed through doors and into walls. Old emotions burned through us, new ones raged.

And memories of a thousand other times.

I held her against the wall and her legs found my waist, wrapped me up. She kissed me so hard I thought I might bleed, but didn't care. Then she gripped my hair and pulled me back. I looked at her swollen lips, stared into those kaleidoscope eyes. She was breathing hard, trembling. Her words came in a fierce whisper.

"What I said before, about it being gone, about me being done. . . ." Her eyes slid to my chest, back up. "That was a lie."

"I know."

"Just tell me this is real."

I told her, and when we found the bed, it could have been the floor or the kitchen table. It didn't matter. She was on her back, her fingers twisted into the sheets when I saw that she was crying again.

"Don't stop," she said.

"Are you okay?"

"Make me forget."

She meant the loneliness, I knew, the five-year stretch of nothing. I rose to my knees and ran my eyes down the length of her; she was lean and hard, a broken fighter. I kissed her damp cheeks, traced her body with my hands, and felt the tension in her collapse. Her arms came up from the bed and there was no strength in them, just lightness and heat that seemed to mirror some desperate part of her. I slipped one arm beneath the small of her back and crushed her against me as if I could drive the demons out by sheer, brute force. She was light and small, but she found her rhythm and the strength to rise beneath me.

# *Eighteen*

I fell asleep with Robin's head on my chest. It felt familiar and warm and right, and those things scared the hell out of me. I didn't want to lose her again. Maybe that's why I dreamed of another woman. I stood at a window, looking down on Sarah Yates and moonlit grass. She was walking, and carried her shoes in one hand. A white dress stirred around her legs, and her skin flashed silver as she looked up once and raised a hand as if she held a penny on her palm.

I woke in gray silence. "Are you awake?" I whispered.

Her head moved on the pillow. "Thinking," she said.

"About?"

"Grantham."

I shook off the dream. "He's coming after me, isn't he?"

"You didn't do anything wrong." She was trying to convince herself that it was that simple, but we both knew better. Innocent men go down all the time.

"Nobody likes to believe in rich man's justice, but that's what people see. They want payback."

"It won't happen like that."

"I'm convenient," I said.

She shifted beside me, the hard curve of her thigh pressing against mine. This time she did not contradict me. Her words slipped into the air between us. "Did you think about me?" she asked. "All those years in New York."

I considered, and then gave her the painful truth. "At first, all of the time. Then I tried not to. It took a while. But it's like I said, I buried this place. You had to go, too. It was the only way."

"You should have called. Maybe I'd changed my mind about coming with you." She rolled onto her side. The covers slipped off her shoulder.

"Robin . . ."

"Do you still love me?"

"Yes."

"Then love me."

She laid her lips against my neck, reached down, and I felt the light touch of her hand. We started slowly, in the shadow of those words, and the looming gray of a tentative dawn.

At ten o'clock I took Robin back to her car. Her fingers squeezed mine and she pressed against me. She looked strangely vulnerable and I knew that she probably was.

"I don't take half measures, Adam. Not on things that matter. Not on us. Not on you." She laid her palm on my face. "I'm on your side. Whatever it takes."

"I can't commit to Rowan County, Robin. Not until I see where things go with my father. I need things to be right with him. I don't know how to get there."

She kissed me. "You can consider my choice made. Whatever it takes."

"I'll be at the hospital," I said, and watched her go.

I found Miriam in the waiting area. She was alone, eyes closed. Her clothing rustled as she made small movements. When I sat, she grew still and showed me half of her face.

"You okay?" I asked.

She nodded. "How about you?"

Miriam had grown into a beautiful woman, but you had to

look carefully to see it. She seemed smaller, in all things, than she actually was. But I understood. Life, for some, was just hard.

"I'm glad to see you," I told her. She nodded, her hair swinging forward. "You really doing okay?" I asked.

"Don't I look it?"

"You look fine. Is someone with Grace?"

"Dad. He thought that it might help Grace to have me here. I've been in once already."

"How's she doing?" I asked.

"She screams in her sleep."

"How about Dad?"

"He's like a woman."

I didn't know what to say to that.

"Look, Adam, I'm sorry that we haven't talked much. I've wanted to. It's just been . . ."

"Yeah. Weird. You told me."

She smoothed her hands across her thighs, pushed herself straighter, so that her back was bent into less of a question mark. "I am happy to see you again. George told me that you thought maybe I wasn't. I'd hate for you to think that."

"He's grown into a good man," I said.

She lifted her shoulders, gestured down the hall with a bitten fingernail. "Do you think she'll be okay?"

"I hope so."

"Me, too."

I put my hand on her forearm and she twitched, jerked it away, then looked sheepish.

"Sorry," she said. "You startled me."

"You okay?" I asked.

"This family is coming apart." She closed her eyes. "There're cracks all over the place."

When my father came out of Grace's room, he moved slowly and nodded at me as he sat. "Hello, Adam." He turned to Miriam. "Will you sit with her for a while?"

She looked at me once and then disappeared down the hall. My father patted me on the knee.

"Thanks for being here."

"Where's Dolf?"

"We're taking turns."

We settled back against the wall. I gestured after Miriam. "Is she doing all right? She seems . . ."

"Dark."

"I beg your pardon?"

"Dark. She's been like that since Gray Wilson's death. He was a bit older, a bit rougher, but they were close, ran with the same group in school. When you were tried for his murder, the group cut her off. She's been very alone since then. She couldn't handle college. Came back from Harvard after one semester. But that just made it worse. Grace tried once or twice to bring her out of it. Hell, we all did. She's just . . ."

"Dark."

"And sad."

A nurse passed us. A tall man rolled a gurney down the hall.

"Do you have any idea who might have killed Danny?" I asked.

"No clue."

"He was heavy into gambling. His father is a drug dealer."

"I don't like seeing it that way."

"Who is Sarah Yates?" I asked.

He went rigid, and the words came slowly. "Why do you ask me that?"

"Grace was talking to her shortly before the attack. They looked like they might be friends."

He relaxed marginally. "Friends? I doubt it."

"Do you know her?"

"No one really knows Sarah Yates."

"That's pretty vague."

"She lives on the fringe. Always has. She can be warm

one day, mean as a snake the next. As far as I can tell, there's not much that Sarah Yates cares about."

"So, you do know her."

He faced me, lips tight. "I know that I don't want to talk about her."

"She says that I was a lovely boy." My father turned in his seat, and his shoulders squared up. "Do I know her?" I asked.

"You should stay away from her."

"What do you mean?"

"I mean that you should stay the hell away from her."

I went shopping for Grace. I bought flowers, books, and magazines. None of it felt right; it was all guesswork, and I had to face the truth of it once again. I didn't know her anymore. I felt restless, and drove around town for a bit. Every road was layered in memory, so textured that the past was physical. That was another thing about home.

I was almost back to the hospital when my cell phone rang. It was Robin. "Where are you?" I asked.

"Look in your mirror." I looked and saw her car twenty feet behind me. "Pull over. We need to talk."

I hung a left into a quiet, residential area that had been developed in the early seventies. The houses were low with small windows. The yards were neat and trim. Two blocks down, kids rode bikes. Someone in yellow pants kicked a red ball. Robin was all business.

"I spent the morning making very quiet inquiries," she said. "Reached out to people I trust. Asked them to keep me in the loop. I just got a call from a detective friend who was about to testify in Superior Court when Grantham showed up and spoke to the judge."

"Judge Rathburn?"

"Yeah. Rathburn called a recess and took Grantham into chambers. Ten minutes later he canceled court for the day." She paused.

"You know why, don't you?"

"This came from one of the clerks. It's solid. Grantham presented the judge with an affidavit in support of an arrest warrant. The judge signed off on it."

"A warrant for whose arrest?"

"Unknown, but given what we know, I suspect that it has your name on it." Distant laughter rolled over us, the high squeal of children at play. Robin's eyes were filled up with worry. "I thought that you might want to call that lawyer."

Grace was sleeping when I returned to the hospital. Miriam had left and my father was in the room with his eyes closed. I put the flowers by the bed and the magazines on a table. I stood for a long minute, looking at Grace and thinking of what Robin had told me. Things were coming to a head. "You okay?" my father asked. His eyes were red from sleep. I pointed at the door, and when I left, my father followed me out. He scrubbed a hand over his face.

"I've been waiting for you to get back," he said. "I told Janice that I want to have everyone to the house for dinner. I want you to come."

"Janice didn't like that, I bet."

"It's what families do. She knows that."

I looked at my watch. Afternoon was upon us. "I need to speak with Parks Templeton," I said.

My father's face twitched with sudden worry. "What's going on?"

"Robin thinks that Grantham has an arrest warrant with my name on it."

He understood immediately. "Because they've identified your prints on Dolf's gun."

I nodded.

"Maybe you should leave."

"And go where? No. I'm not running again."

"What are you going to do?"

I looked at my watch again. "Let's have a drink. On the porch. Like we used to do."

"I'll call Parks from the car."

"Tell him he should get here sooner rather than later."

We walked outside and turned for the parking lot. "There's one more thing I'd like for you to do," I said.

"What's that?"

I stopped and he did, too. "I want to speak with Janice. In private. I want you to make it happen."

"May I ask why?"

"She testified against me in open court. We've never talked about that. I think we need to get it behind us. She won't want to have the conversation."

"She's scared of you, son."

I felt the familiar anger. "How do you think that makes me feel?"

Back in the car, I pulled out the postcard sealed in its plastic bag. Danny never made it to Florida; I was pretty certain of that. I studied the photo on the card. Sand too white to be real, and water so pure it could wash away sin.

SOMETIMES IT'S JUST RIGHT.

Whoever killed Danny Faith had mailed this postcard to try and hide the crime. It could very well have prints on it. I wondered for the hundredth time if I should tell Robin about it. Not yet, I decided. Mostly for her own good. But it was more than that. Somebody, for reasons unknown, had killed Danny Faith. Someone pointed a gun and squeezed the trigger; lifted Danny up, and dumped him down that great dark hole.

Before I went to the cops, I needed to know who.

In case it was someone I loved.

We gathered on the porch, all of us, and though the liquor was expensive, it felt thin and false, like the assurances we traded. None of us believed that everything would be all right, and when the words dried up, which they often did, I studied faces that were naked in the hard rays of the bright, falling sun.

Dolf lit up, and loose tobacco settled on his shirt. He flicked at the small, moist pieces with an utter lack of care. Yet he wore his larger concerns like he wore his boots, as if he'd be lost without them; my father could have been his brother in that regard. They were pared down, the both of them, scoured clean.

George Tallman watched my sister like some part of her might fall off, and he'd need wariness and great speed to catch the piece before it struck and shattered. He kept an arm pressed against her, and leaned low when she spoke. Occasionally, he looked at my father, and I saw adoration in his face.

Jamie sat darkly next to a row of empty bottles. His mouth dipped at the corners, and hard shadow filled the sockets of his eyes. He spoke infrequently and in a low rumble. "It's not fair," he muttered once, and I assumed that he was speaking of Grace; but when I pressed, he shook his head, and tipped back the brown bottle of whatever foreign beer he'd chosen.

Janice, too, looked tortured, with chipped nails, dark circles, and hollow eyes. She'd deteriorated even over the past day. Her words came often and forced, and they were as brittle as the rest of her. She played the role that my father had imposed upon her, that of hostess, and, to her credit, she tried. But it was a brutal thing to see; and there was little mercy in my father's eyes. He'd told her what I wanted and she did not like it. The fact of it was all over her.

I kept an eye on the long drive, looking for dust behind bright metal. I hoped for the lawyer to make it first, yet expected Grantham and his deputies to arrive at any moment. A lawyer friend once said that it was easy to hate lawyers until you needed one. At the time I'd found him glib, but not now.

Now he was a goddamn genius.

The day settled as our conversation dwindled to nothing. There was danger in words, trip wires and blind spots where great harm could be done. Because the reality of murder was more than the concept of it. It was the loose, damp corpse of a man we'd all known. It was the questions that sprung up, the theories that we'd all turned over, yet not once discussed. He was killed here, where the family lived and breathed, and that danger alone should be enough; but there was also Grace.

And there was me.

No one knew what to do with me.

When Janice spoke to me, her voice was too loud, her eyes directed somewhere over my shoulder. "So, what are your plans now, Adam?" Ice clattered in the fine crystal beneath her white-tipped fingers, and when our eyes finally met, there was a sudden filling of the space between us, as if countless wires connected us, as though they all started humming at once.

"I plan to have a conversation with you," I said, and did not mean for the words to sound like such a challenge.

The smile slipped off her face, taking most of her color with it. She wanted to look at my father, but did not. "Very well." Her voice was cool and even. She smoothed her skirts and rose from the chair as if an unseen force lifted her. She could have carried stacked books on the crown of her head, even as she leaned in to kiss my father on the cheek. She turned at the door, more calm, I thought, than she had ever been. "Shall we go to the parlor?"

I followed her into the cool interior, down the length of the long hall. She opened the door to her parlor and motioned me ahead of her. I saw pastel colors and rich fabrics, a bag of incomplete needlepoint on what my mother would have called a "fainting couch." I took three steps into the room and turned to watch her as she gentled the door shut. Her thin fingers spread out on the dark wood, then she turned and slapped me. Pain flared like a match head.

Her finger rose between us, and the damaged paint shone on her nail. Her voice wavered. "That's for having your father lecture me about the meaning of family." She stabbed her finger in the direction of the porch. "For insulting me in my own home." I opened my mouth, but she spoke over me.

"For calling me on the carpet in front of my own family like I was some wicked, wicked child." She lowered her hand, tugged at the waist of her pale yellow silk jacket, and suddenly, she was shaking. Her next words fell into the room like petals from a dying flower.

"I refuse to be frightened, and I refuse to be manipulated. Not by you and not by your father. Not anymore. Now, I'm going upstairs to rest. If you tell your father that I struck you, I'll deny it."

The door closed with the faintest click, and I think that I would have followed her out, but it didn't happen. The cell phone vibrated in my pocket, even as I took the first step. I recognized Robin's number. She was out of breath.

"Grantham just left with three deputies. They plan to execute the warrant."

"They're coming here?"

"That's my information."

"When did they leave?"

"Fifteen minutes ago. They'll be there any minute."

I took a deep breath. It was happening again. "I'm on my way," Robin said.

"I appreciate the thought, Robin, but whatever is going to happen will be long done by the time you get here."

"Is your lawyer there?"

"Not at the moment."

"Just do me one favor, Adam." I waited, said nothing. "Don't do anything stupid."

"Like what?"

A pause. "Don't resist."

"I won't."

"I mean it. Don't antagonize him."

"Jesus."

"Okay. I'm rolling."

I closed the phone, rattled a vase on a side table as I passed down the hall. I walked into the sudden warmth of sunset and saw Parks Templeton climbing the steps. I pointed at him and then at my father. "I need to see you two inside, right now."

"Where's your mother?" my father asked.

"Stepmother," I said automatically. "This is not about her."

"What is it?" Parks asked.

I looked around the porch. Every eye was on me, and I realized that discretion was irrelevant. It would happen soon and it would happen right here. I put my eyes on the horizon one more time, and saw just how few seconds were actually left.

It looked like three cars. Lights on, sirens off.

I met the lawyer's eyes. "You're going to earn your money today," I said. He looked perplexed and I pointed. The lights flashed brighter as the day darkened around us. They were close; two hundred yards. Engine noise reached out and touched us. It swelled as my family came to its feet around me, and I heard the sound of rocks being thrown against metal, the dull clank and bang of cars moving too fast on gravel. Ten seconds out, the lead car killed its lights; the others followed suit. "They're here to serve an arrest warrant," I said.

"You're sure?"

"I am."

"Let me do the talking," the lawyer replied, but I knew that he would be useless. Grantham would not care about subtleties. He had his warrant, and it was enough. I felt a hand on my shoulder; my father. He squeezed hard, but I did not turn around; and no words found their way past his lips. "It's going to be all right," I said, and his fingers tightened.

That's how Grantham found us—an unbroken line. His hands settled on his hips, and his deputies formed up around him, a wall of brown polyester and black belts that angled low on one side.

Parks stepped into the yard, and I followed him down. Dolf and my father joined us. The lawyer spoke first. "What can I do for you, Detective Grantham?"

Grantham dipped his chin to peer across the tops of his glasses. "Afternoon, Mr. Templeton." He shifted slightly. "Mr. Chase."

"What is it that you want?" my father asked.

I looked at Grantham, whose eyes shone intently behind the same thick and dirty glasses. There were four men, not a single expression between them, and I knew then that there was no stopping it.

"I'm here lawfully, Mr. Chase, warrant in hand." His eyes found mine and his fingers spread out. "I don't want any trouble."

"I'd like to see the warrant," Parks said.

"Momentarily," Grantham replied, his eyes still on me. He'd not once looked away.

"Can you stop this?" my father asked the lawyer in a low voice.

"No."

"Goddamn it, Parks." Louder.

"We'll have our moment, Jacob. Be patient." He spoke to Grantham. "Your warrant had best be in perfect order."

"It is."

I stepped forward. "Then get on with it," I said.

"Very well," Grantham replied. He turned to my left, the cuffs coming out. "Dolf Shepherd, you are under arrest for the murder of Danny Faith."

Light flashed on steel, and when it circled his wrists, the old man bent under the weight of it.

This was wrong. In almost thirty years I'd never seen Dolf raise his hand or his voice in anger. I pushed toward him and deputies drove me back. I called Dolf's name, and the batons came out. I heard my name; my father yelling for me to calm down, to not give them an excuse. When his hands, thick and speckled, finally gripped my shoulders, I allowed him to pull me back. And I watched as Dolf was stuffed into one of the marked cars.

The door slammed, lights pulsed on the roof, and I closed my eyes as a sudden roar filled my head.

When it died, Dolf was gone.

He'd never once looked up.

# Nineteen

I called Robin from the car and told her what had happened. She wanted to meet us at the jail but I told her no. She was already in this thing too deep. She fought me about it, and the more we argued, the more convinced I became. She'd made her choice—me—and I wasn't going to let that choice hurt her. We agreed to meet the next day, once I had some idea just what the hell was going on.

We went downtown to the Rowan County Detention Center; Parks, Dad, and me. Jamie said he couldn't handle it, and I knew what he meant. The bars, the smells. The fact of it. Nobody tried to talk him out of it. He'd been sullen all afternoon and there was little love lost between him and Dolf. The building loomed against the descending sky. We crossed against traffic, mounted broad steps, and passed through security. The front room smelled of hot glue and floor cleaner. The door fell shut behind us, a crash of metal, and lukewarm air sighed out from ceiling vents. Four people sat in orange plastic chairs along the wall, and I took them in at a glance: two Hispanics in grass-stained clothes, an old woman in expensive shoes, and a young man biting his nails bloody.

Parks stood out in his immaculate suit, but no one was impressed, least of all the sergeant who sat behind the scuffed bulletproof glass. Parks drew himself up and played the lawyer card and asked to see Dolf Shepherd.

"No." The response was unequivocal, offered with the tired indifference of long practice.

"I beg your pardon?" The lawyer appeared truly offended.

"He's in interrogation. Nobody sees him."

"But I am his lawyer," Parks said.

The sergeant pointed to the long row of molded chairs. "Help yourself to a seat. It'll be a while."

"I demand to see my client now."

The sergeant leaned back in his chair and crossed his arms. Age had put its mark on the man: deep frown lines and a belly like a suitcase. "Raise your voice to me one more time and I will personally put you out of this building," he said. "Until I hear otherwise, no one sees him. That's the word from the sheriff himself. Now, sit down or leave."

The lawyer settled back onto his heels, but the hard edge did not leave his mouth. "This is not over," he said.

"Yes, it is." The officer rose from his chair, walked to the back of the room, and poured a cup of coffee. He leaned on a counter and stared at us through the bulletproof glass. My father put a hand on the lawyer's shoulder.

"Sit down, Parks."

The lawyer stalked to a far corner and my father tapped on the glass. The sergeant put down his coffee and came over. He was more respectful to my father. "Yes, Mr. Chase?"

"May I speak with the sheriff?"

The man's features relaxed. In spite of everything that had happened in recent years, my father was still a force in this county and respected by many. "I'll let him know you're here," he said. "No promises."

"All I'm asking for."

My father moved away and the sergeant lifted a phone off its cradle. His lips moved minutely, and he hung up. He looked at my father. "He knows you're here," he said.

We gathered in the corner. Parks spoke in a low whisper. "This is intolerable, Jacob. They cannot keep an attorney from his client. Even your sheriff should know that."

"Something's off," I said.

"Meaning what?"

I read the frustration in the lawyer's eyes. My father was paying him three bills an hour and he could not get past the front desk.

"We're missing something," I said.

Parks paled. "That's not much help, Adam."

"Nevertheless . . ."

"What are we missing?" my father asked.

I faced him, saw that he was close to the edge. Dolf may as well have been his brother.

"I don't know. Dolf knows that Parks is here. And Parks is right. Even this sheriff knows better than to interrogate a suspect with his attorney cooling his heels in the lobby." I looked at the lawyer. "What's our recourse here? What can we do?"

Parks settled down, looked at his watch. "It's after-hours, so we can't go to the courts for relief. Not that they could do anything. The warrant looked solid. Other than barring my entry, the sheriff is acting within his authority."

"What can you tell us about the warrant?" I asked.

"Short version? Dolf's .38 fired the shot that killed Danny Faith. They seized the gun when they searched the house. Ballistics confirmed it as the murder weapon. According to the warrant, it has Dolf's prints on it."

"Dolf's prints?" I asked.

*Not mine?*

"Dolf's prints," the lawyer confirmed. And then it hit me. Dolf was a meticulous man. He would have cleaned the gun before putting it back in the cabinet. He'd wiped off my prints and left his.

"They can't make a case with just the murder weapon," I said. "For trial, they'll need more. Motive. Opportunity."

"Opportunity won't be a problem," Parks said. "Danny

worked part time for your father. Fourteen hundred acres.
Dolf could have killed him anytime. Motive is another matter. The warrant is not specific in that regard."

"So, what?" my father asked. "We just sit here?"

"I'll make some calls," Parks said.

My father looked to me. "We wait," I said. "We talk to the
sheriff."

We sat for hours. Parks rousted one of his assistants at
home and instructed him to begin drafting a motion to sup-
press evidence based on the denial of right to counsel. That
was all he could do, which was basically as good as doing
nothing. At nine fifteen the sheriff walked through the security door. An armed deputy flanked him. He held up his hand
and spoke before Parks could launch into a tirade.

"I'm not here to debate or discuss anything," he said.
"I'm well aware of your complaint."

"Then you know that it is a constitutional violation to interrogate my client out of my presence."

Color rose in the sheriff's face. He stared the lawyer down.
"I have nothing further to say to you," he said, and paused a
beat. "You are irrelevant." He spoke to my father. "Before you
get all riled, Jacob, you may as well hear what I have to say.
Dolf Shepherd has been charged with the murder of Danny
Faith. He has been advised of his right to counsel and has refused that right." He looked at Parks and smiled. "You are not
his attorney, Mr. Templeton. Therefore, there has been no constitutional violation. You will not be going further than this
lobby."

My father's words exploded in a rush. "He doesn't want a
lawyer?"

A smile spread above the uniform. "Unlike some, Mr.
Shepherd seems unwilling to hide behind lawyers and their
tricks." His eyes swiveled onto me.

My stomach churned. A familiar feeling.

"What are you saying?" Parks demanded. "That he's confessed?"

"I'm not speaking to you," the sheriff replied. "I thought I'd made that clear."

"What *are* you saying?" my father asked.

The sheriff held my father's gaze, then turned slowly to me, the smile sliding into obscurity. There was no reading his face. "He wants to see you," he said.

"Me?"

"Yes."

Parks interrupted. "And you'll allow that?"

The sheriff ignored him. "I can take you back whenever you're ready."

"Just a minute, Adam," Parks said. "You're right. This doesn't make sense."

The sheriff shrugged. "You want to see him or not?"

Parks gripped my arm and pulled. He spoke in a whisper. "Dolf's been in custody for what, three or four hours? He's refused counsel, yet asked for you. Unusual, to say the least. Most troubling, though, is the sheriff's willingness to go along with that request." He skipped a beat, and I saw that he was deeply concerned. "Something is definitely wrong."

"But what?" I asked.

He shook his head. "I can't see it."

"It doesn't change anything," I said. "I can't refuse."

"You should, though. Legally speaking, I don't see what can be gained."

"It's not always about the law."

"I advise against it," Parks stated.

"Dad?" I asked.

"He wants to see you." Hands shoved deep into pockets, the implication was clear in his face. Refusal was not an option.

I walked back to the sheriff, studied his face for some kind of hint. Nothing. Dead eyes and a flat slash of mouth. "All right," I said. "Let's go."

The sheriff turned, and something flickered on the face of the deputy beside him. I looked back at my father. He raised a hand, and Parks leaned toward me. "Listen to what he has to say, Adam, but keep your mouth shut. You have no friends in there. Not even Dolf."

"What are you saying?" I asked.

"A murder charge has been known to turn friends against each other. It happens all the time. The first to deal is the first to walk. Every D.A. in the country plays that game. And every sheriff knows it."

My voice was unforgiving. "Dolf's not like that."

"I've seen things you wouldn't believe."

"Not this time."

"Just watch yourself, Adam. You beat one of the biggest murder charges ever brought in this county. That's been eating at the sheriff for five years. Politically, it hurt him, and I guarantee he's lost sleep over it. He still wants a piece of you. That's human nature. So, remember: without me in the room there's no attorney-client privilege attached to your conversation. Assume that you're being overheard, even recorded, no matter what they say to the contrary."

It was a needless warning. I'd been through the door before, and I had no illusions. Two-way mirrors, microphones, hard questions. I remembered. The sheriff paused at the door. A buzzer sounded. A lock clicked open.

"Look familiar?" the sheriff asked.

I ignored the smirk, and stepped through the door. After five long years, I was back inside.

I'd spent a lot of time here, and I knew it like I knew my own home: the smells, the blind corners, the guards with quick tempers and ready clubs. It still smelled of vomit, antiseptic, and black mold.

I'd sworn I would never come back to Rowan County; but I had. And now I was here, in the pit. But it was for Dolf; and I was not in custody. A big difference.

We passed prisoners in jumpsuits and flip-flops. Some moved freely; others traveled the halls in cuffs and under guard. Most kept their eyes down, but some stared, a challenge; and I stared back. I knew how it worked, the rules of engagement. I'd learned how to spot the predators. They'd come at me on day one. I was rich, I was white, and I refused to look away. That was really all it took, and they decided early on to beat me down.

I had three fights in the first week. It took a broken hand and a concussion to earn my place in the pecking order. I wasn't at the top, not even close, but judgment had been made.

Tough enough to be left alone.

So, yeah. I remembered.

The sheriff led me to the largest interview room and stopped at the door. I saw a slice of Dolf through the small glass window, then the sheriff blocked the view. "Here's how it works," he said. "You go in alone and you get five minutes. I'll be out here, and in spite of what your lawyer said, you'll have your privacy."

"That right?"

He leaned close and I saw the sweat on his face, the close-cropped gray hair and the sunburned scalp beneath it. "Yeah. That's right. Hard thing to screw up. Even for you."

I leaned left and peered through the glass. Dolf was bent, staring at the tabletop. "Why are you doing this?" I asked.

He twisted his lips and lowered fleshy eyelids. He turned and shoved a key into the broad lock, twisted it with a practiced motion. The door swung free. "Five minutes," he said, and stepped aside. Dolf did not look up.

My skin crawled when I walked into the room, and it seemed to burn when the door clanged shut. They'd grilled me for three days, same room, and I saw it like it was yesterday.

I took the chair opposite Dolf, the cop side of the table. It grated when I dragged it over the concrete floor. He sat immobile, and although the jumpsuit hung on him, his wrists still looked massive, his hands thick and competent. The light was brighter in here because the cops wanted no secrets, but the color still seemed off, and Dolf's skin looked as yellow as the linoleum floor outside. His head was bent, and I saw the hump of his nose, the white eyebrows. Cigarettes and a foil ashtray sat on the table.

I said his name, and he finally looked up. I don't know why, but I expected to see something distant in him, a barrier between us; but that's not how it was. There was warmth and depth in him; a wry smile that surprised me.

"Hell of a thing, huh?" His hands moved. He looked at the mirror and rotated his neck. His fingers found the smokes and shook one out. He lit it with a match, leaned back, gestured at the room with a hand. "Is this how it was for you?"

"Pretty much."

He nodded, pointed at the mirror. "How many back there, do you think?"

"Does it matter?"

No smile this time. "Guess not. Is your dad out there?"

"Yes."

"Is he upset?"

"Parks is upset. My father is distraught. You're his best friend. He's scared for you." I paused, waited for some hint of why he'd asked to speak with me. "I don't understand why I'm here, Dolf. You should be talking to Parks. He's one of the best lawyers in the state and he's right out there."

Dolf made a vague motion with the cigarette, causing pale smoke to dance. "Lawyers," he said vaguely.

"You need him."

Dolf waved the thought away, leaned back. "It's a funny thing," he said.

"What's that?"

"Life."

"Meaning what?"

He ignored me, ground out the cigarette in the cheap foil tray. He leaned forward, and his eyes were very bright. "Would you like to know the most profound thing I've ever seen?"

"Are you okay, Dolf?" I asked. "You seem . . . I don't know . . . scattered."

"I'm fine," he said. "The most profound thing. Would you like to know?"

"Sure."

"You saw it, too, although I don't think you fully appreciated it at the time."

"What?"

"The day your father went into the river after Grace."

I don't know what was on my face. Blankness. Surprise. It was not what I'd expected to hear. The old man nodded.

"Any man would have done the same," I said.

"No."

"I don't understand."

"Other than that day, have you ever seen your father in the river or in a pool? In the ocean, maybe?"

"What are you talking about, Dolf?"

"Your father can't swim, Adam. Guess you never knew that about him."

I was shocked. "No. I never knew."

"He's scared of water, terrified; been that way since we were boys. But he went in without hesitation, headfirst into a debris-choked river so swollen it was all but over its banks. It's a miracle they didn't both drown." He paused, nodded again. "The most profound thing I have ever seen. Unequivocal. Selfless."

"Why are you telling me this?"

He leaned forward and grabbed my arm. "Because you're like your father, Adam; and because I need you to do something for me."

"What?"

His eyes burned. "I need you to let it go."

"Let what go?"

"Me. This. All of this." New force moved into his words, a conviction. "Don't try to save me. Don't start digging. Don't get your teeth into it." He released my arm and I rocked back. "Just let it go."

Then Dolf rose to his feet and took quick strides to the two-way mirror. He looked back with still bright eyes and a voice that broke. "And take care of Grace." Sudden tears appeared in the seams of his face. "She needs you."

He rapped on the glass, and turned away, tilted his face to the floor. I found my feet, reaching for words and failing. The door opened with a clang. The sheriff came in; deputies filled the space behind him. I held up my hand. "Wait a second," I said.

Some emotion moved in the sheriff. Color flooded his face. Grantham appeared over his shoulder, paler, more distant.

"That's it," the sheriff said. "Time to go."

I studied Dolf: the straight back and the bent neck; a sudden, racking cough and his arm in that orange sleeve wiping across his mouth. He spread his fingers on the mirror and lifted his head so that he could see my reflection. His lips moved, and I could barely hear him.

"Just go," he said.

"Come on, Chase." The sheriff reached out with his hand, as if he could pull me from the room.

Too many questions, no answers; and Dolf's plea a clatter inside my head.

I heard a plastic rattle, and two deputies rolled in a video recorder on a tripod.

"What's going on?" I asked.

The sheriff took my arm, pulled me through the door. The pressure eased when the door clanged shut; I shrugged my arm out of his grip. He let me watch through the narrow glass as deputies aimed the camera. Dolf moved to the table, looked once in my direction, and sat. He lifted his face to the camera as the sheriff turned the key and dropped the bolt.

"What is this?" I asked.

He waited until I looked at him. "A confession," the sheriff said.

"No."

"For the murder of Danny Faith." The sheriff paused for full effect. "And all I had to do was let him talk to you."

I stared.

"That was his one condition."

I understood. The sheriff knew how much Dolf meant to me and he wanted me to see it: the camera, the old man in front of it, the sudden complacence in his collapsed frame. Parks had been right.

"You fucking bastard," I said.

The sheriff smiled, stepped closer. "Welcome back to Rowan County, you murdering piece of shit."

# Twenty

We left the detention center and stood in wind that brought the smell of distant rain. Lightning flashed silent heat and went dark before the thunder rolled over us like cannon fire. They wanted to know about Dolf, so I stripped my voice down and told them almost everything. I did not mention his plea to me because I could not leave Dolf Shepherd to rot. No way in hell. I told them that the last thing I saw was Dolf sitting in front of a video camera.

"It doesn't make sense," my father finally said. "Dolf took you to the knob, Adam. He all but held the rope. You'd have never found the body without him."

"Your father's right," Parks said, and paused. "Unless he wanted the body to be found."

"Don't be absurd!" my father exclaimed.

"Guilt does strange things to people, Jacob. I've seen it happen. Mass murderers suddenly confess. Serial rapists ask the court for castration. People twenty years in the clear suddenly own up to killing a spouse decades earlier in a jealous rage. It happens."

I heard Dolf's voice in my head; what he'd said to me at the hospital: *Sinners usually pay for their sins.*

"Bullshit," my father said, and the attorney shrugged.

The wind gusted harder, and I held out my hand as the

first raindrops clattered down. They were cold, hard, and hit the steps with a sound like fingers snapping. In seconds, the drops multiplied until the concrete hissed.

My father spoke. "Go on, Parks. We'll talk later."

"I'll be at the hotel if you need me." He dashed for his car, and we watched him go. There was a covered area behind us and we moved out of the rain. The storm was fully engaged. Rain hit hard enough to float a cold mist under the shelter.

"We're all guilty of something," I said, and my father looked at me. "But there is no way that Dolf murdered Danny."

My father studied the rain as if it held a message. "Parks is gone," he said, turning to face me. "So, why don't you tell me the rest?"

"There's nothing else to say."

He ran both hands over his hair, squeezing the water away from his face. "He wanted to talk to you for a reason. So far, you haven't said what that reason is. With Parks here, I could understand that. But he's gone, so tell me."

Part of me wanted to keep it locked up, but another part thought that maybe the old man could shed some light. "He told me to let it go."

"Meaning what?"

"Don't dig. He's worried that I'll look for the truth of what really happened. For whatever reason, he doesn't want me to do that."

My father turned from me and took three steps to the edge of the shelter. One more step and the rain would swallow him whole. I straightened and waited for him to look at me; I needed to see his reaction. Thunder clawed the air as I spoke, and I raised my voice. "I saw his face when we found Danny's body. He didn't do it." The thunder abated. "He's protecting someone," I said.

Nothing else made sense.

My father spoke over his shoulder, and the words he cast at me may as well have been stones. "He's dying, son." He showed me his face. "He's eaten up with cancer."

I could barely process the words. I thought of what Dolf had told me about his bout with prostate cancer. "That was years ago," I said.

"That was just the start. It's all in him now. Lungs. Bones. Spleen. He won't make it another six months."

Pain struck so hard it felt physical. "He should be in treatment."

"For what? To win another month? It's incurable, Adam. Every doctor says the same thing. When I told him that he should fight, he said that there was no need to make a stink of it. Death with dignity, as God intends. That's what he wants."

"Oh, my God. Does Grace know?"

He shook his head. "I don't think so."

I took the emotion and shoved it down deep. I needed a clear head, but it was hard. Then it hit me. "You knew," I said. "As soon as I told you that he'd confessed, you knew why he was doing it."

"No, son. I knew only what you knew; that Dolf Shepherd could never kill anyone. I have no idea who he's protecting; but I do know this. Whoever it is, it's someone he loves." He paused, and I prompted him.

"So?"

He stepped closer. "So, maybe you should do what he asks. Maybe you should let it go."

"Dying in jail is not death with dignity," I said.

"It could be. Depends on why he's doing it."

"I can't leave him there."

"It's not your place to tell a man how to spend his final days—"

"I won't let him die in that hole!"

He looked torn.

"It's not just Dolf," I said. "There's more."

"More what?"

"Danny called me."

He was vague in the gloom, dark hands at the end of long, pale sleeves. "I don't understand," he said.

"Danny tracked me down in New York. He called three weeks ago."

"He died three weeks ago."

"It was a strange thing, okay? The call came out of nowhere, middle of the night. He was hopped-up, excited about something. He said that he'd figured out how to fix his life. He said that it was something big, but that he needed my help. He wanted me to come home. We argued."

"Needed your help with what?"

"He refused to say, said he wanted to ask me face-to-face."

"But—"

"I told him that I would never come home. I told him that this place was lost to me."

"That's not true," my father said.

"Isn't it?"

He hung his head.

"He asked for my help and I refused him."

"Don't go there, son."

"I refused him and he died."

"Things are not always that simple," my father said, but I would not be swayed.

"If I'd done what he wanted, if I'd come home to help him, then he might not have been murdered. I owe him." I paused. "I owe Dolf."

"What are you going to do?"

I looked at the rain, reached out my hand as if I could pull truth from the void.

"I'm going to turn over some fucking rocks."

# Twenty-one

We rode back to the farm, and I listened to the hard slap of wipers on the old truck. He killed the engine and we sat in the drive. Rain beat itself to mist on the roof. "Are you sure about this, son?"

I didn't answer the question; I was thinking of Danny. Not only had I refused his request, but I'd doubted him, too. It was the ring found with Grace. It made everything so clear. He'd changed, gone dark for the money. His father wanted mine to sell and Danny had played along. Damn! I was so ready to believe it. I forgot the times that he'd stood up for me, forgot the man I knew him to be. In all of the ways that mattered, that was the greatest injustice I had done to him. But he was dead. I had to think of the living.

"This is going to kill Grace," I said.

"She's strong."

"Nobody's that strong. You should call the hospital. It'll hit the papers. Maybe they can keep it from her, at least for a day or two. She should hear about this from us."

He seemed uncertain. "Maybe until she's better." He nodded. "A day or two."

"I've got to go," I said, but my father stopped me with a hand on my arm. My door was open and water cascaded into the cab of the truck. He didn't care.

"Dolf is my best friend, Adam. He's been that for longer than you've been alive; since before I met your mother, since we were kids. Don't think that this is easy for me."

"Then you should feel like I do. We need to get him out."

"Friendship is also about trust."

I waited for a long second. "So is family," I finally said.

"Adam . . ."

I climbed out, leaned in as water thrummed on my back. "Do you think I killed Gray Wilson? Right here, right now . . . do you think I did it?"

He leaned forward and the dome light struck his face. "No, son. I don't think you did it."

Something snapped in my chest, a strap loosened. "Saying that doesn't mean that I forgive you. We have a long way to go, you and me."

"Yes, we do."

I didn't plan to say what came next; it just welled out of me. "I want to come home," I said. "That's the real reason I'm back." His eyes widened, but I wasn't ready to talk further. I slammed the door, splashed through puddles, and slipped into my car. My father climbed onto his porch and turned to face me. His clothes hung wetly from his frame. Water ran down his face. He raised a hand above shadow-filled eyes, and kept it up until I pulled away.

I went to Dolf's house; it was empty and dark. I stripped off wet clothes and flung myself down onto his couch. Thoughts churned through my mind; speculation, theories, despair. Fifteen miles away Dolf would be lying on a hard, narrow bunk. Probably awake. Probably afraid. The cancer would be chewing through him, looking for that last vital bit. How long until it took him? Six months? Two months? One? I had no idea. But when my mother died, and my father, for years, had been lost to me in mourning, it was Dolf Shepherd who made the difference. I could still feel the strength of that heavy hand on my shoulder. Long years. Hard years. And it was Dolf Shepherd who got me through.

If he was going to die, it should be with sunlight on his face.

I thought of the postcard in my glove compartment. If I was right, and Dolf had not killed Danny, then the card could possibly set him free. But who might it implicate? Someone with a reason to want Danny dead. Someone strong enough to conceal his body in the crack at the top of the knob. Maybe it was time to give it to Robin. But Dad was right about one thing: Dolf must have his reasons, and we had no idea what they might be. I closed my eyes and tried to not think of what Parks had said. *Maybe he wanted the body found.* And then Dolf's voice, again: *Sinners usually pay for their sins.* Dark thoughts came with the sound of thunder. If Dolf killed Danny, he would have needed a damn good reason. But could he have? Was it even possible? I'd been gone for a long time. What things had changed in five years? What people?

I chewed on that thought until I fell asleep, and for once, I did not dream of my mother or of blood. Instead, I dreamt of teeth, of the cancer that was eating a good man down.

I woke before six, feeling as if I had not slept at all. Coffee was in the cupboard, so I set it to brew and walked outside to watery, gray light. It was thirty minutes before dawn, silent, still. Leaves drooped under dark beads and the grass was beaten flat. Puddles shone on the drive, as black and smooth as poured oil.

It was a perfect, quiet morning; and then I heard it, the multithroated wail of dogs on the hunt. The ululation of the pack. It was a primal sound that made my skin prickle. It rose above the hills and then faded. Rose and fell, like crazy men speaking in tongues. Then shots crashed out in quick succession, and I knew that my father, too, was restless.

I listened for a minute more, but the dog sounds faded away, and no more shots were fired. So I went inside.

I stopped in Grace's door on the way to take a shower. Nothing had changed and I pulled the door closed. Down the hall, I turned on the water. I washed in swift, economical movements and toweled dry. Steam followed me back to the living room, where I found Robin sitting where I had slept, her fingers splayed on the pillow. She stood, looking small and pale and more like my lover than a cop. "I always seem to find you in the shower," she said.

"Next time, join me." I smiled, but the day was too dark for levity. I opened my arms, felt the cool press of her face against my chest. "We need to talk," she said.

"Let me get dressed."

She had coffee poured by the time I returned. We sat at the kitchen table as mist moved out of the forest and the sun stretched sharp fingers between the trees. "I heard about Dolf's confession," she said.

"It's bullshit." The words came more strongly than I'd intended.

"How can you be certain?"

"I know the man."

"That's not enough, Adam—"

My control slipped. "I've known him my whole life! He all but raised me!"

Robin kept her calm. "You didn't let me finish. That's not enough if we're going to help him. We need a crack in the story, some place to start chipping."

I studied her face. There was no reticence in her. "I'm sorry," I said.

"Let's talk about what we can do."

She wanted to help, but I was in possession of material evidence, a crime, maybe the first of many. "Not we, Robin. Just me."

"What are you saying?"

"I'll do whatever it takes to get Dolf out of there. Do you understand what I'm saying? Anything. If you help me, your career might not survive. Other things might not survive. I'll do what I have to do." I paused so she could think about what I was saying. Obeying the law was not one of my priorities. "Do you understand?"

She swallowed. "I don't care."

"You chose me, not Dolf. I don't want you getting hurt. You owe Dolf nothing."

"Your problem is my problem."

"How about this? You help me in ways that don't put you at risk."

She thought about it. "Like what?"

"Information."

"I'm off the case, remember? I don't have much."

"How about motive? Grantham must have some theory on that. Have you heard anything?"

She lifted her shoulders. "Just chatter. Dolf didn't give a motive in his interview. They tried to pin him down, but he was vague. There are two theories. The first is simple. Dolf and Danny worked together. They had a falling-out, an argument that went too far. Happens all the time. The second comes down to money."

"What do you mean?"

"Maybe Dolf was the one killing cattle and torching outbuildings. Maybe Danny caught him doing it and got killed for his trouble. It's thin, but a jury will listen."

I shook my head. "Dolf has nothing to gain one way or another."

Puzzlement twisted Robin's features. "Of course he does. Same as your father. Same as Zebulon Faith."

"My father owns this place. The house, the land. All of it."

Robin leaned back, put her hands on the table's edge. "I don't think so, Adam." She tilted her head, still confused. "Dolf owns two hundred acres, including the house we're sitting in."

I opened my mouth, but no words came. Robin spoke slowly, as if I were not quite right in the head. "That's six million dollars, based on the latest offer. One hell of a motive to squeeze your father into selling."

"That can't be right."

"Check it out," she said.

I thought about it, shook my head. "First of all, there's no way Dolf owns a piece of this farm. My father would never do that. Secondly"—I had to look away—"secondly, he's dying. He wouldn't care about money."

Robin understood what that statement cost me, but she refused to back away. "Maybe he's doing it for Grace." She put her hand on mine. "Maybe he'd rather die on a beach some place far from here."

I told Robin I needed to be alone. She put soft lips on my face and told me to call her later. What she had said made no sense. My father loved this land as he loved his own life. Guarding it was his special trust; keeping it for the family, the next generation. Over the past fifteen years, he'd given partial ownership to his children, but that was for estate planning purposes. And those interests were merely shares in a family partnership. He kept control; and I knew that he would never part with an acre, not even for Dolf.

At eight o'clock, I went to the house to ask my father if it were true, but his truck was gone. He was still out, I thought, still after the dogs. I looked for Jamie's truck, but it was gone, too. I opened the door to a cathedral silence, and followed the hall to my father's study. I wanted something to put context around what Robin had said. A deed, a title policy, anything. I pulled on the top drawer of the file cabinet, but it was locked. All of the drawers were locked.

I paused, considering, and was distracted by a flash of color through the window. I walked to the glass and saw Miriam in the garden. She wore a solid black dress with long sleeves and a high collar, and was clipping flowers with her mother's shears. She knelt in the wet grass, and I saw that her dress was damp from having done so many times. The shears closed around a stem, and a rose the color of sunrise fell to the grass. She picked it up, added it to the bouquet; and when she stood I saw a small but satisfied smile.

She'd piled her hair upon her head; it floated above a dress that might have come from another age. Her movements were so fluid that in the silence, through the glass, I felt as if I were watching a ghost.

She crossed to a different bush, knelt again, and clipped a rose as pale and translucent as falling snow.

As I turned from the window, I heard a noise from upstairs, a sound like something being dropped. It would be Janice. Had to be.

For no reason that I could articulate, I still wanted to speak with her. I guess we had unfinished business. I climbed the stairs, and my feet were quiet on the thick runner. The upstairs hall was bathed in cold light through tall windows. I saw the farm below, the brown drive that cut through it. Oil paintings hung on the walls; a wine-dark carpet ran away from me; and the door to Miriam's room stood ajar. I stood at the crack and saw Janice within. Drawers were pulled open and she stood with hands on her hips, studying the room. When she moved, it was for the bed. She lifted the mattress and apparently found what she was looking for. A small sound escaped her lips as she held the mattress with one hand and scooped something out from underneath. She dropped the mattress and studied what lay in her palm; it glittered like a shard of mirror.

I spoke as I stepped through the door. "Hello, Janice."

She spun to face me, and her hand closed in a spasm; she whipped it behind her back, even as she bit down in obvious pain.

"What are you doing?" I asked.

"Nothing." A guilty lie.

"What's in your hand?"

"That's none of your business, Adam." Her features calcified as she drew herself up. "I think you should leave."

I looked from her face to the floor. Blood was dripping on the hardwood behind her feet. "You're bleeding," I said.

Something in her seemed to collapse. She slumped and brought her hand from behind her back. It was still clenched shut, white at the knuckles in spite of the pain; and blood had, indeed, channeled through her fingers.

"How badly are you hurt?" I asked.

"Why do you care?"

"How badly?"

Her head moved fractionally. "I don't know."

"Let me see."

Her eyes settled on my face, and there was strength in them. "Don't tell her that you know," she said, and opened her hand. On the palm of it lay a double-edged razor blade. Her blood put a sheen on it. It had cut her deeply, and blood welled from perfectly matched wounds on each side of the blade. I lifted the blade and placed it on the bedside table. I took her hand, cupped mine beneath to catch the blood.

"I'm going to take you to the bathroom," I said. "We'll wash this off and take a look."

I ran cold water on the cuts, then wrapped her hand in a clean towel. She stood rigidly throughout the entire process, eyes closed. "Squeeze tight," I said. She did, and her face paled further. "You may need stitches."

When her eyes opened, I saw how close she was to breaking. "Don't tell your father. He can't possibly understand, and she doesn't need that burden, too. He'll only make it worse."

"Can't understand what? That his daughter is suicidal?"

"She's not suicidal. That's not what this is about."

"What, then?"

She shook her head. "It's not your place to hear about it, no more than it's mine to tell. She's getting help. That's all you really need to know."

"Somehow, I don't think that's true. Come on. Let's get you downstairs. We'll talk about it there." She agreed reluctantly. As we passed the tall windows, I saw Miriam driving away. "Where is she going?" I asked.

She pulled up. "You don't really care, do you?"

I studied her face: the set jaw, the new lines, and the loose skin. She would never trust me. "She's still my sister," I said.

She laughed, a bitter sound. "You want to know; fine, I'll tell you. She's taking flowers to Gray Wilson's grave. She does it every month." Another tight sound escaped her. "How's that for irony?" I had no answer, so I kept my mouth shut as I helped Janice down the steps. "Take me to the parlor," she said. I led her into the parlor, where she sat on the edge of the fainting couch. "Do me one last favor," she said. "Go to the kitchen and bring ice and another towel."

I was halfway to the kitchen when the parlor door slammed shut. I was still standing there when I heard the heavy lock engage.

I knocked twice, but she declined to answer.

I heard a high sound that may have been keening.

Miriam was where her mother had said she would be. She knelt, folded into herself, and from a distance it looked as if a giant crow had settled upon the grave. Wind moved between the weathered stones and shifted her dress; all that she lacked was the sheen of feathers, the mournful call. She moved as I watched. Deft fingers sought out weeds and plucked them from the earth; the bouquet was positioned just so. She looked up when she heard me, and tears moved on her skin.

"Hello, Miriam."

"How did you find me?"

"Your mother."

She pulled out another weed and tossed it to the wind. "She told you I was here?"

"Does that surprise you?"

She ducked her head, wiped off the tears, and her fingers left a trace of dark soil beneath one eye. "She doesn't approve of me coming here. She says it's morbid."

I squatted on my heels. "Your mother is very much about the present, I think. The present and the future. Not the past." She studied the heavy sky and seemed oppressed by it. The tears had ceased, but she still looked sunken and gray. Beside her, the bouquet was brilliant and stark and weeping fresh. It leaned against the stone that bore the dead boy's name. "Does it bother you that I'm here?" I asked.

She grew suddenly still. "I never thought you killed him, Adam." She put a tentative hand on my leg; a gesture of comfort, I thought. "It doesn't bother me."

I moved to place my hand over hers, but, at the last second, laid it on her forearm instead. She jerked back and a small hiss of pain passed though her lips. A dark certainty filled me. The same thing had happened at the hospital when I'd touched her arm; she'd told me that I startled her. I doubted that now.

She canted her eyes at the ground, held the arm against her body, as if afraid I might reach for it again. Her shoulders angled away from me. She was frightened, so I spoke softly. "May I see?"

"See what?" Defensive. Small.

I sighed. "I caught your mother searching your room. She found the razor blade." She rolled her shoulders in, made a ball of herself. I thought of the long sleeves she wore, the sweeping skirts, and the long pants. She kept her skin hidden. At first, I'd thought nothing of it, but the blade put everything into a different light.

"She should not have done that. It's an invasion."

"I can only assume that she's worried about you." I waited before I asked again. "May I see?"

She denied nothing, but her voice dwindled even further. "Don't tell Daddy."

I held out an open palm. "It's okay."

"I don't do it much," she said. Her eyes were soulful and afraid, but she held out her arm, half-bent. I took the hand, found it hot and damp. Her fingers squeezed as I pushed up the sleeve as gently as I could. Breath hissed between my teeth. There were fresh cuts and those that had partially healed. And there were scars, thin and white and cruel.

"You weren't at a health spa, were you?"

She shrank away, almost to nothing. "Eighteen days of in-patient treatment," she said. "A place in Colorado. The best, supposedly."

"And Dad doesn't know?"

She shook her head. "It's for me to fix. Me and Mom. If Dad knew, it would only make it harder."

"He should be involved, Miriam. I don't see how hiding this can help anyone."

She lowered her head further. "I don't want him to know."

"Why not?"

"He already thinks something is wrong with me."

"No, he doesn't."

"He thinks I'm twitchy." She was right. He'd used those words.

I asked the biggest question, although I knew that there was no simple answer. "Why, Miriam?"

"It takes away the pain."

I wanted to understand. "What pain?"

She looked at the gravestone, caressed the hard-edged letters of Gray Wilson's name. "I really loved him," she said.

The words caught me off guard. "Are you serious?"

"It was a secret."

"I thought you were just friends. Everybody thought that."

She shook her head. "We loved each other."

My mouth opened.

"He was going to marry me."

# Twenty-two

Miriam had never been what my father thought she should be; she was right about that. She was beautiful in a pale and subdued way, but so reticent at times that one might easily forget that she was in the room. She'd been like that from the earliest days: sensitive and small, easily lost in the shadows. The rest of us were too outgoing perhaps. Maybe her mother wasn't the only one who'd smothered Miriam. Maybe it had been a group effort, unintentional but cruelly effective. And I knew how weakness could compound over time. When she was twelve, some girls at school had been unkind to her. We never learned what the unkindness had been, something typical of girls that age, I'd always imagined. Whatever the slight, she'd gone three weeks without speaking to anyone. My father had been patient at first, then grown frustrated. There was an explosion near the end, harsh words not easily forgotten. She had cried and fled the room, and his apologies, later that night, had been to no avail.

He'd felt horrible about it, but dealing with women had never been his strong suit. He was gruff, spoke his mind when he spoke at all; and there was no place for delicacy in the man. Miriam was too young to understand that. She withdrew further over subsequent years, built the wall higher, salted the ground around her. She confided in her mother, and in Jamie, perhaps. But not in my father, and certainly not in me. It was a small sadness that began easily and grew until we barely noticed it.

Miriam was just quiet. That's how she was.

The relationship with Gray Wilson must have been as precious to her as the memory of sunset to a blinded man. I could understand why she'd have feelings for the kid; he was loquacious and bold, everything that Miriam was not. And I could certainly surmise why they'd kept it a secret. My father would not have approved; Janice, either. Miriam had just turned eighteen when Gray was killed. She was about to start Harvard, and he was in his third month of work at the truck plant one county over. But I could see how the two of them might be together. He was easy and likable, handsome in a thick-boned way. And it could be true, what was said about opposites. He was large and raw and poor; she was small and delicate and destined for great wealth.

It was a shame, I thought. One of many.

Before I left the cemetery, I asked Miriam if she wanted me to stay with her, but she declined. *Sometimes I just want to be alone with him, you know. Alone with the memory.*

Neither one of us mentioned George Tallman, but he was out there, big and real and boring as dirt. George had been in love with Miriam since they were young, but she'd never given him the time of day. He'd been lovesick and desperate and sad. So much so that, at times, it had been painful to watch. She'd settled, I saw that now. Alone and destined to be that way, she'd taken the easy route. She would never admit it, not even to herself; but it was fact, like the sky above was fact, and I wondered what George would say if he could see her here, tear-stained and dressed in black, weeping over the grave of a rival five years in the ground.

We parted with an awkward embrace and my promise to keep quiet about what I'd learned. But I was worried. More than that, I was frightened. She was a cutter, so full of pain that it took her own blood to wash it away. How did it work?

I wondered. A cut an hour? Two a day? Or did they come without pattern, a quick slice when life reared its ugly head? Miriam was weak, as fragile and liable to drop as any of the petals she'd laid on his grave. I doubted that she had the resources to deal with the problem, and wondered if Janice had the requisite commitment. She'd kept it from my father. Was that to protect Miriam or for some other reason? I asked myself one more question, asked because I had to.

Could I keep my promise to stay quiet?

As I drove away, left her alone, I felt a powerful urge to visit Grace. It was not a conscious matter, but one of feeling. They were so different, the two of them. Raised on the same property by two men who could have been brothers, they could not be more opposite. Miriam was as cool and quiet as March rain; Grace had the raw force of August heat.

But I decided against a visit. There was too much to do, and Dolf, for the moment, needed me more. So I drove past the hospital and continued farther into town. I parked in the lot of the Rowan County Municipal Building and took the stairs to the second floor. Grantham thought he had a motive. I needed to take a look at that.

The tax assessor's office was to the right.

I entered through a glass door. A long counter ran the width of the reception area; seven women occupied the space behind it. None of them paid me the slightest bit of attention as I consulted the huge map of Rowan County that was posted on the wall. I found the Yadkin River and traced it until my finger touched the long bend that contained Red Water Farm. I found the right reference number, went to the smaller maps, and pulled the one I needed. I spread it out on one of the large tables. I expected to see a single fourteen hundred and fifteen–acre parcel with my father's name on it. That's not what I saw.

The farm was delineated on the map: *Jacob Alan Chase Family Limited Partnership*. Twelve hundred and fifteen acres.

The southern piece of the farm had been carved away, a

rough triangle with one long side of curving river. *Adolfus Boone Shepherd.* Two hundred acres.

Robin was right. Dolf owned two hundred acres, including the house.

*Six million dollars*, she'd said. *Based on the latest offer.*

What the hell?

I copied the deed book and page numbers onto a piece of scrap paper and replaced the map on its rack. I went to the counter, spoke to a woman. She was middle-aged and round. Thick blue powder rimmed the hollow space beneath her eyebrows. "I'd like to see the deed for this parcel of land," I said, and slipped the scrap of paper onto the counter between us. She did not even bother to look down.

"You need the Register of Deeds, sugar."

I thanked her, went to the Register of Deeds office, and spoke to another woman behind another counter. I gave her the numbers and told her what I wanted. She pointed to the end of the counter. "Down there," she said. "It'll take a minute."

When she reappeared, she had a large book under her arm. She dropped it onto the counter, slipped a thick finger between two pages, and opened the book. She thumbed pages until she found the right one, then spun the book to face me. "Is that what you want?" she asked.

It was a deed of transfer dated eighteen years ago. I skimmed the language; it was straightforward. My father had transferred two hundred acres to Dolf.

"That's interesting," the woman said.

"What?"

She put the same thick finger on the deed. "No tax stamps," she said.

"What do you mean?"

She huffed, as if the question weighed heavily on her. Then she flipped back a few pages to another deed. On the top corner was affixed a number of colored stamps. She pointed. "Tax stamps," she said. "When land is purchased, a tax is paid. The stamps go on the deed." She flipped back to the deed that transferred two hundred acres of Chase land to Dolf Shepherd. She put her finger on the corner. "No stamps," she said.

"What does that mean?" I asked.

She leaned down to read the name on the deed. "It means that Adolfus Shepherd didn't buy this land." I opened my mouth to ask the question, but she forestalled me with an upraised hand and a puff of cigarette breath. She leaned into the deed again, plucked off another name.

"Jacob Chase gave it to him."

Outside, the heat tried to weigh me down. I looked up the street to the next block, where the courthouse sat, timeless and spare under the white sun. I wanted to talk to Rathburn. He'd been at the farm, trying to speak to my father about something. And there was something about Dolf, too. What was it that my father had said? I stopped on the sidewalk, tilted my head as if to better hear the words: *And don't you go talking to Dolf about this either. What I say goes for him, too.*

Something to that effect.

I pushed my feet up the sidewalk, toward the jail. It rose, hard-edged and graceless, with windows as narrow as a woman's face. I thought of Dolf, rotting inside, then was past, and moving up the courthouse stairs. The judges' chambers were on the second floor. I had no appointment, and the bailiffs at security knew damn well who I was. They sent me through the metal detector three times, patted me down so well that I could not have slipped a paper clip past them if I'd put it in my underpants. I took it, like I could take it all day. Still, they hesitated; but the courthouse was public domain. They lacked the authority to keep me out.

The judge's chamber was a different story. It was easy to find—up the stairs, past the D.A.'s office—but getting in was another matter. Nothing public about chambers. You got in if the judge wanted you in. The door was made of steel and bulletproof glass. Two dozen armed bailiffs guarded the building, and any one of them would take me down if the judge told him to.

I looked up and down the empty hall. Beyond the glass, a small woman sat behind a desk. She had a tea-colored face, yellow hair, and severe eyes. When I rang the buzzer she stopped typing. The eyes focused, she lifted a finger, then left the room as fast as her swollen legs could shift her.

Gone to tell the judge who'd come calling.

Rathburn had on a different suit, but looked about the same. A little less sweat, maybe. He studied me through the glass, and I could see the wheels turn. After a few seconds, he whispered to his secretary, who put her fingers on the phone. Then he opened the door. "What do you want?"

"A minute of your time."

"On what subject?" His glasses flashed, and he swallowed. No matter the verdict, he thought I was a killer. He stepped forward until his body filled the crack in the door. "Are we going to have a problem?"

"Why did you come to see my father the other day? That's what I'm here to talk about."

"You can have one minute," he said.

I followed him past the small woman with the hard eyes and stood in front of his desk as he closed the door down to a crack. "She's looking for an excuse to call the bailiffs," he told me. "Don't give her one."

He sat and I sat. A light sweat appeared on his top lip. "What was the argument about?" I asked. "You and my father."

He leaned back and scratched at his toupee with a finger. "Let's get one thing straight first. The law is the law and the past is past. You're in my chambers and I'm the judge. I don't do *personal* in chambers. You step over that line and I'll have the bailiffs in here so fast you won't believe it."

"You locked me up for murder. You locked Dolf up for murder. Hard to keep that from being personal."

"Then you can leave right now. I don't owe you anything."

I tried to calm down. I told myself that I came here for a reason.

The judge's face had gone dark red. A chair creaked in the other room. I leaned back, breathed in, breathed out, and he smiled in a way that made me queasy. "That's good," he said. "That's better. I knew that somewhere there was a Chase that could be reasonable." He smoothed his polished, white hands across the desk. "If you could just talk your father into being equally reasonable."

"You want him to sell?"

"I want him to consider the well-being of this county."

"That's why you went to see him?"

He leaned forward and cupped his hands as if he were holding some great jewel. "There is opportunity here. Opportunity for you, for me. If you could just talk to him. . . ."

"He knows his own mind."

"But you are his son. He'll listen to you."

"That's why you agreed to see me? So I could talk to my father?"

His face closed down, smile gone. "Somebody needs to make him see reason."

"Reason," I said.

"That's right." He tried another smile, but it failed. "Things have gone from bad to worse for your family. Seems to me that this is the perfect opportunity to steer your family in a better direction. Make some money. Help the community . . ."

But I didn't hear all that. My mind was stuck. "Bad to worse . . ." I repeated the phrase.

"Yes."

"What do you mean?"

He opened his hands, lifted the right one, palm up. "Bad," he said, then lifted the left hand. "Worse."

I pointed at the right hand, knew that he could read the tight anger in my voice. Knew that he enjoyed it. "Start with the bad," I said.

"I'll start with the worse." He jiggled that hand. "Another loved one in jail for murder. People getting killed and hurt on the property. An angry town—"

"Not everybody feels that way," I interrupted.

He tilted his head, continued in a louder voice. "Risky business decisions."

"What risky business decisions?"

His mouth twitched at one corner. "Your father's in debt. I'm not sure that he can pay."

"I don't believe it."

"It's a small town, Adam. I know a lot of people."

"And the bad?" I asked.

He lowered his hands, took on a pained expression that I knew was false. "Do I really need to explain it?"

I bit down, hard.

"Your mother was a beautiful woman. . . ."

He was twisting the knife for his own satisfaction. I saw that and refused to participate. I came to my feet, raised a finger, then turned and walked away. He followed me into the antechamber. I felt him behind me as I passed his secretary's desk. "Bad to worse," he said, and I turned to face him. I don't know what his secretary saw on my face, but she was dialing as I closed the door behind me.

# Twenty-three

My father was drunk. He was alone in the house and he was hammered. It took about three seconds for me to figure that out, mainly because I'd never seen it before. His religion was work to excess and all other things in moderation, so that in the past, when I'd come home drunk and bloody, his disappointment shone out like holy fire. This thing that I saw now . . . it was new and it was ugly. His face was loose and drawn, eyes gone wet. He filled the chair like he'd been poured into it. The bottle was open and close to empty, the glass down to half a finger. He stared at something in his hand, and strange emotions moved in him so that his features seemed to flow across the bones of his face. Anger, regret, remembered joy. It was all there in staccato bursts, and it made him look like a soul unhinged. I stood in the door for a long time, and I don't think he blinked once. Were I to close my eyes, I would see the color gray touched with small, cold yellow. An old man in a fractured slice of time. I had no idea what to say to him.

"Kill any dogs this morning?"

He cleared his throat and his eyes came up. He opened the desk's drawer and slipped whatever he'd been holding inside. Then he closed the drawer with something like care and shook his head. "Let me tell you something about scavengers, son. Only a matter of time before they find a streak of bold."

I didn't know if he was talking about the dogs or the people who wanted him to sell, men like Zebulon Faith and Gilley Rat. I wondered if new pressures were being brought to bear. Assault and murder. Dolf in jail. Debt ramping up. What forces now conspired against my father? Would he tell me if I asked, or was I just one more complication? He found his feet and steadied himself. His pants were wrinkled and muddy at the cuffs. His shirt hung out of his belt on one side. He twisted the cap back onto the bourbon and walked it over to the side bar. The day had put a new bend in his back and three decades onto the way he walked. He put the bottle down and dropped a hand around its neck. "I was just having a drink for Dolf."

"Any word?"

"They won't let me see him. Parks went back to Charlotte. Nothing he can do if Dolf won't hire him." He stopped by the side bar, and his pale whiskers caught that small, yellow light so perfectly that it could have been the only color left in the world.

"Has something changed?" I asked.

He shook his head. "Strange things can happen in the human heart, Adam. There's power there to break a man. That's all I know for certain."

"Are we still talking about Dolf?"

He tried to pull himself together. "We're just talking, son." He looked up and straightened a framed photograph on the wall. It was of him and Dolf and Grace. She was maybe seven, teeth too large for her face, laughter all over her. He stared at her, and I knew.

"You told Grace, didn't you?"

His breath leaked out. "She should hear it from someone who loves her."

Sudden despair filled me. Dolf was all she had, and as tough as she pretended to be, she was still a kid. "How is she?"

He sniffed and shook his head. "As far from Grace as I've ever seen her."

He tried to lean a hand on the side bar, but missed. He barely caught himself. For some reason, I thought of Miriam, and how she, too, tottered at the edge of some dark place. "Have you spoken to Miriam?" I asked.

He waved a hand. "I can't talk to Miriam. I've tried, but we're too different."

"I'm worried about her," I said.

"You don't know anything about anything, Adam. It's been five years."

"I know that I've never seen you like this."

Sudden strength infused his joints; pride, I suspected. It stood him up and put a copper flush on his face. "I'm still a long way from having to explain myself to you, son. A long goddamn way."

"Is that right?"

"Yes."

Suddenly, the anger was mine. It was raw and laced with a sense of injustice. "This land has been in our family for more than two centuries."

"You know that it has."

"Passed down from generation to generation."

"Damn right."

"Then why did you give two hundred acres to Dolf?" I asked. "How about you explain that?"

"You know about that?"

"They're saying it's why he killed Danny."

"What do you mean?"

"Owning that land gives Dolf a reason to want you to sell. If you sell, he can, too. Grantham thinks that maybe Dolf was killing cattle and burning buildings. Maybe even writing those threatening letters. He has six million reasons to do something like that. Danny worked the farm, too. If he caught Dolf working against you, then Dolf would have reason to kill him. It's one of the theories they're pursuing."

His words slurred. "That's ridiculous."

"I know that, damn it. That's not the point. I want to know why you gave that land to Dolf."

The strength that had so suddenly filled him vanished. "He's my best friend and he had nothing. He's too good a man to have nothing. Do you really need to know anything more than that?" He lifted the glass and knocked back the last slug of bourbon. "I'm going to lie down," he said.

"We're not finished here."

He didn't answer. He left the room. I stood in the door to watch his back recede, and in the hushed splendor of the great house I felt the tremor of his foot on the bottom stair. Whatever grief my father suffered, it was his, and under normal circumstances, I would never intrude. But these times were far from normal. I sat at his desk and ran my hands across the old wood. It had come from England originally, and had been in my family for eight generations. I opened the top drawer.

There was plenty of clutter: mail, staples, junk. I looked for something small enough to be cupped in a large man's palm. I found two things. The first was a beige sticky note. It sat atop the clutter. On it was a man's name: Jacob Tarbutton. I knew him vaguely, a banker of some sort. I would never have considered it a possible source for my father's anguish, save for the numbers written below the name. Six hundred and ninety thousand dollars. Beneath it he'd scrawled *first payment*, and then a due date less than a week out. Recognition hit me with a twist of nausea. Rathbun was telling the truth. My father was in debt. And then I thought, with guilt, of the buyout he'd insisted upon when he'd driven me off the farm. Three million dollars, wired to a New York account the week after I'd left. Then I thought of Jamie's vines, and of what Dolf had told me. Getting the vines in had taken millions more. He'd sacrificed producing crop to make it happen.

I thought that I finally understood, but then I found the second thing. It was in the very back, lost in the corner. My fingers discovered it almost by accident: stiff and square, with sharp corners and a texture like raw silk. I pulled it out, a photograph. It was old, backed with cardboard and curled at the edges. Faded. Washed-out. It showed a group of people standing in front of the house I'd known as a child. The old one. The small one. It filled the space behind the group with a simplicity that pulled at me. I looked away, studied the people that stood in front of it. My mother looked pale, in a dress of indeterminate color. She held her hands in a clench at her waist, and turned her face in profile to the camera. I touched her cheek with my finger. She looked so young, and I knew that the picture must have been taken shortly before her death.

My father stood beside her. Somewhere in his thirties or forties, he appeared broad and fit, with smooth features, a careful smile, and his hat tipped onto the back of his head. He'd laid a hand on my mother's shoulder, as if to hold her up or to keep her in the picture. Dolf stood next to my father. He smiled broadly, hands on his hips. Unabashedly happy. A woman stood behind him, her face partially obscured by his shoulder. She was young, maybe twenty. She had pale hair, and I could see enough of her face to know that she was beautiful.

It was in the eyes that I saw it first.

Sarah Yates.

And her legs were perfect.

I put the photo back in the drawer and went upstairs to find my father. His door was closed, and I knocked. He did not answer so I tried the handle. Locked. The door was nine feet tall and solid. I knocked harder, and the voice that came back was shorn of emotion. "Go away, Adam."

"We need to talk," I said.

"I'm done talking."

"Dad—"

"Leave me be, son."

He did not say "please," but I heard it nonetheless. Something was eating at him. Whether it was Grace, the debt, or Dolf's hard fall, it didn't really matter. He was forlorn. I left him alone and turned for the stairs. I saw the car coming when I passed the second window. I was in the drive, waiting, when Grantham stepped out.

"Are you here to tell me that you found Zebulon Faith?" I asked.

Grantham put a hand on the top of his car. He had on blue jeans, dusty cowboy boots, and a sweat-stained shirt. Wind riffled his thin hair. The same badge hung on his belt. "We're still looking for him."

"I hope that you're looking hard."

"We're looking." He leaned on the car. "I've been going over your file. You hurt a lot of people over the years, put some in the hospital. I missed that, somehow." He leveled a gaze at me. "I've also been reading up on what happened to your mother. Losing someone that you love, well, that can make a person crazy. All that anger and nowhere to put it." He paused. "Any idea why she did it?"

"That is none of your damn business."

"Grieving never ends for some folks, anger either."

I felt the blood stir, the hot flush in my veins. He saw it, smiled as if he'd figured something out. "Apologies," he said. "Sincere apologies." He looked like he meant it, but I knew that I'd been played. The detective wondered about my temper. Now he knew.

"What do you want, Grantham?"

"I understand that you were at the Register of Deeds this morning. Mind if I ask why?"

I didn't answer. If he knew that I was checking on his theories of motive, then he'd also know where I got the information.

"Mr. Chase?"

"I was looking at maps," I said. "Maybe I'll buy some land."

"I know exactly what you looked at, Mr. Chase, and I've already discussed the matter with the Salisbury City police chief. You can rest assured that Robin Alexander will be excluded from every stage of this investigation from now on."

"She's already off the case," I said.

"She stepped over the line. I've asked for her suspension."

"Is there a purpose to this visit, Detective?"

He took off his glasses and pinched the bridge of his nose. A sudden wind cut channels through tall grass in the fields beyond the barbed wire. Trees bent, then the wind vanished. Heat pressed down.

"I am a rational man, Mr. Chase. I believe that most things follow their own logic. It's just a matter of figuring out what that logic might be. Even insanity has a logic, if you look deeply enough and in the right places. The sheriff is happy with Mr. Shepherd, happy with the confession."

Grantham shrugged, left the rest unsaid. I finished for him.

"But you're not."

"The sheriff dislikes all of you. I assume that it has something to do with what happened five years ago, but I don't know why and I don't really care. What I do know is that Mr. Shepherd has been unable to provide any discernible motive."

"Maybe he didn't kill him," I said. "Did you talk to Danny's old girlfriend? She filed an assault warrant against him. She'd be the logical person to investigate."

"You forget that Mr. Shepherd's gun was used in the murder."

"He never locks his house."

He gave me the same unforgiving look I'd seen before. Then he changed the subject. "Judge Rathburn called the sheriff right after you left his office. He felt threatened."

"Ah."

"The sheriff called me."

"Did you come out here to warn me to stay away from the judge?"

"Did you threaten him?"

"No."

"Is your father home?" The shift was sudden, and it made me nervous.

"He's unavailable," I said.

Grantham's gaze slid across my father's truck, then up to the house. "Mind if I see for myself?" He started for the door, and I pictured my father in his state of fractured dismay. A sense of protectiveness filled me up. A bell started ringing in the back of my mind.

"I do mind," I said, stepping in front of him. "This has been difficult for him. He's in distress. Now is not a good time."

Grantham stopped and his mouth compressed. "They're close, aren't they? Your father and Mr. Shepherd?"

"Like brothers."

"He'd do anything for your father."

I saw it now, the way it could play. Cold infused my voice. "My father is no killer."

Grantham said nothing, kept those washed-out eyes right on me.

"What possible reason could my father have for wanting Danny Faith dead?" I asked.

"I don't know," Grantham replied. "What reason do *you* think he could have?"

"None whatsoever."

"Is that right?" He waited, but I said nothing. "Your father and Zebulon Faith go back a ways, decades. They both own land out here. Both are strong men, and capable, I think, of violence. One wants the deal to go through. The other doesn't. Danny Faith worked for your father. He was caught in the middle. Frayed tempers. Money on the table. Anything could have happened."

"You're wrong."

"Your father owns no handguns, but has access to Mr. Shepherd's house."

I stared at him.

"Mr. Shepherd refuses to take a polygraph. I find it odd that he would confess to a murder and then refuse a simple test that could corroborate his story. It forces me to reevaluate the confession. It leaves me no choice but to consider other possibilities."

I stepped closer. "My father is no killer."

Grantham looked to the sky, then off to the distant trees. "Mr. Shepherd has cancer." He looked back at me. "Are you aware of that?"

"What's your point?"

The detective ignored my question. "I spent twenty years as a homicide detective in Charlotte. There were so many murders toward the end, that I could barely keep track of them. I had murder files on my bedside table, believe it or not. Hard to process that much senseless death. Hard to maintain focus. Eventually, I got one wrong and sent an innocent man to prison. He was shanked in the yard three days before the real killer confessed." He paused and looked hard at me. "I came up here because murder is still somewhat unusual in Rowan County. I have time to dedicate to the victims. Time to get it right."

He took off the glasses, leaned closer. "I take the job very seriously, and I don't necessarily care what my boss has to say about it."

"What are you saying?"

"I've seen a father take the heat for a son, a husband go down for a wife and vice versa. I don't know that I've ever seen one friend take a murder rap for another, but I'm sure it could happen if the friendship is strong enough."

"That's enough," I said.

"Especially if the one going down is dying of cancer and has nothing to lose."

"I think you should leave now."

He opened the door to his car. "One last thing, Mr. Chase. Dolf Shepherd was put on suicide watch this morning."

"What?"

"He's dying. I don't want him killing himself before I get to the bottom of this." He put his glasses back on. "Tell your father that I'd like to speak with him when he feels better."

Then he turned and was gone, lost behind a window that reflected high yellow clouds and the deep blue of a windless sky. I watched him go, and thought of my father's dismay and of the words he'd spoken with such conviction.

*Strange things can happen in the human heart, Adam. There's power there to break a man.*

I still did not know what he was talking about, but suddenly I was worried. I looked from the rear of Grantham's car to the second-floor window of my father's room. It was barely open, no more than an inch at the bottom. At first, there was nothing, then the curtains moved slightly, as if in a breeze.

That's what I told myself.

A breeze.

# Twenty-four

I wanted to talk to Dolf. Needed to. Nothing made sense: not Dolf's confession, not Grantham's suspicions. The only thing that made less sense than Dolf Shepherd killing Danny was the idea that my father had. So I went to the detention center, where I was denied visitation. Visitors are allowed, but only during certain hours and only if your name was on the list, which my name was not. Up to the prisoner, I was informed.

"Who's on the list for Dolf Shepherd?" I asked.

Grace was the only name.

I turned for the door, then stopped. The guard looked bored. "There must be a way," I said.

He regarded me evenly. "Nope."

Frustrated, I went to the hospital. My father had told Grace about Dolf and I could only guess at her thoughts and feelings. In her room, I found an unmade bed and today's newspaper. Dolf's arrest was page one news. They ran his picture under a headline that read: MURDER NUMBER TWO AT RED WATER FARM.

The facts on Danny's death were slim, but the descriptions were lurid. *Partially skeletonized remains were hauled out of a deep crack in the earth on a bright, blue day.* Dolf's confession was more certain. Although the sheriff had scheduled a news conference for the following day, reliable sources were apparently talking. And speculation was rampant. *Five years since another young man was killed on the same farm.*

My picture was on page two.

No wonder my father was drunk.

I closed Grace's door behind me and sought out the nurses' station. Behind the counter was an attractive woman who told me, in clipped tones, that Grace had been discharged from the hospital less than an hour earlier.

"On whose authority?" I demanded.

"On her own."

"She's not ready to leave the hospital," I said. "I'd like to speak to her doctor."

"I'm going to ask you to lower your voice, sir. The doctor would not have allowed her to leave unless he felt that she was fit to do so. You are welcome to speak with him, but he'll tell you the same thing."

"Damn it," I said, and left. I found her sitting on the curb outside of the detention center, a bag of clothing clutched in her lap, her head bent. Hair hung limply over her face and she was rocking gently as cars blew past less than five feet away. I parked as close as I could and got out. She did not look up, not even when I sat down next to her. So I looked at the sky, watched the cars. I'd been here less than an hour ago. We must have just missed each other.

"They wouldn't let me see him," she said.

"You're on the list, Grace. You're the only one he wanted to see."

She shook her head, and her voice was all but gone. "He's on suicide watch."

"Grace . . ."

"Suicide watch." Her voice gave out, she started rocking again, and I cursed Grantham for the hundredth time. She wanted to see Dolf and he wanted to see her. She could ask the questions that I could not; but Grantham had put him on suicide watch. No visitors allowed. I suspected that Grantham's decision had as much to do with keeping Dolf isolated as it did with keeping him alive. It was smart. And it was cold.

The bastard.

I took Grace's hand; it was limp and dry. I felt slickness at her wrist and saw that she had not even taken off the hospital bracelet. The swelling was down in her face, the bruises gone yellow at the edges. "Do you know that he has cancer?"

She flinched. "He didn't talk about it much, but it was always there, like another person in the house. He tried to prepare me."

I had a sudden revelation. "That's why you're not at college."

Tears threatened and she dashed a hand across her eyes before they could spill out. "All we have is each other."

"Come on," I said. "Let me take you home."

"I don't want to go home," she said. "I need to do something. Anything."

"You can't stay here." She lifted her face and I saw the grief. "There's nothing you can do."

I took her back to Dolf's house. The whole time, she held herself as if some deep part of her was frozen. Occasionally, she shuddered. I tried to speak once, but she shut me down. "Just leave me alone, Adam. You can't make this right."

It was pretty much the same thing I'd said to Dolf after my father threatened to kill me.

She allowed me to lead her inside and sit her on the edge of her bed. The bag she'd been carrying fell to the floor, and her hands turned palms up on the bed beside her. I switched on the lamp and sat next to her. Her tan was washed-out, her eyelids heavy. The stitches looked especially cruel on her dry, passive lips. "Can I get you some water?" I asked.

She shook her head, and I saw that some of her hair had gone white, long strands that gleamed as hard as stretched wire. I put an arm around her shoulder and kissed her head.

"I yelled at your father," she said. "He came to the hospital and told me. He wanted to stay with me after he broke the news. He told me I couldn't leave the hospital, that he wouldn't allow it. I said some pretty awful things."

"It's okay," I said. "He understands."

"How can I make this go away?" she asked.

I shook my head. "I don't know why he's doing it, Grace. What I do know is that you should go to bed."

She rose to her feet. "I can't do anything useful in bed. There has to be something to do." She paced three quick turns, then stopped, and stood still. "There's nothing I can do," she said, looking stricken.

I pulled on her hand, drew her back down to the bed. "Can you think of anyone else that might want Danny Faith dead? Anything at all and I'll check it out."

She raised her head, and her eyes held such pain. "You don't understand," she said.

"What do I not understand?"

Her hands tightened on mine and her eyes turned mirror-bright once again. "I think that maybe he did it."

"What?"

She stood abruptly and took hard steps to the far corner of the room. "I should not have said that. Forget it. I don't know what I'm saying."

"Grace, you can trust me. What's going on?"

When she turned, the line of her mouth was unforgiving. "I don't know you anymore, Adam. I don't know if I can trust you or not."

I stood, opened my mouth, but she rode over my words.

"You're in love with a cop."

"That's not—"

"Don't deny it!"

"I wasn't going to deny it. I was going to say that it's not relevant. I would never put Dolf in harm's way." Grace backed into the far corner of the room. Her shoulders drew up, as if to protect the vital parts of her neck. Her fists clenched. "I'm not your enemy, Grace. And I'm not Dolf's. I need to know what's happening. I can help."

"I can't tell you."

I stepped toward her.

"You stay right there!" she said, and I saw how close she was to truly breaking. "I need to figure this out. I need to think."

"Okay. Just calm down. Let's talk about this."

She lowered her hands, and the shoulders came down, too. Resolution moved in her. "You need to leave," she said.

"Grace—"

"Get out, Adam."

"We're not done here."

"Get out!"

I moved for the door and stopped with my hand on the frame. "Think hard, Grace. This is me, and I love Dolf, too."

"You can't help me, Adam. And you can't help Dolf."

I did not want to leave. Things still needed to be said. But she slammed the door in my face, leaving me to stare at thin, blue paint. I wanted to beat the door down. I wanted to shake sense into a frightened woman that should know better. But she was like the paint, so thin in places that I could see raw wood beneath. I slid my hand down the door, and paint flaked away. I blew bits of it from my fingertips.

Things were in motion that I could not begin to understand. Things had changed, people, too; and my father was right about one thing.

Five years was a long time, and I knew nothing about nothing.

I called Robin. She was at the scene of some domestic disturbance and told me that she could not speak for long. In the background, I heard a woman screaming obscenities and a man repeating the words, "Shut up," over and over.

"Did you hear about Dolf?" I asked.

"I did. I'm sorry, Adam. They don't put prisoners on suicide watch without some good reason. I don't know what
to say."

Grantham's words flashed through my mind: *I don't want
him killing himself before I get to the bottom of this.*

He had to be wrong.

About everything.

"It's okay. That's not why I called. I ran into Grantham.
He plans to ask your boss to suspend you. I thought you
should know."

"He already asked. My boss told him to kiss off."

"That's good."

"Well, the storage unit tip you gave me was solid. They
raided it last night and seized over three hundred thousand
dollars of crystal meth. Zebulon Faith may be a bigger player
than we thought. On top of that, they found crates of cold
medicine that they think were hijacked from a distribution
center near the Charlotte airport."

"Cold medicine?"

"Yeah. They use the ingredients to make meth. Long
story. Listen, there's one other thing you should know—" She
broke off, and I heard her voice escalate. She was not talking
to me. "Sit down, sir. I need you to sit down right there.
Now, stay.

"I have to go, Adam. I wanted you to know that DEA is
sending some of its boys around to check out what we
seized. They may want to talk to you. May not. I don't know.
We'll talk later."

"Wait a minute," I said.

"Quickly."

"I need the name of the woman that filed the assault
charge against Danny Faith."

Robin was silent, and I heard the man again. "Shut up.
Shut up. Shut up." And then the woman, who was maybe his
wife, screaming, "Don't tell me to shut up, you lyin' ass,
cheatin' motherfucker!"

"Why?" Robin asked.

"As far as I can tell, she's the last one to see Danny alive. Somebody needs to talk to her. If Grantham won't take the time, I sure as hell will."

"Don't get in Grantham's way, Adam. I've warned you about that. He won't have the patience for it. He'll come down hard if he finds out."

"Are you going to tell me?"

I heard her exhale. "Her name is Candace Kane. Goes by Candy."

"Are you serious?"

Voices escalated behind Robin: two angry lovers ready to tear into each other. "I've got to go," Robin said. "She's in the book."

The car was soft leather and familiar smells, the engine so silent I almost couldn't hear it. I rolled down windows to wash out the heat and felt the overwhelming vastness of the land around me. For a moment, it gave me comfort, but the moment did not last. I needed to talk to my father.

I turned out of Dolf's driveway, and drove to my father's house. His truck was gone, but Miriam was on the porch swing. I stepped out of the car and onto the porch. She looked up, but her eyes told me nothing. I thought of sharp blades and tattered hearts.

"You okay?" I asked.

"Yes."

"What are you doing?"

"Do you ever feel the need to stop, just for a second, before walking into a room? Like you need to take one last breath before you can handle what's on the other side of the door?"

"I guess so."

"I just needed that breath."

"There's a lot going on right now," I said.

She nodded, and I saw that her hair was pulling free from

the comb that held it up. Long, black strands spilled over her collar. "It's frightening," she replied.

She looked so sad, I wanted to touch her, to put an arm around her, but I did not. It might hurt her, or startle her. The past few days had been hard on everyone, but Miriam looked close to transparent. "I guess Dad's not home."

"His truck's gone. It's just Mom, I think. I've been here for a while."

"Miriam," I said. "Do you have an idea who might have wanted to kill Danny?" She shook her head, then stopped, chin cocked sideways. "What?" I asked.

"Well, there was once, about four months ago. Somebody beat him up pretty badly. He wouldn't talk about it, but George said that it was probably a bookie out of Charlotte."

"Is that right? Did George know what bookie?"

"I doubt it. He just said that Danny was finally getting some justly deserved payback. When I asked him what he meant, he said that Danny had been living too large for his own pants and it had finally caught up with him."

"George said that?"

"Yes."

"Do you know where Jamie is right now?"

"No."

"Hang on a second." I dialed Jamie's number on my cell phone. It rang four times before voice mail kicked in. "Jamie. It's Adam. I need the names of those bookies. Call me when you get the message." I closed the phone and placed it on the seat beside me. Miriam looked so fragile, like she might break down at any second. "It'll be okay," I told her.

"I know. It's just hard. Dad's so sad. Mom is upset. Grace . . ."

We were silent for a moment. "Do you think that Dolf could have killed Danny?"

"As God is my witness, Adam, I have no idea. Dolf and I never knew each other that well, and I really didn't know Danny at all. He was older, hired help. We didn't associate."

A sudden thought occurred to me. Miriam said that George described Danny's beating as justly deserved payback. Harsh words, I thought, and pictured George at breakfast the other day, the anger that rose in him as we spoke of Danny.

*Danny said I was a joke. He told Miriam that she shouldn't date a joke.*

I'd suggested that Danny remembered a different George Tallman.

*Fuck him, then. That's what I say.*

I studied Miriam. I did not want to upset her needlessly. As far as I could tell, George Tallman did not have a violent bone in him; but I had to ask. "Miriam, did George and Danny have issues? Problems? Anything like that?"

"Not really. Years ago, they were friends. The friendship ended. One of them grew up, the other didn't. I don't believe there were any issues beyond that."

I nodded. She was right. Danny had a great power to make other men angry. It was the ego in him. Nothing more.

"How about Dad and Danny?" I asked. "Have they had problems?"

"Why would you ask that?"

"The cops doubt Dolf's confession. They think that he might be lying to protect Dad."

Miriam shrugged. "I don't think so."

"Does the name Sarah Yates mean anything to you?" I asked.

"No."

"What about Ken Miller?"

She shook her head. "Should it?"

I left her on the porch swing, wondering if she had a blade tucked away somewhere. Wondering if her talk of "one last breath" was just talk.

I turned the car toward town, called information and got

the number and address for Candace Kane. I knew the spot, an apartment complex near the college. I dialed the number and let it ring ten times before hanging up. I'd try again later. When the road forked, I pulled onto the gravel shoulder and stopped. The cops were not going to look beyond my family to explain Danny's death. I refused to accept that. I had two possible leads, people who shared a history of violence with Danny Faith: Candace Kane, who swore out an assault warrant, and whoever it was that beat Danny so badly four months ago. Candy was out somewhere and Jamie was not answering his phone. I had nowhere to go. Frustration put knots in my back. There had to be other avenues.

But there were not. Zebulon Faith was off the radar. Dolf would not talk to me. My father was gone.

Damn.

My mind turned to the other issue that bothered me. It was smaller, less urgent, but still, it ate at me. Why did Sarah Yates seem so familiar to me? How did she know who I was? I put the car in gear, and at the fork in the road, I went left. Davidson County was to the left.

So was Sarah Yates.

I crossed the river and forest marched beside me as I struggled to get my head around this powerful sense of knowing her. I turned off the road and onto the narrow track that led to her place on the river. When I came out of the trees, I saw Ken Miller in a lawn chair by the purple bus. He was in jeans, with bare feet stretched out in the dirt, and his head tilted back to catch the sun on his face. He stood when he heard the car, shaded his eyes, then stepped into the road to block my passage. He held out his arms as if crucified, and frowned with great commitment.

When I stopped, he bent low to peer inside, then stepped to my window. Anger put an edge on his words.

"Haven't you people done enough for one day?" he demanded. His fingers gripped the window frame. Earth grimed his neck and gray hairs protruded from his shirt collar. Swelling closed one of his eyes. The skin shone, dark and tight.

"What people?"

"Your goddamn father. That's what people."

I pointed at the eye. "He did that?"

"I want you to leave." He leaned in closer. "Now."

"I need to speak with Sarah." I put the car in gear.

"I have a gun inside," he said.

I studied his face: the hard line of his chin, the vein that pulsed at the temple. He was angry and scared, a bad combination. "What's going on, Ken?"

"Do I need to get it?"

I stopped at the blacktop. It was empty, a long slice of hard black that curved away in a two-mile bend. I turned left for the bridge, window down, noise level ramping up. I came out of the bend doing fifty. Any faster and I would have missed it.

Sarah's van.

It was parked at the back corner of a concrete biker bar called the Hard Water Tavern. She'd nosed it in beside a rusted Dumpster. All but hidden, it was definitely hers. Same maroon paint, same tinted windows. I slowed the car, looking for a place to turn around. It took another mile, then I whipped into a gravel drive, backed out, and gunned it. I parked next to her van and got out. Sixteen Harleys were lined up between the door and me. Chrome threw back sunlight. Studs gleamed on black leather saddlebags. The bikes angled out with military precision.

Inside, it was dark and low. Smoke hung above pool tables. Music blasted from a jukebox to my left. I went to the bar and ordered a beer from a weary woman who looked sixty, but was probably not much older than I. She stripped the cap off a longneck and put the bottle down hard enough to bring foam out of the mouth. I sat on a vinyl swivel stool and waited for my eyes to adjust. It didn't take long. Lights hung over green felt. Hard light pushed in from the edges of the door.

I pulled on the beer, set it down on the moisture-stained bar.

It was a one-room, three-table joint with a concrete floor and drains that would serve equally well for washing down booze, vomit, or blood. Ten feet down, a fat woman in shorts slept with her head on the bar. Two of the pool tables were in play, circled by men with beards so black they looked polished. They handled the cues with calm familiarity, and looked my way between shots.

Sarah Yates sat at a small table in the back corner. Chairs had been pulled aside to accommodate her wheelchair. Two bikers shared the table with her. They had a pitcher of beer, three mugs, and about fifteen empty shot glasses. As I watched, the bartender threaded her way across the room and delivered three more shots of something brown. They clinked glasses, said something I could not hear, and knocked them back. The bikers slammed the empties down. Sarah lowered hers between two delicate fingers.

Then she looked at me.

There was no surprise in her face. She bent a finger to summon me over. The bikers made room for me to pass, but not much. Hard cues brushed my shoulders, smoke exploded in my face. One man had a teardrop tattoo on the edge of his left eye. I stopped at Sarah's table, and the pool games resumed. Her companions were older than most of the other bikers. Prison tats on thick arms had faded to powder gray. White streaked their beards, and lines carved their faces. They wore thick rings and heavy boots, but appeared neutral. They would take their cue from Sarah. She studied me for half a minute. When she spoke, her voice carried.

"Do you doubt that any of these boys would split your head if I asked him to?" She gestured around the room.

"Because you're their dealer?" I asked.

She frowned, so did the bikers next to her. "Because I'm their friend," she said.

I shook my head. "I don't doubt it."

"I ask because I don't want a repeat of the same kind of crap your old man pulled. I won't tolerate it."

"What did he pull?" I asked.

"Is that why you're here?"

"Partly."

She looked at the two bikers. "It's all right," she said. They got up, huge men smelling of smoke and booze and sunbaked leather. One of them pointed at the bar and Sarah Yates nodded. "Sit down," she said to me. "Want another beer?"

"Sure," I said.

She caught the bartender's eye, lifted the pitcher, and pointed at me. The bartender brought a clean glass and Sarah poured. "I don't normally drink in the afternoon," she said. "But your father put a kink in my day."

I looked around. "Is this your regular place?"

She laughed. "Once, maybe." She gestured with a finger, swept it across the room. "When your life revolves around ten square miles for as long as mine has, you get to know pretty much everybody."

I studied the big men with whom she'd been drinking. They sat with their backs to the bar, feet on the floor like they could still cross the room in seconds. Unlike the others, they watched us closely. "They seem to care about you," I said.

She sipped her beer. "We share a similar mind-set. And we go way back."

"Can we talk?"

"Only if you take back the dealer comment. I don't deal."

"Then I take it back."

"What do you want to talk about?"

In spite of the empty glasses, she did not appear to be drunk. Her face was soft and unlined, but a hardness underlay all of that, a metallic glint that sharpened the edge of her smile. She knew something about hard living and tough choices. I saw it in her measuring gaze and in the way she kept a thin line of contact with the boys at the bar. They watched and they waited.

"Two things," I said. "How do you know me and what did my father want?"

She leaned back and adjusted herself in the chair. Fingers found an empty shot glass and spun it slowly on the table. "Your father," she said. The glass twisted in her long fingers. "A stubborn, self-righteous, son of a bitch. A hard man to like, but an easy man to appreciate." She showed small teeth. "Even when he behaves like the world's biggest asshole.

"He didn't want me talking to you. That's why he came out to see me this morning. He rolled up like the Second Coming of Jesus Christ. Angry, cold. Started barking at me like he had the right. I don't accept that kind of behavior. Our conversation got a little heated. Ken, poor bastard, tried to intervene when he should have known better. First, because I didn't need it. Second, because your father won't tolerate another man laying hands on him."

"He hit Ken?"

"Might have killed him on a different day."

"Why was he so angry?"

"Because I'd been talking to you."

"You talk to Grace all the time."

"That's different."

"Why?"

"Because you're the issue, boy."

I leaned back, frustrated. "How do you know me? Why does he care if we talk?"

"I made him a promise once."

"I found a picture of you in my father's desk. It was taken a long time ago. You were with Dolf and my parents."

She smiled wanly. "I remember."

"Tell me what's going on, Sarah."

She sighed and looked at the ceiling. "It's about your mother," she said. "It's all about your mother."

A pain detonated somewhere in my gut. "What about her?"

Sarah's eyes were very bright in the gloom. Her hand fell away from the shot glass and flattened on the table. "She really was a beautiful woman," Sarah said. "We were very different, so I couldn't admire everything about her, but what she had, she had in spades. Like you, for instance. I've never seen a woman be a better mother or love a child more than she did you. In that way, she was born to be a mother. In other ways, not so much."

"What do you mean?"

Sarah knocked back the rest of her beer and spoke over me. "She couldn't get pregnant," she said. "After you, she had seven miscarriages. The doctors couldn't help. She came to me and I treated her."

"Did I see you? You look very familiar."

"Once, maybe. I usually came at night, when you were asleep. I remember you, though. You were a good kid."

She raised her hand to the bartender, who delivered two shots as if she'd been waiting with them in hand. Sarah raised hers and inclined her head toward the other. I lifted it, tapped her glass, and swallowed liquor that burned all the way down. Sarah's eyes had gone distant.

"But my mother . . . ?"

"She wanted a baby so badly. She ached for it. But the miscarriages were wearing her down, physically and emotionally. By the time I got to her, she was already depressed. When she conceived, though, the spark came back."

Sarah stopped speaking and studied me. I had no idea what she saw. "You sure you want to hear this?"

"Just tell me."

"This one went to the second trimester before she lost it. But she did lose it, and lost a lot of blood in the process. She never got over it, never got her strength back. Depression ate her down to nothing. You know the rest."

"And my father didn't want me to know this?"

"Some business is between a man and his wife and nobody else. He came out today because he didn't want me telling you. He wanted to make sure I remembered my promise."

"Yet, you did tell me."

Heat flashed in her eyes. "Fuck him for not trusting me."

I thought about what she'd said. "It still doesn't make sense. Why would he care that much?"

"I've told you all I'm going to tell."

My hand came down on the table, hard. I didn't even know I'd moved it. Her eyes grew still, and I saw that her friends were on their feet. "Careful," she said softly.

"It doesn't make sense," I repeated.

She leaned closer, laid her hands upon my own, and lowered her voice. "Her complications stemmed from a difficult delivery," she said. "Problems when you were born. Do you see it now?"

Some invisible hand twisted a wrench in my heart. "She killed herself because of me?"

She hesitated and squeezed with her fingers. "That's exactly what your father did not want you thinking."

"That's why he wanted me to stay away from you."

She leaned away from me, brushed her hands along the table's edge. Whatever sympathy I'd seen in her disappeared. "We're done now."

"Sarah . . ."

She lifted a finger and her biker friends crossed the room and stood behind me. I felt them there, a wall. Sarah's face was unforgiving.

"You should leave now."

The day exploded on me as I walked outside. Sunlight drilled into the back of my skull and the booze churned in my empty stomach. I replayed her words and the look on her face. The cold, hard pity.

I made it to the car before I heard footsteps.

I spun, hands up. It was that kind of place. One of the bikers from Sarah's table stood five feet away. He was six two, in leather chaps and wraparound shades. The white in his beard looked more like yellow in the sun. Nicotine streaks at the corners of his mouth. I put his age at sixty. A hard, brutal sixty. The handgun wedged in his pants was chrome-plated.

He stretched out a hand, a folded scrap of paper between two fingers. "She wants you to give this to the guy in jail."

"Dolf Shepherd?"

"Whatever."

I took the paper, a folded napkin. Handwriting stretched loosely over three lines, blue ink that leeched into soft paper. *Good people love you and good people will remember what you stand for. I'll make sure.*

"What does it mean?" I asked.

He leaned forward. "None of your fucking business."

I looked past him to the door. He saw me thinking and dropped a hand to the pistol in his belt. Muscles twisted under his leather skin.

"That's not necessary," I said.

Yellow whiskers moved at the corners of his mouth. "You upset Sarah. Don't bother her again."

I stared him down, and his hand stayed on the gun.

"You can consider that a warning."

I crossed the Salisbury line late in the afternoon. My head hurt and I felt emptied out. I needed something good, so I called Robin, who answered on the second ring. "Are you finished for the day?" I asked.

"Wrapping up a few things. Where are you?"

"In the car."

"Are you okay? You sound bad."

"I think I'm going crazy. Meet me for a drink."

"Usual place?"

"I'll be at the bar," I said.

We'd not been to our usual place in five years. It was

almost empty. "We don't open for ten more minutes," the hostess told me.

"How about I just sit at the bar?" She hesitated, so I said thanks and headed for the bar. The bartender had no problem starting a few minutes early. She had tall hair, a long nose, and poured with a heavy hand. I put away two bourbons before Robin finally showed. The bar was still empty and she kissed me like she meant it.

"No word on Dolf," she said, then asked, "What's wrong?"

Too much had happened. Too much information. I couldn't try to spin it. "Everything," I said. "Nothing I want to talk about."

She sat and ordered one of what I was having. Her eyes were troubled and I could tell that her day had been no picnic either. "Am I causing you problems?" I asked.

She shrugged, but too quickly. "Not many cops share a history with two murder suspects. It complicates things. I'd forgotten how it felt to be on the outside. People are treating me differently. Other cops."

"I'm sorry, Robin."

"Don't worry about it." She held up her glass. "Cheers."

We finished our drinks, had dinner, and went back to her place. We climbed into bed and pressed close. I was done, cashed out for the day, and so was she. I tried not to think of Dolf, alone, or of the things that Sarah had said. For the most part, I succeeded. My last thought before sleep came was that Jamie had never returned my call. After that, the dreams found me pretty damn quick. They came in staccato waves. Visions. Memories. I saw blood on the wall and a white deer that moved with the sound of crashing stone. Sarah Yates, face up and smiling on a night as bright as day. My mother under the dock, her eyes on fire. A leather man with a silver pistol.

I woke reaching for the gun tucked under the biker's belt, came halfway out of bed with a scream balled in the back of my throat. Robin reached for me in her sleep, pressed a smooth hot breast against my ribs. I took shallow breaths and forced myself to lie still. Sweat slicked my skin and hard, black air pushed against the windows.

*She killed herself because of me. . . .*

# Twenty-five

It was still dark when Robin kissed my cheek. "Coffee's on," she said. "I'm out of here."

I rolled over. Her face was a blur. I smelled her skin and her hair. "Where are you going?" I asked.

"I'm going to find Zebulon Faith."

I blinked. "Are you serious?"

"Bad things have been piling up on us. We need something good to happen. I've stayed out of it because it's a county case, but I'm tired of waiting for them to break it. I'll do it myself."

"You'll piss off Grantham."

"I'm starting to feel like you do. Screw Grantham. Screw the politics."

"Do you think Zebulon Faith attacked Grace?"

"At first, I didn't. Too obvious. Now, I'm not so sure. He has a lot of things to answer for. Bottom line, I want to talk to him. I tend to trust my instincts."

"What about DEA?"

"They looked at the drugs we seized and confirmed that the cold meds were stolen. They'll ask around, but they're useless on this."

I sat up in bed and looked at the clock. Five forty-five.

"He's gone to ground," she said, "but I don't think he's

gone far. His son is dead, his drugs are seized, and he knows we're looking; but he's stupid and he's mean and he still thinks there's some way out of all this. He has thirty acres worth seven figures. He'll be in some dark hole close by, at least until the power company's deal is off the table. I'll start with known associates. I'm not scared to squeeze."

"Let me know," I said.

Robin left and my mind raced until the gray light found me. At eight o'clock, I walked out under heavy clouds and found George Tallman sitting in a parked cruiser. He got out when he saw me. He looked like he'd been up all night. Wrinkles marred the perfection of his dark blue uniform. He watched me with bloodshot eyes. "Morning," I said.

"Morning."

"You waiting for me or Robin?"

"You."

His face was meaty and pale under two days' worth of beard. "How'd you know I was here?"

"Come on, Adam. Everybody knows. It's the talk of the police department, probably of the town."

"What do you want, George? It's early."

He leaned against the hood of his car, spread his hands on the paint, and looked suddenly grave. "It's about Miriam," he said. "She told me that you know."

"About the cutting?"

He looked away, as if from the word itself. "Yeah."

"There's no bullshit in that, George. The issues that drive it . . . I can't begin to guess what it all means. Can you handle it? Do you want to handle it?"

"It's like I said the other day, Adam. Miriam needs me. Fragile, beautiful." He held the imaginary teacups again, then opened his fingers like a conjurer. "She's got issues. Who doesn't? She has the soul of an artist, and that doesn't come without cost. She feels pain more than most of us would."

He was clearly shaken, and I sensed the depth of his feeling for her. "Do you know why she does it, George?" I was thinking of Gray Wilson, and of how she mourned over his grave.

He shook his head. "She'll tell me when she's ready. I know better than to push."

"My father should not be out of the loop on something so important."

"He can't help Miriam. I love him, but he can't. He's a hard man and she needs a soft touch. He'd tell her to grow up, be strong, and that would just make it worse. She cares what he thinks. She needs his approval."

"Janice can't handle this on her own."

His feet clicked pavement. "First of all, Janice is not handling this on her own. I'm dealing with this, too. Miriam sees a counselor in Winston-Salem. She goes to inpatient treatment three or four times a year. We're taking care of her, doing what needs to be done."

"Just make sure you pay damn close attention." He started to speak, but I cut him off. "I mean it, George. It's no game."

He rose up, indignant. "Do you even realize the nerve it takes for you to say that to me? Where have you been this whole time? Off in your big-city life, living large on your father's money. I've been here for her. I've picked up the pieces time after time. I've held her together. Me. Not you."

"George—"

"Shut up, Adam, or I will shut you up myself. I will not stand here and be judged."

I gave myself a few seconds. He was right. "I'm sorry, George. I'm out of touch, out of the loop. I just worry. She's family. I love her, hate to see her in pain. I have no right to judge how you and Janice are handling the problem. I'm sure that she's seeing the best people she can."

"She's getting better, Adam. I have to believe that."

"I'm sure you're right, and I apologize again. What can I do for you, George? Why are you here?"

He took a deep breath. "Don't tell your father, Adam.

That's what I'm here to ask you. We haven't slept. She cried all night long."

"Miriam's asking?"

He shook his big head. "She's not asking, Adam. She's begging."

I tried to call Jamie from the car and got his voice mail again. I left a message, and doubted that my voice sounded kind. He'd been unusually scarce and I guessed that he was either drunk, hungover, or avoiding me. Miriam was right, I realized. The family was tearing itself apart. But I couldn't worry about Miriam now, or even Grace. I had to concern myself with Dolf first. He was still in jail, still not talking to any of us. There were things that I did not know, things going on, and I needed to get to the bottom of it, preferably before Grantham did. Today, I told myself, and Candace Kane was a good place to start. I found her apartment at eight thirty.

It was an old development, two stories high, redbrick, with a balcony running along the façade. It filled a skinny lot a block away from the college: thirty units, mostly blue-collar local. Forty years' worth of broken beer bottles had been ground to powdered glass under ten thousand tires. The whole lot looked like spilled glitter when the sun hit it right.

Candace's apartment occupied the back corner, second floor. I parked and walked. Rough concrete grated beneath my shoes as I hit the stairs. From the balcony, I could see the tall spire of the college chapel, the magnificent oak trees that stood above the quad. The numbers were off the door, but I saw a trace of the number "sixteen" in the discolored paint. Desiccated tape covered a drilled-out peephole. A corner had folded up in the heat, and I saw where someone had packed the hole with tissue before taping it up. A plastic garbage bag leaned against the wall, smelling of sour milk and Chinese takeout. I knocked on the door, got no answer. A minute later, I tried again.

I was halfway to my car, sun finally breaking through,

glass shards lighting up on the tarmac, when I saw the woman cutting across a parking lot two hundred feet away. I watched her: mid-twenties in pink shorts and a shirt too small to contain either her breasts or the penny-roll of fat around her waist. I thought of Emmanuel's description: *White. Kind of fat. Trashy.* Looked about right. She had a paper bag in one hand, a half-smoked cigarette in the other. Bleached hair straggled out from under a baseball cap.

I heard her flip-flops.

Saw the scar on her face.

She pulled up when we were ten feet apart. Her mouth opened into a small circle and the eyes went wide, but the expression didn't last. Her face closed down and she changed the line of her walk just enough to miss me. I cut the corner and said her name. She narrowed her eyes, rolled up on the balls of her feet. Up close, she was prettier than I expected, even with the scar. Clear, blue eyes framed a slightly upturned nose. Her lips were full, skin clear. But the scar hurt her. It was tight and pink, glossy as a vinyl skirt. Three inches long, it had a jagged kink in the middle that spoke to me of emergency room surgery.

"Do I know you?" she asked.

Two keys hung on a ring at her waist, the plastic key fob shoved under the elastic of her shorts. I smelled breakfast in the bag and guessed she'd walked to the local barbecue joint for takeout.

"You're Candace, right?"

Much of the initial fear had left her. It was early morning next to a busy street. Five thousand college kids were no more than a block away. "Candy," she corrected me.

"I need to talk to you about Danny Faith."

I expected her face to pinch, but instead, it loosened. Her lips spread to show a single, corrupt tooth on the right side. Tears widened her eyes and her breakfast hit the ground. She clamped her hands over her face, hiding the bright pink rip in her otherwise flawless skin.

She shook, a weeping wreck.

It took her a minute. When the hands came off, her face was splotched white where fingers had pressed too hard. I picked up the warm bag and handed it to her. She fished out a napkin and blew her nose. "I'm sorry," she said. "I just found out yesterday that he was dead."

"Do you care?" I asked. "He gave you that scar," I said. "You filed an assault warrant against him."

Her head dipped. "It don't mean that I didn't love him." She sniffed, trailed a dry corner of the napkin beneath one eye, then the other. "People fix mistakes all the time. People move on. People get back together."

"May I ask what you were fighting about?"

"Who are you again?"

"Danny and I were friends."

She made a damp sound, raised a finger. "You're Adam Chase," she said. "He talked about you a lot. Yeah. He said you were friends, said you could never have killed that boy. He said so to anybody that'd listen. He got in fights about it sometimes. He'd get drunk and angry. He'd talk about how great you were and how much he missed you. Then he'd go out and look for people saying things about you. Five times, six times. Maybe more. I can't remember all the times he came back bloody. A lot. It used to scare me."

"Blood can have that effect."

She shook her head. "Blood don't bother me. I have four brothers. It was what came after."

"What do you mean?"

"After he calmed down, washed the blood off, he'd sit up late and drink by himself. Just sit in the dark and get all weepy. Not like he was really crying." She made a face. "It was just kind of pitiful."

The thought of Danny standing up for me hit hard. After five years of silence, I'd assumed that he'd written off the friendship, moved on with his life. While I tried to bury things, Danny was protecting the memory. It made me feel worse, if possible. I'd interpreted my exile as a mandate. Do whatever it took to get through the hours. Forget your family and your friends. Forget yourself.

I should never have doubted him.

I should have kept the faith.

"He called me," I said. "You don't know what he wanted, do you?"

She gave a head shake. "He never mentioned anything." Her eyes were red, but drying. She sniffed. "Want a cigarette?" she asked. I declined and she pulled a crumpled pack from the back of her shorts. "He has a picture of you in his room. The two of you, I guess I should say. He had his arm around you, but not like he was sweet on you or anything. You were all muddy, laughing."

"Dirt biking," I told her. "I remember."

She took a drag, and the smile died on her face. She shook her head, and there was such meaning in the gesture. I thought that she might cry again.

"What did you and Danny fight about?" I asked.

She dropped the cigarette, crushed it with a green, rubber sandal and I saw how pink polish had chipped away from her toenails. She did not look up. "I always knew he had other girls," she said. "But when he was with me, he was completely and totally with me. See? Those other girls didn't matter. I knew I was the one. He told me so. None of them others would last. It's just the way Danny was. And it's not like I could blame them." She laughed wistfully. "There was something about him. Something that made me put with it. With all of it."

"All of what?"

"The girls. The drinking. The fights." She broke down again. "He was worth it. I loved him."

Her voice fell off and I prompted her. "He hit you?" I asked.

"No." Weak voice. "He didn't hit me. That's just what I said. I was mad."

"What happened?"

"I wanted to hurt him, but you can't tell the cops, okay? They asked me the other day, and I told 'em that he had. I was scared to change my story." She paused. "I just wanted to show him."

"You were angry."

When she looked up, I saw the black gulf behind shining, blue eyes. "He tried to break up with me. He said it was over. What happened to my face. . . . That was my fault. Not his."

"How so?"

"He didn't hit me, like I told the cops. He was trying to walk away and I was pulling on his arm. He jerked it and I tripped on a stool. I fell into that window."

"It doesn't matter now," I said. "He's gone. The warrant means nothing."

But she was crying slow, oily tears, her head loose on her neck. "I put the cops on him. I chased him into hiding. Maybe that's what got him killed."

"Was he into something illegal?"

She shook her head violently, either answering in the negative or refusing to answer at all. I couldn't tell. I asked her again. No answer.

"Gambling?"

A nod, eyes closed.

"Is that who beat him up four months ago? The people that took his bets?"

"You know about that?"

"Who handled his bets, Candy?"

She choked up. "They beat him so bad—"

"Who?" I pushed.

"I don't know. Danny said they'd been looking for him. They went to the motel. They went to the farm. He went missing for a while beforehand. I think he was hiding from them. You should ask Jamie. He's your brother, right?"

"Why should I ask Jamie?"

"He and Danny ran around a bunch. Went to the ball games and the gambling clubs. Dogfights somewhere out in the county. Cockfights. Anything they could bet on. They came home with a new car once, won it from some guy over in Davidson County." She smiled thinly. "It was a junker. Two days later, they traded it for beer and a moped. They were friends, but Danny said once that he couldn't trust Jamie the way he trusted you. Said Jamie had a cruel streak in him." She shrugged. "He really missed you."

She was still crying a little, and I needed to think about what she'd said. She was the second person to think that Jamie and Danny were mixed up in gambling together. George Tallman had said basically the same thing. I considered the implications. I gave her a second. The hard question was coming up. "Why was he breaking up with you, Candy?"

She tilted her head so far to the side that I saw nothing but baseball cap and dry hair bleached to the color of soap. When she spoke, I could tell that the words hurt. "He was in love. He wanted to change his life."

"In love with who?" I asked.

"I don't know."

"No idea?"

She looked up, unforgiving, and the scar twisted when she spoke. "Some whore."

I called Robin as Candy Kane walked away from me. I heard traffic sounds when she answered. "How's it going?" I asked.

"Slowly. The good news is that the sheriff's office has, indeed, been looking for Zebulon Faith. I've spoken to some of the same people, covered a lot of the same ground. Bad news is, I'm getting the same answers. Wherever Faith went to ground, it's out of his name or off the grid."

"What do you mean?"

"I checked with the utility companies for Rowan and surrounding counties. As far as I can tell, he has no other properties, nothing with a phone or power hookup. I've got other irons in the fire. I'll keep you posted."

"I just spoke to Candace Kane."

"Grantham spoke to her yesterday."

"What did she tell him?"

"I'm off the case, remember? I'm the last person Grantham will talk to. All I know is that he tracked her down."

"She told Grantham that Danny hit her and that she hated him for it. That's not entirely the truth. She loved him. He dumped her right before he died. Could be a motive."

"You think she's capable?"

"Of murder?" I looked up as Candace mounted the stairs. Her long legs pumped beneath pink, terry cloth shorts. The extra weight on her jiggled. "I don't see it," I said. "But she has four brothers. They may not like the scar on her face."

"That's a viable motive, but again . . . it was Dolf's gun. I'll run the names and see if any of them have a sheet. Who knows? Maybe we'll get lucky."

She did not sound hopeful, and I understood. It all came back to the gun. It only made sense if Danny took the gun himself and somehow lost control of it. And that was thin. Danny knew how to handle himself. "Do you think Faith knows that his son is dead?"

"That depends on how deep he's hiding."

"Danny might have been into gambling. It looks like somebody beat him pretty badly four months ago. Might be gambling related."

"Says who?"

"Candace Kane. George Tallman."

"George, huh?"

I heard the disdain in her voice. "What do you have against him?"

"He's an idiot."

"Seems like more than that."

She hesitated and I knew she was thinking about the question. "I don't trust him."

"Any particular reason?"

"It's complicated."

"Try me."

"I've been a police office for more than a few years. I know a lot of cops and a lot of criminals, and, in some ways, the two aren't that different. Criminals have their good sides, if you can find them. Cops can run dark. You understand? Cops can't be saints. The job won't allow it. Too many bad people in your life. Too many bad days, bad decisions. It accumulates. Likewise, criminals are rarely bad all the time. They have kids. They have parents. Whatever. They're human. Spend enough time around anyone, and you should see hints of both sides. That's human nature. You see what I'm saying?"

"I think so."

"I've worked with George Tallman for four years. I've never seen his dark side."

"What's your point?"

"Nobody is that easy. Nobody is that level, least of all a cop."

She was wrong. I'd known George since he was in high school. He could not hide a feeling if he had to. I let it go, chalked it up to cynicism born of long years wearing a shield. "What about the gambling? Do you think there could be some tie-in there? Something to link it to Danny's death? Candace Kane said that these bookies came looking for Danny. They went to the motel. They went to the farm. Have you seen anything that might support that kind of motive? Danny was killed on the farm."

"There are some big game-makers in Charlotte. Highly profitable, highly illegal. If he was in over his head, it could get ugly."

"Is anybody going to check it out?"

Her voice was not without pity. "Dolf confessed. Nobody is looking for alternate explanations. Any jury in the country would convict him."

"Grantham has doubts about motive," I said.

"It's not up to Grantham. It's up to the sheriff and he isn't going to waste time or money when he already has what he wants."

"Grantham thinks that Dolf might have confessed to protect my father." Robin was silent. "That's stupid, right?"

More silence.

"Robin?"

"Grantham's smart. I'm trying to see this from his perspective. I'm thinking."

"Well, think out loud."

"Whoever killed Danny would have to know about the crack up on the knob."

"That could be anybody. We used to have parties up there. Shoot skeet. I could name a hundred people that have been up there."

"I'm just playing devil's advocate, Adam. Danny's killer would have to be strong enough to get the body in the hole. Your father has no handguns of his own, but has access to Dolf's gun cabinet. Danny worked for him off and on. Plenty of opportunity for problems to fester. Did he have any reason to be upset with Danny?"

"I have no idea," I said, but then thought of Jamie's gambling. Danny was a bad influence. The family was short on cash.

"Then I don't know what to tell you. Nothing makes sense without a motive."

"For now, I'm going to assume that Danny's death has something to do with the power plant or with his gambling. Whoever took his bets has already assaulted him once. I need to look into that."

"Don't. Not in Charlotte. Those guys are heavy hitters. They don't like people messing around in their business. Cross the wrong one down there and you may find yourself in a world of trouble. I'm not kidding. I won't be able to help you."

I pictured Danny, spoiling for a fight, then coming home to drink alone. Dolf, in a cell. Grace crumbling from the inside out. Grantham's insinuation that Dolf was lying to protect my father. There was a piece missing, and somebody, somewhere knew what it was. I had no choice but to dig where I could. Deep down, Robin had to recognize that.

"I have to do something," I said.

"Don't, Adam. I'm asking you."

"I'll think about it," I said, and continued before she could question the lie. "You'll check on the brothers?"

"Yes."

"Anything else I should know?"

"I doubt it means anything, but I'm guessing that Candy Kane wasn't the only woman Danny dumped."

"What do you mean?"

"Danny lived at the motel. We went through his room after his body was found. One of the windows was broken, patched with cardboard from a shoe box. On a dresser we found a rock sitting on top of a note. The note was yellow paper, unfolded, rock sitting on it like a paperweight. Looked like someone had wrapped the note around the rock and tossed it through the window. The rubber band was still on the rock. The Mexican guy, Emmanuel, thought he remembered that happening shortly before Danny went missing."

"What did the note say?"

" 'Fuck you, too.' "

"How do you know it was from a woman?"

"Lip prints where a signature should be. Bright red lipstick."

"Perfect," I said.

"Sounds to me like Danny Faith was cleaning house."

# Twenty-six

I called Jamie and got his voice mail. I left another message. Call me. Now. We need to talk. I hung up the phone, took a couple of steps, then opened it again. The fire was in me, and Jamie was part of it. Candace said he was still gambling, he and Danny. He'd lied to me about that. He should have called me back yesterday. I hit redial, and he answered on the second ring. I heard his breath first, then his voice, sullen and petulant. "What do you want, Adam?"

"Why didn't you call me back?"

"Look, I've got shit to do."

"I'm going to cut to the chase, Jamie. I found Danny's girlfriend."

"Which one?"

"The one that filed the warrant. Candace Kane."

"Candy? I remember Candy."

"She says that you're still gambling. She says that you and Danny would take any game you could find. You lied to me about that."

"First of all, I don't answer to you. Second, that wasn't gambling. That was a hundred bucks here and there. Just an excuse to get out and do something."

"So, you're not gambling?"

"Hell, no."

"I still need the names of those bookies."

"Why?"

"Danny got beaten up a while back. You remember?"

"He didn't talk about it, but it was hard to miss. He couldn't walk for a week. I'm not sure his face ever got over it."

"I want to talk to whoever did that. Maybe he still owed. Maybe they came looking for him."

"Well . . ." The word drew out, like there was nothing coming after it.

"I need them now."

"Why do you care, Adam? Dolf admitted that he killed Danny. He's going to fry for it. Fuck him, I say."

"How can you even think that?"

"I understand that you see sunshine coming out of his ass, but there's never been any love between me and that old man. In fact, he's always been a pain. Danny was a buddy of mine. Dolf says he killed him. Why are you messing with that?"

"Do I need to come find you in person? I will do it. I swear to God, I'll track you down if I have to."

"Jesus, Adam. What the hell? Just chill."

"I want the names."

"I haven't really had time to find them."

"That's crap, Jamie. Where are you? I'm coming there. We'll go get them together."

"Okay, okay. Jeez. Keep your pants on. Let me think." He took more than a minute, then gave me a name. "David Childers."

"White guy or black guy?"

"Redneck guy. Keeps a pistol in his desk drawer."

"He's in Charlotte?"

"He's local."

"Where?"

"You sure you want to do this?" Jamie asked.

"Where do I find him, Jamie?"

"He owns the Laundromat by the high school. There's an office in the back."

"Is there a back door?"

"Yeah, but it's steel. You'll have to go in the front."

"Anything else I should know?"

"Don't mention my name." The phone clicked off.

The Laundromat filled a shady place between an apartment complex surrounded by hurricane fencing and a grand old home on the verge of decay. Nondescript and small, it was easy to miss. Glass windows threw back a rippled reflection of my car as I turned into the lot. I did not park in front, though. Instead, I slipped down the narrow space beside the building and parked where fencing sealed off the back. I climbed the fence, dropped to the other side, and crossed a litter-strewn square of pavement hidden from the street. The steel door stood open, wedged with a cracked chunk of cinder block. The gap was less than a foot wide, air still and damp. I smelled laundry detergent and something along the lines of rotting fruit. Bass-heavy music pumped through the crack in the door.

I edged to the door and looked in. The office was dim and paneled, papers stacked on cabinets, big cheap desk with a fat bald man behind it, swivel chair spun sideways. His pants hung off one ankle. Head tilted back, eyes squeezed tight in a red face. The woman was on her knees, head working like a steam piston. Slender, young, and black, she could pass for sixteen. He had one hand twined in her oily hair, the other locked onto the chair arm so hard I saw tendons popping through the fat.

A limp twenty hung off the corner of the desk.

I kicked the cinder block away and slammed the door open. When it clanged against brick, the fat man's eyes flew open. For a long second he stared at me as the girl continued to work. His mouth rounded into a black hole and he said, "Oh, God."

The girl stopped long enough to say, "That's right, baby." Then she went back to work. I stepped into the room as he pushed the girl away from his crotch. I caught a glimpse of her face and saw the void in her eyes. She was wrecked on something. "Damn, baby," she said.

The fat man wallowed to his feet, hands clutching at his pants, leg trying to find the hole. His eyes never left mine. "Don't tell my wife," he said.

Slowly, the girl came to realize that they weren't alone. She stood, and I saw that she was no child. Twenty-five, maybe, dirty and bloodshot. She wiped a hand across her mouth as the man's pants came up. "This counts," she said, and reached for the twenty.

She smiled as she moved past me: gray teeth, crack-pipe lips. "Name's Shawnelle," she said. "Just ask around if you want some of the same."

I let her go, stepped in, and closed the door. He was working the belt, tugging hard to get it closed up. Forty, I thought. Fifty, maybe. It was hard to tell with the sweat and the fat and the shining, pink scalp. I watched his hands and I watched the drawer. If there was a gun there, he had no intention of going for it. But he was firming up now that he had his pants on. The anger was in there, buried, but waking. "What do you want?" he asked.

"Sorry to bother you," I said.

"Yeah, right." There it was. "You working for my wife? Tell her she can't get blood from a stone."

"I don't know your wife."

"Then what do you want?"

I stepped in, closer to the desk. "I understand you take bets."

A nervous laugh gushed out of him. "Jesus. Is that what this is? You should come in from the front, damn it. That's how it's done."

"I'm not here to bet. I want you to tell me about Danny Faith. You take his bets?"

"Danny's dead. I saw it in the papers."

"That's right. He is. Did you handle his bets?"

"I'm not going to talk about my business to you. I don't even know who you are."

"I can always talk to your wife."

"Don't call my wife. Christ. The final hearing is next week."

"About Danny?"

"Look, there's not much I can tell you, okay? Danny was a player. I'm small-time. I run football pools, handle the payoff on illegal video poker machines. Danny moved out of my league two or three years ago. His action's in Charlotte."

I felt a sudden, sickening twist in my stomach. Jamie lied to me. This was a wild-goose chase. "What about Jamie Chase?" I asked.

"Same thing. He's big-time."

"Who handles their play in Charlotte?"

He smiled an unclean smile. "You going to try this shit down there?" The smile spread. "You're gonna get smoked."

There was no backdoor sneaking at the place he sent me. It was a cinder-block cube on the east side of Charlotte, set back off an industrial four-lane that reeked of freshly poured tar. I got out of the car, saw sun glint off downtown towers three miles and a trillion dollars east. Two men loitered at the front door, a row of pipes scattered against the wall in easy reach. They watched me all the way in, a black guy in his thirties, white guy maybe ten years older.

"What do you want?" the black guy asked.

"I need to talk to a man inside," I said.

"What man?"

"Whoever's running the place."

"I don't know you."

"I still need to talk to somebody."

The white guy held up a finger. "What's your name?" he asked. "You look familiar." I told him. "Wallet," he said. I handed him my wallet. It was still stuffed with hundreds. Travel money. His eyes lingered on the sheaf of bills, but he didn't touch them. He pulled out my driver's license. "This says New York. Wrong guy, I guess."

"I'm from Salisbury," I said. "I've been away."

He looked at the license again. "Adam Chase. You had some trouble a while back."

"That's right."

"You related to Jamie Chase?"

"My brother."

He handed back the wallet. "Let him in."

The building was a single room, brightly lit, modern. The front half was fashioned into a reception area: two sofas, two chairs, a coffee table. A low counter bisected the room. Desks behind the counter, new computers, fluorescent lights. A rack of dusty travel brochures leaned against the wall. Posters of tropical beaches hung at uneven intervals. Two young men sat at computers. One had his foot on a pulled-out drawer.

A man in a suit stood at the counter. He was white, sixty. The guard from outside approached and whispered in the man's ear. The man nodded, shooed the guard away. The older man smiled. "May I help you?" he asked. "A trip to the Bahamas? Something more exotic?" The smile was bright and dangerous.

I stepped to the counter, feeling eyes on my back. "Nice place," I said. The man shrugged, palms up, smile noncommittal. "Danny Faith," I said. "Jamie Chase. These are the men I'm here to speak about."

"These names should be familiar to me?"

"We both know that they are."

The smile slid away. "Jamie is your brother?"

"That's right."

He sized me up with eyes as predatory as a snake's. Something told me that he saw things that other men would not. Strengths and weaknesses, opportunity and risk. Meat on a scale. "I've pulled Danny Faith out of a hole once or twice, rat that he is. But he is of no interest to me. He settled his debts about three months ago and I haven't seen him since."

"Settled?"

He showed teeth too white and straight to be real. "Paid in full."

"He's dead."

"I know nothing about that. I concern myself with those that owe, which brings us to your brother. Are you here to pay off his debt?"

"His debt?"

"Of course."

"How much?" I asked.

"Three hundred thousand."

"No," I said, as cold twisted through me. "I'm not here to pay off his debt."

He waved a hand. "Then get the hell out."

The guard moved behind me, so close I could feel his heat. The old man turned away.

"Wait," I said. "You pulled Danny Faith out of a hole. What hole?"

He turned back, a twist of displeasure on his thin lips. "What are you talking about?"

"You said that you pulled Danny out of a hole. I'm looking for his father. Maybe he's hiding in the same hole."

He shook his head, frowning. "Get him out of here."

"I'll pay for the information."

"Fine. Three hundred thousand dollars is the price. You got that on you? Thought not. Now, get lost." A hand fell on my shoulder. The young men behind the counter rose to their feet.

Outside, the sun seared down, tar smell everywhere. The black guy still propped up the wall. The other shoved me toward my car, following two steps behind. "Just keep walking," he said. Then, five feet from the car, in a quiet hiss, "Five hundred bucks."

I turned, put my back against hot metal. His eyebrows pulled together. He turned his head fractionally, casting a glance at the man against the wall. "Yes or no?"

"Five hundred for what?"

He positioned himself so that he stood between me and the other man, shielded me. "Your boy, Danny, was late on thirty large. We spent most of a week looking for him. When we found him, we beat the crap out of him. Not just because he owed, because we had to look so damn hard to find him. We were pissed." He tilted his head again. "You put five hundred dollars in my hand right now and I'll tell you where we found him. Maybe it's the hole you're looking for."

"Tell me first."

"It's about to go up to a grand. One more word out of your mouth and it's fifteen hundred."

I pulled the wallet out of my back pocket.

"Hurry up," he said.

I thumbed five bills out of the wallet, folded them, handed them over. He hunched his shoulders and shoved them in the front pocket of his jeans. He gave me an address. "It's a shit-box skinny out in the middle of nowhere. The address is good, but it's a bitch to find."

He started to turn. "How did he manage to pay off thirty thousand dollars?" I asked.

"What do you care?" His voice was mostly sneer.

I held out one more bill. "Another hundred," I said.

He rolled back, snatched the bill, and leaned in close. "We track him down. We mess him up a bit. Eight days later he shows up with thirty thousand in cash. Brand-new bills, still in the sleeves. He tells us that's it, he's done gambling. We never hear from him again. Not a whiff. Not a peep. All cleaned-up and proper."

The drive out of Charlotte was a sun-baked nightmare. I kept the windows down because I needed wind on my face, eighty miles an hour of hard North Carolina air. It kept

me sane as heat devils twisted the horizon and my insides
roiled with the cold hard fact of my brother's deceit. He was
a gambler, a drunk, and a stone-faced liar. Three hundred
thousand dollars was a mint of money and there was only
one way he could hope to put his hands on it. That was if my
father sold. Jamie's stake would be ten percent, call it a million five.

Coin to spare.

And he had to be desperate. Not just to save himself a
beating like Danny's, but also to keep the truth from my father, who'd already bailed him out once. But how desperate
was he?

Just how black was his soul?

I tried to stay calm, but could not escape one simple fact.
Somebody attacked Grace, beat her half to death to make a
point. *Tell the old man to sell.* That's what the note said. It
was Jamie or Zebulon Faith who did it. One or the other. Had
to be. Please, I prayed. Don't let it be Jamie.

We would not survive it.

# *Twenty-seven*

The address for Zeb Faith's "shit-box skinny" was two counties over in an area bedridden by two decades of a failed blue-collar economy. A hundred years ago, it was some of the most productive farmland in the state. Now it was wild and overgrown, littered with shuttered plants, crumble-down mill houses, and single-wides on dirt tracks. Fields lay fallow and the forest pushed out scrub. Chimneys rose from piled debris. Kudzu slung long arms over phone lines as if to pull them down.

That's where Faith's hideaway was, deep in the ruined green.

It took two hours to find it. I stopped three times for directions, and the closer I got, the more the countryside seemed to sweat poverty and despair. The road twisted. Single-lane and cracked, it slipped between low hills and thick-smelling bogs, ended in a two-mile loop that wrapped the edges of a dead-end hollow with more cold shade than most.

I was forty miles from Salisbury, one of the richest towns in the state, less than sixty from the silver towers of Charlotte, and I could have been in a different country. Goats stood hock-deep in wire pens full of shit. Chicken coops settled on bare dirt yards in front of houses with plastic bag windows and unpainted, plywood siding. Cars bled rust. Slat-sided dogs lolled in the shade while barefoot kids tempted fleas and worms with blank-eyed disregard. In all my life, I'd never seen anything like it. Black or white, it didn't matter.

The drain emptied here.

The hollow was a mile across, maybe two dozen shacks, some by the road, others no more than mildewed hints behind hooked brambles and trees that waged stiff-armed war for precious light. The road was a loop through hell. I followed it until it spit me out at the beginning. Then I started again, more slowly, and felt eyes in the dark places behind torn screens. I heard a door slam, saw a milk-eyed woman with a dead rabbit, and drove on, looking for a number.

I rounded a bend and found a little boy with skin so black it was purple. He had no shirt, a round belly, and a sharp stick in one hand. Beside him, a dusty brown girl in a faded yellow print pushed a doll on a tire swing. They stared at my car with lowered lids and slack, parted lips. I slowed to a stop, and a giant woman avalanched through the tarpaper door. She had thick, rolled ankles and was clearly naked beneath a parchment dress devoid of shape or color. In one hand, she held a wooden spoon dripping sauce as red as uncooked meat. She scooped the little boy under one arm, and raised the spoon as if she might flick sauce at me. Her eyes were tucked into deep flesh.

"You get on out of here," she said. "Don't you be botherin' these children."

"Ma'am," I said. "I don't intend to bother anybody. I'm looking for number seventy-nine. Maybe you can help me."

She thought about it, eyelids puckered, lips pushed together. The boy still hung from her arm, bent at the waist, arms and legs dangling straight down. "Numbers don't mean much around here," she finally said. "Who you looking for?"

"Zebulon Faith."

Her head rolled on the stump of her neck. "Name don't mean a thing."

"White guy. Sixties. Thin."

"Nope." She started to turn away.

"His son has red hair. Mid-twenties. Big guy."

She pivoted on one foot, lowered the boy by a wrist. He picked up his stick and stole the doll off the tire swing. The girl raised an arm and cried muddy tears.

"That red one," she said. "Pure trouble."

"Trouble?"

"Drinking. Howling at the moon. Got a ten-foot pile of shot-up bottles back there. What you want him for?"

"He's dead. I'm looking for his father." It did not answer her question, but seemed to satisfy her. She sucked on a gap in her teeth and pointed up the road. " 'Round that bend you'll see a track off to the right. Got a pie plate nailed to a tree. That's what you want."

"Thanks," I said.

"Just stay away from these children."

She snatched the doll from the boy and handed it back to the little girl, who smeared tears with a forearm, kissed the plastic face, and smoothed her small hand over plugs of ragged, vinyl hair.

The pie plate had seven bullet holes in it. The track was almost invisible, guarded by two things: the massive tree to which the plate was nailed, and the knee-high grass that grew between the wheel ruts. Whatever was down there, I doubted anyone used it very often. I drove my car around the tree and parked it out of sight of the road. Once out of the car, the smell of the place intensified, the fecund reek of stagnant water, still air, and damp earth. The track curved left, disappeared around a shoulder bone of wood and granite. Suddenly, I doubted the wisdom of coming here. It was the silence. The sense of hushed expectancy. A raptor called in the distance, and I shrugged the feeling off.

The ground was spongy, tire tracks recent. Grass stems were broken and bent. Within the last day or two, I guessed.

I hugged the left side until I came to the bend and pressed against the granite outcrop. The track cut hard left, back into the trees. I risked a glance, pulled back, then looked again and studied Zebulon Faith's shit-box skinny. The trailer was old, probably thirty, which is about three hundred in trailer years. It canted to the right on cinder-block legs. No phone line. No power line. A lifeless shell.

There was no car, either, which made it unlikely that anyone was here. Nevertheless, I approached cautiously. The trailer was hard-used. Somebody brought it in new a lifetime ago or hauled it off a junk heap last year. Six one way, half dozen the other. Whatever the case, here it would linger until the earth managed to consume it. It sat in the middle of a jagged gash in the trees. Vines grew over the back corner. The pile of shot-up bottles was more two feet tall than ten.

I could see, in the grass, where a car had been parked.

Slick steps led onto a sagging square of wood at the front door. There was a single plastic chair, more bottles in the grass, and a lot of give under my feet as I stepped up. I peered in the window, got the vague impression of peeled vinyl floors and Dumpster furniture. Beer bottles ringed the kitchen table, fast-food wrappers and lottery tickets on the counter.

I tried the door—locked—then circled the trailer, stepping over discarded furniture and other refuse. The back looked like the front with one exception, a generator under a limp tarp weighted with bricks. I checked all the windows. Two bedrooms, one empty, the other with a box spring and mattress on the floor. There was one bathroom. It had toothpaste on the counter and dirty magazines on a stool. I checked the main room again and saw a rabbit-ear television with a VCR and a stack of tapes, ashtrays on the floor, couple bottles of vodka.

It was a flophouse, a place to hide from the world, which made sense if you were a man like Zebulon Faith. I wanted to break in and tear it down. I wanted to burn it.

But I knew that I'd be coming back, so I left it.

No point in scaring him off.

I drove toward the farm, sun low and in my face. I called Robin, talked about a lot of nothing, and said I'd see her tomorrow. No mention of Zebulon Faith. Some things are best done in the dark, and I did not want her involved. Period. I turned off the phone and pushed harder into the scorching orange. The day was dying, and I wondered what it would take with it.

I saw my father's truck from a distance, parked across the drive from Dolf's house. I pulled in behind him and got out. He was in old clothes bleached by the sun. Miriam sat next to him, looking exhausted.

I leaned in the window. "You okay?" I asked.

"She won't talk to us," he said.

I followed the direction of his nod and saw Grace in the side yard. She was barefoot in faded jeans and a white tank top. In the soft light, she looked very hard, very lean. She'd put the archery target a hundred feet out. The compound bow looked huge in her hands. I watched her draw back and release. The arrow moved like thought, buried its head in the target's center. Six arrows nested there, a thick knot of fiberglass, steel, and bright, feathered flights. She nocked another shaft, steel head winking. When it flew, I thought I could hear it.

"She's good," I said.

"She's flawless," my father corrected me. "She's been at this for an hour. Hasn't missed yet."

"You've been here that whole time?"

"We tried twice to speak to her. She won't have it."

"What's the problem?"

His face worked. "Dolf made his first appearance in court today."

"She was there?"

"They brought him in wearing full chains. Waist, ankle, wrists. He could barely walk in all that. Reporters everywhere.

That dickhead sheriff. The D.A. Half dozen bailiffs, like he was a threat. Goddamn. It was intolerable. He wouldn't look at any of us. Not at me, not at Grace, not even when she tried to get his attention. She was jumping up and down . . ."

He paused. Miriam shifted uncomfortably.

"They offered him the chance for counsel and he turned it down again. Grace left in tears. We came out here to check on her." He nodded again. "This is what we found."

My eyes swung back to Grace. Nock and release. Smack of hardened steel on stuffed canvas. The feel of split air. "Grantham has been looking for you," I said. "He seems to think there are still things to discuss."

I studied him closely. He continued to watch Grace and his face did not change. "I have nothing to say to Grantham. He tried to talk after court, but I refused."

"Why?"

"Look what he's done to us."

"Do you know what he wants to talk about?"

His lips barely moved. "Does it matter?"

"So, what's going to happen with Dolf? What's next?"

"I talked to Parks about that. The district attorney will go for an indictment. Unfortunately for Dolf, the grand jury is sitting this week. The D.A. won't waste time. He'll get the indictment. The dumb bastard confessed. Once the grand jury returns the indictment, he'll be arraigned. Then they'll figure out whether or not the death penalty is on the table."

I felt a familiar chill. "Rule twenty-four hearing," I said flatly. "To determine if a capital charge is appropriate."

"You remember."

He couldn't meet my gaze. I knew the steps from the inside. It had been one of the worst days of my life, listening for long hours as the lawyers argued over whether or not I'd get the needle if convicted. I shook the memory off, looked down, and saw my father's hand settle on a sheaf of pages on the seat next to him. "What's that?" I gestured.

He picked up the pages, made a sound in his throat, and

handed them to me. "It's a petition," he said. "Sponsored by the chamber of commerce. They gave it to me today. Four of them. Representatives, they called themselves, like I haven't known them all for thirty years and more."

I riffled the pages, saw hundreds of names, most of which I knew. "People that want you to sell?"

"Six hundred and seventy-seven names. Friends and neighbors."

I handed the pages back. "Any thoughts on that?"

"People are entitled to their opinions. None of it changes mine."

He was not going to discuss it further. I thought of the debt he had to repay in a few short days. I wanted to talk about it, but couldn't do it in front of Miriam. It would embarrass him.

"How are you, Miriam?" I asked.

She tried a smile. "Ready to go home."

"Go on," I said to my father. "I'll stay."

"Be patient with her," he said. "She's too proud for the load she's carrying."

He turned the key. I stood in the dust and watched him go, then sat on the hood of my car and waited for Grace. She was smooth and sure, bending arrows with quiet resolve. After a few minutes I pulled the car into the driveway, went inside, and came back out with a beer. I dragged a rocking chair to the other side of the porch, where I could watch her.

The sun sank.

Grace never lost her rhythm.

When she finally came up onto the porch, I thought that she would walk past without speaking, but she stopped at the door. Her bruises were black in the gloom. "I'm glad to see you," she said.

I didn't get up. "Thought I'd make dinner."

She opened the door. "What I said before. I didn't mean it."

She was talking about Dolf.

"I'm going to take a shower," she said.

I found ground beef in the refrigerator and had dinner on

the table by the time she came out. She smelled like clean water and flowered soap. Wet hair brushed the robe she wore and the sight of her face shot new barbs through my chest. The eyes were better, but the torn lips still looked raw, the stitches black and stiff and wrong. The bruises had eggplant hearts fading to green at the edges. "How bad is it?" I asked.

"This?" She pointed at her face. "This is meaningless." She looked at the water I'd poured for her, then pulled a beer out of the fridge. She cracked it, took a sip, and sat. She pushed up her sleeves to eat, and I saw the wreckage of her left forearm. The bowstring had chewed it up, put long welts across a ten-inch stretch. Grace caught me staring.

"Jesus, Grace. You're supposed to wear arm guards."

She took a bite, unflinching, and pointed at my plate. "You going to eat that?"

We ate dinner, drank beer, and barely spoke. We tried, but failed, and the silence grew close to comfortable. The company mattered. It was enough. When I said good night, her eyes were heavy. I lay on the guest bed, thinking of Jamie's deceit and of tomorrow's conversation, of all the things that lived with such force in this place. The sheer volume made the room spin. Life, in all its complications, seemed to funnel down from a vast, high place, so that when Grace opened the door, it felt ordained.

She'd lost the robe, wore a cobweb gown that could have been nothing. When she moved into the dark, she was a whisper.

I sat up. "Grace—"

"Don't worry, Adam. I just want to be near you."

She crossed on swift feet and climbed under the comforter, being careful to keep the sheet between us. "See?" she said. "I'm not here to spoil you for other women." She moved close and I felt her heat through thin cloth. She was soft and she was hard and she pressed upon me in near perfect stillness. It was then, in the dark and the heat, that revelation found me. It was the smell of her, the way her breasts flattened against me, the hard curve of her thighs. It came with an audible snap, the sound of pieces slipping into place. Danny's call three weeks ago. The urgency in his voice. The need. And there was Grace's friend, Charlotte Preston, who worked at the drugstore and told Robin of some unknown boyfriend. She'd said that there were issues, something that made Grace unhappy. Other pieces shifted and clicked. The night that Grace stole Danny's bike. The wormlike twist of a tight, pink scar and the words that Candace Kane spilled with such venom when I'd asked why Danny had left her.

*He was in love. He wanted to change his life.*

What had been void mere seconds ago now brimmed with bright, dripping color. Grace was not the girl who lived in my head. Not the child I remembered. She was a grown woman, lush and complex.

*The hottest thing in three counties,* Jamie had said.

There were still gaps, but the shape was there. Danny worked the farm, he probably saw her every day. Danny would know that she loved me. I rolled away and turned on the bedside light. I needed to see her face.

"Danny was in love with you," I said.

She sat up, pulled the comforter to her chin. I knew that I was right.

"That's why he was breaking up with his other girl-friends," I said. "That's why he was clearing his debts."

An edginess moved into her face, a stiffness that spoke of defiance. "He wanted to prove himself. He thought he could convince me to change my mind."

"You dated him?"

"We went out a few times. Motorcycle races on the park-way. Late nights in Charlotte, dancing at the clubs. He was fearless, charming in a way. But I wouldn't go where he wanted to go." She lifted her chin. Her eyes glittered, hard and proud.

"You wouldn't sleep with him?"

"That was part of it. The start. Then he got crazy. Wanted to spend our lives together, talked about having kids." She rolled her eyes. "True love, if you can believe that."

"And you weren't interested."

She put her eyes on mine, and her meaning was unmistakable. "I'm waiting for someone."

"That's why he called me."

"He wanted me to know that you weren't coming back. He thought that if you told me that yourself, I might actually believe it. He said I was wasting my life waiting for something that would never happen."

"Jesus."

"Even if you'd done what he wanted, come home and told me face-to-face, it wouldn't have made a difference."

"That night you took Danny's bike . . . ?"

She shrugged. "Sometimes I just need to see the dotted line go solid white. Danny didn't like me doing it without him. I took the bike all the time. I just never got caught."

"Why do you think Dolf may have killed him?"

She tensed. "I don't want to talk about that."

"We need to."

She looked away.

"He hit you," I said. "Didn't he? Danny got mad when you told him no."

It took her a minute. "I laughed at him. I shouldn't have, but I did."

"And he hit you?"

"Once, but it was pretty hard."

"Damn it."

"He didn't break anything, just bruised me. He was immediately sorry. I hit him back and hit him harder. I told Dolf as much."

"So, Dolf knew."

"He knew, but we worked it out, Danny and me. I think Dolf understood that. At first, anyway."

"What do you mean?" I asked.

"Danny was stubborn, like I said. He wouldn't take no for an answer. Once things calmed down, he went to Dolf, to ask for my hand in marriage. He thought Dolf could convince me." She barked a laugh. "The nerve."

"What happened?"

"Dolf thought it was the worst idea he'd ever heard and he said as much to Danny. He said there was no way he'd let me marry a hitter, not even a one-time hitter. No matter what. No way. Danny was drunk at the time, trying to get his nerve up, I guess. He didn't like it. They argued and it got ugly. Danny took a swing and Dolf laid him out. He's tougher than he looks. A day or two later, Danny was just gone."

I thought about what she'd said. I could see it. Grace was Dolf's pride and joy. He'd have been furious at the thought of anyone laying a hand on her. And Danny trying to force a relationship on her. . . . If he kept pushing . . .

Grace waited until I looked at her. "I don't really think that Dolf killed him. I just don't want anybody thinking he might have had a reason."

She lay down, put her head on the pillow. "Did you love him at all?" I asked, meaning Danny.

"Maybe a little." She closed her eyes, sunk lower in the covers. "Not enough to matter."

I watched her for a moment. She was done talking. I was, too. "Good night, Grace."

"Good night, Adam."

I turned off the light and lay back down. We were both stiff and aware, not just of each other's proximity, but of all the things still unsaid. It took hours to fall asleep beneath the open window.

When I woke, it was to the smell of fire.

# *Twenty-eight*

I sat up fast. Dead-of-night darkness spilled through the window, and with it came the taint of smoke. I shook Grace. "Get up," I said.

"What is it?"

"You smell that?"

She reached for a lamp. "Don't," I said. I swung my legs over the bed and pulled on pants, snatched up my shoes. Grace climbed out, too. "Get dressed."

Grace ran for her clothes and I passed down the dark hall, out onto the porch, the screen door screeching like a night bird. A solid black sky pressed down: no stars, no moon. The wind came over the hilltop, the charred smell so faint I could almost miss it. Then the wind gusted and brought smoke thick enough to taste. When Grace came out, seconds later, she was dressed and ready. "What are we doing?" she asked. I pointed north, where sudden orange stained the bottoms of low clouds.

"Get in the car."

I flung gravel as I slammed the pedal down, fishtailed out of the drive. We raced down a dark tunnel, Grace's hand clenched on my shoulder. As we came over a hill, the glow expanded. It was still distant, a mile or more, and then we were almost to my father's house.

"I'll drop you at the house. Wake everybody up. Get the fire department out here."

"What are you going to do?"

"Find out where the fire is. I have my cell. I'll call the house once I know for certain. You can direct the trucks once they get here."

I barely stopped at the house. Grace sprang for the steps as I gunned it. I hit the tree line in seconds, engine revving as I overpowered on the loose gravel. I got the car under control, pointed it at the long winding hill that sliced through the forest. The glow intensified as I approached the crest. I exploded over the top of the hill, out of the woods, and slammed on the brakes, sending the car into a long, stuttering drift. When I came to rest, I spilled out into the hot air, smoke like a blanket. The valley below was raging. It was the vineyard, the hundred acres that Dolf had shown me. Orange tongues licked at the sky. Black shadows danced as heat and flame sucked in great drafts of air and pushed smoke skyward. A third of the vineyard flamed.

And suddenly I understood.

Jamie's truck was skewed across the road less than twenty yards from the flames, driver's door open. Windows reflected the hard yellow boil. The paint danced. When I looked for Jamie, I saw him halfway across the bowl, moving like a locomotive through unburned rows near the fire's outer edge. The fire had cut him off from the truck and he was in full flight, arms driving. I thought I saw him look back, but couldn't be sure.

I was already in a full sprint.

I cut downslope, aiming to catch him on the other side of the vineyard, near the slide of dark water. Loose earth turned under my feet. I stumbled, then ran harder. I wanted to catch him. That's what I told myself, but some deeper part of me knew that if I just ran hard enough, fast enough, then I could escape the truth of my brother's betrayal. For an instant it worked; my mind went blank, then black with pure, sweet anger. Then something caught my foot and I went down in a hard sprawl of limbs and cascading earth. I struck my head on a root, tore skin from my hands. When I found my knees, I needed to vomit and it was not because of the pain. The truth filled me up, the ugly, bitter swell of it in the center of my soul. I'd been wrong all along. It wasn't Zebulon Faith. It was Jamie. My brother. My own damn family.

And I was going to make that right.

No matter what.

I choked down the nausea and pushed myself up. It took a second to find my legs, but gravity was on my side and I hit the bottom of the hill in a dead run. I leapt an irrigation ditch and crashed into the vineyard, heat on my back. I ducked vines and turned onto a long row where light jigged and twisted with nightmare precision. Smoke cooked my throat, but I was sucking hard and couldn't stop. Jamie flashed through a gap twenty feet in front of me. His arms beat at vines in his path. He stumbled once and almost fell. Then he was gone behind the green, and I ran harder, the great roar of consumption behind me.

I flicked a glance left, saw a gap in the rows, and ducked through it. When I came out, Jamie was ten feet in front of me, feet thudding into the earth, giant arms churning. I must have screamed, because his head whipped around, even as I closed the gap and took him down. He was huge and hard as oak. I drove my right shoulder into the small of his back and felt his body whiplash as his knees dug into the ground. Momentum propelled us, and as I came down on his back I drove a forearm into the back of his head and slammed his face into the dirt.

Most men would be stunned, but it didn't faze him. He rolled sideways, over me, came to his feet with a rock in his hand. He raised it, emotion bending his features, then he recognized me, and we faced off beneath the wall of flame. He dropped the rock.

"What the fuck are you doing, Adam?"

But I was in no mood to talk. "Son of a bitch," I said, and

stung him on the hard bone over his eye. His head snapped back.

"Goddamn it, Adam."

"What the hell is wrong with you, Jamie?"

Something moved in his eyes. He started to straighten, and I saw red. He recognized it. "Wait—" he said, but I was already on him, hands lashing out. Quick jabs and crushing blows he couldn't avoid. He was huge, but I was a fighter.

And he knew it.

He backed off, but the third jab opened a cut over his eye, blinded him, and I hammered the ribs. It was like hitting the heavy bag.

I just hit harder.

He was backpedaling, saying something, but I'd moved beyond that. I saw Grace, shattered, felt the heat of this fire that was gutting four years of my father's life. And for what? Because Jamie was a gambler and a coward. A weak-ass son of a bitch that put himself first. Well, fuck that.

The blows ran together. Any other man and he'd be done. But he wasn't. He tucked his head, charged, and this time, I wasn't fast enough. He got those arms around me, bore me down. Our faces were inches apart. Pressure came on my ribs. His voice rose to a scream. My name. He kept yelling my name. Then something else.

"Zebulon Faith!" he yelled. "Damn it, Adam. It was Zebulon Faith! I almost had him!"

I felt like I was coming out of a tunnel. "What did you say?"

"Are you going to hit me?"

"No. We're done."

He rolled off me and climbed to his feet, wiping blood out of his eye. "Faith was heading for the river." He looked off, into the darkness. "But he's gone now. We'll never find him."

"Don't try to confuse me, Jamie. I know about your gambling."

"You don't know what you're talking about."

"You're in the hole for three hundred thousand dollars."

He opened his mouth to argue, then he lowered his head, condemned by the truth of it.

"Did you think that burning the vines would force Dad to sell? Was that the plan?"

His head snapped up. "Of course not. I would never do that. The vineyard was my idea." He pointed at the flames. "Those are my babies burning."

"Don't bullshit me, brother. You lied about your gambling. You sent me on a wild-goose chase to keep me from finding out about it, but I did. Three hundred thousand dollars and Danny was beaten half to death by the same people for a debt one-tenth that size. Who knows what else you're involved in? You're drinking day and night, sullen and unhelpful, all too eager for Dolf to take the fall. For all I know, your name is on that damn petition."

"That's enough, Adam. I told you before, I don't answer to you."

I stepped closer, and had to look up to meet his eyes. "Did you attack Grace?" I asked.

"That's enough," he repeated, angry but shaken.

"We'll see," I said. "We'll find Zebulon Faith and then we'll see."

Jamie threw up his hands. "Find him?" He looked out at the dark. "We'll never find him."

"Yes, we will." I stepped closer. "You and me."

"How?"

I jabbed him in the chest. His eyes opened, wide and yellow-bright. "You'd better be right," I said.

A sallow dawn threatened the dead-end hollow by the time we parked under the shot-up pie plate. Four hours had passed since I sat up, smelling smoke. Then the fire trucks, my father's helpless rage, and the battle to save what remained of the vineyard. They dropped a line into the Yadkin and used its mud-choked water to extinguish the flames. That was the one good thing, the proximity of limitless water. Otherwise, the whole thing would have burned. Everything.

We got out of there before the cops came. I took Jamie by the arm and pulled him into the darkness. Nobody saw us go. Jamie was hard-faced and sullen, his skin the color of ash. Crusted blood made a sharp ridge over his left eye and finger-wide streaks of red smeared his face. We'd barely spoken, but the important words still hung between us, and would do so until this was over.

Until we found Zebulon Faith, and settled things once and for all.

He got in the car when I pointed, opened his mouth when I stopped at Dolf's and came out with the 12-gauge and a box of shells. Once, ten minutes out, he said, "You're wrong about me."

I cut my eyes right, knew my voice was brutal. "We'll see," I said.

Now, knee-deep in bent grass at the end of the civilized world, Jamie looked scared. His hands spread on the top of my car and he watched me crack the barrel and shove in two thick, red shells. "What is this place?" he asked, and I knew what he saw. The gray light was unforgiving, and the road in was a hard, fast slide to the bottom rung of the human experience.

"Just a place," I said.

He looked around. "Ass end of nowhere."

I breathed in the stagnant water smell. "Not everybody was born lucky."

"You preaching at me now?"

"Faith has a trailer just around that bend. If I'm wrong about you, I'll apologize and I'll mean it. Meantime, let's just do this."

He came around the car. "What's the plan?"

I closed the gun with a metallic click. "No plan," I said, and started walking.

He fell in behind me, stiff-legged and clumsy. We came

to the bend, the granite shoulder cold and damp under my
fingers. We couldn't see it yet, but dawn bulged on some far
horizon. Birds trilled from the deep woods, and color rose in
the earth as the cold gray began to die.

I rounded the corner and the low drone of the diesel generator rolled over me. Lights burned in the trailer, weak yellow
and a television flicker. A mud-stained Jeep was parked near
the front door. Jamie stumbled behind me, nodded once, and I
sidled up to the back of the Jeep. Gasoline cans lined the floor
behind the front seats. I pointed with my chin, made sure that
Jamie saw them. He raised his eyebrows as if to say, I told you
so. But I wasn't sold yet. Could be diesel for the generator.

Metal slipped across my hip as I moved. Dried mud crumbled to rubble and fell in the grass. I laid my hand on the hood
and found that it still held some engine heat. Jamie felt it, too.
I nodded and pointed to the front porch. We crossed the last of
the clearing and knelt beneath the windows. Jamie was eager,
and started for the steps. I stopped him, remembering how the
wood had sagged. We had almost five hundred pounds between the two of us, and I did not want the porch to collapse.
"Slowly," I whispered.

I went first, stock of the gun against my hip, twin barrels angled in front of me. A night sweat slicked the steps. The generator put a vibration into the structure, so that it thrummed at a
cellular level. Rust scaled the siding next to my face. From inside came a dull and rhythmic thump that felt wrong. It was too
regular, too hollow.

The door stood open a crack, screen door closed behind
it. Up close, the thumping sound grew louder. I thought that
if I put my hand on the wall, I'd probably feel it. We knelt
beside the door.

I stood, looked in the window.

Zebulon Faith was sprawled across the floor, his back
propped against one of the decomposing chairs. Mud darkened his jeans, shoes in a corner. A burn on his forearm
glowed with cherry heat. His left hand held a near empty

bottle of vodka stuffed with lime wedges. He raised it, wrapped his lips around the neck, and swallowed three huge slugs, choking. Thin tears pushed out from under tight-squeezed lids and he slammed the bottle back down. He opened his mouth and shook his head. The television stained the room with a *Twilight Zone* flicker.

The gun was in his right hand, a black, thick-barreled revolver, probably the same one he'd tried to kill me with at the river. The fingers held it loosely until he shook off the vodka chug and opened his eyes. Then the fingers closed and he started pounding the butt of the pistol against the trailer floor. Up and down, lift and slam, once every five seconds. The thumping sound. Wood and metal on a sagging floor.

The room looked the same. Trash, strewn paper, the overwhelming sense of neglect and decay. Faith fit right in. Vomit stained the front of his shirt.

He stopped pounding the gun on the floor, looked at it, tilted it, then began tapping it against his head. He smoothed it over his cheek, a look of sensual awareness captured in the lines of his open mouth. Then he struck harder, against the temple, strong enough to twist his head sideways. He chugged more vodka and lifted the gun, stared into the muzzle, and then, in a most disturbing manner, reached out a tongue to taste it.

I ducked down.

"He's alone?" Jamie whispered.

"And fucked-up. Stay behind me."

I got my feet under me, clicked the safety off the 12, and went through the door smooth and fast. He didn't even notice. One second I was on the porch and then I was on the vinyl floor of his kitchen, maybe ten feet between us. I had the gun up and he was still oblivious. I watched the revolver. His eyes were wrinkled shut, the television pure snow.

Jamie crowded in behind me. The trailer shifted under his weight and Faith opened his eyes. The gun didn't move. I stepped forward and to the side, squaring up my line of fire.

He smiled the most hateful smile I'd ever seen, like I didn't know a smile could be. The hate filled him up, then drained away. In its place rose a deep, liquid hopelessness like I'd seen only once before.

And the gun began to rise.

"Don't," I said.

He hesitated, took a last mighty suck on the vodka bottle. Then his eyes glazed as if he was already gone. I leaned into the stock, finger so tight on the trigger I felt it creak.

But deep down, I knew.

The gun came up, straight and smooth and unstoppable. The hard round mouth settled against the bellow of flesh beneath the old man's chin.

"Don't," I said again, but not very loudly.

He pulled the trigger.

Painted the ceiling with red mist.

Sound crashed through the tight space, and Jamie staggered back, collapsed into a kitchen chair. He was in shock, mouth open, eyes wide and dilated. "Why'd you wait?" he finally asked, voice uneven. "He could have shot us."

I propped the shotgun against the wall, looked down on the crumpled ruin of a man I'd known for most of my life. "No," I said. "He couldn't have."

Jamie stared. "I've never seen so much blood."

I took my eyes off Faith, looked hard at my brother.

"I have," I said, and walked outside.

When Jamie came out, he held onto the loose rail like he might bend over it and hurl. "You didn't touch anything?" I asked.

"Hell, no."

I waited until he looked at me. "Faith had soot all over him, a nasty burn on his arm. The whole room stank of gasoline." Jamie saw where I was going. I put a hand on his shoulder. "I owe you an apology," I said.

He waved a hand, but did not speak.

"I'm serious, Jamie. I'm sorry. I was wrong."

"The gambling is my problem," he said. "Not anybody else's. I'm not proud of it, and I have no idea what I'm going to do about it, but I would never do anything to hurt Dad or Grace or anybody else." He paused. "It's my problem. I'll fix it."

"I'll help you," I said.

"You don't have to."

"You're my brother and I owe you. But right now we've got to figure out what to do."

"Do? We get the hell out of here. That's what we do. He's just a crazy old drunk that killed himself. Nobody's even got to know we were here."

I shook my head. "No good. I was here yesterday, asking questions. Prints in the house, probably. And even though the windows we passed on the way in were dark, I guarantee we didn't come this far in unseen. This place knows a stranger. We'll have to call it in."

"Damn, Adam. How's that going to look? The two of us here at the crack of dawn. In his house with a 12-gauge."

I allowed myself a small smile. "Nobody has to know about the 12." I stepped into the trailer and retrieved the gun. "Why don't you go lock this in the trunk? I'm going to look around."

"Trunk. Good idea."

I caught him by the arm. "We had our suspicions about the fire. We came out here to ask a few friendly questions. We knocked on the door and walked in just as he killed himself. Nothing different from what happened. Just no gun."

I went back inside and studied the scene. The old man was on his side, the top of his head opened up. I crossed the last few feet, careful of where I stepped. His face was largely clean of blood. Except for a slight lengthening, it looked the same.

I left the TV on. Vodka soaked into the ratty carpet. The newspaper was on the floor beside him: a picture of his son on page one.

The story of his murder.

Jamie came back into the trailer. "Check the other rooms," I said.

It did not take him long. "Nothing," he said. "Just a bunch of junk."

I pointed at the paper, saw the photograph register on Jamie's face. "He's been holed up here for days. I'm guessing he got the paper tonight."

Jamie stood over the body. "I don't see him doing this over Danny. He was a shitty father. Selfish. Self-absorbed."

I shrugged, took another look at the body, thinking of Grace. I expected to feel something. Satisfaction. Relief. But standing over a broken old man in a dump trailer at the shit end of the universe, what I felt was empty. None of it should have happened.

"Let's get out of here," Jamie said.

"In a minute."

There was a message here somewhere, something about life and the living of it. I bent to take one last look at the face of a man I'd known since I was a kid. He died twisted and bitter. I felt something turn in my chest, and looked deep, but there was no forgiveness in me. Jamie was right. He was a shitty father, a bad man, and I doubted that he would have killed himself over the murder of his only son. There had to be more.

I found it in his left hand.

It was squeezed into his palm, a wad of newsprint, crumpled and damp. He'd been holding it between his hand and the vodka bottle. I pulled it from spread fingers and twisted it toward the light.

"What is it?"

I met Jamie's eyes. "A notice of foreclosure."

"Huh?"

"It's for the land he bought on the river." I riffled through the newspaper on the floor, found where he'd ripped it out. I checked the date, then balled the scrap back up, and replaced it in his hand. "Looks like his gamble didn't pay off."

"What do you mean?"

I took a last look at the crumpled husk of Zebulon Faith. "He just lost everything."

# Twenty-nine

We spent the next six hours slapping bugs and talking to stone-eyed men. Local cops responded first, then Grantham and Robin, in separate cars. They had no jurisdiction, but the locals let them stay when they learned about all the reasons they had an interest: murder, assault, arson, methamphetamines. That was real crime, hard-core stuff. But they would not let them talk to us. The locals had a body, here, now; so, the locals came first, and Grantham didn't like it. He argued and he threatened, but it was not his jurisdiction. I felt his rage from across the clearing. This was the second body I'd called in. First the son, now the father. Grantham sensed something big, and he wanted me.

He wanted me now.

He cornered the lead investigator on three different occasions. He raised his voice and made violent arm movements. He threatened to make calls. Once, when it looked like the locals might back off, Robin intervened. I could not hear what was said, but Grantham's color deepened, and when he spoke to her, there was little movement in him. The obvious frustration had been tamped down, contained, but I could feel the tension, the resentment, and his gaze was sharp on her back as she walked away.

The locals asked their questions and I gave my answers. We knocked. We opened the door. Bang. End of story.

Simple.

Drug enforcement rolled up just before noon. They looked sharp in matching jackets and would have been there sooner, but they got lost. Robin could hide neither her contempt nor her amusement. Nor could she hide her feelings toward me. She was angry, too. I saw it in her eyes, the line of her mouth, her stance. Everywhere. But it was a different kind of emotion, more personal, laced with hurt. As far as she was concerned, I'd crossed a line, and it had nothing to do with the law or the things I did. This was about the things I did *not* do. I did not call her. Did not trust her. And again, I had to face the dangers of that two-way street.

She'd made her choice. Now she had to wonder about mine.

So I watched Grantham stew as the sun rose higher and the locals ran the investigation as they saw fit. Cops moved in and out of the trailer. The medical examiner made his appearance, and the morning faded into heat and damp. They carried Zebulon Faith out in a dull, black body bag. I watched the long car disappear, and the day stretched on. None of the people who lived on the loop showed themselves. No bystanders. No flipped curtains. They kept their heads down and hid like squatters. I couldn't blame them. Cops did not do community outreach in places like this. When they showed up, it was for a reason, and none of them were good.

The hard questions came in due course, and they came from Grantham. The rage in him had died to a colorless implacability, and he was pure professional by the time the locals gave him the nod to talk to us. I watched him approach, and knew what was coming. He'd separate us and hammer for weak spots. Zebulon Faith was dead. So was his son. I had a history with each of them and had been the first on scene with both bodies. He doubted Dolf's confession, and was ready to tear into me with a saw. But he'd be cagey. I knew something about cops and cop questions, so he'd try to be subtle. I was sure of it.

But he surprised me.

He walked straight up to me and spoke before he stopped. "I want to see what's in your trunk," he said.

Jamie twitched and Grantham saw it. "Why?" I asked.

"You've been sitting on it for six hours. In the sun. Un-moving. Your brother has looked at it nine times in the past hour. I'd like to see what's inside."

I studied the detective. He'd put on a bold air, but it was all bluff. I'd watched him, too. In six hours he'd made at least a dozen calls. If he could have secured a search warrant for the trunk, he'd have it in hand right now.

"I don't think so," I said.

"Don't make me ask again."

"That's really the word, isn't it? *Ask*. As in permission." His features compressed, and I continued. "You need per-mission or probable cause. If you had cause, you'd have a warrant. I won't give you permission."

I remained calm as his composure slipped. I watched him fight for the kind of control he normally took for granted. Robin hovered at a distance. I risked a glance and saw a warn-ing in her eyes. Grantham stepped closer, and when he spoke, the words came in a low, dangerous voice. "People are lying to me, Mr. Chase. You. Mr. Shepherd. Others, undoubtedly. I don't like it and I'm going to get to the bottom of it."

I stood and looked down on the detective. "Do you have questions for me?"

"You know that I do."

"Then ask them."

He straightened, and fought to regain his composure. It did not take long. He separated us and started with Jamie. He led him across the clearing, and I watched, guessing that Jamie was made of sterner stuff than Grantham anticipated. It took a while. Jamie looked scared, but in control of him-self. He'd tell it just like it happened, only no gun. The detective was pale and grim when he came back for me. His questions came fast and hard. He scoured for weak spots in the story. Why were we here? How did we find this place? What happened? What did we touch?

"You didn't touch the body?"

"Just the paper in his hand. The newspaper next to him."

"Did you touch the handgun?"

"No."

"Did Mr. Faith tell you to come inside?"

"The door was open. The screen door was cracked. I nudged it, saw him with the gun against his head."

"There was a fire. You thought Faith set it. Why did you think that?"

I told him.

"And you were angry?"

"I was upset. Yes."

"Did you come here to harm Mr. Faith?"

"I came to ask a few questions."

"Did he say anything?"

"No."

He continued, firing questions with speed, backtracking, probing for inconsistencies. Jamie paced thirty feet away and gnawed at his fingernails. I sat on the warm metal of my car's trunk. I looked occasionally at narrow blue sky, and I told the truth about almost everything. Grantham's frustration grew, but no law barred us from coming here as we did, and we crossed no line when Faith pulled the trigger. None, at least, that Grantham could find. So I took what he had to give. I answered his questions and I covered my ass. I thought I saw the end, but I was wrong.

He saved the best for last.

"You quit your job three weeks ago."

It was not a question. He stared so hard at my face, that I could almost feel the touch of his eyes. He waited for me to speak, but I had no response. I knew where he would go.

"You worked at McClellan's Gym on Front Street in

Brooklyn. N.Y.P.D. checked it out. I talked to the manager myself. He says you were dependable, good with the young fight-
ers. Everybody liked you. But three weeks ago you dropped off
the radar. Right about the time that Danny Faith called you. In
fact, nobody saw much of you after that. Not your neighbors.
Not your landlord. I know that Dolf Shepherd is lying to me. I
assumed that was to protect your father. Now, I'm not so sure."
He paused, refused to blink. "Maybe he's protecting you."

"Is that a question?"

"Where were you three weeks ago?"

"I was in New York."

His chin dipped. "You sure about that?"

I stared at him, knowing what was already in motion.
They'd pull my credit card records, A.T.M. records, check
for traffic citations. Anything that could put me in North
Carolina three weeks ago.

"You're wasting your time," I said.

"We'll see."

"Am I under arrest?"

"Not yet."

"Then we're done."

I turned and walked away, half-expecting to feel his hand
on my shoulder. Jamie looked shot. I put a hand on his arm.
"Let's get out of here," I said.

We went back to my car. Grantham had moved from the
trunk to the hood. One of his fingers brushed the word carved
into the paint. *Killer,* it said, and Grantham smiled when he
saw me looking at him. He rubbed his fingers together, then
turned back to the trailer and the bloodstained floor.

Robin approached, expressionless, as I opened the car
door. "You going back to town?" she asked.

"Yes."

"I'll follow you."

I closed the door, and Jamie got in next to me. The engine
turned over and I drove us out of there. "Any trouble?" I asked.

He shook his head. "I kept waiting for them to search the car."

"He couldn't. Not without permission or probable cause."

"But what if he had?"

I smiled tightly. "No law against having a gun in the trunk."

"Still . . . small miracles, man."

I looked at him. He was clearly upset. "I'm sorry I doubted you, Jamie."

He flexed, but his voice was weak. "Guns, baby."

He fooled nobody.

We drove for ten minutes, both of us dealing with the morning in our own way. When he spoke, he didn't sound any better. "That was scary stuff," he said.

"What part?"

"All of it."

He was pale, glassy-eyed, and I knew that he was reliving another human being's last second in this world. Violence and hate. Hopelessness and red mist. He needed something.

"Hey, Jamie," I said. "About the fire and all. What happened in the field . . ." I held out until he looked at me, waited for the eyes to focus. "I'm sorry I had to kick your ass like that. That was probably the scariest part, huh?"

It took him a moment, then the tension bled out of his face, and I thought he might actually smile. "Fuck you," he said, and punched me on the arm so hard it hurt.

The rest of the drive was gravy.

Almost.

Robin hit the lights seconds after we crossed the city limits. I wasn't surprised. Her turf. Made sense. I pulled into a convenience store parking lot and killed the engine. It was going to get ugly and I didn't blame her. We met on the tarmac by the front of her car. She was a small package of hard lines and displeasure. She kept her hands down until she was close enough, then she slapped me, hard.

I rolled with it, and she did it again. I could have dodged the second one, but did not. Her face was full of fierce anger and the hint of tears. She opened her mouth to speak, but was too keyed up. She walked away and stopped, her body leaning away from me. When she turned, the emotion was back under armored glass. I saw hints of it, dark swirls, but her voice was immaculate. "I thought we'd settled this. You and me. A team. I made the choice. We talked about that." She came closer and I saw where anger faded to hurt. "What were you thinking, Adam?"

"I was trying to protect you, Robin. I didn't know how it would go down and I didn't want you involved."

"Don't," she said.

"Anything could have happened."

"Do not insult me, Adam. And do not think for a minute that Grantham is an idiot, either. No one believes you were out there for a friendly chat." She lowered her hands. "They'll take a hard look. If they find anything to incriminate you, then God himself won't be able to help you."

"He torched the farm," I said. "He attacked Grace, tried to kill me."

"Did he kill his own son?" The words came, cold. "There are other elements in play. Things we don't understand."

I refused to back down. "I'll take what I can get."

"It's not that easy."

"He deserved it!" I yelled, stunned by the force of my reaction. "That bastard deserved to die for what he did. That he did it himself makes the justice that much more perfect."

"Damn it!" She paced, turned back, and I saw black mist where the armored glass had buckled. "What gives you the right to claim anger like you're the only one that's ever been hurt? What's so special about you, Adam? You've lived your whole life this way, like the rules don't apply to you. You cherish the anger like it *makes* you special. Well, let me tell you something—"

"Robin—"

She raised a fist between us. Her face was drawn tight. "Everybody suffers."

That was it. She left in disgust, left me with nothing but the anger she held in such contempt. Jamie looked a question at me when I got back in the car. I felt heat on my face, the hard twist in my stomach. "Nothing," I said, and took him home. We sat in the car for a long minute. He was in no hurry to get out.

"We okay?" he asked. "You and me?"

"I was wrong. You tell me."

He did not look at me. Color, I saw, had returned to his face. When he turned, he held up a fist, kept it there until I tapped my knuckles on his. "Solid," he said, and got out of the car.

When I got to Dolf's house, I found it empty. Grace was gone. No note. I took a shower, sluiced off dirt, sweat, and the smell of fire. When I got out, I pulled on clean jeans and a T-shirt. There were a million things to do, but not one that was in my power. I pulled two beers out of the refrigerator and took the phone onto the porch. The first beer disappeared in about a minute. Then I called my father's house. Miriam answered.

"He's not here," she said when I asked for my father.

"Where is he?"

"Out with Grace."

"Doing what?"

"Looking for dogs." Her voice was bleak. "It's what he does when he feels helpless."

"And Grace is with him?"

"She's good with a gun. You know that."

"Tell him that I'd like to see him when he gets back." Silence. "Miriam?" I asked.

"I'll tell him."

The day moved around me. I watched the light stretch long and the low places fill. Two hours. Five beers.

Nothing to do.

Mind on overdrive.

I heard the truck before I saw it. Grace was driving. They were both in high color, not smiling exactly, but refreshed, as if they'd managed to dodge the worst parts for a few hours. They climbed onto the porch and the sight of me killed the light in them. Reality check.

"Any luck?" I asked.

"Nope." He sat next to me.

"Do you want dinner?" Grace asked.

"Sure," I said.

"How about you?"

My father shook his head. "Janice is cooking." He raised his palms. I would not be invited.

Grace looked at me. "I need to go to the store. Take your car?"

"You lost your license," my father said.

"I won't get caught."

I looked at my father, who shrugged. I gave her the keys. As soon as the car engine started, my father turned. His question cut. "Did you kill Zebulon Faith?"

"Robin called you."

"She thought I should know. Did you kill him?"

"No," I said. "He did it himself, just like I told the cops."

The old man rocked in the chair. "He's the one that burned my vines?"

"Yes," I said.

"All right."

"Just like that?" I asked.

"I never liked him anyway."

"Grantham thinks Dolf's confession is bullshit."

"It is."

"He thinks that Dolf is protecting someone. Maybe you."

My father faced me. He spoke slowly. "Grantham's a cop. Thinking up paranoid, bullshit theories is what he does."

I rose from the chair and leaned against the rail. I wanted to see his face. "Does he have a reason to?"

"To what?"

"Protect you."

"What the hell kind of question is that?"

My father was rough-and-tumble, salt of the earth, but he was also the most honest man I'd ever known. If he lied to me now, I'd know it. "Do you have any reason to want Danny Faith dead?"

The moment drew out. "That's an absurd question, son."

He was angry and offended—I knew how it felt—so I let the question go. I'd said it before. My father was no killer. I had to believe that. If not, then I was no better than him. I sat back down, but the tension grew. The question still hung between us. My father made a disgusted sound and went inside for five long minutes. When he finally came out, he had two more beers. He handed one to me. He spoke as if the question had never happened. "They're going to bury Danny tomorrow," he said.

"Who made the arrangements?" I asked.

"Some aunt from Charlotte. The service is at noon. Graveside."

"Did you know that he was in love with Grace?" I asked.

"I think we should go."

"Did you know?" I repeated, louder.

My father stood and walked to the rail. He showed me his back. "She's too good for him. She was always too good for him." He turned, lifted an eyebrow. "You're not interested in her, are you?"

"Not like that," I said.

He nodded. "She has precious little in this world. Losing Dolf will kill her."

"She's tough."

"She's coming apart."

He was right, but neither one of us knew what to do about it, so we watched the shadows pool and waited for the sun to detonate behind the trees. It occurred to me that he had not answered my second question, either.

When the phone rang, I answered. "He's here," I said, and handed it to my father. "Miriam."

He took the phone and listened. His mouth firmed into an uncompromising line. "Thanks," he said. "No. Nothing you can do for me." More listening. "Jesus, Miriam. Like what? There's nothing you can do for me. Nothing anyone can do. Yes. Okay. Goodbye."

He handed me the phone, drained his beer. "Parks called," he said.

I waited.

"They indicted Dolf today."

# *Thirty*

D inner was painful. I fought for words that meant something while Grace tried to pretend that the indictment didn't cut the world out from under her. We ate in silence because we could not discuss the next step, the rule twenty-four hearing. Arguments would be made and it would be decided. Life or death. Literally. The night pressed down and we could not get drunk enough, forgetful enough. I told her to not give up hope, and she walked outside for most of an hour. When we went to bed, a blackness hung over the house, and hope, I knew, had abandoned us.

I lay in the guest room and put my hand on the wall. Grace was awake. I thought that Dolf probably was, too. My father. Robin. I wondered, just then, if anybody slept. How anyone possibly could. Sleep did eventually come, but it was a restless one. I woke at two o'clock and again at four. I remembered no dreams, but woke each time to churning thoughts and a sense of mounting dread. At five o'clock, I rose, head pounding, no chance of sleep. I dressed and slipped outside. It was dark, but I knew the paths and fields. I walked until the sun came up. I looked for answers, and failing that, I scrounged for hope. If something did not break soon, I would be forced onto another path. I would have to find some way to convince Dolf to recant his confession. I would need to meet with the lawyers. We'd have to start planning some kind of defense.

I did not want to go through something like that again.

As I crossed the last field, I planned my assault on the day. Candy's brothers were still out there and somebody needed to talk to them. I'd try to see Dolf again. Maybe they'd let me in. Maybe he'd come to his senses. I did not have names for the bookmakers in Charlotte, but I had an address and descriptions. I could identify the two who had attacked Danny four months earlier. Maybe Robin could talk to somebody at Charlotte P.D. I needed to talk to Jamie. Check on Grace.

The funeral was at noon.

The house was empty when I returned. No note. The phone rang as I was about to leave. It was Margaret Yates, Sarah's mother.

"I called your father's house," she explained. "A young woman told me I might find you at this number. I hope you don't mind."

I pictured the old lady in her grand mansion: the withered skin and small hands, the hate-filled words she pushed out with such conviction. "I don't mind," I said. "What can I do for you?"

She spoke smoothly, but I sensed great hesitation. "Did you find my daughter?" she asked.

"I did."

"I wondered if I could prevail upon you to come see me today. I know it's an unusual request. . . ."

"May I ask why?"

Her breath was heavy over the line. Something clattered in the background. "I didn't sleep last night. I haven't slept since you came to my house."

"I don't understand."

"I tried to stop thinking about her, but then I saw your picture in the paper; and I asked myself if you'd seen her. What you'd talked about." She paused. "I asked myself what might be good in the life of my only daughter."

"Ma'am—"

"I believe that you were sent to me, Mr. Chase. I believe that you are a sign from God." I hesitated. "Please, don't make me beg."

"What time did you have in mind?"

"Now would be ideal."

"I'm very tired, Mrs. Yates, and I have a great many things to do."

"I'll put on coffee."

I looked at my watch. "I can give you five minutes," I said. "Then I'll really have to go."

The house was as I'd last seen it, a great white jewel on a bed of green velvet. I paused on the porch, and the tall doors split as the right side swung open. Mrs. Yates stood in the dim space, bent at the neck, somber in crisp gray flannel and a lace collar. The smell of dried orange peels wafted out, and I wondered if anything ever changed in this place. She held out a hand that felt dry and hollow-boned. "Thank you so much for coming," she said. "Please." She stepped aside and swept an arm toward the dim interior. I walked past her and the door settled into its frame.

"I can offer you cream and sugar for your coffee, or something harder if you prefer. I'm having sherry."

"Just coffee, please. Black."

I followed her down a wide hall full of somber art and fine-grained furnishings. Heavy drapes defended the interior from excessive sunlight, but ornate lamps burned in every room. Through open doors, I saw leather that gleamed and further hints of subdued color. A grandfather clock ticked somewhere in the vastness.

"You have a lovely home," I said.

"Yes," she agreed.

In the kitchen, she lifted a tray and carried it into a small sitting room. "Sit," she said, and poured coffee from a silver service. I sat on a narrow chair with hard arms. The china cup felt as light as spun sugar.

"You think me cold," she said without preamble. "In the matter of my daughter, you think me cold."

I lowered the cup to its saucer. "I know something of family dysfunction."

"I was rather harsh when last we spoke of her. I would hate for you to think me either senile or without heart."

"It can get complicated. I would not presume to judge."

She sipped her sherry, and the crystal stemware made a sound like bells as she set it on the silver tray. "I'm not a zealot, Mr. Chase. I do not condemn my daughter because she worships the trees and the dirt and God knows what else. I would be heartless, indeed, to cast out my only child for reasons as intangible as mere differences of faith."

"Then, may I ask why?"

"You may not!"

I leaned back, laced my fingers. "With all due respect, Mrs. Yates, you broached the subject."

Her smile was tight. "You're right, of course. The mind wanders and the mouth, it seems, is more than willing to follow."

She trailed off, looked suddenly uncertain. I leaned forward so that our faces were close. "Ma'am, what is it that you want to discuss with me?"

"You found her?"

"I did."

She lowered her gaze and I saw powder blue lines in the paper-thin eyelids. Her lips pursed, thin and bloodless under lipstick the color of a December sunset.

"It's been twenty years," she said. "Two decades since last I saw or spoke to my daughter." She lifted the sherry and drank, then lay a light hand on my wrist. Her eyes widened as her voice cracked. "How is she?"

I leaned away from the desperation in her face, the quiet, weak hunger. She was an old woman, alone, and after two decades, the wall of anger had finally crumbled. She missed her daughter. I understood. And so I told her what I could.

She sat perfectly still and absorbed everything I said. I sugarcoated nothing. By the end, her eyes were down. A large diamond spun loosely on her finger as she twisted the ring.

"I was in my mid-thirties when I had her. She was . . . unplanned." She looked up. "She was more child than woman the last time I saw her. Half her life ago."

I was confused. "How old is your daughter?" I asked.

"Forty-one."

"I assumed that she was much older."

Mrs. Yates frowned. "It's the hair," she said, gesturing at her own hair, thin and white and lacquered. "An unfortunate family trait. Mine turned white in my early twenties. Sarah was even younger."

She levered herself out of the chair and crossed the room on stiff ankles. From a shelf beside the fireplace, she took down a photograph in a polished, silver frame. A smile bent the lines in her face as she stared at it. One finger trembled on the glass as she traced something I could not see. She came back to her seat and handed me the photograph. "That's the last one I ever took of her. She was nineteen."

I studied the picture: the animal grin and stark green eyes, the blond hair shot with white. She rode bareback on a horse the color of a northern sea. Fingers twisted into the mane. One hand lay flat on the animal's neck as she leaned forward as if to whisper in its ear.

I felt a momentary disconnect, as if the words that came were not my own. "Mrs. Yates, earlier, I asked about the reasons that you and your daughter stopped speaking."

"Yes." Hesitant.

"I'd like to ask you again." She balked, and I glanced again at the photo. "Please," I said.

She folded her hands in her lap. "I try not to think of it."

"Mrs. Yates . . . ?"

She nodded. "Perhaps it will help," she said, but a minute passed before she spoke again. "We fought," she finally said. "That may seem normal to you, but we did not fight as most mothers and daughters would. She knew how to hurt me at an early age, knew where to put the knife and how to twist it. In honesty, I suppose I hurt her, too, but she refused to obey the rules. And they were good rules," she said quickly. "Fair rules. Necessary ones." She shook her head. "I knew she was destined for great failure. I just didn't think that it would find her so young."

"What failure?"

"She was already confused. Running all over the county like some kind of druid. Arguing with me about the meaning of God. Smoking pot and God knows what else. I swear to you, it was enough to make a mother weep for a daughter's soul."

She refilled her sherry, drank a large swallow. "She was twenty-one when the baby came. Unmarried and unrepentant. Lived in a tent in the woods. With my grandbaby!" She shook her head. "I wouldn't have it. Couldn't have it." She paused, gazing inward. "I did what I had to do."

I waited, knowing more or less how the story would end.

She sat up straighter. "I talked to her, of course. I tried to make her see the error of her ways. I invited her back into my home, told her I would help her raise the child properly. But she wouldn't listen. Said she was going to build a cabin, but she was deluding herself. She had no money, no resources." The old lady sipped sherry and sniffed. "I got the authorities involved . . ."

The words trailed off. I was about to prompt her when she spoke, loudly. "She ran away. With my grandbaby. California, I heard, on a quest for like-minded people. Freaks, if you ask me. Witches and pagans and drug abusers." She nodded. "Well, let me tell you"—she nodded again, repeated herself—"let me tell you . . ."

"California?"

She finished the sherry. "She was high when she went off the road. High on pot with the baby in the car. Sarah never walked again. And I never saw the child, either. My grandchild died in California, Mr. Chase. My daughter came back a cripple. I never forgave her and we've not spoken since."

She stood abruptly, swiping at her eyes. "Now, how about something to eat?"

She rustled her way into the kitchen, where she stood with her hands pressed flat on polished granite, head bowed. She did not move. She did not open her eyes. Food, I knew, would not be prepared.

I stood and placed the photograph back on the shelf. I tilted it to catch what light there was.

It was all there.

So clear to me now.

I lay a finger on the glass, traced the line of her bright smile, and understood, finally, why she seemed so familiar to me.

She looked just like Grace.

I cut into the trees from a bright, empty stretch of road, passed by Ken Miller's bus without slowing down. When I pulled to a stop in front of Sarah Yates's cabin, a cloud of red dust hung in the air behind my car. I crossed the porch in two strides, and my hand was loud on the door. No answer. But the van was here, canoe at the dock. I pounded again and heard a noise inside, a low muffle that swelled into footsteps.

Ken Miller opened the door.

He wore a towel around his waist. Sweat matted the hair on his chest. A hot flush infused his face. "What the hell do you want?" he asked.

Beyond him, shadows filled the main room. The bedroom door stood ajar.

"I'd like to speak with Sarah," I said.

"She's indisposed."

Then, from within, Sarah's voice. "Who is it, Ken?"

He yelled over his shoulder. "It's Adam Chase, all hot and bothered about something!"

"Ask him to wait a minute, then come and help me."

"Sarah . . ." He was displeased.

"Don't make me repeat myself," Sarah said.

When Ken looked back at me, there was murder in his eyes. "I am so tired of you," he said, then pointed at the row of chairs on the porch. "Wait over there." Five minutes later, the door opened again. Ken pushed past me without looking up. His jeans were unbuttoned, shoes untied. He walked off without once looking back. A few moments later, Sarah rolled her chair onto the porch.

Her words came as a matter of course. "No man likes being interrupted in flagrante delicto." She wore a flannel robe and slippers. The back of her hair was still wet with sweat. "That's the nature of the beast."

She rolled to a stop and set the brake on her chair.

"You and Ken . . . ?" I said.

She shrugged. "When it suits."

I searched her face, looking for hints of Grace, and wondering how I'd ever missed it. They had the same heart-shaped face, same mouth. The eyes were a different color, but had the same shape. Sarah was older, her face more full, the white hair . . .

"Well, spit it out," she said. "You're here for a reason."

"I saw your mother again today."

"Good for you."

"She showed me a picture of you when you were young."

"So?"

"You looked just like Grace Shepherd. You still do in a lot of ways."

"Ah." She said nothing else.

"What does that mean?"

"I've been waiting twenty years for someone to notice that. You're the first one. I guess it's no surprise. I don't see many people."

"You're her mother."

"I've not been her mother for twenty years."

"Your child did not die in California, then?"

She turned sharp eyes on me. "You covered some ground with my mother, didn't you?"

"She misses you."

Sarah waved a loose hand. "Bullshit. She misses her youth, misses the things she's lost. I'm no more than a symbol of all that."

"But Grace is her granddaughter?"

Her voice rose. "I would never allow her to raise a child of mine! I know what that road looks like: narrow and sharp and unforgiving."

"So you lied about the accident?"

She rubbed her lifeless legs. "That was no lie. But my daughter survived."

"And you gave her up?"

The smile was cold, eyes like green stone. "I'm no mother. I thought that maybe I could be, but that was just self-deception." She looked away. "I was unqualified in every way."

"Who's the father?"

She sighed. "A man. Tall and fine and proud, but just a man."

"Dolf Shepherd," I said.

She looked frightened. "Why would you believe that?"

"You gave him the child to raise. In the note you gave me, you wrote of good people who love him. Of good people who will remember."

Her face hardened.

"There's no other reason you would do that."

"You know nothing," she said.

"It fits."

She measured me, debating her words. When she spoke, it was with determined finality. Like she'd made some brutal decision.

"I should have never spoken to you," she said.

* * *

They buried Danny Faith under a featureless, steel sky. We settled into folding chairs that could have been formed from the same metal. Heat percolated through everything so that clothing grew damp and flowers drooped. Women I'd never seen moved crenellated fans before faces done up in hard-won perfection. The funeral was planned and paid for by an aunt of Danny's whom I'd never met. I picked her out easily enough—she had the same red hair—and I pegged the rest of the women as her friends. They'd come in old cars with smallish men, and their diamonds struggled for luster in the empty light.

His aunt looked pained, but I watched her in silent admiration. The coffin cost more than her car. Her friends had traveled far to be with her.

A good woman, I thought.

We sat for a while in near perfect silence, waiting for the appointed time and the words that would follow Danny into the ground. I saw Grantham at the same time that his eyes found me. He stood at a distance in a dark, buttoned coat. He watched the gathering, studied faces, and I tried to ignore him. He was doing his job—nothing personal—but I saw that my father was watching him, too.

The preacher was the same who'd buried my mother, and the years had been cruel to him. Sadness spilled from his eyes. His face stretched, long and careworn. Yet his words still had the power to comfort. Heads moved in accord. A woman crossed herself.

For me, the irony was hard. I found Danny in one hole so he could be put into another. But I nodded at times, and the prayers rolled off my lips, too. He'd been my friend and I'd failed him. So, I prayed for his soul.

And I prayed for mine.

I watched Grace as the preacher finished his talk of salvation and eternal love. Her face showed nothing, but she had eyes as blue as Dolf's. She held herself rigidly and clasped a small purse against her black dress. It was obvious why Danny loved her, why anyone would. Even here, at this place, eyes seemed to find her. Even the women paid attention.

When the preacher finished, he gestured to Danny's aunt, who moved slowly to the graveside and laid a white flower on the coffin. Then she turned and began making her way down the row of seats. She took hands, said thankful words to my father, to Janice, and to Miriam. Her face softened when she stopped before Grace. She took one of her hands in both of hers, and paused, so that everyone recognized the moment.

In that space of time, she beamed. "I understand that he loved you very much." She let Grace's hand fall, and tears slipped down the withered planes of her face. "You would have made a beautiful couple."

Then she sobbed and walked away, a bent figure under a stained metal sky.

Her friends followed, climbed into the old cars with their silent husbands. My family left, as well, but I lingered for some reason. No, I told myself. That was a lie.

I knew the reason, and I fooled no one. Not my father. Not the preacher.

No one.

I sat on the small metal chair until all were gone but the gravediggers, who lingered at a respectful distance. I regarded them as I stood: rough men in hard-worn clothes. They would wait as long as it took. They were used to it, got paid for it. Then, when all had left, they would lower Danny into the earth.

I looked for Grantham, but he was gone. I laid a hand on my friend's coffin, felt the smooth perfection, then turned down the long slope that led, in the end, to the stone that bore my mother's name. I knelt in the grass and listened to the distant sound of Danny's descent. I bowed my head and said one last prayer. I stayed there for a long time, reliving what memories I had. I often came back to that day under the dock, when slanting light set her eyes on fire. She'd said that there was such magic in the world, but she was wrong. Most of it died with her.

When, finally, I stood, I saw the preacher.

"I'm sorry to disturb you," he said.

"Hello, Father. You're not disturbing me." I gestured toward Danny's grave. "You gave a nice service."

He moved to stand beside me, stared at my mother's stone. "I still think of her, you know. Such a shame. So young. So full of life . . ."

I knew where his mind had gone. *So full of life until she'd taken her own.* The peace I'd felt vanished. In its place rose the familiar anger. Where was this man, I asked myself, this preacher? Where was he when the darkness consumed her?

"Those are just words, Father." He saw the emotion in me. "Words count for nothing."

"There's no one to blame, Adam. Other than memories, words are all we have. I did not mean to upset you."

His regret rolled off of me, and looking at the lush grass that covered my mother, I felt an emptiness like I had never known. Even the anger was gone.

"There's nothing you can do for me, Father."

He clasped his hands in front of the vestment he wore. "A loss like this can do untold damage to troubled souls. You should look to the family you still have. You can be of comfort to each other."

"That's good advice." I turned to leave.

"Adam." I stopped. His eyes held a troubled look. "Believe it or not, I normally stay out of other people's affairs, unless, of course, I'm asked. So, I'm hesitant to intrude. But I am confused about something. May I ask a question?"

"Of course."

"Am I right to understand that Danny was in love with Grace?"

"That's right. He was."

He shook his head, and the look of troubled perplexity deepened. Melancholy came off him in waves.

"Father?"

He gestured toward the distant church. "After the service, I found Miriam kneeling at the altar, crying. Weeping, actually." He shook his head again. "She was barely coherent. She damned God, right there in front of me. I'm worried. I still don't understand."

"Don't understand what?"

"She was crying for Danny." He unclasped his fingers, spread his palms like wings. "She said they were going to be married."

# *Thirty-one*

I pictured the scene as I started the car. Miriam in her sweeping black dress, her face full of hate and secret hurt. I saw her crumpled beneath the shining cross, hands clenched as she damned God in his own house and shunned the help of an honest priest. I thought I understood, saw the ugly bits of it. It was Grace, in perfect stillness, head tilted skyward as Danny's aunt said, *I understand that he loved you very much.* And it was Miriam's face beyond her, the sudden slackness, the dark glass that covered her eyes as those words rolled over Danny's coffin and mournful strangers tipped their heads in silent condolence for a great love lost.

She'd told the preacher that she and Danny were going to be married. She'd said the same to me, but about Gray Wilson.

*He was going to marry me.*

Danny Faith. Gray Wilson.

Both were dead.

Everything took new meaning; and while nothing was certain, a sense of dread overtook me. I thought of the last thing the preacher had told me, the last words Miriam had said before she fled the church and its minister.

*There is no God.*

Who would say something like that to a man of faith? She was gone. Lost.

And I'd been so willing to *not* see it.

I tried to call Grace, but got no answer. When I called my father's house, Janice told me he was out after dogs again. No, she said. Miriam was not there. Grace either.

"Did you know that she was in love with Danny?" I asked.

"Who?"

"Miriam."

"Don't be absurd."

I hung up the phone.

She knew nothing, not a damn thing, and I drove faster, accelerated until the car felt light beneath me. I could still be wrong.

*Please, God, let me be wrong.*

I turned onto the farm. Grace would be there. Outside, maybe, but she'd be there. I crossed the cattle guard and stopped the car. My heart hammered against my ribs, but I did not get out. The dog on the porch had tall triangular ears and a filthy black coat. He lifted his head and stared at me. Blood soaked his muzzle. Teeth glinted red.

Two more dogs came around the corner of the house, one black, the other brown. Burrs and hitchhikers infested their matted coats, snot ringed their nostrils, and one had shit caked in the long fur on his back legs. They loped along the wall, kept their snouts down, but teeth showed at the sides. One lifted his head and panted in my direction, pink tongue out, eyes as eager and quick as darting birds.

I looked back to the dog on the porch. Big. Black as hell. Bloody rivulets dripped from the top step. No movement in the house, door closed fast. The other dogs joined the first, up the stairs and onto the porch. One passed too close and suddenly the first was on it, a whirl of black fur and gnashing teeth. It was over in seconds. The interloper made a noise like a human scream, then scuttled away, tail down, one ear in shreds. I watched him disappear around the house.

That left two dogs on the porch.

Licking the floor.

I opened the cell, called Robin. "I'm at Dolf's," I told her. "You need to get out here."

"What's happening?"

"Something bad. I don't know."

"I need more than that."

"I'm in the car. I see blood on the porch."

"Wait for me, Adam."

I looked at the blood dripping down the steps. "I can't do that," I said, and hung up. I opened the door slowly, watching. One foot out, then the other. The 12-gauge was in the trunk. Loaded. I reached for the trunk latch. The dogs looked up when it popped, then went back to what they were doing. Five steps, I guessed. Five steps to the shotgun. Fifteen feet to the dogs.

I left the door open, backed along the side of the car, feeling for the loose trunk. I got a finger under the metal and lifted. It rose in silence and I risked a glance inside. The gun pointed in, barrel first. My hand closed around the stock. Eyes on the dogs.

The gun came out, smooth and slick. I cracked the barrel to check the loads. Empty. Damn. Jamie must have unloaded it.

I looked at the porch. One dog was still muzzle-down, but the big one stared at me, unmoving. I risked a glance in the trunk. The box of shells was on the far side, tipped over, still closed. I stretched for it, lost my view of the porch. The stock clanged against the car and my fingers closed on the box. I straightened, anticipating the hard silent rush, but the dog was still on the porch. He blinked, and the painted tongue spilled out.

I fumbled at the lid, opened the box. Smooth, plastic shells. Brass caps bright against the red. I got two between my fingers and slipped them in, eased the gun closed, flipped the safety off. And just like that, the dynamic changed.

That was the thing about guns.

I put shoulder to stock and made for the porch, checking

the far corners for other dogs. More than three dogs in the pack. The others had to be somewhere.

Ten feet, then eight.

The alpha dog lowered its head. Lips rippled, black and shiny on the inside, jaws two inches apart. The growl rumbled in its throat, grew louder so that the other dog looked up and joined in; both of them, teeth bared. The big one stepped closer and hair rose on my neck. Primal, that sound. I heard my father's words: *Only a matter of time before they find a streak of bold.*

Another step. Close now. Close enough to see the floor.

The pool of blood spread wide and deep, so dark it could pass for black. It was smeared where they'd licked it, stepped in it, but parts of it were smooth, like paint cut with fine lines where it slipped between the boards. From the pool to the front door I could see drag marks and bloody handprints.

Blood on the door.

But this was not a dog attack. I knew that at a glance. It was the way the blood pooled, how it had already turned as tacky as glue.

Scavengers, I told myself. Nothing more.

I angled to the side of the steps and the dogs tracked every step, shoulders hunched, heads low. I gave them plenty of room, but they did not move. We froze like that. Gun up, teeth bared.

Then the alpha dog flowed down the stairs and across the yard. He stopped once and seemed to grin, and the other dog joined him. They loped over the grass and disappeared into the trees.

I mounted the steps, still watching for the dogs, and crossed the porch as quietly as I could. The smell of copper filled my nose, bloody paw prints streaked the floor. I turned the knob slowly, pushed the door with a fingertip.

Grace curled on the floor, blood around her, black dress dark and wet with it. She clutched her stomach. Her feet pushed feebly against the floor, church shoes slipping in the fine, red film. Blood welled from between her fingers. I followed her eyes.

Miriam sat on the edge of a white chair across the room, facing Grace. She leaned forward, elbows on her knees, hair hanging over her face. The gun dangled from her right hand, a small automatic, something blue and oiled. I stepped into the room, pointed the 12 at Miriam. She straightened, flicked the hair from her face, and pointed the pistol at Grace. "She took him from me," Miriam said.

"Put the gun down."

"We were going to be married." She paused, scrubbed away tears. "He loved *me*." She jabbed with the gun. "Not her. That bitch aunt was lying."

"I'll listen, Miriam. I want to listen to everything. But put the gun down first."

"No."

"Miriam—"

"No!" she screamed. "You put it down!"

"He used you, Miriam."

"Put it down!"

I took another step. "I can't do that."

"I'll put the next one in her chest."

I looked at Grace: the slick, red fingers, the agony in her blued-out face. She shook her head, made a wordless sound. I lowered the gun, put it on the table, and held out my hands. "I'm going to help her," I said, and knelt next to Grace. I took off my jacket, folded it over the stomach wound, and told her to push. Pain burned in her eyes. She groaned as she pushed. I kept my hand on hers.

"She's nothing special," Miriam said.

"She needs a doctor."

Miriam stood. "Let her die."

"You're not a killer," I said, and realized immediately that I was wrong. It was the way her eyes glittered, sparks of crazy light. "Oh, my God."

I saw it all.

"Danny broke up with you."

"Shut up."

"He was breaking up with all of his girlfriends. He wanted to marry Grace."

"Shut up!" Miriam yelled, stepping closer.

"He used you, Miriam."

"Shut up, Adam."

"And Gray Wilson—"

"Shut up, shut up, shut up!" All but incoherent. Rising to a scream. Then the pistol jumped in her hand. One slug tore into the floor, peeled back bright, white splinters. The other struck my leg, and pain exploded through me. I hit the floor next to Grace, hands clutching the wound. Miriam dropped beside me, face twisted with worry and wild regret.

"I'm sorry," she said, fast and loud. "I'm so sorry. I didn't mean to. It was an accident."

I struggled to pull off my belt. Blood jetted onto the floor before I got the belt around my leg. The flow diminished. The pain did not.

"Are you okay?" Miriam asked.

"Jesus . . ." Agony rifled through me, hot, acid spikes of it. Miriam found her feet. She paced rapid circles, the gun in agitated motion, black eye spinning away from me and then back. I watched it anxiously, waiting for it to wink red.

The pacing slowed, the color fell out of Miriam's face. "The things Danny did to me. The way he made me feel." She nodded. "He loved me. He had to have loved me."

I couldn't help myself. "He loved lots of women. That's who he was."

"No!" An angry scream. "He bought me a ring. He said he needed money. A lot of money. He wouldn't say what it was for, but I knew. A woman can tell. So, I loaned it to him. What else would he use it for? He bought a ring. A fine, for-ever ring. He was going to surprise me." She nodded again. "I knew."

"Let me guess," I said. "Thirty thousand dollars."

She froze. "How could you know that?" Her face twisted. "He told you?"

"He used it to pay off a gambling debt. He didn't love you, Miriam. Grace did nothing wrong. She didn't even want Danny."

"Oh! She's so fucking special." Something flooded into Miriam's face, a new awareness. "You think you know everything," she said. "Think you're so damn smart? You know nothing. Nothing!" She paused, suddenly crying. Bewildered. She rocked from foot to foot. "Daddy loves her more."

"What . . . ?"

"More than you!" Her voice trailed off. "More than me. . . ." She rocked again, tapped the gun against her head the way that Zebulon Faith had.

A voice came from the open door. "That's not true, Miriam." It was my father. I'd not heard his approach. He filled the door, wearing muddy snake-boots and thorn-proof pants. He held the rifle low, but pointed at Miriam. His face was gray under the tan, his finger inside the trigger guard. When Miriam saw him, she jerked, pointed the gun at Grace again. The tears welled harder.

"Daddy . . ." she said.

"It's not true," my father repeated. "I've always loved you."

"But not like her," Miriam said. "Never like her."

My father stepped into the room. He looked at Grace, then at Miriam. He did not deny it again.

"I hear the things you say," she said. "You and Dolf, talking at night. You never notice me. You wouldn't see me if I sat down next to you. Oh. But not Grace. Perfect, darling Grace! It's like a light comes off her. . . . That's what you like to say, isn't it? She's so pure. So different from everybody else. Different from me." She beat the gun against her head again. "Better than me." Her voice dropped, and when she looked up, she could have shared a bloodline with any of those wild dogs. "I know your secret," she said.

"Miriam—"

"Your filthy, disgusting secret!"

My father stepped closer. The rifle did not waver.

"You ruined me," she said. Then she screamed again. "Look how you ruined me!" She tore at the front of her dress, buttons flying until she ripped it open. She held the pieces spread, showing us her pale body.

Her pale, cut body.

Every inch. Every curve. The scars shone like all the hurt the world had ever known. Her stomach. Her thighs. Her arms. Every place that clothing could cover had been cut and cut again.

The word *pain* carved over her heart; *deny* cut into her stomach.

I heard my father, like he was choking. "Dear God," he said, and looking at her, I knew that the cutting was not something she'd done for five years. Not since the death of Gray Wilson. No chance. This had gone on for a long, long time.

Miriam looked at me, and her face was an open wound. "She's his daughter," she said.

"Stop, Miriam."

But she would not. Pain twisted her face. Loss. Anguish. She looked at Grace, and I saw jealousy and hatred. Dark emotions. So very dark.

"All these years." Her voice broke. "He always loved her more."

The pistol started up.

"Don't," my father said.

The pistol wavered. Miriam looked from Grace to my father, and her face crumpled. Tears. Rage. Those same sparks of crazy light. The barrel moved, tracked across the floor toward Grace.

My father spoke, and desolation was in his voice. "For God's sake, Miriam. Don't make me choose."

She ignored him, turned to me. "Do the math," she said. "He ruined you, too."

Then she brought the gun up, and my father pulled the trigger. The barrel leapt, shot out fire and noise enough to end the world. The bullet struck Miriam high on the right side of her chest. It spun her twice, like a dancer, and flung her across the room. She went down, boneless, and I knew, at a glance, that there would be no getting up.

Not now.

Not ever.

Smoke hung in the room. Grace cried out.

And my father wept for the fourth time in his life.

# *Thirty-two*

Grace was still alive when the paramedics arrived. Alive, but barely. They worked on her as if she could die any second. At some point, she winked out. The eyes rolled white, red fingers opened. I didn't know that I was banging the back of my head against the wall until Robin put a hand on me. Her eyes were calm and very brown. I looked at Grace. One of her legs twitched, fine shoe clicking on the wood floor as they forced air down her throat and beat unmercifully on her chest. I barely heard the sound of her breath when they got her back, but somebody said, "She's good," and they bundled her out of there.

I met my father's eyes across the floor. He sat against one wall. I was propped against the other. As badly as I hurt, and as near as Grace was to death, my father, I think, suffered the most. I watched him as a paramedic bent over my leg. He'd checked Miriam's body once, then held on to Grace as if he was strong enough to hold her soul in place. The paramedics had to pull him away to work on her. He was soaked with her blood, in plain, open anguish, and I knew that part of it came from what he'd done, and part of it was born from the truth of what Miriam had said with her last breath. He knew what it meant, and I did, too.

Grace was his daughter. Fine. Fair. Happens all the time.

Looking back, it made sense. His love for her had never been an understated thing. But she didn't come to the farm until two years after my mother's death. I'd never done the math. It had never occurred to me. But I knew Grace's birthday, and I saw it now, Miriam's gift.

Truth in a dark box.

Grace was born two days before my mother killed herself, and that could not be coincidence.

Miriam was right.

He'd ruined me, too.

My father lifted his arm and opened his mouth as if he might speak, but I couldn't have that. I put a hand on the paramedic's shoulder. "Can you get me out of here?" I asked.

I glanced once more at my father, and when he saw my face, he closed his mouth.

I woke in hospital sheets: dim lights, drugged, no memory of the surgery they'd done on my leg. But I remembered the dream of young Sarah Yates. It was the same one that I'd had several nights before. Almost the same. She walked in the moonlit yard, dress loose around her legs. When she turned, she raised her hand as if a penny lay flat upon it. In the past, that's where the dream ended. Not this time. This time I saw it all.

The hand rose up and she touched her fingers to her lips. She smiled and blew a kiss, but not to me.

The dream was no dream. It was memory. Standing at my window, a boy, I saw it all. The windblown kiss, the secret smile; and then my father, shoeless in the pale, damp grass. How he scooped her up and kissed her for real. The raw, naked passion that I recognized even then.

I'd seen it, and I'd buried it, tucked it away in some small place in that boy's mind. But I remembered it now, felt it like a tear in my soul. Sarah Yates was not familiar to me because she looked like Grace.

I knew her.

I thought of what the preacher had said to me about the nature of my mother's death. "There's no one to blame," he'd said, and in the shadow of the church I'd always known, those words made some kind of sense. But not now.

I'd been angry for twenty years, unsettled, restless. It was like I had a shard of glass in my mind, a red blade that twisted through the soft parts of me, traveled the dark roads, cutting. I'd always blamed my mother, but now I understood. She'd pulled the trigger, yes, done it in front of me, her only child. But what I'd said to my father was true. She'd wanted *him* to see it, and now I understood why. Eight years of miscarriages. Constant failure until it wore her down to nothing.

Then, somehow, she knew.

And pulled the trigger.

The anger, I finally realized, was not at my mother, whose soul had simply withered beyond her capacity to restore. Being angry at her was unfair, and in that, I'd failed her. She deserved better. Deserved more. I wanted to weep for her, but could not.

There was no place in me for gentle emotion.

I pressed the call button for the nurse, a large woman with brown skin and indifferent eyes. "People are going to want to talk to me," I said. "I don't want to speak to anyone until nine thirty. Can you make that happen?"

She leaned back, a twist of smile on her face. "Why nine thirty?"

"I need to make some calls."

She turned for the door. "I'll see what I can do."

"Nurse," I said. "If Detective Alexander comes, I'll speak with her."

I looked at the clock. Five forty-eight. I called Robin at home. She was awake. "Did you mean what you said about choice?"

"I think I was pretty plain."

"Words are easy, Robin; life is hard. I need to know if you

really mean it. All of it. The good and the bad. The consequences."

"This is the last time I'm going to say it, Adam, so don't ask me again. I made my choice. You're the one holding back. If you want to talk about choice, then we need to talk about you. It can't be a one-way street. What's the point?"

I gave myself a second, and then I committed, for better or worse. "I need you to do something for me. It means putting what matters to me over what matters to the cops."

"Are you testing me?" She sounded angry.

"No."

"It sounds serious."

"Like you would not believe."

"What do you need?" No hesitation.

"I need you to bring me something."

She was in the room an hour later, the postcard from my glove compartment in her hand. "You okay?" she asked.

"Angry. Messed up. Mostly angry."

She kissed me, and when she straightened, she left the card on the bed. I looked at the blue water, the white sand. "Where did you get that?" she asked.

"Faith's motel."

She sat, slid the chair close. "It's postmarked after Danny died. Whoever mailed that is complicit in his murder, at least after the fact."

"I know."

"Will I get it back?"

"I don't know."

"Are you serious?"

I looked at the clock. "We should know in a few hours."

"What do you plan to do?"

"Tell me about Grace," I said.

"You're not making this easy."

"I can't talk about what I'm going to do. I just need to do it. It's not about you. It's about me. Can you understand that?"

"Okay, Adam. I understand."

"You were going to tell me about Grace."

"It was close. A few more minutes and she'd have died. Probably a good thing you didn't wait for me."

"How did it happen?"

"She came back from the funeral and went inside. Half an hour later, somebody knocked on the door. She opened it and Miriam shot her. Never said a word. Just pulled the trigger and watched as Grace dragged herself back inside."

"Where'd she get the gun?" I asked.

"Registered to Danny Faith. A little peashooter. He probably kept it in his glove compartment."

"Why do you say that?"

"Charlotte P.D. found his truck in long-term parking at Douglas Airport. I saw the inventory yesterday. He had a box of .25-caliber shells in the glove compartment, but no gun."

"Miriam killed him," I said. "She used Dolf's gun to do it, then put it back in the gun cabinet. She must have found the .25 when she ditched the truck."

I saw the wheels turn, small lines at the corners of her eyes.

"There are a lot of gaps in that theory, Adam. It's a big jump. How do you figure?"

I relayed the things that Miriam had said about her and Danny. I paused, then told her the rest of it: Grace, my mother. I kept my face neutral, even when I spoke of my father's long deception.

Robin kept her own mask up and nodded only as I finished. "That lines up with your father's statement."

"He told you? All of it?"

"He told Grantham. It wasn't easy for him, but he wanted Grantham to understand why Miriam snapped. Even though she was dead, he wanted the blame for it." She leaned forward. "It's killing him, Adam. He's eaten up over this, like it's all his fault."

"It is his fault."

"I don't know. Miriam's father ran out on her when she was very young. That's a tough thing for a little girl. When your father stepped in, she put him on a pretty high pedestal. A long way to fall."

I wasn't ready to go there. "Killing Danny is only part of it," I said. "She's the one that attacked Grace. She beat her bloody because Danny loved her." I looked away. "And because she's my father's daughter."

"You can't know that."

"I suspect it. I plan to prove it."

I felt her eyes on my face, could not imagine what she must be thinking. "Are you okay?" she asked.

"It's true, what Miriam said." I paused. "My father always did love Grace best."

"You're missing the one piece of good in all this."

"Which is?"

"You have a sister."

Something fragile spread in the void of my chest. I looked out the window, watched hard blue fill up the morning sky. "Miriam killed Gray Wilson," I finally said.

"What?" Robin was stunned.

"She was infatuated with him."

I told her about finding Miriam at Gray Wilson's grave. How she went there every month with fresh-cut flowers, how she claimed that they were going to be married. The same thing she'd said about Danny. It could not be coincidence.

"He was handsome and popular, everything she was not. She probably spent months working up the courage to tell him how she felt, fantasizing about his response. Playing it out in her mind. Then the party happened." I shrugged. "I think she tried to seduce him and failed. He said something belittling. Laughed, maybe. I think she bashed his head in with a rock when he tried to walk away."

"Why do you think that?"

"It's what happened to Danny, more or less."

"I'd like something more."

"Ask me again in three hours."

"Are you serious?"

"Right now, it's just theory."

She looked at the postcard. It was material evidence in what could easily be a capital case. She could be fired, prosecuted. She picked it up. "If this has prints, it could set Dolf free. Have you considered that?"

"He'll walk, regardless."

"Are you willing to gamble on that?"

"I know reasonable doubt when I see it. You do, too. Miriam shot two people in a fit of jealousy over Danny. She used the gun taken from his abandoned truck, gave him thirty thousand dollars, thought he was going to marry her." I shook my head. "The case will never go to trial."

"Will you at least tell me what you're planning?"

"You made a choice. I made a choice. It's time for my father to do the same thing."

"Is this about forgiveness?"

"Forgiveness?" I said. "I don't even know what that word means."

Robin stood and I reached for her hand. "I can't stay here," I said. "Not after this. Not knowing what I do. When the dust settles, I'm going back to New York. I want you to come with me this time."

She bent and kissed me. She left two fingers on my jaw as she straightened. "Whatever you're doing," she said, "don't screw it up."

Her eyes were wide and dark, but that was no kind of answer, and we both knew it.

# Thirty-three

I called George Tallman at home. The phone rang nine times and he dropped the receiver when he tried to answer. "George?" I asked.

"Adam?" His voice was thick. "Hang on." He put the phone down. I heard it strike wood. Most of a minute passed before he picked it up again. "I'm sorry," he said. "I'm not dealing with this very well."

"You want to talk about it?"

He knew most of what had happened, and sounded like a man in full-blown shock. He kept using the present tense when he spoke of Miriam, then he'd apologize, embarrassed. It took a few minutes for me to realize that he was drunk. Drunk and confused. He did not want to say anything that would hurt Miriam's memory. Saying that made him cry.

Her memory.

"Do you know how long I'd been in love with her?" he finally asked.

"No."

He told me, in fits and starts. Years. All the way back to high school, but she'd never wanted anything to do with him. "That's what made it so special," he explained. "I waited. I knew it was right. I stayed true. Eventually, she knew it, too. Like it was meant to be."

I waited for a dozen heartbeats. "May I ask a question?"

"Okay." He sniffed loudly.

"When Miriam and Janice flew back from Colorado, they spent the night in Charlotte and stayed there the next day."

"To shop."

"But Miriam wasn't feeling well." It was a guess. I wanted corroboration.

"She was . . . how did you know that?"

"You took Janice shopping and left Miriam at the hotel."

Suspicion crept into his voice. "Why are you asking about this?"

"Just one more question, George."

"What?" Still doubtful.

"What hotel did they use?"

"Tell me why you want to know." He was sobering up, suspicion growing, so I did what I had to do. I lied.

"It's a harmless question, George."

A minute later, I hung up, and for two more, I did nothing, just closed my eyes and let everything wash over me. The pain climbed to the next level as the drugs wore thin. I thought about the morphine pump, but kept my hand on the bed. When I felt able, I called the hotel in Charlotte. "Concierge desk, please."

"One moment." The phone clicked twice, then another man's voice. "Concierge."

"Yes. Do you have cars available for your guests?"

"We have a private limousine service."

"Do you loan cars to your guests? Or rent them?"

"No, sir."

"What car rental company is nearest to your hotel?" He told me. It was one of the big ones.

"We can take you there in a shuttle," he said.

"Can you give me their phone number?"

The woman who answered at the rental desk was standard corporate issue. Monotone. Unflappable. Unhelpful when I asked my question. "We cannot give out that information, sir."

I tried to stay calm, but it was difficult. I asked three times. "It's very important," I said.

"I'm sorry, sir. We cannot give out that information."

I hung up the phone, caught Robin on her cell. She was at the station house. "What is it, Adam? Are you okay?"

"I need some information. I can't get it. They'd talk to the police, I think."

"What kind of information?"

I told her what I wanted and gave her the number of the car rental company. "They'll have records. Credit card confirmations. Something. If she jerks you around, you can always try the corporate office."

"I know how to do this, Adam."

"You're right. I'm sorry."

"No need to apologize. I'll let you know. Stay by the phone."

I almost smiled. "Was that a joke?"

"Cheer up, Adam. The worst part is over."

But I was thinking of my father. "No," I said. "It's not."

"I'll call you."

I sank into the pillow and watched the big clock on the wall. It took eight minutes, and I knew in the first second that she'd gotten what I wanted. Her voice had that keen edge. "You were right. Miriam rented a green Taurus, license plate ZXF-839. Miriam's credit card. Visa, to be precise. Rented that morning, returned that afternoon. One hundred and seventeen miles on the odometer."

"That's round-trip to the farm and back."

"Almost to the mile. I checked."

I rubbed my eyes. "Thanks," I said.

She paused. "Good luck, Adam. I'll come see you this afternoon."

The next call had to wait until business hours. I called at nine. The woman who answered the phone was dangerously happy. "Good morning," she said. "Worldwide Travels. How may I be of service?"

I said hello and got straight to the point. "If I wanted to fly from Charlotte to Denver," I asked, "could you route me through Florida?"

"Where in Florida?"

I thought about it.

"Anywhere."

I watched the clock while she tapped keys. The answer came in seventy-three seconds.

I closed my eyes again, shaky, strangely out of breath. The pain in my leg climbed like it might never stop: sharp spikes that radiated outward in waves. I buzzed the nurse. She took her time.

"How bad is this going to get?" I asked.

I was pale and sweaty. She knew what I meant, and there was no pity in her face. She pointed with a well-scrubbed finger. "That morphine pump is there for a reason. Push the button when the pain gets too bad. It won't let you overdose." She started to turn. "You don't need me holding your hand."

"I don't want any morphine."

She turned back, one eyebrow up, voice dismissive. "Then it's gonna get a lot worse." She pursed her lips and left the room on wide, slow-moving hips.

I pushed into the pillows, dug my fingers into the sheets as the pain bared its teeth. I wanted the morphine, wanted it badly, but I needed to stay sharp. I fingered the postcard.

SOMETIMES IT'S JUST RIGHT.

And sometimes it's wrong.

My father arrived at ten.

He looked horrible: drained eyes, broken posture. He looked like a damned soul waiting for the floor to drop.

"How are you?" he asked, and shuffled into the room.

Words failed me. I looked for the hate and couldn't find it. I saw the early years, and how the three of us had been. *Golden.* The feeling rose in me and I almost cracked.

"It's true, isn't it?"

He said nothing.

"Mom knew about Sarah and the baby. That's why she killed herself. Because of what that did to her. That betrayal."

He closed his eyes and bowed his head. He didn't have to say it.

"How did she find out?" I asked.

"I told her," he said. "She deserved that much."

I looked away from him. Some part of me had been hoping that this was all a mistake. That I could still come home. "You told her and she killed herself."

"I thought it was the right thing to do."

"A little late to worry about that."

"I never stopped loving your mother—"

I cut him off. Did not want to hear it. "How did Miriam find out? I'm pretty sure you never told *her.*"

He turned his palms up. "She was always so quiet. She lingered around corners. She must have heard Dolf and me talking about it. We did from time to time, usually late at night. She probably figured it out years ago. It's been at least a decade since I spoke of it out loud."

"A decade." I could barely get my head around the way Miriam must have suffered with that knowledge, what she must have felt when she saw the old man's face light up every time Grace walked into the room. "You hurt so many people. And for what?"

"I'd like a chance to explain," he said, and like that, the glass in my mind started tumbling.

"No," I said. "I don't want to hear you justify what you did. I would either throw up or come out of this bed and beat you where you stand. There is nothing you can say. I was wrong to even ask. My mother was weak, worn down by poor health and disappointment, already on the edge. She found out you had a daughter and it pushed her over. She killed herself because of you." I paused under the weight of what I was about to say. "Not because of me."

An invisible force seemed to crush him. "I've had to live with it, too," he said.

Suddenly, I could not stand it. "Get out of here," I said. He started to turn, and the ice flowed back into me. "Wait. It's not going to be that easy. Tell me what happened. I want to hear it from you."

"Sarah and I—"

"Not that part. The rest of it. How Grace came to live with Dolf. How you lied to both of us for almost twenty years."

He sat without asking, dropped from the knees. "Grace was an accident. It was all an accident."

"Damn it . . ."

He tried to straighten. "Sarah thought she wanted the child. Thought it was fate, meant to be. She took her to California to start a new life. Two years later she came back, crippled, disillusioned. She didn't much care for being a parent. She wanted me to take the child."

"Why do you keep saying 'the child' when you mean Grace?"

He tilted his head. "Grace is not her real name. I gave her that name."

"Her real name . . . ?"

"Sky."

"Jesus."

"She wanted me to take the child, but I had a new family." He paused. "I'd already lost one wife. I didn't want to lose another. But she was my daughter. . . ."

"So you bribed Dolf to raise her. You gave him two hundred acres to help hide your secret."

"It wasn't like that."

"Don't—"

"The land was for Grace to inherit! She deserved it. None of this was her fault. As for Dolf, he was lonely. He wanted the job."

"Bullshit."

"It's true. His wife left him years ago. He never sees his own daughter. Grace has done great things for him."

"Even though it's all a lie."

"He was in a dark place, son. We all were after your mother died. That child was like the sun rising."

"Does Grace know?"

"Not yet."

"Where's Janice?" I asked.

"She already knows, son. I told her. There's no need to drag her into this."

"I want to see her."

"You want to hurt me. I understand."

"This is not about you. We're done with that. This is something else entirely."

"What do you mean?"

"Get Janice," I said. "Then we'll talk."

New pain flooded his face. "I killed her daughter last night. She's sedated, and even if she weren't, I doubt that she is ready to speak with either one of us. She's not doing well at all."

"I need her to be here."

"Why, for God's sake? None of this was her fault, either."

I felt disconnected from his suffering. "Tell her that I'd like to talk about Florida."

"That makes no sense."

"Just do it."

# *Thirty-four*

Grantham came an hour later, and I gave my statement. He pushed for details on the shooting and I told him that my father had had no choice. That was no favor to the old man, just simple truth.

Grace or Miriam.

Hard, brutal choice.

He also wanted to talk more about the death of Zebulon Faith. He wanted to know why I had a shotgun in the trunk of my car. But that was another county. Not even his case. I told him to leave me alone, and he had no choice but to comply. I was not Danny's killer. Nor was I Zebulon Faith's. He knew that now.

When he left, I thought I might go for the morphine after all, push the button before I did what I had to do. I was in such agony that, at times, it made me shake. I almost folded, but Robin called and the sound of her voice helped. "It's been over three hours," she said.

"Patience," I told her, and tried to will it on myself.

They showed up two hours later.

My father.

My stepmother.

She looked worse, if possible, than he did. Her lids drooped and one hand clutched at air as if she saw something to hold on to where the rest of us did not. Uneven lipstick, hair in disarray. It looked like he'd pulled her straight out of bed. But when she sat and faced me, I saw the fear in her, and knew, then, that I was right.

"Close the door," I said to my father. He closed it and sat. I faced Janice. I wanted to be angry, and part of me was. The rest, however, was overcome by melancholy.

She was a mother first, and she had her reasons.

"Let's talk about the night that Gray Wilson was killed."

Janice started to rise, then stopped. She sank back down. "I don't understand. . . ."

"Miriam was covered in his blood. She brought it into the house after she killed him. That's why you said it was me. That's why you testified against me. To protect Miriam."

"What?" Her eyes went wide and white. Hands clawed into the fabric of her skirt.

"If you said it was somebody else, and the cops found blood in the house, then the story would collapse. It could not be a stranger. It had to be someone with access to the house. Upstairs, especially. It couldn't be Jamie or my father. It had to be me. I was the only one you weren't close to."

My father finally stirred, but I raised a hand before he could speak. "I always thought you believed it. I thought you saw someone that you honestly mistook for me." I paused. "But that's not it. You *had* to testify against me. Just in case."

My father spoke. "Are you insane?"

"No. I'm not."

Janice put her hands on the chair and pushed herself up. "I refuse to listen to this," she said. "Jacob, I'd like to go home."

I pulled the postcard from beneath the sheet, held it up so that she could see it. One hand settled at her throat, the other reached for the chair. "Sit down," I said. And she did.

"What's that?" my father asked.

"Gray Wilson, unfortunately, is ancient history. Dead and

buried. I can't prove a thing. But this"—I waved the card—
"this is a different matter."

"Jacob . . ." She reached for his arm, fingers curling
around his wrist. My father repeated the question. "What is
that?"

"This is choice," I said to him. "Your choice."

"I don't understand."

"Whatever demons pursued Miriam, they'd been after her
for a long time, and Janice knew all about them. Why she hid
them, I can't pretend to understand. But Miriam was sick. She
killed Gray Wilson because she thought she loved him and because he didn't want anything to do with her. Same thing with
Danny Faith." I paused. "The knob is hard to get to. You'd
need a truck for the body, and Danny was a large man."

"What are you talking about?" my father asked.

"Miriam couldn't get Danny into that hole all by herself."

"No," he said. But he knew. I saw it in his face.

"I don't think Miriam mailed this card, either." I flipped
the card so he could read the back. *Having a blast,* it said. "It
was mailed *after* Danny died."

"This is ridiculous," Janice said.

"Janice took Miriam to Colorado within a day or two of
Danny's death. You can route through Florida on your way to
Denver. I made some phone calls this morning. An hour and
forty minutes to change planes. Plenty of time to drop a
postcard in the mail. The police can verify the travel itiner-
ary. The dates will match." I held my father's eyes. "I doubt
that this card has Miriam's prints on it."

My father was silent for a long time. "It's not true," Janice
said. "Jacob . . ."

He did not look at her. "What does any of this have to do
with choice?"

"Whoever mailed this card was trying to conceal the fact
that Danny was dead. The police will want to speak with the
person that mailed this card."

He came to his feet, voice loud, and Janice twitched when he spoke.

"What choice, goddamn it?"

The moment drew out, and I took no pleasure in it. But it had to be done. Too many wrongs littered the road behind us: betrayal and lies; murder and complicity. A mountain of grief.

I placed the card on the edge of the bed.

"I'm giving it to you," I said. "Burn it. Hand it over to the police. Give it to her." I pointed to Janice and she shrank away. "Your choice."

They both stared at the card. Nobody touched it.

"You made other phone calls?" he asked. "What other calls?"

"Janice and Miriam flew back from Colorado the night before Grace was attacked. They stayed the night in a hotel in downtown Charlotte. George drove in the next morning and spent the day with Janice—"

"He took me shopping," Janice interrupted.

"And Miriam stayed behind."

"At the hotel," Janice said.

I shook my head. "She rented a car two hours before Grace was attacked. A green Taurus. License plate ZXF-839. The police know about that, too."

"What are you saying?" my father asked.

"I'm saying that she was still angry about Danny. She'd had eighteen days to think about Grace and Danny together, about how Danny dumped her for Grace. I'm saying she was still angry about that."

"I don't . . ." He was lost, so I drove the point home.

"Two hours after Miriam rented that car, someone stepped from behind a tree and beat Grace with a club."

He looked at the card, looked at me. Janice squeezed his arm so hard I thought she might draw blood. "But what about Danny's ring? The note . . . ?"

"She probably kept the ring when she killed Danny. She may have left it with Grace as some kind of strange message. Or maybe, like the note, she was covering her tracks, hiding the true nature of Grace's assault. The ring implied that Danny was involved in the attack, even that he was still alive. If people didn't buy that, or if Danny's body was found, then the note would steer them to people with a stake on the river. I think it was simple misdirection. Something she learned from watching her mother."

My father looked at his wife.

"I'm sorry," I said.

He picked up the card and our eyes met. He tried to speak, but gave up when nothing came. Janice pulled herself up by my father's sleeve. He looked at her one last time, then turned like a very old man, and left. Janice bent her head and trailed in his wake.

I waited until their footsteps died away, then reached for the morphine trigger. I pushed the button and warmth gushed into me. I kept my thumb on the trigger, even after the morphine ceased to flow.

My eyes glazed.

The button clicked in the empty room.

Robin returned as the sun fell through the earth. She kissed me and asked how it went. I told her everything and she was silent for a long time. She opened her phone and made some calls. "He hasn't called," she said. "Not Salisbury P.D. Not the sheriff's office."

"He may not."

"You okay with that?"

"I don't know anymore. I hate what Janice did to me, but Miriam was her daughter. She did what she felt she had to do."

"You're kidding."

"I've never had a child, so I can only imagine, but I'd lie for Grace. I'd lie for you. I'd do worse, if necessary."

"Sweet talker." She stretched out on the bed with me, put her head on the pillow next to mine.

"About New York," I said.

"Don't ask me about that yet."

"I thought you'd made your choice."

"I did. But that doesn't mean that you get to make every decision for the rest of our lives." She was trying to keep it light.

"I really can't stay here," I said.

Her head turned on the pillow. "Ask me about Dolf."

"Tell me."

"The D.A. is close to dropping the charges. Most people think he has no choice. It's just a matter of time."

"Soon?"

"Maybe tomorrow."

I thought of Dolf, pictured the way he'd turn his face to the sun when he walked out.

"Have you seen Grace yet?" she asked.

"She's still in ICU and they're limiting visitation. But that's okay. I'm not ready."

"You'll confront your father and Janice, but you're hesitant to talk to Grace? I don't understand."

"She'll need time to get her head around this. Besides, it's hard."

"Why?"

"I have something to lose with Grace. I had nothing left to lose with my father." She stiffened beside me. "What?" I asked.

"Not very long ago, I'd have said the same thing about you."

"That's different."

She rolled onto her side. "Life is short, Adam. We don't get many people that truly matter. We should do whatever it takes to hang on to the ones we have."

"What are you saying?"

"I'm saying that we all make mistakes."

We lay in the darkened room and at one point I drifted. Her voice startled me. "Why did Miriam agree to marry George Tallman?"

"I talked to him this morning. He was pretty messed up. I asked him how it happened. He'd been in love with her for years. They went out, but she would never say yes. She called him on the day before she left for Colorado. She told him to ask her again, and she said yes, just like that. He already had the ring.

"It was Janice's idea, I think. If the body did turn up, few would suspect a cop's fiancée. She didn't plan to go through with it."

"Why do you say that?"

"The first thing she did when she got back was send him shopping with her mother so she could sneak back here and beat the hell out of Grace. He was cover. That's all he would ever be."

"It's sad," Robin said.

"I know."

Robin closed her eyes, pushed closer. She slipped her hand under my shirt. Her palm lay cool on my chest. "Tell me about New York," she said.

# Thirty-five

I got out of the hospital on the same day that Dolf got out of jail. He picked me up and drove us to the edge of the quarry outside of town. The granite was gray in the shade, pink where the light touched it. Crutches dug into my arms as I stood and looked down on clear water in the bottom of the quarry. Dolf closed his eyes and held his face to the sun. "This is what I thought about while I was inside," he said. "Not the farm or the river. This place, and I've not been here for decades."

"No memories here," I said. "No ghosts."

"And it's pretty."

"I don't want to talk about my father," I said, and looked at him. "That's the real reason you brought me here. Isn't it? So you could do his dirty work for him."

Dolf leaned against the truck. "I would do anything for your father. Would you like to know why?"

I turned and started limping down the hill. "I'm not going to listen to this."

"It's a long way back to town."

"I'll make it."

"Damn it, Adam." Dolf caught my arm. "He's human. He messed up. It was a long time ago." I pulled my arm away, but he kept talking. "Sarah Yates was young and beautiful and willing. He made a mistake."

"Some mistakes you have to pay for," I said.

"I asked if you'd like to know why. Well, I'm going to tell you. It's because he's the best man I've ever known. Being his friend has been a privilege, a goddamn honor. You're blind if you don't see that."

"You're entitled to your opinion."

"Do you know what he sees when he looks at Grace? He sees a grown woman and a lifetime of memories, an amazing human being that would not be here without the mistake you're so ready to damn him for. He sees the hand of God."

"And I see the death of the finest woman I ever knew."

"Things happen for a reason, Adam. The hand of God is everywhere. Haven't you figured that out yet?"

I turned, started walking, and knew that he was right about one thing. It was a long way back to town.

I spent the next four days at Robin's place. We ordered in. We drank wine. We did not talk about death or forgiveness or the future. I told her all that I could about New York City.

We read the papers together.

The shooting was big news, and articles ran across the state. Red Water Farm was described as a North Carolina landmark. Three bodies in five years. Six towers. Billions at stake. It did not take long for the wire services to pick it up. One enterprising reporter wrapped the story into a larger piece about nuclear power, rural desecration, and the price of unstoppable growth. Others spoke of obstructionism. Editorials ran hot in all of the major papers. People clamored for my father to sell. Environmentalists protested. The situation escalated.

On the fourth day, the power company announced that it had settled on a secondary site in South Carolina. Better water supply, they claimed. Just as convenient. But I had my own suspicions. Too much controversy. Too much heat.

In the wake of the announcement, a stunned silence rippled across the county. I felt the pop of vacuum as imaginary wealth was sucked back into the ether. That was the day I called Parks. The day I decided to put the problems aside and do what I could to help. We met for coffee at a restaurant ten miles down the interstate. After a few cautious words, he asked me to get to the point.

"How deep is my father's debt?" That was my question.

He looked at me for a long time, trying to figure me out. I knew that he and my father had spoken. He'd told me as much.

"Why do you want to know?"

"The farm has been in my family for two centuries. Much of the vineyard has burned. My father is in debt. If the farm is at risk, I want to help."

"You should be talking to your father," Parks said. "Not going through an intermediary."

"I'm not ready to do that."

He drummed long fingers on the table. "What do you propose?"

"He bought me out for three million. I'll buy back in for the same price. It should be enough to see him through."

"You have that much left?"

"I made good investments. If he needs more, I have it."

The lawyer rubbed his face, thought about it. He looked at his watch. "Are you in a rush?" he asked.

"No."

"Wait here."

I watched him through the window. He stood in the parking lot, cell phone to his ear, and argued with my father. His face still held the heat when he came back to the table. "He said no."

"Did he say why?"

"I can't talk about that."

"But he gave you a reason?"

The lawyer nodded. "A pretty good one."

"And you won't tell me what it is."

He spread his hands and shook his head.

* * *

It was Dolf who finally explained it to me. He showed up at Robin's the next morning. We spoke in the shade of the building, at the edge of the parking lot. "Your father wants to make things right. He wants you to come home, but not because you have a financial interest. Not to protect your investment."

"What about the money he owes?"

"He'll refinance, leverage more acreage. Whatever it takes."

"Can he do it?"

"I trust your father," he said, and the statement had layers of meaning.

I walked with Dolf to his truck. He spoke to me through the open window. "Nobody's seen Jamie," he said. "He hasn't been home." We both knew why. Miriam was his twin, and our father had shot her down. Worry filled Dolf's eyes. "Look for him, will you?"

I called my broker in New York and arranged to transfer funds to a local branch. When I went looking for Jamie, I had a cashier's check for three hundred thousand dollars in my pocket. I found him at one of the local sports bars. He sat in a booth in the back corner. Empties stretched from one end of the table to the other. As far as I could tell, he had neither shaved nor bathed in days. I limped to the table, slipped in across from him, and propped the crutches against the wall. He looked destroyed.

"You okay?" I asked.

He said nothing.

"Everybody's looking for you."

When he spoke, he slurred, and I saw in him the kind of anger that had all but destroyed me. "She was my sister," he said. "Do you understand?"

I did. As different as they had been, they were still twins.

"I was there," I said. "He had no choice."

Jamie slammed a bottle on the table. Beer shot out and spattered my sleeve. People stared, but Jamie was oblivious. "There's always a choice."

"No, Jamie. Not always."

He leaned back, rubbed giant, callused hands over his face. When he looked at me, it was like looking into a mirror. "Go away, Adam. Just go away." He put his head in his hands and I slipped the check across the table.

"Anything you need," I said, and hobbled out. I turned once at the door and saw him there. He held the check in his fingers, then put it down. He found me across the room and raised his hand. I would never forget the face that he showed me.

Then he looked down and reached for another beer.

When I went to see Grace, it was easier than I thought. I did not see my mother when I looked at her. In that, at least, my father had been right. It was not her fault, and I loved her no less. She looked worn, but the truth rested more lightly on her than it did on me. "I always thought my parents were dead," she explained. "Now I have two, and a brother."

"But Dolf's not your grandfather," I said. "You lost that."

She shook her head. "I couldn't love him any more than I already do. Nothing will change for us."

"What about you and me? Is that weird?"

It took her a minute to answer. When she did, I felt the confusion in her. "Hope dies hard, Adam. It hurts. I'll get used to it because I don't have a choice. I'm just glad you didn't sleep with me."

"Ah. Humor."

"It helps."

"And Sarah Yates?"

"I like her, but she abandoned me."

"Almost twenty years, Grace. She could have lived anywhere, but chose a place three miles upriver. That was no accident. She wanted to be near you."

"Near is not the same."

"No, it's not."

I guess we'll see where it goes."

"And our father?"

"I look forward to walking that road." Her gaze was so level that I had to look away. She put her hand on mine. "Don't leave, Adam. Walk it with me."

I withdrew my hand, moved to the window, and looked out. A canopy of trees spread above the neighborhood behind the hospital. I saw a thousand shades of green. "I'm going back to New York," I said. "Robin's coming. We want you to come with us."

"I told you before. I'm no runner."

"It's not running," I said.

"Isn't it?"

# Thirty-six

They buried Miriam on an unseasonably cool day. I went to the funeral and stood with Robin at my side. My father was there with Janice, both of them looking sleepless, weathered, and bleak. Dolf stood between them like a rock. Or a wall. They did not look at each other, and I knew that grief and blame were chewing them down. Jamie lingered on the fringe, sunken, with splotches of red on his cheeks. He was drunk and angry, with no forgiveness in his face when he looked at my father.

I listened to the same preacher who buried my mother, buried Danny. He wore the snowy vestment and spoke similar words, but they brought me no comfort. Miriam knew little peace in life, and I feared that her soul might share the same predilection. She died a killer, unrepentant, and I hoped that she'd found a better place.

I looked across her grave.

I prayed for mercy on her wounded soul.

When the preacher finished, my stepmother folded herself against the coffin and shook like a leaf in high wind. George Tallman stared into nothing as tears slipped off his chin to stain his dress blues dark.

I moved away from the small gathering and my father

joined me. We stood alone under a distant sun. "Tell me what to do," he said.

I looked at what remained of my family, and thought of Miriam's prophetic words. The family had torn itself apart.

*Cracks all over the place.*

"You haven't called the police." I was speaking of the postcard.

"I burned it." He looked down and repeated himself. "I burned it."

Then he, too, began to tremble.

And I walked away.

# Thirty-seven

Idiscovered something over the next year. New York with someone you love is better than the same city all alone. Ten times better. A thousand. But it wasn't home. That was fact, simple and pure. I tried to live with it, but it was hard. When I closed my eyes, I thought of open spaces.

We had no idea what we would do with the rest of our days, only that we would spend them together. We had money and we had time. We talked about getting married. "One day," she said.

"Soon," I countered.

"Kids?"

I thought of my father and she recognized the pain. "You should call him back," she said.

He called every week. Sunday night. Eight o'clock. The phone would ring and the number would appear on the handset. Every week he called. And every week I let it ring. Sometimes he left a message. Sometimes, not. We got a letter once. It contained a copy of his divorce decree and a copy of his new will. Jamie still had his ten percent, but my father left control of the farm to Grace and me. He wanted us to protect its future.

Us.

His children.

Grace and I spoke regularly, and things got better with time. The relationship began to feel normal. We asked her to visit, but she always refused. "One day," she said, and I understood. She was walking blind on a new road. That took concentration. She spoke, once, of our father. "He's hurting, Adam."

"Don't," I said, and she never raised the subject again.

Dolf came twice, but did not care for the city. We went out to dinner, hit a few bars, told some stories. He looked better than I thought he would, but refused to talk about what the doctors were saying. "Doctors," he'd say, then change the subject. I asked him once why he'd taken the blame for Danny's murder. His answer did not surprise me.

"Your dad had a fit when I told him that Danny hit Grace. In all of my life I'd never seen him that angry. Danny went missing right after that. I thought maybe your father killed him." He shrugged, looked at a pretty girl on the sidewalk. "I was dying anyway."

I thought about that often: the power of their friendship. Fifty years and more. A lifetime.

His death almost broke me.

I didn't see it coming, and I wasn't there when it happened. I went back to Rowan County for one more funeral, and my father told me that Dolf died with the sun on his face. Then he lifted his arms and asked me to forgive him, but I could not speak. I was crying like a child.

When I came back to New York, I was not the same. Not for days. Not for weeks. I dreamed three times of the white deer, and each dream came with more power than the last. His antlers were as smooth as bone, and a gold light shone between them. He stood at the edge of the forest and waited for me to follow, but I never did. I could not face what he wanted to show me, and was wary of what lay beyond the hard, black trees.

I tried to explain the dream to Robin, the power of it, the sense of awe and fear that all but choked me when I bolted up in the dark. I told her that Dolf was trying to tell me something, or maybe my mother; but she shrugged that off. She wrapped me up and said it meant that good still moved in the world. Plain and simple. I tried my best to believe her, but there was a hole in me. So she said it again, whispered with the voice that I loved, *Good still moves.*

But that's not what it meant.

There was something behind those trees, some secret place, and I thought I knew what I might find there.

When my mother killed herself, she killed my childhood, too. She took the magic with her. It was too much for me to forgive, too destructive, and in the absence of forgiveness, the anger filled me up, twenty years' worth, and only now was I beginning to understand. She did what she did, but hers was a sin of weakness, as was my father's; and while the repercussions of his misdeed were enormous, the sin itself was one of human frailty. That's what Dolf tried to tell me, and I knew now that his words were not just for my father's sake, but also for mine. My father's failing is where the anger started, that's what set the glass spinning, and every day it seemed a smaller thing. So, I held my woman close, and I told myself that when next I dreamed, I would follow a flash of white. I would walk the dark trail, and I would look at what I feared to see.

Maybe it was magic.

Or forgiveness.

Maybe it was nothing.

At dusk the next Sunday, Robin said that she was going for a walk. She kissed me hard and put the phone in my hand.

I stood at the window and looked at the river. It was not the one I loved. Different color. Different shores. But the water moved. It wore things down and it restored itself, emptied into the same vast sea.

I thought of my own mistakes and of my father, then of

Grace and of the things that Dolf had said; how human is human and the hand of God is in all things.

The phone would ring in ten minutes.

I wondered if tonight I would pick it up.

Turn the page for an excerpt from

JOHN HART's latest thriller

# THE LAST CHILD

–Now Available

from Thomas Dunne Books!

Detective Hunt sat at the cluttered desk in his small office. Files spilled from cabinet tops and unused chairs. Dirty coffee cups, memos he'd never read. It was 9:45. The place was a mess, but he lacked the energy to deal with it. He scrubbed his hands across his face, ground at the sockets of his eyes until he saw white streaks and sparks. His face felt rough, unshaven, and he knew that he looked every bit of his forty-one years. He'd lost so much weight that his suits hung on his frame. He'd not been to the gym or the shooting range in six months. He rarely managed more than one meal a day, but none of that seemed to matter. Everything was different now.

In front of him, he'd spread his office copy of the Alyssa Merrimon file. A well-thumbed duplicate was locked in a desk drawer at home. He flipped pages methodically, reading every word: reports, interviews, summaries. Alyssa's face stared out at him from an enlarged copy of her school photograph. Black hair, like her brother's. Same bone structure, same dark eyes. A secret kind of smile. A lightness, like her mother had, an ethereal quality that Hunt had tried and failed to identify. The way her eyes tilted, maybe? The swept-back ears and china skin? The innocence? That's the one that Hunt came back to most often. The child looked as if she'd never had an impure thought or done an ill deed in her entire life.

And then there was her mother, her brother. They all had it, to one degree or another; but none of them like the girl.

Hunt scrubbed his face one more time.

He was too close, he knew that, but the case had a grip on

him. A glance at the office showed the depth of his fall.
There were cases here that needed work. Other people. Real
people who suffered just like the Merrimons did; but those
cases paled, and he still did not know why. The girl had even
found her way into his dreams. She wore the same clothes
she had on the day she disappeared: faded yellow shorts, a
white top. She was pale in the dream. Short hair. Eighty
pounds. A hot spring day. There was no lead-up when it happened; the dream started like a cannon shot, full-blown,
color and sound. Something was pulling her into a dark
place beneath the trees, dragging her through the warm, rot-
ten leaves. Her hand was out, mouth open. He dove for the
hand, missed, and she screamed as long fingers drew her
down into some dark, seamless place, the entrance to which
he could never find.

When it happened, he woke sheeted in sweat, arms
churning as if he were digging through leaves. The dream
found him two or three nights a week, and it was the same
every time. He'd climb from bed sometime close to three,
shaky and wide-awake, then put cold water on his face and
stare long into bloody eyes before going downstairs to pore
through the file for whatever hours remained before his son
woke up and the day put its own long fingers on his skin.

The dream had become his personal hell, the file a ritual,
a religion; and it was eating him alive.

"Well, good morning, Sunshine."

Hunt jerked, looked up. In the door stood John Yoakum,
his partner and friend. "Hey, John. Good morning."

Yoakum was sixty-three years old, with thinning brown
hair and a goatee shot with gray. Thin but very fit, he was
dangerously smart, cynical to a fault. They'd been partners
for four years, worked a dozen major cases together, and
Hunt liked the guy. He was a private man and a smartass, but
he also brought rare insight to a job that demanded nothing
less. He worked long hours when they needed to be worked,

watched his partner's back; and if he was a little dark, a little private, Hunt was okay with that.

Yoakum shook his head. "I'd like to live the night that made you look like this."

"No, you wouldn't."

Yoakum's grin fell off and his words were brisk. "I know that, Clyde. Just messing with you." He gestured over his shoulder. "I have a call you might want to take."

"Yeah. Why is that?"

"Because it's about Johnny Merrimon."

"Seriously?"

"Some lady who wants to talk to a cop. I told her that I was the only real cop here today. I said, emotional wrecks, yeah, got one of those. An obsessive compulsive that used to look like a cop. She could have that guy, too. Both, in fact. At the same time."

"What line, smartass?"

Yoakum showed his fine, porcelain teeth. "Line three," he said, and left with an easy swagger. Hunt lifted the phone and punched the flashing button for line three. "This is Detective Hunt."

At first there was silence, then a woman's voice. She sounded old. "Detective? I don't know that I need a detective. It's not that important, really. I just thought someone should know."

"It's okay, ma'am. May I have your name, please?"

"Louisa Sparrow, like the bird."

The voice fit. "What's the problem, Ms. Sparrow?"

"It's that poor boy. You know, the one that lost his sister…"

"Johnny Merrimon."

"That's the one. The poor boy…" She trailed off for an instant, then her voice firmed. "He was just at my house… just this minute…"

"With a picture of his sister," Hunt interrupted.

"Why, yes. How did you know?"

Hunt ignored the question. "May I have your address, please, ma'am?"

"He's not in trouble, is he? He's been through enough, I know. It's just that it's a school day, and it's all very upsetting, seeing her picture like that, and how he still looks just like her, like he hasn't grown at all; and those questions he asks, like I might have had something to do with it…"

Detective Hunt thought about the small boy he'd found at the grocery store. The deep eyes. The wariness. "Ms. Sparrow…"

"Yes."

"I really need that address."

Hunt found Johnny Merrimon a block away from Louisa Sparrow's house. The boy sat on the curb, his feet crossed in the gutter. Sweat soaked his shirt and plastered hair to his forehead. A beat-up bike lay where he'd dropped it, half on the grass of somebody's lawn. He was chewing on a pen and bent over a map that covered his lap like a blanket. His concentration was complete, broken only when Hunt slammed the car door. In that instant the boy looked like a startled animal, but then he paused. Hunt saw recognition snap in the boy's eyes, then determination and something deeper.

Acceptance.

Then cunning.

His eyes gauged distance, as if he might hop on his bike and try to run. He risked a glance at the nearby woods, but Hunt stepped closer, and the kid sagged. "Hello, Detective."

Hunt pulled off his sunglasses. His shadow fell on the boy's feet. "Hello, Johnny."

Johnny began folding the map. "I know what you're going to say, so you don't have to say it."

Hunt held out his hand. "May I see the map?" Johnny froze, and the hunted animal look rose again in his face. He looked down the long street, then at the map. Hunt continued: "I've heard about that map, you see. I didn't believe it at first, then didn't know what to make of it; but people have told me." Hunt's eyes were hard on the boy. "How many times is it now, Johnny? How many times have I talked to you about this? Four? Five?"

"Seven." His voice barely rose from the gutter. His fingers showed white on the map.

"I'll give it back."

The boy looked up, black eyes shining, and the sense of cunning fell away. He was a kid. He was scared. "Promise?"

He looked so small. "I promise, Johnny."

Johnny raised his hand and Hunt's fingers closed on the map. It was worn soft and showed white lines in the folds. He sat on the curb, next to the boy, and spread the map between his hands. It was large, purple ink on white paper. He recognized it as a tax map, with names and matching addresses. It only covered a portion of the city, maybe a thousand properties. Close to half had been crossed off in red ink. "Where did you get this?" he asked.

"Tax assessor. They're not expensive."

"Do you have all of them? For the entire county?" Johnny nodded, and Hunt asked, "The red marks?"

"Houses I've visited. People I've spoken to."

Hunt was struck dumb. He could not imagine the hours involved, the ground covered on a busted-up bike. "What about the ones with asterisks?"

"Single men living alone. Ones that gave me the creeps."

Hunt folded the map, handed it back. "Are there marks on other maps, too?"

"Some of them."

"It has to stop."

"But—"

"No, Johnny. It has to stop. These are private citizens. We're getting complaints."

Johnny stood. "I'm not breaking any laws."

"You're a truant, son. You're ditching school right now. Besides, it's dangerous. You have no idea who lives in these houses." He flicked one finger at the map; it snapped against the paper and Johnny pulled it away. "I can't lose another kid."

"I can take care of myself."

"Yeah, you told me that this morning."

Johnny looked away, and Hunt studied the line of his narrow jaw, the muscles that pressed against the tight skin. He saw a small feather tied to a string around Johnny's neck. It shone whitish-gray against the boy's washed-out shirt. Hunt pointed, trying to break the mood. "What's that?"

Johnny's hand moved to his neck. He tucked the feather back under his shirt. "It's a pin feather," he said.

"A pin feather?"

"For luck," Johnny added.

Hunt saw the kid's fingers go white, and he saw another feather tied to the bike. The feather was larger, mostly brown. "How about that one?" He pointed again. "Hawk? Owl?" The boy's face showed nothing, and he kept his mouth shut. "Is that for luck, too?"

"No." Johnny paused, looked away. "That's different."

"Johnny…"

"Did you see in the news last week? When they found that girl that was abducted in Colorado? You know the one?"

"I know the one."

"She'd been gone for a year and they found her three blocks from her own house. She was less than a mile away the whole time. A mile from her family, locked up in a dirt hole dug into the wall of the cellar. Walled up with a bucket and mattress."

"Johnny…"

"They showed pictures on the news. A bucket. A candle. A filthy mattress. The ceiling was only four feet high. But they found her."

"That's just one case, Johnny."

"They're all like that." Johnny turned back, his deep eyes gone darker still. "It's a neighbor or a friend, someone the kid knows or a house she walked past every day. And when they find them, they're always close. Even if they're dead, they're close."

"That's not always true…"

"But sometimes. Sometimes it is."

Hunt stood as well, and his voice came softly. "Sometimes."

"Just because you quit doesn't mean that I have to."

Looking at the boy and at his desperate conviction, Hunt felt a great sadness. He was the department's lead detective on major cases, and because of that, he'd taken point on Alyssa's disappearance. Hunt had worked harder than any other cop to bring that poor child home. He'd spent months, lost touch with his own family until his wife, in despair and quiet rage, had finally left him. And for what? Alyssa was gone, so gone they'd be lucky to find her remains. It didn't matter what happened in Colorado. Hunt knew the statistics: most were dead by the end of the first day. But that made it no easier. He still wanted to bring her home. One way or another. "The file is still open, Johnny. No one has quit."

Johnny picked up his bike. He rolled up the map and shoved one end into his back pocket. "I have to go."

Detective Hunt's hand settled on the handlebar. He felt specks of rust and heat from the sun. "I've cut you a lot of slack. I can't do it anymore. This needs to stop."

Johnny pulled on the bike but couldn't budge it. His voice was as loud as Hunt had ever heard it. "I can take care of myself."

"But that's just it, Johnny. It's not your job to take care of yourself. It's your mother's job, and frankly, I'm not sure she can tend to herself, let alone a thirteen-year-old boy."

"You may *think* that's true, but you don't *know* anything."

For a long second the detective held his eyes. He saw how they went from fierce to frightened, and understood how much the kid needed his hope. But the world was not a kind

place to children, and Hunt had reached the limit with Johnny
Merrimon. "If you lifted your shirt right now, how many
bruises would I see?"

"I can take care of myself."

The words sounded automatic and weak, so Hunt lowered
his voice. "I can't do anything if you won't talk to me."

Johnny straightened, then let go of his bike. "I'll walk,"
he said, and turned away.

"Johnny."

The kid kept walking.

"Johnny!"

When he stopped, Hunt walked the bike over to him. The
spokes clicked as the wheels turned. Johnny took the handlebars when Hunt offered the bike back to him. "You still have
my card?" Johnny nodded, and Hunt blew out a long breath.
He could never fully explain his affinity for the boy, not even
to himself. Maybe he saw something in the kid. Maybe he
felt his pain more than he should. "Keep it with you, okay?
Call me anytime."

"Okay."

"I don't want to hear about you doing this again."

Johnny said nothing.

"You'll go straight to school?"

Silence.

Hunt looked at the clean, blue sky, then at the boy. His hair
was black and wet, his jaw clenched. "Be careful, Johnny."

People were not right. The cop had that part straight.
Johnny had peered over more fences and into more windows than he could count. He'd knocked on doors at all hours,
and he'd seen things that weren't right. Things that people did
when they thought they were alone and no one was watching.
He'd seen kids sniff drugs and old people eat food that fell on
the floor. He once saw a preacher in his underwear, red-faced
and screaming at his wife as she cried. That was messed up.
But Johnny was no idiot. He knew that crazy people could

look like anybody else. So, he kept his head down. He kept his shoes laced tight and a knife in his pocket.

He was careful.

He was smart.

Johnny did not look back until he'd gone two full blocks. When he did turn his head, he saw that Detective Hunt still stood in the road, a distant speck of color next to a dark car and green grass. The cop was still for an instant, then one arm rose in a slow wave, and Johnny rode faster, careful to not look back again.

The cop scared him, and Johnny wondered how he knew the things he knew.

*Five.*

The number popped into his head.

*Five bruises.*

He pedaled harder, pumped his legs until the shirt on his back clung like a second skin. He went north to the far edge of town, to the place where the river slid beneath the bridge and widened out until the current went flat. He rode his bike down the bank and dropped it. Blood pounded in his ears and he tasted salt. His eyes burned from it, so he wiped at them with a grubby sleeve. He used to fish here with his father. He knew where to find the bass and the giant cats that hugged the mud five feet down, but none of that mattered. He never fished anymore, but he still came here.

This was still his place.

He sat in the dust to untie his shoes. His fingers shook and he did not know why. The shoes came off, then he touched the feather to his cheek and wrapped it in his shirt. The sun put fierce heat on his skin, and he looked at the bruises, the largest of which was the size and shape of a large man's knee. It wrapped around the ribs on his left side and he remembered how Ken had held him down with that knee, shifted his weight whenever Johnny tried to squirm out.

Johnny rolled his shoulders, tried to forget about it, the knee on his chest, the finger in his face.

*You'll fucking do what I fucking say...*

Open hand slaps to Johnny's face, first one side, then the other, his mother passed out in the back room.

*You little shit...*

Another slap, harder.

*Where's your daddy now...*

The bruise had yellowed out on the edges, gone green in the middle; and it hurt when he pushed it with a finger. The skin went white for a second—another perfect oval—then the color rushed in. Johnny scrubbed more salt from his eyes, and when he moved for the river, he stumbled once. He stepped in and river bottom pushed between his toes; then he dove, and warm water closed above him. It wrapped him up, shut out the world, and bore him tirelessly down.

Johnny spent two hours at the river, too worried about Detective Hunt to risk more of his search, too ambivalent about school to make going worth his time. He swam across the river and back, made shallow dives from flat rocks baked hot by the sun. Driftwood lay in silver stacks and wind licked off the water. By late morning he was physically worn, stretched out on a flat rock forty feet downriver from the bridge, invisible behind a willow that dragged long strands in the black water. Cars made the bridge hum. A small stone clattered on the rock beside his head. He sat up and another pebble struck him on the shoulder. He looked around and saw no one. A third rock glanced off his leg. It was large enough to sting. "Throw another and you're dead."

Silence.

"I know it's you, Jack."

Johnny heard a laugh, and Jack stepped from the wood's edge. He wore cutoff jeans and filthy sneakers. His shirt was yellow-white, with a picture of Elvis in black silhouette. He had a backpack on his back and more loose stones in his hand. One side of his mouth turned a sharp edge, and his hair was slicked back. Johnny had forgotten that it was Friday.

"That was for ditching without me." Jack walked over, a small boy with blonde hair, brown eyes, and a seriously messed-up arm. The right one was fine, but it was hard to miss the other. Shrunken and small, it looked like someone had nailed the arm of a six-year-old to a kid twice that age.

"Are you angry?" Johnny asked.

"Yes."

"I'll give you a free hit to make it even."

Jack held the hard smile. "*Three* hits," he said.

"Three with your girl arm."

"Two with the hammer." Jack cocked his good fist, and his smile thinned. "No flinching." He stepped closer and Johnny flexed his arm, pulled it tight to his side. Jack spread his legs, drew back the fist. "This is going to hurt."

"Do it, you pussy."

Jack punched Johnny in the arm, twice. He hit hard, and when he stepped back, he looked satisfied. "That's what you get."

Johnny rolled his arm, tossed one of the pebbles, and Jack ducked it. "How'd you know I'd be here?"

"It's not rocket science."

"Then, what took you so long?"

Jack sat on the rock next to Johnny. The pack came off and he stripped off the shirt, too. His skin was burned red, peeling on the shoulders. A silver cross hung on a thin steel chain. It spun as he opened the pack, winked silver in the sun. "I had to go home for supplies. Dad was still there."

"He didn't see you, did he?" Jack's father was a serious, hard-ass cop, and Johnny avoided him like the plague.

"Do I look like an idiot?" Jack's good hand disappeared inside the pack. "Still cold," he said, and pulled out a can of beer. He handed it to Johnny, then pulled out another.

"Stealing beer." Johnny shook his head. "You're going to burn in hell."

Jack flashed the same sharp smile. "The Lord forgives small sins."

"That's not what your mom says."

He barked a laugh. "My mom is one step away from foot-washing and snake-handling, Johnny man. You know that. She prays for my soul like I might burst into flame at any moment. She does it at home. She does it in public."

"Get out."

"That time I got caught cheating? Remember?"

Three months ago. Johnny remembered. "Yeah. History class."

"We had a meeting with the principal, right? Before it was done, she had him on his knees, praying for God to show me the path."

"Bullshit."

"I don't think he's a praying man, he was just too scared to tell her no. You should have seen his face, all scrunched up, one eye squinting out to see if she was looking at him while he did it." Jack popped the top, shrugged. "Still, can't blame him. She's gone off the deep end and is trying just as hard to take me down with her. She had the preacher over last week to pray for me."

"Why?"

"In case I'm touching myself."

"I don't believe it."

"Life is a comedy," Jack said, but there was no smile left. His mother was scary religious, born again and taking no prisoners. She was on Jack all the time with threats of hell-fire and damnation. He played it off, but the cracks showed.

Johnny opened his beer. "Does she know your dad still drinks?"

"She says that the Lord disapproves, so Dad put a beer re-frigerator in the garage, his liquor, too. That seems to have settled it."

Jack chugged. Johnny took a sip. "That's some crap beer, Jack."

"Beggars and choosers, man. Don't make me hit you

again." Jack chugged the rest of his beer, then stuffed the empty in the pack, and pulled out another.

"Did you do your history paper?"

"What did I say about small sins?"

Johnny scanned the area behind Jack. "Where's your bike?"

"I don't know…"

"What do you mean, you don't know?"

"I didn't feel like riding it."

"It's a six-hundred-dollar Trek."

Jack looked away, shrugged. "I miss the old one. That's all."

"Still no sign, huh?"

"Stolen, I guess. Gone for good."

The power of sentiment, Johnny thought. Jack's old bike was piss-yellow with a three gears and a banana seat. His dad had bought it second-hand and it had to be fifteen years old. It had been gone for a long time. "Did you hop the train?"

Johnny's eyes slid to the stunted arm. Jack had fallen from the back of a pickup when he was four and shattered the arm, which turned out to have a hollow bone. He'd had an operation to fill the hollow core with cow's bone, but the surgeon must have been pretty bad, because it never really grew after that. The fingers didn't work that well. The limb had little strength. Johnny gave him hell about it because it made the arm a non-issue between the two of them. But that was just cover-up. When it came down to it, Jack was sensitive. He saw the glance.

"You don't think I can handle a train jump?" Angry.

"I was just thinking of that kid, you know."

They both knew the story, a fourteen-year-old from one of the county schools that tried to hop the same train and lost his grip. He'd fallen under the wheels and lost both legs: one at the thigh, one below the knee. He was a cautionary tale for kids like Jack.

"That kid was a wimp." Jack rooted through one of the outer pockets of the backpack and came out with a pack of menthols. He pulled out a cigarette with his bad arm and held it between two baby fingers as he lit it with a lighter. He sucked in smoke and tried to blow a ring on the exhale.

"Your dad buys crap cigarettes, too."

Jack looked at the perfect, blue sky and took another drag. The cigarette in his small hand looked unnaturally large. "You want one?" he asked.

"Why not?"

Jack handed Johnny a smoke and let him light it off the coal on the end of his own. Johnny took a drag and coughed. Jack laughed. "You are *so* not a smoker."

Johnny flicked the butt into the river. He spat into the dirt. "Crap cigarettes," he repeated. When he looked up, he caught Jack staring at the bruises on his chest and ribs.

"Those are new," Jack said.

"Not so new." Johnny watched the current carry a log past their rock. "Tell me again," he said.

"Tell you what?"

"About the van."

"Damn, Johnny. You know how to suck the joy out of a day. How many times do we need to go over it? Nothing's changed since the last time. Or the time before that."

"Just tell me."

Jack pulled in smoke and looked away from his friend. "It was just a van."

"What color?"

"You know what color."

"What color?"

Jack sighed. "White."

"What about dents? Scratches? Anything else you re-member?"

"It's been a year, Johnny."

"What else?"

"For fuck's sake, man. It was a white van. White. Like I

told you. Like I told the cops." Johnny waited and eventually Jack settled down. "It was a plain, white van," he said. "Like a painter would use."

"You never said that before."

"I did."

"No. You described it: white, no windows in the back. You never said it looked like a painter's van. Why would you say that now? Was there paint spilled on the side?"

"No."

"Ladders on the roof? A rack for ladders?"

Jack finished the cigarette and flicked his own butt into the river. "It was just a van, Johnny. She was two hundred yards away when it happened. I wasn't even sure it was her until I found out she was missing. I was coming home from the library, same as her. A bunch of us had been there that day. I saw the van come over the hill and stop. A hand came out of the window and she walked up to the side. She didn't look scared or anything. She just walked right up." He paused. "Then the door opened up and somebody grabbed her. A white guy. Black shirt. Like I've said a hundred times. The door closed and they took off. The whole thing took like ten seconds. There's just nothing else for me to remember."

Johnny looked down, kicked at a stone.

"I'm sorry, man. I wish I'd done something, but I just didn't. It didn't even look real."

Johnny stood and stared at the river. After a minute, he nodded once. "Give me another beer."

They drank beer and swam in the river. Jack smoked. After an hour, Jack asked, "You want to check some houses?"

Johnny skimmed a rock and shook his head. Jack liked the game of it, the risk. He liked creeping around and seeing things that kids were not supposed to see. For Jack, it was an adrenaline thing. "Not today," Johnny said.

Jack walked to Johnny's bike, where the map was wedged into the spokes of the front tire. He pulled it out, held it up. "What about this?" Johnny looked at his friend, then told him about his run-in with Detective Hunt. "He's all over me."

Jack thought it was bullshit. "He's just a cop."

"Your dad's a cop."

"Yeah, and I steal beer from his fridge. What does that tell you?" Jack spat in the dirt, a universal sign of disgust between the two boys. "Come on. Let's do something. It makes you feel better. We both know it. And I can't sit out here all day."

"No."

"Whatever," Jack said, and shoved the map back between the spokes. He saw the feather tied to Johnny's bike. It dangled from a cord looped around the seat post. He took it in his hand. "Hey, what's this?"

Johnny stared at his friend. "Nothing," he said.

Jack ran the feather between his fingers. Light made it glisten at the edges. He tilted it against the light. "It's cool," he said.

"I said, leave it alone."

Jack saw the new angle in his friend's shoulders, and he let the feather drop. It swung once on its cord. "Jeez. It was just a question."

Johnny loosened his fingers. Jack was Jack. He meant no harm. "I heard that your brother picked Clemson."

"You heard that?"

"It was all over the news."

Jack picked up a rock, rolled it from his good hand to his bad. "He's already being scouted by the pros. He broke the record last week."

"What record?"

"Career home runs."

"For the school?"

Jack shook his head. "The state."

"Guess your old man is proud," Johnny said.

"His son is gonna be famous." Jack's smile looked real,

but Johnny saw how he tucked his bad arm more tightly against his ribs. "Of course he's proud."

They went back to drinking. The sun crawled higher, but the daylight seemed to dim. The air grew cool, as if the river itself had chilled. Johnny got halfway through his third beer, then put it down.

Jack got drunk.

They spoke no more of his brother.

It was noon when they heard the car downshift on the road above them. It stopped at the bridge, then turned onto the old logging road that led to the high bank above them. "Shit." Jack hid the beer cans. Johnny pulled on his shirt to hide the bruises, and Jack pretended that it was a normal thing to do. It was an old argument between them, whether or not to tell.

A high, metal grill pushed through the weeds that grew between the ruts of the track, and Johnny saw that it was a pickup, waxed. Chrome threw off glints of sun and the windshield was mirrored. When it stopped, the engine revved, then died. Three of the four doors opened. Jack stood up straighter.

Blue jeans. Boots. Thick arms. Johnny saw all of that as the older kids circled to the front of the truck. He'd seen them around. They were high school kids. Seventeen, eighteen years old. Grown men, or close to it. One had a pint of bourbon in his hand. All three were smoking cigarettes. They stood on a lip of earth where the bank fell away to the water. They looked down on Johnny, and one of them, a tall blond kid with a raspberry birthmark on his neck, nudged the driver. "Look at this," he said. "Couple of junior high faggots."

The driver's face showed no emotion. The guy with the bourbon took a pull on the bottle. Jack said, "Fuck off, Wayne."

Birthmark stopped laughing.

"That's right," Jack said. "I know who you are."

The driver thumped the back of his hand on Birthmark's chest. He was tall and well-built, handsome in a postcard way. He regarded Wayne coolly, then pointed at Jack. "That's Gerald Cross's brother, so show him a little respect."

Wayne made a face. "That little dip-shit? I don't believe it." He took a step, leaned over the bank, and raised his voice. "Your brother should have signed with Carolina," he said. "You tell him Clemson is for pussies."

"Is that where you'll be going?" Johnny asked.

The driver laughed. So did the kid holding the bourbon. Wayne's face darkened, but the driver stepped forward, cut him off. "I know you, too," he said to Johnny, then paused and took a drag on his cigarette. "I'm sorry about your sister."

"Wait a minute," Wayne said, and pointed. "That's this guy?"

"Yes, it is."

The words came without visible emotion, and the blood fell out of Johnny's face. "I don't know you," Johnny said.

Jack touched Johnny's arm. "That's Hunt's son. The cop's son. His name is Allen. He's a senior."

Johnny looked up and saw the resemblance. Different hair, but the same build. The same soft eyes. "This is our place," Johnny said. "We were here first."

Hunt's son leaned out over the bank, but was clearly not disturbed. He spoke to Jack. "Haven't seen you around in a while."

"Why would you?" Jack said. "We've got nothing to say to each other. Gerald either for that matter."

Johnny looked at Jack. "He knows your brother?"

"Once upon a time."

Allen straightened. "Once upon a time," he said, and there was no emotion in the words. "We'll find another place." He turned around, stopped, and spoke to Jack. "Tell your brother I said hi."

"Tell him yourself."

Allen paused, then offered an empty smile. He gestured to his friends, then got in the truck and started the engine. They backed up the dirt track, disappeared; then it was just the river, the wind.

"That's Hunt's son?" Johnny asked.

"Yeah." Jack spat in the dirt.

"What's the problem with him and your brother?"

"Nothing," Jack said, then looked out over the river. "Water under the bridge."

The mood soured after that. They caught a garter snake and let it go, shaved driftwood with their knives, but it was no good. Johnny was talked out and Jack sensed it, so that when a distant whistle announced the south-bound freight, Jack pulled on his shoes and packed up. "I'm going to split," he said.

"You sure?"

"Unless you want to pedal me back to town on your handlebars." Johnny followed Jack up the bank. "You want to hook up later?" Jack asked. "Catch a movie? Play some videogames?"

The whistle called again, closer. "You'd better roll," Johnny said.

"Just call me later."

Johnny waited until he was gone, then unwrapped the pin feather from his shirt and slipped the string over his neck. Dipping his hands in the river, he dabbed water on his face, then smoothed the feather on his bike. The water made it gleam, and it slid between his fingertips, crisp and cool and perfect.

Johnny skimmed some more stones, then went back to the rock and lay down. The sun was warm, the air a blanket, and at some point, he dozed. When he woke, it was with a start. The day had slid to late afternoon: five o'clock, maybe five-thirty. Dark clouds piled up on the far horizon. A breeze carried the smell of distant rain.

Johnny hopped off the rock and went to find his shoes. He had them in his hand when he heard the whine of a small engine. It approached from the north, fast. The whine climbed to a scream, a motorcycle, pushing hard. It was almost to the bridge when Johnny heard another engine. This one was big and running wide-open. Johnny craned his neck, saw the concrete abutment that ran along the bridge and beyond that a slice of green leaves and sky gone the color of ash. The bridge began to shake, and Johnny knew that he'd never heard anything hit it so fast.

They were halfway across when metal hit metal. Johnny saw a shower of sparks, the top of a car and a motorcycle that cartwheeled once before the body came over the rail. One of the legs bent impossibly, the arms churned, and Johnny knew that it was a mistake, a pinwheel that screamed with a man's voice.

But then it hit.

It landed at Johnny's feet with a wet thump and the double-snap of breaking bones. It was a man in a muddy shirt and brown pants. One arm twisted under his back, angle all wrong, and his chest looked caved in. His eyes were open, and they were the most amazing blue…

Brakes squealed on the road. Johnny stepped closer to the injured man, saw skin torn from one side of his face, right eye starting to go bloody. His good eye locked on Johnny like the boy could save him.

Up on the road, the big engine gunned. Tires barked in reverse. Johnny felt the vibration when the car rolled back onto the bridge.

The injured man's jaw worked. "He's coming back…"

"It's okay," Johnny said. "We'll help you." He knelt in the dirt. The man held out his hand and Johnny took it. "It's going to be okay."

But the man ignored Johnny's words. With a surprising strength, he pulled the boy closer. "I found her."

Johnny focused on the man's lips. "You found who?"

"The girl that was taken…"

Johnny felt cold shock. The man's body seized, and blood shot from his mouth onto Johnny's shirt. Johnny barely noticed. "Who?" he said again, then louder. "Who?"

"I found her…"

Above them, the big engine idled. The injured man rolled his eyes up, his fear obvious. He pulled Johnny so close that he smelled blood and crushed organs. The man's eyes crinkled at the edges, and Johnny heard a single word. A whisper.

"Run…"

"What…?"

The man's grip tightened. Johnny heard how the big engine rumbled and spat, then something like steel on concrete. The man's hand clenched so hard that nails cut Johnny's skin.

"For God's sake…"

The body seized again, spine locked tight, broken arm twisting.

"Run…"

Johnny looked down, saw a boot heel push dirt, and something clicked in his mind.

*This was not an accident.*

Johnny looked at the bridge and saw a hump of movement: a head and a shoulder, a man moving around the front of the car. It was a shadow man, a cutout. Johnny felt the blood on his hands, sticky-wet and going cold…

*Not an accident.…*

The man's body seized, head slamming dirt, boot heel drumming. Johnny tried to pull his hand free, had to jerk with all he had. Noise on the bridge. Movement. Fear was a knife that went in low and touched some deep place in him. Johnny had never been so scared in all of his life, not the day he woke up to find his father gone, not the times his mom winked out and Ken got that gleam in his eye.

Johnny was terrified.

Frozen.

Then, he turned and ran, along the river, down the trail. He ran until his throat closed, until his heart tried to claw free from his chest. He ran fast and he ran afraid. He ran until the giant black monster stepped from the shadows and grabbed him up.

Then Johnny screamed.